TALES OF THE OUTER ISLANDS

Neil Gardner

TALES OF THE OUTER ISLANDS

©Neil Gardner 2023

The author asserts the moral right to be identified as the author of this book, so bloody well watch out.

ISBN: 978-0-6457808-0-2
Cover and inside illustrations: Ryan Curtis
Design and typesetting: Julia Knight
Printed by: Ingram Spark

Published by Quelnge Creations 2023

125 Pottery Road
Lenah Valley
Tasmania 7008
Australia

Dedication

For my grandson Archie

This novel is a work of fiction. Any follies, failings or foibles it contains, remain the property of the author.

The Cumberland Archipelago

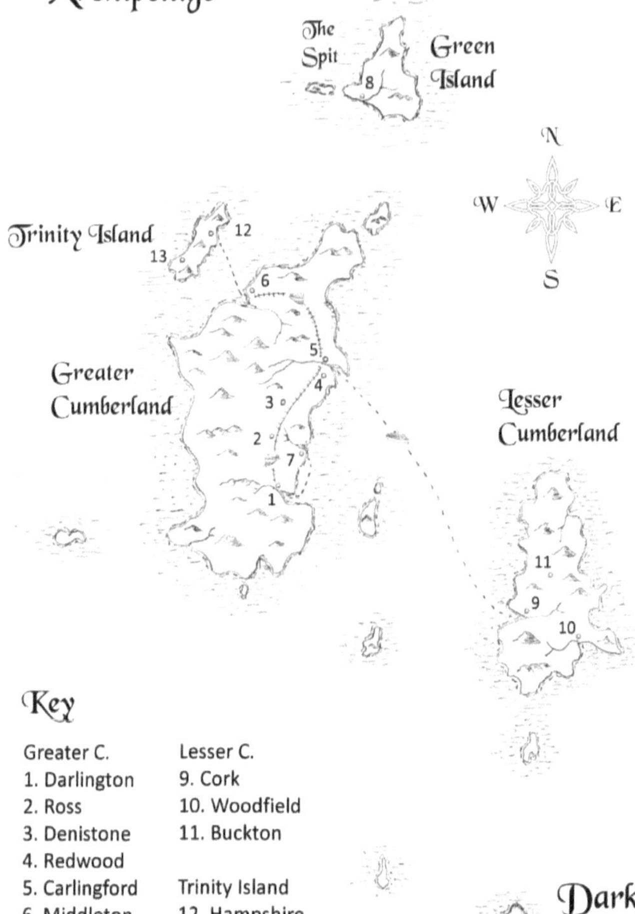

Key

Greater C.	Lesser C.
1. Darlington	9. Cork
2. Ross	10. Woodfield
3. Denistone	11. Buckton
4. Redwood	
5. Carlingford	Trinity Island
6. Middleton	12. Hampshire
7. Kempton	13. Willow Bend

Green Island	Dark Tor
8. Whiteford	14. Irishtown

1: A Broken Evening

One day was pretty much like another to Hugh Conroy. He liked it that way and did his best to ensure that his life followed a comfortable, predictable pattern. That isn't to say he found life dull or boring. On the contrary, it was lit from within by his own personal vision - a bright and private faerie world. It was this vision which sustained him during the boring hours of his working day and the solitary evenings at home in his flat.

He had always used games as a refuge. During his early school years, the family had lived close by the school and he had quickly slipped into the habit of going home at recess and lunch times to continue the games he had commenced that morning or the night before. From there, the games followed him back to school and lived on in his mind as he paid lip service to the routine of school life.

All of this meant that he was an indifferent scholar with few friends. Except for the rare occasions when the demands of education coincided with the yearnings of his inner world, he showed little or no promise in any subject. He was only able to make the transition from school to working life relatively painlessly because a friend of his father secured him a junior clerk's position with the Darlington City Council in 1968. His father thought that the sudden shock of moving to the capital city, living on his own and working for a living, would oblige him to grow up.

The nature of Hugh's games became more romantic and sophisticated as he embarked upon adolescence, but the essential technique of living at one remove from the **real** world remained unchanged. He was not alone in his private world however. Two children who had lived across the street from his childhood home were the friends of his infancy. They were Brian McInerney, a boy of his own age, and Brian's sister Maggie who was two years younger. They shared the games of Hugh's formative summers and, like small bright insects in amber, they became caught up in and transfixed by the alchemy of his daydreams.

The young McInerneys had been virtually abandoned by their school teacher parents who had left them in boarding schools here in the Cumberland Archipelago and gone back to the British Isles to pursue their teaching careers. This meant that Brian and Maggie came to spend their school holidays with Hugh in his flat in Gracechurch Street.

When he installed Hugh in the flat, Hugh's father had asked Mrs Malleson, the lady in the downstairs flat, who acted for the landlord, to let him know if Hugh got into any difficulty or trouble. Mrs Malleson was a very unobtrusive neighbour but she became a friend to Hugh and particularly to Maggie who was fascinated by her garden.

From an early age Hugh and Maggie had been lovers and in her final years at boarding school, she had become his Guinevere. They had exchanged passionate letters celebrating their love and the glorious long vacation they had spent together with Brian (their Merlin) in the summer of 1968. Hugh's kitchen was still hung with the bunches of herbs that Maggie had harvested from Mrs Malleson's garden. Sitting in the kitchen with her latest scented letter in his hands and surrounded by the heady aroma of dried flowers and orris root, he could conjure up his sweetheart from the memory of her presence. It was as if that previous summer had never ended or left that room. In this way Hugh stored up the glittering memories of past happiness as little vignettes caught like dew drops in a spider's web. That was his world. He felt at peace there and had no desire to leave it.

It was for these reasons that he was quite content at dusk on that July day walking from the bus stop to his flat. Mist was gathering down on the river but up in the suburban foothills of Mount Cameron, the air was frosty and clear. Territorial blackbirds buffeted each other on the shadowy lawns of daphne scented gardens, occasionally thrilling the air with triumphant outbursts of silver song.

At about eight o'clock that night, when the surrounding gardens were given over to the stirrings of small night creatures and blackbirds slept, Hugh, in the blue silk "wizard's" dressing gown that Maggie had made for him, was enjoying a glass of sherry before bed. There was a game that he often played at this time. His flat was a kind of winged ship, becalmed and surrounded by sleeping monsters. He would tiptoe down the stairs to the front door, open it cautiously and creep outside (past the sleeping monsters) to put the empty milk bottles near the gate post. Then he would creep back inside, close the door behind him and go back upstairs and get into bed. As his head hit the pillow, the monsters would wake and his ship would take flight, bearing him off to sleep and safety.

On this particular July night, much to his surprise, when he gently opened the door, there were three figures standing on the doorstep, one of them just about to knock. The shock of finding actual monsters at his door and wanting to get in, completely shattered Hugh's composure.

'Do you live in the upstairs flat?' asked one of the monsters, a dark haired girl in duffle coat and glasses.

'Yes' said Hugh, clutching his milk bottles defensively to his chest.

'Could we go upstairs and talk?' asked the girl, 'before the old lady in the downstairs flat comes out?'

Because he had lost control of the situation, Hugh consented. Thus his castle and keep were overthrown at the first attempt without a blow being struck. Shutting the door behind them, he ushered the three strangers up the stairs to his flat, wishing for the moment that Maggie hadn't embroidered moons and stars all over his dressing gown.

Hospitality was going to be a problem. For one thing there were only three chairs, one each for himself, Maggie and Brian. The guests sat down on these while Hugh tried unsuccessfully to look relaxed, lounging next to the mantelpiece. However, one of the visitors, a thinly bearded individual in a duffle coat and a black beret, soon got up and began to walk around the room, breaking leaves off the dried herbs, crushing them, sniffing them, naming them and then dropping them on the floor.

'Basil,' he said; 'eau de cologne mint, sage, horehound, feverfew, comfrey - that's good for setting broken bones. Not much point hanging parsley to dry. You're better off leaving it fresh in the ground. Spanish lavender, yarrow, and you probably think that's chamomile but it's not. It's just a common form of daisy. It fools a lot of beginners. Lady's mantle, that's good for menstrual disorders but they shouldn't trouble you.'

The stranger went on with the relentless momentum that only the most truly insensitive people are able to maintain. Hugh took an instant dislike to him.

During the dissertation on herb-lore, the third stranger who was dressed in motor cycle leathers, was examining the bookshelf which housed Hugh and Maggie's collection of Enid Blyton books.

'Is there a kid living here?'

Blushing, Hugh, the man who was determined to remain always proudly a child, mumbled something like,

'One stays here sometimes.'

With this betrayal of his sweetheart and his secret world burning his cheeks, he tried to regain control of the situation.

'Is there something I can do for you people? I was just about to go to bed.'

'Oh it's only early yet,' said the herbalist, whose name was Robert. He was making much of eating a nasturtium.

'These are good in salads.'

'I suppose we'd better introduce ourselves,' said the girl. 'My name's Lucy and this is Robert and Jim.' Jim put down his crash helmet and shook Hugh's hand very firmly in what seemed more of a challenge than a greeting.

'And you,' said Robert 'are Hugh Conroy. You see we already know quite a bit about you. But we're more interested in this house or rather in who owns it.'

'Yes,' said Lucy. 'Do you ever see your landlord?'

'No I pay my rent to Mrs Malleson downstairs.'

'Ah yes, the Malleson dragon,' said Robert. 'We've met.'

'She's a very good friend of mine,' said Hugh, feeling he had to defend someone since he had betrayed Maggie.

'Look,' said Jim. 'If we are going to get anywhere we have to tell him everything. What we want to do is illegal after all.'

'It's not that bad,' said Lucy, a little embarrassed. 'But I guess you are right. You see we think that this house and the people who own it are part of an amazingly well kept secret. How well do you know the City?'

'How well do you know your Cumberland history?' Robert butted in.

'I did it to matriculation level, 'said Hugh rather testily.

'Ah right, you'd have been fed the standard line then and they don't always get that right.'

In a patronising school teacher's chant, Robert began the following discourse.

'In 1807, a ship called the Dryad left England with a cargo of mainly Irish convicts. She was bound for Botany Bay. The ship was last heard of when it took on supplies at Rio De Janeiro. The Dryad never reached her destination and was presumed lost at sea.

'In 1815 the Remote, a ship of the Royal Navy, en route from Port Jackson to Hobart Town, was caught and disabled in a violent storm. She was swept miles off course. A combination of strong winds and a previously unknown ocean current caused the vessel to run aground on one of an uncharted group of islands. In this way the Cumberland Archipelago was discovered. To their amazement, the Captain and crew of the Remote found what appeared to be a well established community of European settlement on the island. It seemed that the Dryad had been wrecked on the same Island eight years earlier. Although the ship had been lost, there was no loss of life and most of the ship's cargo had been retrieved before she broke up.

'The Dryad's captain, Edward Jamieson, won the respect and loyalty of crew and convicts alike because of the concern and leadership he showed in rescuing everyone on board. It quickly became clear to Jamieson that the loyalty and co-operation of the convicts would be essential if the party was to survive. He took the radical step of provisionally granting them their freedom in all things but the right to bear arms. The gamble paid off and a successful settlement was established.

'The commander of the Remote was so impressed with what he found that, on his return to England with Captain Jamieson, the two men were able to argue successfully for a free pardon for all the convicts. As it happened, none of them wanted to return to the British Isles anyway.   And that is how the Cumberland Archipelago became a part of the British Empire. Well that's the primary school version anyway. But I think the real story might be a bit different. You see I'm doing my thesis on Cumberland History and I believe there's been a cover up.

'What started me thinking was a painting of Darlington Village done by an artist who was an officer on the Remote. The painting is on permanent display at the Museum. You ought to look for yourself. It was done from sketches made in 1815 which was supposedly only 8 years after the wreck of the Dryad. The painting shows a number of cottages, one or two more substantial houses and some public buildings. There's also a small schooner being unloaded from a wharf. All of it is overlooked by Mount Cameron. In the right foreground there are some well established trees that look to me like oak trees.

'Now it seems remarkable to me that one boat load of people could salvage enough from a single shipwreck to establish such a prosperous looking community in only 8 years. What are the odds that a small group of convicts, predominantly male, and a ship's crew would contain the necessary blend of skills, let alone the tools, to build such solid houses and a schooner and support themselves independently in such a short space of time? By comparison, the Sydney settlement wasn't properly able to feed itself for well over twenty years. It remained dependent on supplies from England for years after the arrival of the first fleet. I've also asked a couple of botanists to examine the trees in the painting. They both estimate the oak trees to be more than 40 years old.'

Robert paused theatrically to draw breath. Lucy and Jim said nothing and gave him plenty of space. It was a story that they were obviously very familiar with. They held their peace but surreptitiously studied Hugh's reaction to the performance. The more he heard, the more Hugh felt his interest beginning to stir. Like most people in the Cumberlands, he had grown up accepting the traditional account of his country's origins. Being a person who invented his own reality, he was excited by any ideas that seemed to challenge the conventional reality.

Robert continued. 'My tutors and lecturers went out of their way to discourage my ideas - Professor Meadows in particular. They pointed out that the painting was probably completed at a later date in England, from his original sketches and that it was a work of art rather than an historical record. Some even thought that the artist may have returned ten years later and finished it then. There are paintings that he is known to have done in Sydney and Hobart at about that time.

'The trees were dismissed as being native acacias. They pointed out that in the early days of settlement, European artists had difficulty depicting antipodean vegetation. When I pointed out that the oak trees are still there to this day, they said that they were probably planted after the painting was completed.

'I raised the matter of the schooner and questioned where they would have obtained sail cloth and rigging and why, with a ship at their disposal , they didn't try to return to civilization. Their response was that the schooner was only big enough to sail to other islands in the archipelago and that its sails and rigging were probably salvaged from the wreck of the Dryad. In short, they said that, while my suggestions were interesting, there were plausible alternative explanations for every point I raised.'

'So what did you do then?' asked Hugh.

'I concluded that there must have been some kind of settlement already established in the Cumberlands before the wreck of the Dryad. In some way, the pre-existing community was able to disguise itself and blend in with the survivors of the wreck by the time the Remote arrived. I wondered if they might have been French or Dutch, but there doesn't appear to have been any official sighting of the Cumberlands by any other power before 1815. Then the idea occurred to me to try and track down the names of the convicts and crew of the Dryad's last voyage and compare them with names in the official land and property records from the early years.

'I went to the National Archives to see what I could find and was most surprised when the Chief Archivist did his level best to discourage me. He said that the older records were in a fragile state and not available for use by the general public. I told him I was a serious student of history but he said I would need a signed letter from one of the history lecturers at the university in Ross. Fortunately after the Chief had gone, one of the junior archivists who had been listening, took me aside and offered me access to the records on Wednesday afternoons which was when his boss played golf every week.'

At this point in Robert's narrative, Lucy asked if she could make herself a cup of coffee.

'I'll have one too,' said Robert, and, before Hugh could intervene, Lucy had Maggie and Brian's cups down off their hooks and was boiling the kettle.

'Would you have anything stronger?' asked Jim, looking up from the open copy of "Alice in Wonderland" which Hugh had been reading at tea time.

'Well there is some sherry if you'd like,' said Hugh taking the chance to replenish his own glass and give Brian's to Jim, thus enabling Maggie's glass to remain inviolate. He sensed that Jim probably had something more macho in mind when he asked for something stronger to drink, but that couldn't be helped. Outside, the Moon was making gold of the roof tops while the mist down on the river grew heavier. Robert, in the mean time, was suitably refreshed by his coffee and eager to continue his story.

'When Captain Jamieson returned from England with his commission as Governor, he set about drawing up a record of land ownership. The older land title documents are still referred to as Jamieson Titles today. I've spent many hours poring over old maps and deeds of title. Much of the land was assigned as farming plots to sailors and convicts. Their names tallied with the names on the ship's register. However a number of much larger properties, including whole islands in other parts of the Archipelago, were owned by people whose names don't appear in the ship's register as either convicts or crew.

There were about twenty families with names like Fairchild, Barlow, Meadows, Weaver, Penruddock, Lanthorne, Malleson and Fairbrother.

'They were in marked contrast to the predominantly Irish Burkes, Hogans, McInerneys, Mahoneys, O'Hallorans, Slatterys and Rileys of the convicts. To this day, the big land owners in Cumberland are predominantly drawn from that group of families which didn't arrive on the Dryad. It seems to me that the small holdings in Captain Jamieson's titles were, in actual fact, granted to the convicts and sailors by the landed families that were already there, rather than being grants from the Crown.'

'You must be wondering what this history lesson is leading up to,' said Lucy, taking her glasses off to clean them. Hugh was taken by the attractiveness of her features when the unflattering, dark framed spectacles were removed.

'I am,' said Hugh, still torn between resentment at his apartment being overrun by strangers, and a nagging feeling that something of genuine importance might lie behind their intrusion.

'Well you see,' said Lucy, 'Robert has been able to establish that there was some kind of settlement here before the convicts arrived. We're fairly sure of their names, but the big mystery is, where did they come from and what sort of people were they? And for that matter what are they like now? Well I had been following a private line of enquiry which sort of ties in with Robert's research and that's where this house comes in. An art teacher of mine once drew my attention to a style of architecture he believes is unique to the Cumberlands, to Darlington in particular. This house is an example. It's a bit unusual because it's on its own. Normally you find them in clusters in secluded cul-de-sacs.

'I became particularly interested because there was a group of them quite near the house where I grew up. I started researching the location and age of the houses and trying to find out who owned and built them. My curiosity was prompted by something strange I remembered from my childhood.

'Our house and yard backed onto a bunch of these houses in a cul-de-sac in West Darlington, Montrose Court. The boundary fence was a very high brick wall. Now once when I was little, I hit a tennis ball over the wall. I got my dad's step ladder, climbed up and jumped over. Fortunately, the long grass was soft and springy on the other side.

'To start with I was busy looking for the ball. When I eventually found it, I decided to have a bit of a look around. The houses in the cul-de-sac appeared to have a big semi-circle of common ground behind them. It was like a park full of huge old trees. At the back of each house there was a private, walled garden and courtyard.

'After I'd spent a few minutes looking around, I realized that there was a little girl, about my size, standing under an old apple tree, silently watching me. We were both a bit shy at first, but she was really sweet and we played quite happily for half an hour or so. Then she invited me in to have a look at her dolls. She took me into the courtyard behind one of the houses and told me to wait while she went into the house.

'While I was waiting, I began to have a look around the courtyard and I noticed a flight of steps leading underground. Because there was no one around, I decided to have a closer look. It felt like going down into the hold of a ship. At the bottom, there were some low wooden benches and there was a kind of lantern or brazier suspended from the ceiling. It was sort of like a sanctuary lamp at church. The whole thing seemed very churchy but there were no familiar holy pictures or crucifixes.

'My eyes had just begun to get accustomed to the different light when this woman suddenly came down the stairs. I think she was more surprised than I was. She had me out of there very quickly and wanted to know what I was doing. I was beginning to explain myself, when the little girl came back out of the house with her dolls. They were incredibly beautiful, so lifelike, and the costumes were like nothing I'd ever seen before. It was like having a pre-conceived notion of what angels were like, then suddenly seeing the real thing and knowing it for what it was.

'I think the woman had been shocked rather than angry. While we played with the dolls, she brought us out a glass of milk and an apple each, but not before she shut the door that led down to the cellar. After a while she came out again and said it was time for me to go home. They led me down a side path to the street in front of the house and I never saw inside the place again.

'On a few occasions, I climbed to the top of the fence and saw the little girl again, but she said I mustn't come over the fence any more. Sometimes she had friends from the adjoining houses playing with her in the long grass among the old trees. They had very long braided hair and a kind of old world look about them. They were always friendly though, but they could never ask me over. We just did a lot of shy smiling at one another and that was it.'

Lucy smiled wistfully.

'And tell him the girl's name,' urged Robert, who clearly still had things to say.

'It was Marigold,' said Lucy, 'Marigold Fairchild.

'Anyway, getting back to the present, I did a lot of work on the building records of the Darlington City Council. I discovered that the houses in this style were mostly built about eighty years ago on remnants of the farming estates that surrounded the original settlement of Darlington. The farming estates were quite large holdings that ultimately gave their names to the suburbs that later engulfed them - names like Springfield, White Thorn and Mill Farm.

'Eventually, because of the expansion of the city, the big estates were dismantled and these strange houses were built on the sites of the original homesteads. Generally they were built around cul-de-sacs with an area of parkland held in common. That parkland seems to be the overgrown remains of the homestead gardens of the original farms.

'That's probably why you are able to harvest such a rich variety of herbs from the grounds of this place. I assume that's where all these dried herbs come from. Often there is a small stream passing close by. That stands to reason as the original settlements would have been located close to the nearest available fresh water.

'The significant thing is that all these houses were owned and built by members of the families that were already here before the wreck of the Dryad. There were a few similar houses which didn't quite fit the pattern. For the most part, we think that they were just imitations. It is quite an attractive style after all. We thought that this house was one like that at first because it was on its own.

However a bit of research into plans and building approvals showed that this house was originally intended to be part of a cluster, but for some reason, work didn't proceed on the other houses. This one appears to be the last of its kind ever built. It also seems to be the only one of its kind to have been rented out to someone from outside that original group of families.'

'That makes you something special,' said Jim with a smile - his first since their arrival.

'And where do you fit into all this?' asked Hugh, anxious to approach Jim who, of the three visitors, seemed the most authoritative, perhaps because he'd said the least.

'Lucy's got a bit more to tell,' said Jim.

'Not much really - only that the plans for all these houses were drafted by someone called Norian Fairchild.'

'There's that name again,' said Robert champing at the bit. 'The pre-convict families for the most part derive their income from the land. But some are involved in professions like the law, surveying and architecture - all related to property, the establishment and positions of control. A few enter politics but not as many as you might expect. They are probably able to wield all the power they need from behind the scenes because they own so much of the means of agrarian production.

'But the funny thing is they are not very conspicuous in the high society of Cumberland. There's never been a governor from amongst them for example and they're never prominent at Vice Regal Balls and the like, although that's to their credit if you ask me. But you do hear stories about their own private society, especially on some of the islands they own completely. I've heard that they live in a different world like some aristocracy from eighteenth century Europe. The local government records show that positions on some of the Island Councils are never contested at elections. They are virtually hereditary, staying in the same families year after year.'

'You hear lots of stories about the Outer Islands though,' said Hugh. 'Some people reckon they're crawling with inbred hillbillies and weird religious sects. It all sounds a bit hard to believe.'

'None of what we are talking about is easy to believe,' said Jim, helping himself to another glass of sherry. 'I find my own story particularly hard to believe but it happened nevertheless. I'd been working on a fishing boat down south of Seal Island. To this day I can't explain what happened.

'All I can remember is being woken in the middle of the night and told we were sinking. We had trouble getting the lifeboat down and in the end I had to just jump overboard in a life jacket. Of the other four crew members, three made it into the life boat. The fourth man, the owner of the boat, went down with it. We think he was trying to retrieve some valuables from the cabin.

'I got separated from the lifeboat and things after that are a bit of a blur. I don't know how long I was in the water for. I can remember agonising about whether to let myself drown. Rescue seemed to be completely out of the question. Then a mist sprang up out of nowhere and this beautiful, white yacht sailed out of it and I passed out completely.

'I don't know how long it was before I fully regained consciousness. I can vaguely remember being scrubbed down with warm water and some sort of soothing cream being rubbed into my face. A couple of times I was given a kind of liquor to drink and after that I didn't have a care in the world.

'When I woke up, I felt like I'd been asleep for days. Apart from feeling very weak and having very dry and cracked lips, I was in pretty good shape. For the first time I was able to focus clearly on the person who had rescued me. He looked quite young, very young in fact. He had fair hair and very striking eyes – a kind of golden green colour. The first thing he said to me was something like –"Well you're back. You very nearly crossed over but now you're back." I'd apparently been asleep for about three days and we were one day out from land.

'The whole time I was on the boat, I didn't see anyone else but my rescuer. He served me my meals and made sure I was comfortable. He had washed and dried my original clothes and I changed into them at dusk on the day I came ashore. When we rowed towards the beach, I remember seeing the name of the yacht painted on the bow. She was called "Dandillion."

'Before I went ashore, my rescuer gave me some money to pay my way back home. I told him I wanted to repay him when I had the means but he just laughed and said "don't be silly". Then I said at least tell me who you are. He laughed again and said something like "O'Ryan" but because he had an almost Irish sounding accent, like the people from the outer islands, it sounded like "Orion" - and he added "But it won't mean anything to you".

'He said goodbye, wished me luck and started to row back to the Dandillion out in the bay. I've never met anybody like him before or since. It was all very unsatisfactory to see him going away like that. My curiosity about him far outweighed my desire to get back home and I almost wanted to swim back out to him. But then I suddenly felt this horror of the sea which was probably not surprising given my recent past. I stood there ankle deep in foam, crying like a child.

'There was a crescent moon setting at the time and it bathed everything in a sort of mystical, golden light, - the white yacht, the foam, the rocks and the sand. All I could hear was the wind, the waves and the occasional cry of seabirds in the darkness overhead. I stood there until he boarded the yacht and set sail.

'The tide was going out and I was soon left standing on bare sand. In the distance I could see the lights of a village so I started walking towards it. I'd been put ashore on "Dark Tor", the outermost of the Cumberlands. I reached the village at about nine thirty. The place was called Irishtown, and it looked like something from the old country. Some of the cottages even had thatched rooves.

'The pub was an old stone place with low ceilings and long, low wooden benches drawn up around blazing log fires. The locals were very friendly and eager to hear my story. They were drinking a heavy stout that was brewed on the premises. It was beautiful stuff with a head on it like porridge. My first drink was on the house but when I went to pay for my second I noticed something odd about the money "O'Ryan" had given me. The pound note felt crisp and new but it was quite old. It had old Jack Mahoney's portrait on it which meant that it was at least sixty years old.

'Anyway, the locals listened sympathetically to my story. A lot of the men worked on fishing boats themselves so we had some common ground. However something strange came over them as I started describing my rescue. When I mentioned the name of the boat, the "Dandillion", they seemed to lose interest in what I had to say. They were still friendly but not as interested. They began to talk among themselves as if I wasn't there.

'Since I was pretty weak from all that had happened, I asked the Publican for a room when I finished my second drink. Before I got ready for bed I took out all the money that "O'Ryan" had given me. There were half a dozen florins all of which pre-dated 1918. There were five old Jack Mahoney pound notes, so they had to be pre 1920. But they were all fresh and crisp.

'Then I looked at the change I had been given downstairs in the bar. There were about four shillings and three sixpences. The dates on those coins varied from 1954 through to 1966 and none of them looked new. It was only the money that "O'Ryan" had given me which was old and yet still in mint condition.

'The next day, I asked the Landlord about how to get back to the mainland. It turned out that the only regular contact was a mail boat that came twice a week. It had left that morning and wasn't due back for three days. So I used that time to explore the Island.

'The Island itself is a forbidding looking place - a huge, solemn mass of black rock rising sheer out of the sea, with just the barest skirt of land at its feet on which a few villages and jetties are perched. At the southern end of the Island there is a long spit of land which runs down to the beach where I was put ashore.

'At first I thought the Islanders earned their living exclusively from fishing, but when I climbed the steep track up the mountain side I was surprised to find a considerable expanse of pastureland on the summit. In a couple of places I found small flocks of sheep grazing. They were tended by women or children.

'I found the same cautious reserve in their manner that I'd noticed in the pub on the first night. They were always polite. It would be hard, with their accents, to sound anything else. They really throw back to the original Irish. One of the kids was actually playing a tin whistle. I tell you, I wasn't sure which hemisphere I was in, or which century for that matter.

'There was plenty of time to think about my rescue and what it signified. But, in that exotic atmosphere, I began to suspect my mind of playing tricks. What I desperately wanted was to make some contact with the real twentieth century world. On the second night in the pub, I had the good fortune to run into a teacher from the local school. He was from Darlington and, unlike the locals, was quite willing to talk. He had only been on the Island for three years and hadn't yet become one of the locals. Nevertheless he had been able to learn a lot about the Island and its people. He loved the place and told me all sorts of interesting things about it.

'Apparently on the northern tip of the island there's a commune of Gaelic speaking hippies who came out from Wales in the early sixties. The teacher reckoned they must have subsisted on a diet of kelp and marijuana. It appears that after eight years they still hadn't been assimilated, but they were tolerated.

'Some of them even sent their kids to school to learn English. A kind of hybridized Celtic superstition had developed among the kids of the school. I enjoyed the teacher's company but something stopped me from telling him everything about my rescue. I think, by then I wanted to find out more for myself before I gave anything else away.'

Jim took out his wallet.

'I know it doesn't prove anything but I've saved all that was left of the money "O'Ryan" gave me by the time I got home.'

Hugh picked up the two pound notes and readily acknowledged that they had the powdery crispness of new notes.

'Now since I got back from Dark Tor, I've searched high and low for information about the "Dandillion". I've tried yacht clubs and marine boards on all the main islands in the Cumberlands and I could find nothing. I went back as far as I could, and especially to the years when those pound notes would have been issued, but with no luck.

'Then one afternoon on Lesser Cumberland I was sitting in the Shipwright's Arms in Cork, after an unsuccessful examination of the harbourmaster's files, when I found what I'd been looking for and it turned out to be much older. There had been a flood in one of the cellars and some of the things that had been stored there were drying in front of the fire in the bar. Amongst them were some old paintings of sailing boats. And there it was, winning some event at the Cork Regatta of 1837, complete with caption – "Dandillion skippered by N Fairchild." '

There was a theatrical pause as Jim waited for what he said to sink in. Robert hovered fretfully on the edge of the conversation, but even he respected the silence and waited for Jim to continue. Hugh was by now spellbound. Jim toyed absently with the pages of "Alice in Wonderland".

'Now if you want to know what we've come here for, we need to swear you to complete secrecy. We think we're onto something big, something really big.'

Hugh faltered at the mention of secrecy. As the incredible stories of his visitors had been unfolding he'd imagined himself telling Maggie and Brian. He shared everything with them.

'There are two really close friends of mine. They share this place with me when they're on vacation from school, I mean university.'

'Nobody else is to know,' said Jim emphatically.

'I suppose that'd be all right,' said Hugh sounding hesitant and torn. Robert appeared ready to accept that and was drawing breath to launch into the next part of the narrative. But Jim silenced him.

'No we'll let him think about it for a while. Give it some serious thought. I promise you that what we are onto could change our lives forever but, for the moment, secrecy is vital. I'll be away on a fishing boat for the next couple of weeks but we'll come and see you again when I get back.' Then, in less than two minutes, the visitors had gone and the extraordinary encounter was over. Hugh washed up the cups and glasses and went to bed. But his head was too full of the evening's conversation for him to get much sleep.

2: The Thousand Fires of St Francis

It was mid morning on a cold, clear July day. The last traces of morning mist clung to the small streams and ponds of the countryside and in some shaded areas there were still patches of heavy frost. High up in the tree tops beside the highway, a convocation of crows was involved in an animated debate.

The sleek, black birds were too preoccupied to notice the wayfarer who came walking down the highway. Coincidently, his appearance had something of the crow about it too. He wore black, stove pipe jeans, black boots with high heels and elastic sides, an old black frock coat with tails that flapped about in the chill air as he sauntered along, and a dilapidated black top hat. The wayfarer had been listening intently to the crows and their debate.

The case for the "ayes" was being argued by an eloquent and excitable bird who was becoming rather agitated in putting her point across. Every statement that she made was bluntly dismissed by her opponent with a short series of cynical and contemptuous monosyllables. A third and rather scholarly individual chimed in occasionally but seemed to forget the point he was trying to make and his voice would trail off absently to nothing. Several others provided a kind of Greek chorus.

The wayfarer listened - fascinated. The inflexion and the punctuation in what the crows were saying seemed so close to human speech that he thought it must be possible to understand it. When it didn't become immediately clear to him (like many a venerable politician before and since) he still felt that he could contribute to the debate.

He sided with the eloquent female because her opponent was too dismissive and kept offering the same old response while she was able to continually raise new arguments. He copied her plaintive call - rather well he thought - and for the first time, the birds became aware of his presence.

They left off their debate and studied the intruder in curious silence. For his part, the intruder felt that a few well chosen words might resolve their dispute and restore peace. He cleared his throat, dusted his hat, put it back on his head, clasped his hands behind his back and began to pace around beneath the trees in which the birds were sitting.

'Sister Raven, Brother Crow, I have listened with much interest and some dismay to your argument. Life is too short to waste on such disputation and animosity. You are immeasurably blessed. Like the lilies of the field, you neither reap nor sow. Look at me for example. I've got a History tutorial at two o'clock this afternoon but the university is in Ross. If you wanted to attend the tutorial, you could all just take flight now and you'd be there in plenty of time. It's thirty miles by road but probably only about ten as the crow flies - if you'll pardon the expression. I'll never make it unless some kind person gives me a lift. I spent my last ten bob buying drink for a party last night so I can't afford to travel by bus or train.'

The Greek chorus seemed to think the History tutorial might be worth a look and they took to their wings. The intellectual crow thought he'd try to restate his case for the benefit of the wayfarer but again became lost in the complexities of his argument and his voice trailed off to nothing.

'Now I'm sure that if you gave up your arguing and flew along the highway for a bit, you'd find a nice fresh road kill, some new slain knight to furnish your breakfast. That's something else I'll have to go without until I get back to college. So what do you say? Forgive and forget? Live and let live?'

The female flew off, reiterating her argument as she did so. This left the ponderous crow and his phlegmatic comrade to sit and watch the performance which showed no sign of abating. They also saw a small white sports car coast silently down the highway and come to a halt a few yards behind the orator who was by now warming to his task and quite oblivious to everything else. He continued to declaim, now in English, now in Crow, about a wide variety of subjects. He put his hands in his coat pockets and began to flap his elbows like wings. The two remaining crows continued to watch him with interest.

'Doctor Doolittle I presume,' said the driver of the sports car.

Frightened out of his wits, the Crow Man turned around hastily to see a young girl trying, not very successfully, to keep a straight face.

'I suppose you must be wondering what I was doing,' said the Crow Man who had turned crimson with embarrassment.

'You don't have to talk about it if you don't want to,' said the girl choking back a laugh. 'Your secret's safe with me.'

Her laughter was infectious and there was nothing derisive about her smile so the Crow Man began to relax.

He had quickly recognized her as someone he'd seen around the uni, someone he rather fancied in fact.

'I didn't hear you drive up.'

'Obviously. But that's not your fault. The engine wasn't running.'

'Well how were you managing to move from one place to another?'

'I'd run out of petrol.'

'Oh so that means we're both stranded then.'

'No I knew it was going to happen. I've got some more here in a little can. The fuel gauge is dodgy and I wanted to see how far it would run on a single tank. I'm thinking of buying it from my cousin.'

'What, petrol?'

'No! The car you goose. So you see I'm not stranded and the car is a two seater.'

'But a young girl like you shouldn't go offering lifts to strange ... ah to strangers. You shouldn't take risks like that.'

'I haven't offered you a lift. I just said the car has got two seats. And if you're that concerned about my safety, I won't offer you a lift. Although I must say you look pretty harmless to me - totally loopy but quite harmless.'

The girl set about emptying the can of petrol into the tank.

'Your name's Kate isn't it?' ventured the Crow Man, feeling rather awkward and useless looking on while she was being so practical and efficient.

'That's right,' she said as she replaced the lid on the can. 'Now, I don't know about you but I've got a political science lecture at twelve so I can't wait around. If you think I'll be safe you're welcome to a lift.'

'Well I must admit it would come in handy.'

'That's settled then. Jump in. You can hold the can.'

After a couple of tentative splutters, the engine fired and they sped off down the highway leaving the little glade in the custody of the two remaining crows. Conversation was difficult over the roar of the engine but the Crow Man was content to enjoy the wind in his hair and to marvel at his good fortune. He had admired Kate from a distance in History and English lectures all year but the opportunity to introduce himself had never arisen.

'Do you drive?' She shouted.

'No, I might kill somebody.'

'What sort of an answer is that?' Kate said, laughing again. 'I thought perhaps you might...you know...fly....like a crow.' She studied the road intently and smiled a smile of quiet mischief to herself.

'I'll have you know that was something of a mystical experience back there. It was like something out of the "Thousand Fires of Saint Francis." '

'The what?'

'You know. Saint Francis of Assisi. *"The Mille Fiori of Saint Francis."* '

'You don't mean the *"Fioretti"* by any chance?'

'It's the same thing isn't it?'

'Fioretti doesn't mean "fires". It means "little flowers".'

'Are you sure of that?'

'Positive.'

'Ah well. You know what I mean.'

The conversation faltered as Kate, noticing the time, put her foot down and concentrated on driving. For some time, the Crow Man was content to sit back and enjoy the mingled excitement and bliss of the moment, stealing the occasional sidelong glance at Kate who was pre-occupied with her driving.

She was wearing blue denim jeans with just the right degree of weather-beaten fade, a cream camisole which showed just the right amount of cleavage, an exotic looking embroidered astrakhan jacket and riding boots. Sadly, the Crow Man knew the journey would end all too quickly and he was desperately racking his brain for some way of maintaining contact. As much as he admired all of womankind, and Kate in particular, he was very inexperienced when it came to expressing that admiration in useful and constructive terms.

He forgot himself a few miles down the road when a farmer on a tractor waved as they passed. He instinctively rose in his seat and administered a kind of papal blessing with one hand whilst clutching the windshield with the other.

'You twit. Do you always greet passing strangers like that?' Kate asked, looking up momentarily from the highway.

'Only in sports cars. And of course only when the hood is down.'

Kate cast another brief glance in his direction and shook her head, raising her eyebrows in amused disbelief.

Conversation became easier as they approached the outskirts of Ross and slowed down to accommodate the speed limit.

'Well what do you think of the car?' ventured the Crow Man.

'You haven't told me your name,' said Kate.

'It's Brian - Brian McInerney.'

'I like it very much Brian, but I'm not sure how practical it is. I've always wanted to own a bug eye but I'm very fond of my Mini.'

'Yes I'm rather partial to minis myself.'

His mind was pre-occupied with the memory of Kate in a dark-green, suede mini-skirt with just the right degree of "brevity and skimpiness" that, for him, had brightened many a lecture on 18th Century English literature.

'Where do you want to be let off? I'm going straight to my lecture.'

'I'd better go back to Trinity and have a shower.'

'Yes you look like you spent the night in a haystack.'

'So I did. Well it was a barn actually. Look you must let me repay you.'

'Don't worry about it,' said Kate as she pulled up outside the college. 'It's been a highly entertaining interlude.'

'I'll see you later then,' said Brian, beginning to feel frustrated and forlorn.

'Bye,' said Kate, and she accelerated down the street towards the campus.

<div align="center">~~~§~~~</div>

Half an hour later, after a shower and something to eat, Brian's natural optimism had resurfaced and he was sharing his excitement with Maxwell Tynan, a friend and fellow student two rooms down at Trinity College. Theirs was an interesting friendship between opposites. Maxwell was a serious student who actually spent long hours studying. The only real uncertainty in academic life that he had experienced so far, was in deciding which branch of engineering would set him up with the most secure and affluent life-style. Loneliness never posed a problem for him because study was always there to productively fill any vacuum. There was also Brian who frequently needed someone to share the news of his latest exploits with.

Brian displayed no traits of sober industry. All his life, people had told him he was bright. He had breezed through primary and secondary school with a minimum of effort and report cards which declared he was capable of much more. Rightly or wrongly he assumed that university would be no different. He felt that Maxwell was missing the point of university.

Brian and Maxwell viewed each other with a kind of affectionate condescension. Maxwell was, in some respects, a stabilising influence in Brian's life and Brian's anecdotes were as much as Maxwell needed to know about the excitement of student life. Two things they had in common were a love of folk music and an innocent awe of womankind. Maxwell felt that a successful career path and a substantial pay packet would ultimately ensure a satisfactory result in the area of mating and marriage. Brian on the other hand was a complete romantic who believed that marriages were made in Heaven.

Kate was an extremely attractive girl with her long, strawberry blonde hair and hazel eyes. In Brian's eyes, she was a goddess and the only woman he could ever love. He had been sure of this before they met, and the interlude with the crows and the sports car only served to confirm the fact. He was superstitious by nature and he regarded coincidences, especially fortuitous coincidences as manifestations of destiny. He said as much to Maxwell a number of times during that conversation.

'I mean I've always wanted to introduce myself, but there was no way I ever could, and now it's just happened. I tell you its fate.'

He didn't say anything about the part the crows played in the encounter. He'd always had an affinity with crows and thought of them fancifully as Celtic birds of good omen. But Maxwell had no imagination and he wouldn't understand. Hugh, on the other hand was a different proposition. He might just write to old Hugo and tell him. Maxwell let Brian talk until 1:45 and then, pointing out that they both had tutorials to attend, pushed him out the door.

<div align="center">~~~§~~~</div>

Hugh got the letter from Brian three days later. While he exchanged letters with Maggie on a regular basis, letters from Brian were a rarity and he opened it with considerable interest. It had been three weeks since the mysterious visitation from the three conspirators. The visit had unsettled him and undermined the security of his private world. He couldn't decide whether or not he believed the tales told by the strangers and, because of the undertaking of secrecy, he couldn't attempt to resolve his uncertainty by sharing the information with his two closest friends. His complicity in the secret also seemed to inhibit his ability to communicate with Maggie about the everyday matters and interests which formed the basis of their friendship and correspondence.

He felt alienated and vulnerable, and his apartment with its store of treasured memories, no longer seemed able to protect him. The intrusion by the visitors, especially Jim, had left him feeling an embarrassed disbelief about the interests and intimate experiences he held most dear.

There was a time when his regular correspondence with Maggie would have provided all the re-assurance that he needed, but in his present frame of mind that avenue of support had failed him. For the first time in over a year, he had allowed more than two days to elapse before replying to one of Maggie's letters. He hoped that the letter from Brian would somehow restore things.

Sadly, although Brian's letter was full of his own joyous excitement, it didn't hold any joy for Hugh. It contained too many indications that Brian had flown the nest and been let loose on the wide world. At any other time he would have seen the letter as the confidences of a friend, but in his present frame of mind it was just another unwelcome manifestation of inescapable change.

The air of un-reality surrounding the visit of the three conspirators increased with every day that passed. When they had left him on that first evening, their talk of secret civilizations and alternative histories had sounded tantalizingly plausible. He had begun to nerve himself to face potentially far-reaching changes in his life. Now, after three weeks, he wished it had never happened. He desperately wanted to re-establish the frontiers of his private world. In fact, as he drank to the health of Maggie and Brian at bed time that night, he resolved to have nothing more to do with the strangers.

Hugh didn't feel that he was seriously violating that resolution when, two days later as something to do during his lunch break, he visited the Darlington Museum. The painting of Darlington Village was just as Robert had described it. Of course he had no idea whether the village depicted in the painting could have been built from scratch within eight years.   It did look very well established but he couldn't pretend to having a trained eye.

One of the buildings in the painting was the Town Hall where Hugh worked. It was recognisably the same building although there had been a number of additions over the years. Apart from the Town Hall, there were only two other buildings he could recognise. One was a three storey red brick town house which presently housed the head office of the Cumberland Times, the main newspaper in the Archipelago.

The other was a colonnaded structure which now formed part of the Museum itself. In front of that building were the two young trees Robert had alluded to. It seemed highly probable to Hugh that they were youthful images of the two massive oak trees that now dominated the little square of parkland outside the museum.

The dominant feature of the painting was Mount Cameron. It's rugged crown stretched like the spine of some vast sleeping reptile above and behind the settlement. The mountain was unmistakably the same. Together with Brian and Maggie, Hugh had spent many enjoyable hours in the icy solitude of the mountain top, with its eerie landscape of tumbled boulders, stunted trees and misty drifts of cloud.

On one side, Darlington lay spread out far below. On the other was a rugged and mountainous landscape; a wilderness as far as the eye could see. Hugh loved the Mountain. It was a divide, a threshold between two worlds; a dam that held back the ancient and primitive tide of nature and kept it from engulfing the mundane and complacent urban world of the city. But in Hugh's mind, the Mountain itself was also a manifestation of that ancient power - to those with eyes to see.

He had grown up in Middleton, a small saw milling town in the far north west of Greater Cumberland. The forest that encircled the town extended, virtually unbroken for a hundred and fifty miles down the western side of the Island and was the same forest that covered the slopes of Mount Cameron itself. In the previous century there had been mining ventures in isolated pockets within that wilderness. But the mines were now spent and the forest had reclaimed them.

Hugh had lived all his life in the shadow of the silent, brooding presence of the forest. He was not afraid of it but he seldom ventured far into it. He was satisfied just knowing it was there. Whoever had painted this picture could obviously sense the same magic - the otherness of that landscape, the hidden presence which the Mountain held at bay. That was where Hugh's loyalty lay. He re-affirmed his decision to reject the three conspirators and their oath of secrecy. His true loyalty lay with Maggie and Brian. He would tell them whatever he wanted.

While he was studying the painting, Hugh noticed out of the corner of his eye, that someone else had walked into the gallery. He turned around and saw that it was Lucy in a nurse's uniform. She recognized him and quickly left the room without saying a word. Although he had just decided to reject Lucy and her two co-conspirators, Hugh still felt peeved that she appeared to snub him. As he walked back to work he began to feel anxious and hurt about the apparent loss of her confidence.

At home that night, Hugh wrote to Maggie. He began with the clear intention of telling her everything but, try as he might, he was unable to put it into words. In the end, he contented himself with a mysterious allusion to an amazing secret that he would share with her when next they met. At about seven thirty, he sealed the letter and went to post it in the letter box on the corner. It was a cold night and a light but chill rain began to fall as he performed the task and turned for home.

They were waiting at the front gate when he returned. Lucy seemed awkward and anxious, while Robert was subdued to the point of being morose and seemed happy to let someone else do the talking.

'We were wondering if you'd let us buy you a drink,' said Jim, 'to repay your hospitality from last time.'

'My wallet's inside,' replied Hugh, looking for an excuse.

'The drinks are on me. I got paid this morning when we got back to port. What's your local?'

'O'Brien's' said Hugh, meaning the place where he bought his sherry. He had never set foot inside the bar. The pub was about a quarter of a mile from the flat and they retraced his steps past the letter box, where the letter to Maggie lay quietly with its commitment to betray the secret.

O'Brien's was a small Georgian pub which had seen little change to its décor and clientele since the 1940's. A few old timers sat around the warm and smoky bar. Some played crib and others just talked quietly and listened to the night trots and dog races on the wireless. The arrival of the young foursome was a minor sensation. Strangers were a rarity at O'Brien's. The middle-aged barmaid, promptly informed them that she could not serve them in the bar with a young lady.

'If the men want to swear or anything they should be left on their own to do it in the bar. But you're quite welcome to go in the saloon.'

'What if I want to swear as well?' asked Jim.

'That's up to you but the young lady has to go in the saloon.'

The young lady in question had taken off her glasses to wipe away the rain. Her colour, heightened by this attention, enhanced her features. For a second time Hugh was struck by how pretty she looked without her spectacles. Some of the old patrons seemed a little wistful about her having to leave as well.

They found the saloon in darkness. The fireplace was cold and the room was deserted.

'Now what can I get you,' said the barmaid as she turned on the lights. After some awkward confusion, Jim was able to order a pint of ale for himself. Robert, speaking for the first time that night since they had met Hugh, declined the offer of a beer and muttered something about his medication. Along with Lucy, he opted for a lemon squash and Hugh accepted a sherry.

'I'll have to go back to the bar to pull the beer for you, so just bear with me.'

Eventually they were all served and they had the room to themselves.

'Right' said Jim. 'You've had time to consider our story. Are you prepared to come in with us?'

'What will that involve exactly?' Hugh countered, resenting the pressure that was being applied.

'Well we've told you what we've discovered already. Our separate enquiries have brought Robert and Lucy and me together, and the trail has led us to the house where you live. If we are to find out any more, we need the co-operation of someone living on the premises. Mrs Malleson obviously wouldn't be suitable and so that leaves you.'

'But you've already seen inside my flat. I don't see what else I can do.'

'Do you have access to the courtyard?' asked Robert scarcely looking up from staring gloomily at his lemon squash.

'No wait a minute,' said Jim. 'Are you in with us?'

Hugh looked at the three faces. Robert remained glum and uncommunicative, seeming to care little that Hugh hadn't responded to his question. Lucy had been very quiet and aloof. He hadn't forgotten her hasty departure from the gallery that afternoon. However, in the middle of all the tension, her awkwardness softened into a brief compassionate smile.

She didn't seem to like this kind of pressure. Perhaps she had been subjected to something similar herself. Hugh had no idea where it would leave his commitment to betray the secret to Maggie and Brian. He had no idea about anything anymore. He found himself saying "yes" to Lucy and, after a long searching pause, Jim reached across the table and shook his hand. 'Right you're in. This calls for another drink.'

Another round was ordered and the little group began to relax a little. Jim and Lucy were clearly relieved that another stumbling block had been removed. Robert showed little interest or enthusiasm. Hugh had simply given up worrying about it anymore. The drinks were served and Jim proposed a toast to "the project".

'I don't know how much detail you remember from the other night,' he continued, 'but Lucy's story has the most significance for where we go next. That cellar room in the courtyard of the house she visited when she was a kid seems to be central to the secret of the pre-convict families. Remember how keen the woman was to get Lucy out of the downstairs room which seemed kind of churchy?'

Hugh nodded. Jim took a sip of ale and Lucy continued the narrative.

'All the pre-convict homes in those cul-de sac clusters appear to have had those little cellars. I've checked the plans of most of them at the Council offices. But try as we might we've never been able to get another look inside one of them. About three years ago two clusters were set for demolition to make way for the new motorway. We got into those one night after they had been vacated but in all of them, the cellar rooms had been filled with rubble, presumably by the residents.'

'And that brings us to your place of abode,' said Jim. 'Do you have access to the courtyard at the back of your place?'

'Yes,' said Hugh. 'That's where the clothesline is.'

'And is there a cellar door in the courtyard?'

'There is a door, yes.'

'Is it locked?'

'I haven't paid it that much attention. It's none of my business really.'

'Well,' said Jim. 'It is now. We want you to perform a burglary for us. Don't worry. We'll help you. It'll be easier having you on the inside so to speak. Now what do you know about Mrs Malleson's movements?'

'She keeps to herself. I see her on the stairs sometimes, and I pay my rent to her every fortnight. She often invites me in for a cup of tea. She's a nice old thing.'

'Does she ever go out. Something regular or predictable?'

'She goes to stay with her sister sometimes. She asks me to feed her cat then. But it's been a while since she's done that.'

'Does she have any other visitors or family?'

'I think she's got a son in Australia. There's no one else that I've noticed. But she might during the day when I'm at work.'

'Well what we want you to do is find out whether that door has a lock. It would be better if we could get in and out without her knowing. We don't want to upset her if we can help it.'

'I should think so,' said Hugh with some heat. 'I still have to live there after all.'

The barmaid came in to clear the table and advise them that it was closing time.

'Friday and Saturday we have a late licence. You can stay til eleven then.'

They took this as a sign of acceptance and made their way out onto the street.

'Well,' said Jim. 'We'll meet back here same time next Wednesday and you can report to us.'

With that, the three co-conspirators took their leave of Hugh and walked off into the darkness together, leaving him to make his way home alone.

He heard Mrs Malleson moving about in her apartment as he climbed the stairs and his heart sank. Under the influence of two sherries he had begun to warm to the idea of a little intrigue. But now, on his own, it was all too much trouble and he felt put upon. He didn't even know where any of them lived. They could just descend on him from nowhere with all their impositions and obligations and oaths of secrecy and then fade away into the darkness.

They were controlling him. And now they were moving on from fascinating tales of an alternative history to proposals that were against the law and which, at the very least, could get him evicted, if not arrested. He took some aspirin in anticipation of the headache he was sure would afflict him in the morning, and then he went to bed. No milk bottles and monsters at the door tonight - he had completely forgotten about the milk and the monsters had taken up permanent residence.

3: Metamorphosis

After the incident with the crows, Brian became unusually conscientious in his attendance of lectures. He was desperate for the chance to talk to Kate again but the opportunity didn't present itself. In English lectures, she always sat near the front with a group of girl friends. Brian generally entered from the back of the lecture theatre and the opportunity for eye contact didn't present itself. He had to content himself with listening to the sound of her laughter as she and her friends chatted while they waited for the lecturer.

In his frustration, he wistfully thought back to the crows, the "highway ravens" as he affectionately called them. Surely fate was at work. That wonderful day couldn't have been just coincidence or could it? He had been thinking about Kate almost constantly since then, and he couldn't bear to countenance the possibility that she might not have given him another thought since she drove off that day and left him outside Trinity College.

The lecturer eventually arrived and began an arid dissertation on *Joseph Andrews*. Brian actually enjoyed reading Fielding, when he had the patience to concentrate. But Doctor Dudley Spotswood, had the unhappy ability to kill any interest in his subject stone dead within seconds. Brian had been attending the good Doctor's lectures since March and hadn't understood a single word. Eventually the bell went and there was a stampede for the exits, prompted in part by the fact that it was lunch time and in part by the general desire to escape the anaesthetic torpor induced by Doctor Spotswood.

Rather than try to get close in the crush, Brian stayed in his seat and watched Kate and her friends leave by the side door. He took a little comfort from the fact that there never seemed to be any close male associates in her little circle. He sat for a few minutes in silence in the empty theatre and then suddenly remembered that he had a lunchtime concert to attend.

He raced off to grab a salad roll, a cup of coffee and a good seat. There was quite a dedicated folk music society on the campus, made up of an inner circle of performers, their friends and an outer circle of interested spectators. Today's bill of fare was to consist of three short brackets by club members and a special appearance by Mervan Mithras all the way from Darlington.

Cumberland University was set in the rural tranquillity of Ross - an old fashioned university town. Even though it was generally accepted as being the senior academic institution in the Country, the university suffered from a certain provincial stigma when compared with younger establishments like the Art School and Teachers College in the City of Darlington. Mervan Mithras was not only from the capital city, he was also rumoured to have performed overseas in places as far afield as Sydney, Melbourne and Auckland. The Folk Music Society was particularly pleased with itself for having secured the services of a genuinely cosmopolitan troubadour.

<div align="center">~~~§~~~</div>

Maxwell had kept a seat for Brian and they waited expectantly for the rest of the audience to be seated. In his anticipation of the concert, Brian had momentarily stopped thinking about Kate. However the distraction was short lived, for the young lady in question came into the room. She joined her friends and made herself comfortable in a seat, that had clearly been saved for her, in the front row.

Brian noted, to his dismay, that on this occasion, not all of her companions were female. Two were male. Both were members of the Folk Music Society and one of them, who happened to be sitting next to Kate, was a support act for the concert. Brian's customary optimism was almost completely snuffed out by this development. The salad roll, which he had been thoroughly enjoying, immediately lost its flavour and tasted of ashes. He miserably sipped his gall flavoured coffee and wished that it was hemlock.

The appointed time arrived and the club president introduced the opening act - a duo loosely modelled on Ian and Sylvia, Nina and Frederick and Peter, Paul and Mary minus either Peter or Paul. It was their first public appearance. They were a little nervous and self conscious to begin with but they warmed to their task and were enthusiastically supported by the audience.

The second artist was Angela Moriarty, a medical student who had the voice and face of an angel. With very long, braided flaxen hair and moonstone eyes, she projected an image of fragile innocence in deadly peril - singing poignant, tragic songs about substance abuse while looking as though she'd never taken anything stronger than a barley sugar in her life. She used this device to very good effect and almost every male in the audience wanted to rush to her protection while a number of the ladies present wished that the silly cow would just do away with herself and be done with it.

By the time Miss Moriarty had concluded her bracket with *Needle of Death*, Brian's passions had been distracted, if not soothed. However, his gloom returned as Mark Denham, the man at Kate's side, got to his feet and began to tune his guitar. Introduced as needing no introduction, Mark was clearly at the top of the Folk Music Society's pecking order and given pride of place among the support acts on the programme. Brian would normally have agreed that this position of honour was warranted, but he spent most of the bracket looking not at the artist but at the seat he had vacated.

Denham performed with his usual confidence and poise. He was a very competent guitarist with a voice to match and he was determined to give the star attraction a run for his money. He did songs by Dylan and Gordon Lightfoot with an easy and confident line of patter in his introductions. The crowd, with one possible exception, loved it.

As a change of mood for his third song, he played Woody Guthrie's *Car- Car*, which he dedicated to his white Austin Healey Sprite. He also took the opportunity to point out that the Sprite was for sale and that anyone interested in a test drive could see him after the show.

Brian had probably never enjoyed a song so much as that performance of *Car-Car*. Mark Denham was her cousin!! The salad roll instantly became a salad roll fit for the gods and, although it was now cold, the coffee could well have been ambrosia. Mark Denham concluded his bracket with *Don't Think Twice* but was called back for an encore. He obliged with *Four Strong Winds* and then, amid resounding applause, resumed his seat alongside his pretty cousin. Performer and audience alike, seemed satisfied with his efforts and everyone was ready for the main feature.

The president led the star of the show from the back of the room where he had been quietly watching the last two acts. Mervan Mithras had what could almost be called a shambling gait. His denim jeans and jacket had a genuinely road-weary and travel-stained look about them which some of the fresh faced members of the audience were trying hard to cultivate in their own attire. His guitar case was plastered with airline and shipping stickers which suggested that he was a genuine wayfaring stranger. The guitar it contained was a Martin and those members of the audience who were musicians were, impressed.

With silent composure, he ignored the audience while he assembled his mouth organ in its harness and tuned up his guitar. He adopted a no nonsense style with brief almost terse introductions to the first few songs he played, which happened to be a selection of Donovan songs. In contrast to his introductions, the songs were delicately and sensitively executed. They were well received and he began to relax and talk more to his audience. He concluded that part of the performance with *Desolation Row* and the audience was eating out of his hand.

He took a few sips from a mug of coffee and actually told a joke as he prepared for the finale of his performance. It was the genuinely funny sort of story that a seasoned entertainer would be expected to tell. But if anyone had looked closely, they would have noticed that there was no laughter in the performer's eyes. There was an underlying melancholy in his demeanour which lent a particular tension to his performance.

Thus far into the bracket, Mervan Mithras had confined his efforts to familiar songs by established artists. This had ensured a positive reception for him whilst lulling his audience into a sense of false security. The time had now come to play some original compositions. The first few songs were similar in style and content to the Donovan and Dylan songs which he had already performed. But there was to be a sting in the tail of this performance. Mr Mithras intended to bare his soul.

The final song seemed to be autobiographical in nature. At first glance it appeared to be a song of un-requited love. But this was not a poignant song of wistful and tender frustration like *Catch the Wind*. It was a song about a green eyed angel who had "promised Mr Mithras her heart"; a green eyed angel who then "ate Mr Mithras' soul; popped Mr Mithras' veins and blew Mr Mithras' mind apart." The song then went on to suggest that Mr Mithras was "wasting his dying breath" but - fortunately perhaps - he didn't have time to tell his audience "all the things he knew about death."

The song and the performance ended with an emotionally drained Mervan Mithras and a bemused and slightly embarrassed audience which wasn't sure how to respond. The president of the Folk Music Society, who had seen Mervan perform at "The Drinking Gourd" in Darlington, knew the wonderfully restorative effect that an encore would produce and successfully manufactured a groundswell of stamping and clapping. Mervan Mithras responded accordingly with another song of unrequited love but this time he appeared to be dishing out the heartache rather than being on the receiving end. The audience applauded enthusiastically.

The President then spirited him away and the majority of the audience - Brian and Maxwell included - dispersed to resume their academic careers. The support artists and friends - Kate included - joined the President and Mervan for wine and cheese in the common room.

At about four o'clock that afternoon, a taxi deposited Mervan Mithras at the Ross railway station and he waited for the 'up train' to Darlington. The Island of Greater Cumberland was served by a comprehensive, if leisurely, railway network. The dual flagships of the line were a pair of comfortable, almost stately, passenger trains which traversed the Island from top to bottom 6 days a week. The two trains crossed paths and exchanged crews near the centre of the Island around midday.

To the confusion of many visitors, the train travelling north away from the capital was called the "Down Train" while the southbound train to Darlington was known as the "Up Train". Mervan was aware of the potential for a blues composition about substance abuse with a railway hobo theme, based on the names of the two trains. But the comfort level of the 'Up' and the 'Down' trains with their plush green or maroon upholstered seats far surpassed the level of creature comfort enjoyed by Mervan's American heroes of the depression years.

The hostesses on those worthy trains would have been appalled to hear that the service they provided was being in any way compared with the lonesome desolation of derelict travellers on American freight trains. That isn't to say that Emily Oldfield, the chief hostess, didn't think that some of her younger patrons - Mr Mithras included - were beginning to dress and behave like tramps and hoboes. Emily could remember a time when the beer provided by the buffet service only needed re-stocking once a week. However, in recent years, to her dismay, she had noticed that on some occasions, particularly at the beginning and end of university terms, the train could be drunk dry in a single day.

On this particular afternoon, his performer's fee burning a hole in his pocket, Mervan ordered scotch. His attempts to play the rough diamond - the quietly spoken gentleman vagabond - only served to further dismay and disturb the hostess who hurried back to the buffet car pining for those bygone days when she had a nicer sort of passenger to deal with.

Mervan sipped his scotch and watched the passing countryside. It was sheep country mainly. Occasionally, a bend in the track would reveal a glimpse of the lights of Darlington up ahead clustered under the brooding shadow of the Mountain. The cabin lights came on and his attention shifted from the sheep in the gathering dusk outside, to the moody reflection of himself that stared back pensively from the window.

There were people in Mervan's circle of acquaintance who prided themselves on their hedonism. However Mervan's great gift - the gift of being a troubadour - meant that, rather than living purely for life's pleasures he had to chronicle and savour life's more melancholy aspects. For one thing, songs like that were much easier to write. He had chosen a lonely profession but it had its compensations, because he believed that he was destined for greatness.

Born Mervyn Purvis, the son of working class parents, his childhood had been fairly nondescript and was characterised by an awkward shyness that made him the subject of ridicule at school and everywhere else. His parents were aware of his difficulties and tried to support him but he was reclusive and not an easy child to help.

As a small boy, Mervyn was interested in music. His grandfather had owned an old concertina which he used to play at country dances in his youth. Mervyn had discovered the old instrument in a store room in his grandparents' farmhouse. He had spent a whole afternoon trying to coax a tune out of it and was blissfully happy with his achievements. But the bliss had not been shared by other members of the household. Next morning, in circumstances that were never fully explained, the concertina was found crushed beyond hope of restoration under the rear wheels of his Uncle's roadster.

Despite this setback, the child Mervyn retained his interest in music. It was a weekly ritual in the Purvis household for the entire family to spend Sunday afternoon listening to the top 40 on the radio. Being a child of the fifties and early sixties, this meant that on those Sunday afternoons, Mervyn was exposed to a number of powerful musical influences. He absorbed everything he heard, but it was not until he was seventeen that these musical influences found a means of expression when he again picked up a musical instrument and began to teach himself to play the guitar.

The fact that he found other peoples' songs hard to play led him to try composing songs of his own. It was perhaps a happy accident, although Mervan believed it to be something more cosmic and providential, that the cult of the singer-songwriter was beginning to emerge at that time.

Mervyn began to dream of becoming the Cumberlands' answer to Bob Dylan and the true voice of his Nation's soul. He believed that there was a future in protest music. However, the fact that the Cumberlands did not have a military presence in Vietnam took some of the relevance out of anti-war songs at home.

The young singer-songwriter made a few journeys to Australia and New Zealand to further his cause, and found some work plying his trade, but his successes had been modest. He was also mindful of the fact that, if he took up permanent residence in Australia, he ran a very real risk of being conscripted and possibly tasting the horrors of war at first hand. It was this understandable instinct of self preservation that finally led him to return home to the Cumberlands. Sadly, he felt that in doing so, he was giving up the certainty of fame and greatness that he believed were there for the taking.

For a time, he returned to the family home to lick his emotional wounds and consider his future. The family lived on Trinity Island, to the north-west of Greater Cumberland. It consisted of three large triangular mountains connected and surrounded by a low plain. To Hugh, Brian and Maggie, those peaks, when seen in the blue distance from their primary school playground on the mainland, were the pyramids of Egypt. There were very extreme tides between the smaller island and the Mainland and at low tide the seabed between the two land masses was exposed. At such times, the illusion of the pyramids surrounded by sand was complete.

Trinity Island supported a timber industry and a dairy industry and Mervyn's father was a clerk at the butter factory. Mr Purvis had hoped that his son's appraisal of his future prospects would include consideration of getting regular employment somewhere. When, after six weeks of appraisal, his son's thoughts didn't appear to be moving in that direction, he suggested that perhaps they should do so fairly quickly. He even lined up a job at a nearby sawmill. Unfortunately, Mervyn feared for his musician's fingers. He felt there were far too many sawmill employees on the Island with one or more digits missing. In fact, to be only one or two digits short wasn't even considered a disability by most of the locals.

Mervyn remembered the first time, as a very small child, when he had seen a man at Mass whose right index finger was just a stump. In hushed tones, he had asked his father what had happened to it. In equally hushed tones, his father had solemnly whispered, 'that's what happens to people who pick their nose.'

Rather than take the job at the sawmill, Mervyn decided to head for the mainland. It was during that sojourn with friends in an old terrace house in North Darlington that he experienced what he believed to be a revelation. He had always been fascinated by Arthurian legend. On his way back from *Sydney*, he had bought a copy of *The Crystal Cave*, Mary Stewart's novel about Merlin. The book contained many omens and prophesies which captured his imagination. Often a merlin would appear or suddenly take flight at some crucial moment in the young wizard's story. Through reading the book, Mervyn had discovered that his birthday coincided with the feast day of Merlin's god - the soldier's god Mithras.

One afternoon he put down the book and went out into the back garden to check the washing. The fence behind the clothesline was overgrown with a tangled mass of blackberry vines and plum trees. Mervyn heard a scrabbling sound coming from the undergrowth and went to investigate. To his amazement, he found a young hawk caught up in a tangled grotto of withered leaves and thorny branches. A young hawk in the middle of the city!!

Mervyn was no ornithologist so he was unable to tell whether the hawk was a merlin or not. He didn't even know if merlins inhabited the southern hemisphere. But he was convinced that the hawk was a supernatural manifestation. He was afraid to go any closer. The thorny tangle of vines looked impassable and he was also afraid of the savage beauty of the bird.

Back inside the house, the implications of what he had seen, began to dawn on him. His very name, "Mervyn" was not unlike "Merlin". His parents had named him after his uncle Mervyn, the champion axe man. But names were caught up in destiny and bestowed where the gods intended. Perhaps he was Merlin come again. He went back out to see if the young hawk was still there, but it had gone. Then he went inside and helped himself to his hosts' whiskey. He had a definite, cosmic purpose. He was somebody special - a creature of destiny and his destiny lay here in the Cumberlands!

Mervyn decided that he needed to change his name to better reflect his new found identity. It took a few attempts to get it right. Those attempts were recorded on posters for various folk clubs and concerts around the country at that time. Maxwell Tynan was an avid collector of such memorabilia and his poster collection reflected the complete metamorphosis.

To begin with, there were the early posters promoting Mervyn Purvis. Then there were some posters featuring Mithras Purvis. For a while he tried Merlin Purvis. None of these incarnations seemed to adequately capture his new persona. Then one night, in his sleep, the inspiration came to him. He would change the spelling of Mervyn to Mer*van* - a subtle tribute to one of his heroes, Dono*van*. Next morning, when he shed the skin of his sleeping bag, he rose to greet the new day - a Purvis no longer. Mervan Mithras had been born!!

The "Up Train" crossed the River and began to pass through the outskirts of the City, stopping at a succession of small suburban stations. Mervan was just finishing his third whiskey when the train reached journey's end at Darlington Central. He quickly picked up his guitar, stepped onto the platform and moved through the milling crowd of ordinary mortals who stood waiting for their luggage and greeting loved ones. Of course he loved them all dearly, believing himself to be the voice of their nation's soul, but tonight his mind was concerned with other things and he was content to impress them all with his latent fame and travel weary, cosmopolitan demeanour as he melted quietly into the darkness.

As it happened, his passing was only noted by one person on the crowded platform, and that person was far more widely known in the city than Mervan was ever likely to be. A stooped but dapper little man in grey sports trousers, hounds tooth coat and a trilby hat, was busily surveying the scene on the platform looking left and right smiling a smile of mischievous contentment at everything he saw.

His left arm cradled a large teddy bear and in his right hand he held a bunch of flowers. He was waiting, as he often did, to present the flowers to Emily Oldfield when she alighted from the train. He was commonly known as Lester and theories to explain him and his eccentricities abounded.

Darlington, although a capital city, was still small enough to ensure that anything unusual was quickly noticed and Lester had a particular gift for getting himself noticed rather more than most people. His visits to the station were a case in point. Emily Oldfield appeared to take his salutations in good part and certain unkind porters often joked that a half-wit like Lester was the only kind of man she was ever likely to attract.

Lester watched the departing figure of Mervan. In particular he studied the troubadour's shoulder length hair, and proclaimed in a surprisingly loud and theatrical voice to no one in particular

'King Charles the First was floored in his execution!!'

Oblivious, Mervan considered a taxi as he walked by the rank outside the old sandstone terminal building but thought better of it. A brisk twenty minute walk would see him home and sharpen his appetite. His home was a flat consisting of four attic rooms and a downstairs bathroom in a house next to a service station. Apart from his stereo and records; a sleeping bag and mattress; a stove in the kitchen and an old electric radiator with an imitation coal fire, the flat did not contain any furniture.

The thought of the cold reception that awaited him there, coupled with the continued smouldering of the day's pay in his pocket, prompted him to hang the expense and have dinner at a little Italian restaurant not far from where he lived. The restaurateur, Giacomo Montini was an old friend of the Purvis family. When he had first arrived in the Cumberlands in the early fifties he had worked on a swamp reclamation project on Trinity Island and one of Mervan's cousins had taken the young immigrant under his wing.

Giacomo, or Jack as he was known, treated Mervan like family. The young minstrel's meal was always washed down with free chianti and the two would talk and drink until long after the other patrons had left. Jack was a naturally gregarious person. His restaurant was famous throughout the country for its food, its hospitality and its distinguished clientele. Mervan was able to indulge his nascent fame by being a regular patron and basking in Jack's undisguised admiration of his musical ability.

Jack had written some words of his own about his native village in Italy and how he would return there some day. On more than one occasion he had wistfully asked Mervan to set it to music for him. For some reason that Mervan did not fully understand himself, he was reluctant to comply with the request. He always changed the subject whenever it was raised.

Perhaps it was because of the reverent affection he had for Jack. The little Italian's memories were too precious, or perhaps they were too real and the minstrel doubted his own credibility. The subject was broached on this night, as always, but quickly passed over and the conversation moved on to other things. They traded dreams and compliments, childhood memories, past heartaches, earnest aspirations and fond regrets.

After the waiters and kitchen staff had gone, a pest controller arrived and began to lay a potent mixture of toxic powders on the carpet. This was the only time that the work could be done without disrupting trade. The wine continued to flow freely as Jack and Mervan talked on and a pungent vapour began to rise up around their knees.

It was in the early hours of the new morning that Mervan Mithras, with a belly full of pasta, chianti and toxic fumes, finally climbed the stairs to his apartment. An hour or two after he had collapsed on his bed, the minstrel's head began to spin with a blinding, nauseous brightness. The Voice of his Nation's Soul staggered back downstairs to the bathroom and, in a long and painful encore, crouched over the toilet bowl and vomited until eventually, a fitful shivering sleep brought down the curtain on the day's performance.

<div align="center">~~~§~~~</div>

A heavy mist lay over the City and it was bitterly cold. Down on the river, a fishing boat was cautiously nosing its way in to the dock. Jim and a crewmate were drinking brandy and playing cards in the wheel house. This was Jim's favourite part of every voyage. He loved Darlington and felt that to enter the city in this way was to celebrate, and become a living part of, its maritime past.

The blanket of fog obscured the taller, twentieth century additions to the Darlington Skyline. All that was visible was the assortment of old sandstone warehouses and pubs on the dockside and, above the mist, the snow-capped summit of Mount Cameron just beginning to reflect the glow of the rising sun.

Interest in the card game petered out and they were called to help with docking. This was followed by three hours hard work unloading the catch before the skipper paid them off at 9:30. The crew prepared to adjourn to the Crown and Anchor, a well known early opener on the waterfront. As usual, Jim declined the invitation. He would meet them there for a drink before they set out for the next voyage but for now he had other things to do. The crew had grown accustomed to this habit and assumed that he must have a woman waiting for him. Jim said nothing to discourage this assumption.

Slinging a bag over his shoulder, he headed off through the still fogbound inner city and began to climb up into the hilly suburban streets of West Darlington. He was heading for a house in Cranwell Street. As the crow flies, it was about a quarter of a mile from Hugh's flat. That young man was already at his desk in the City Hall preparing accounts and payment vouchers for authorisation by the City Treasurer. A boring, dreary day opened out in front of him while Jim looked forward to a meal of bacon and eggs and the pleasures of a warm bed with clean sheets and feather pillows.

Cranwell Street was quite high up and Jim was able to turn and look back down on the wall of fog as it streamed out through the river valley to the sea, like the ghost of the massive ancient glacier that carved its way across that part of the world in pre-historic times.

Then he turned his attention to the street with its little sandstone cottages. On the downhill side was a terrace that had been built as officers' quarters in 1817. Jim knocked on the door of number four. It opened almost immediately and he was ushered fondly into the warm, bright kitchen with its familiar smell of freshly baked bread, fried egg and bacon.

There was a single brief kiss then he went to the bathroom to wash his hands while she poured the tea and served his breakfast. He opened the door to his room to sling his bag on to the bed. Then he sat down at the kitchen table. She didn't make much conversation while he ate. They were very comfortable in each other's company and didn't need to say a lot.

He had been on the fishing boats for a couple of years now and they had a routine. She worried the whole time he was away and it was worse after the shipwreck. But each time he returned safely, she suppressed her fears and pampered him. It was no good trying to talk him out of it. That would only harden his resolve. She just wished he would find some nice girl and settle down with a job on dry land. The sea had already taken his father.

At 10:30, while Hugh had his morning tea break and Mervan Mithras staggered back upstairs to his sleeping bag, Jim, freshly showered and clad in clean pyjamas, slipped between the sheets of his warm and comfortable bed. His mother kissed him again and then went down the street to do her grocery shopping.

4: *One for Sorrow Two for Joy*

It was a quarter to nine on a Wednesday morning in August - the coldest month in the Cumberlands' year. Brian made his way down the heavily frosted pathway from Trinity College to the English Department for a tutorial on Defoe. A solitary raven watched his progress from the bare branches of an oak tree in the college grounds.

'Judas' said Brian with frosty breath. He had lost faith in the Celtic birds of good omen. Nearly a month had passed since Kate had seen his little discourse to the highway ravens and he had made no progress with her at all. She obviously wasn't interested in him and he had sadly returned to the company of the Ineligible Bachelors. This was a group of dissolute young men who occupied their spare time drinking far more than was good for them at Insect Corner, a little bar in a pub called the Old Bohemian. However, lack of finances had obliged him to stay in on the previous evening. This meant that, for once, he was reasonably alert and not hung over. However it did not mean that he had actually managed to do any preparation for the tutorial. He would, as usual, have to fly by the seat of his pants, but at least he would be doing so with a clearer head than usual.

Doctor Spotswood arrived in the tutorial room and placed two extra seats in the circle.

'A couple of students from my 10:30 tutorial have asked if they can join us this morning because they have other commitments later in the day - Miss Mahoney and Miss Shelverton. I am sure you will make them welcome.'

The group did make them welcome, except for Brian and another ineligible bachelor, Damian Giltinan. Unaware of the exact time, they had stopped outside for a quick cigarette before the tutorial started.

'Good of you to join us,' was all Doctor Spotswood said to them as the two young blades sheepishly sidled into the room and took their seats ten minutes later. In such circumstances, it generally took Brian about five minutes to stop blushing before he could look directly at the other people in the group. But before he had a chance to do this, he heard Kate's voice involved in the discussion. He looked up and found her sitting opposite him.

He removed his battered top hat and placed it on the floor, desperately trying to compose himself and focus on what she was saying. If only he had done some preparation. And how was old Spotswood going to react? Sometimes he persecuted latecomers and spent the entire tutorial cross examining them. Other times he treated them with cold disdain. Brian prayed that it would be the latter but regretted the fact that, either way, he would look pretty stupid in front of Kate.

He spent the rest of the class studying the floor and trying to follow the line of discussion in case he could make an intelligent contribution. On one or two occasions, he nearly chanced his arm but thought better of it. He didn't know if the gods were with him or not. As it happened, Dr Spotswood chose to ignore him and the tutorial passed without further incident. He was considering waiting around to try and engage Kate in conversation but she and Miss Shelverton were busily pursuing some point with the good Doctor.

Cursing quietly to himself, Brian walked from the room, only to remember that he had left his top hat behind. When he went back to retrieve it, the discussion was still in progress. He heard them laughing about something as he left. Naturally he assumed that they were laughing at him. If only he hadn't abused that crow. "One crow for sorrow".

A few minutes later in the cloak room, his frustration boiled over. He put his books away in his locker, threw his unfortunate top hat on the floor, stamped on it and then kicked it across the room. Anger was an emotion he rarely displayed and when it erupted it was hard to contain. In fact at that moment, things were about to become ugly and the outlook for the top hat was far from bright. Brian was about to give vent to his anger when he heard the caw of a crow.

'Quoth the Raven never more,' he muttered as he turned around fearfully expecting to see the Judas crow perched on top of the lockers. But it wasn't a crow. It was Kate with her cupped hands to her mouth doing a very creditable impersonation.

'That's very good,' he said, on a sudden rush of adrenalin. 'Quite convincing. And I should know I'm fluent in Crow.'

'Well judging from your performance in the tutorial, I was beginning to think that perhaps English wasn't your native tongue.'

'How come you came to my tute?'

'I've got to go into town to buy my father a birthday present.'

'Will you be travelling in your sports car?'

'No I decided against it. I've kept my Mini.'

It was a crucial moment and Brian was nerved up to do something dramatic. On suddenly realising that he was alone with Kate, he was able to draw on the enormous tide of anger and frustration welling up inside him. It gave him confidence.

'I don't suppose you'd have room for a passenger?'

'I don't see why not. I won't be coming back til tomorrow though. Is that a problem?'

'No no. I have friends in the city' he said - a little too grandly.

'OK, I'll pick you up outside Trinity at 10:30. Don't forget your poor old hat.'

<div align="center">~~~§~~~</div>

As Brian and Kate sped out of Ross along the highway to Darlington, a burglary was taking place. Mrs Malleson was away for a few days visiting her sister. She had asked Hugh to feed her cat. It was the opportunity the conspirators had been waiting for. Mrs Malleson caught a taxi to the station at 8:15 and Robert, Jim and Lucy arrived at 9:00. Robert and Jim thought it was a bonus that Hugh had the keys to Mrs Malleson's apartment to feed her cat. They insisted on going through her rooms. Hugh angrily objected but in the end had to content himself with making sure they didn't disturb or damage anything.

Hugh had often been in Mrs Malleson's kitchen, but only her kitchen. He paid his rent to her and she always asked him in for a cup of tea. In spite of himself, he was a little curious to see the rest of her apartment.

The kitchen had the feeling of a farmhouse. It resonated with the remnants of the old kitchen garden and farmyard outside. It was cluttered with cannisters, pot plants, spice racks, old family photographs and china ornaments. Her bedroom on the other hand was sparse - almost monastic. There was a bed, a dresser and a wardrobe all made from a pale coloured pine that was native to the Cumberlands.

There were two framed photographs. One was a man in his early twenties. He had close cropped hair and a strong square face but Hugh could recognize something of Mrs Malleson's softer, sadder, features. It had to be her son who was overseas. The second photograph was quite different. It had the appearance of an icon. It was definitely a photograph but it had been hand coloured to emphasise the fair hair and pale, almost transparent moonstone eyes.

'It's him' said Jim, almost beside himself with excitement. 'It's him. It's the bloke that rescued me.' He took the picture down from the wall.

'I tell you it's him. There *is* a connection. We are onto something!'

'For pity's sake, put it back,' said Hugh, still illogically fearful that Mrs Malleson could walk in at any moment. Jim's excitement and uncharacteristic animation were infectious and the other conspirators gathered around the picture.

'It's like a holy picture,' said Lucy. She had shared Hugh's discomfort about invading Mrs Malleson's apartment but the features in the photograph totally captivated her. The image stared at them calmly with a slightly amused and affectionate expression. The photograph was a head and shoulders portrait, vignetted in an oval frame. It was not possible to distinguish the subject's clothing and there were no clues as to when the photograph had been taken.

'We've got to get a copy of this,' said Jim.

'Over my dead body,' said Hugh. 'I live here. Mrs Malleson is my neighbour. She's...she's a friend of mine.'

'He's right Jim,' said Lucy. 'We really shouldn't be here.'

Jim put the photograph back on the wall.

'But at least you've seen him,' he said as they left the room and went out to the back door and the court yard.

A little to one side of the clothes line that Hugh shared with Mrs Malleson, was a trap door.

'It'll probably be locked,' Hugh muttered as they bent down to examine it.

'See if any of Mrs Malleson's keys fit it,' said Robert. None of them did.

'Well it's not a modern lock, so I think I can manage it,' said Jim, taking a huge bunch of old keys out of his pocket. The other three looked nervously about them as Jim began to try a succession of keys in the lock. As luck would have it, the courtyard was screened from the view of neighbouring premises by high fences and bordering trees and creepers. Nevertheless, Hugh was beginning to wish they had left someone at the front door in case Mrs Malleson should unexpectedly return.

'Got it,' said Jim exultantly. 'Now at last we can see for ourselves.'

Hugh said he would wait on guard outside and the other three went eagerly down the stairs. He fretted. If she had caught the down train, Mrs Malleson would be miles away by now. But he felt that he had betrayed her trust. Here he was putting his neck on the line for these complete strangers, when Mrs Malleson was the closest thing to a friend that he had in the City.

Fifteen minutes passed without any sound from downstairs. Hugh's curiosity began to get the better of him. He ventured down the steps. It felt very much like going down into the hold of a ship. He came down into a room with a low ceiling. It was very dusty and it seemed that they were the first visitors in many years. A semi-circle of benches clustered in one corner of the room around an ornate suspended lantern. Hugh remembered Lucy's description of the room she had seen in her childhood.

The other three conspirators were busy reading an assortment of exercise books that had been left on the benches.

'What do you make of these?' said Jim, thrusting some of the exercise books into Hugh's hands. The books were full of what appeared to be the tentative scrawl of very young children. Each book contained an individual account of the same event.

"There was once a lonely sailor called Norian, who sailed a white ship.

When he was a little boy, his best friend drowned and Norian was very sad."

"Norian was a sailor. He had too many children and he had to take them home on his white boat."

'They all tell the same story,' said Robert. 'It's not dictation. Each kid has used his own words.'

'Or hers,' said Lucy.

'How old do you reckon these books are' said Jim blowing the dust from the yellowed pages. 'The writing is copperplate or trying to be. I reckon they're fifty years old at least.'

"And the people went down the tunnel. Norian held a lantern so they could see. The people went on tip-toe. The tunnel led to a cave by a stream where the white ship was waiting. The cave was hidden by some big trees. It was called the Cypress Gate. The sun went down and the moon came out."

They crowded around. A drawing depicted stick people and the ship was vaguely like a Viking longship.

'Is that like the boat that picked you up?' said Hugh sarcastically. Jim's excited enthusiasm made him seem less intimidating and more vulnerable. He didn't notice the jibe.

They searched through the other twenty books. Several others had illustrations. Some of the young artists were more skilful. From the clothing, the figures they had drawn were clearly meant to be from antiquity.

Lucy put the books she had been reading back on the bench.

'I don't think anyone's been down here for years,' she said as she looked around the room. 'There's no electric light.'

'I suppose they would have used the lantern,' said Jim, going over to examine it.

They were unable to determine how it operated.

'I would have thought it was some kind of oil or spirit lamp, but there's no sign of any blackening around the edge of the glass - no wick either.'

'Is this like the room you saw when you were a kid?' asked Robert.

'It's hard to say,' said Lucy. 'The other room was more lived in. It was bright and clean. This just looks deserted and neglected.'

As their eyes became more accustomed to the gloom, they noticed more. There were a few cupboards against the walls. Most proved to be locked or empty but Lucy found one that was neither. It contained more exercise books but they contained the work of older children. The handwriting was more mature. It was in ink instead of pencil and it was beautiful. It was similar to copperplate but with an elegance of its own. To their immense frustration the pages and pages of flowing script were not written in English. Try as they might none of them could recognise the language let alone begin to interpret it.

'We're going to have to take at least one book with us,' said Robert.

'At the very least,' said Jim. 'She obviously doesn't come down here Hugh. You've got nothing to worry about.'

They continued to examine the room. Apart from some crockery there was nothing else in the remaining unlocked cupboards. In the end wall behind the lantern, there was a locked door. None of Jim's keys or the keys on Mrs Malleson's key ring fitted the lock. The door looked too solid to force open. Jim was frustrated.

'We've got enough to be going on with,' said Lucy. 'We can always come back if you can think of a way to open the door.'

Reluctantly Jim agreed. The door had external hinges. Next time they could bring a screw driver and some other tools. Taking pains to leave the room looking as they found it, the conspirators, with a dozen exercise books, left the cellar and adjourned to the saloon bar at O'Brien's.

<center>~~~§~~~</center>

As the conspirators drank to their morning's work, Kate and Brian were arriving in the city. Their journey had commenced a little awkwardly but by the time they reached Darlington, the conversation was flowing easily and pleasantly between them. Brian wanted desperately to spend as much of the day with Kate as possible. Over a cup of coffee at a road side cafe, he had volunteered his services in selecting the birthday present for her father.

'It takes a man to know what a man would like. It's all a question of taste.'

'And you have taste do you?' said Kate laughing. Even when she was laughing at him, it was music to his ears. 'I somehow don't think you and Dad would have the same tastes,' she continued.

'In clothing?'

'In anything.'

'I still think I should come along to make sure you don't get something inappropriate.'

Kate didn't actually turn down this offer and so when they pulled up outside "Cohen and Cutler's", a very staid old establishment with brass name plates and leadlight windows in Jamieson Street at the expensive end of town, Brian dusted off his top hat and sauntered along at her side. He was a little in awe of the place, never having ventured inside it before. He was also impressed by the way that Kate was obviously well known there and treated with respect and courtesy by the staff.

These were mostly elderly gentlemen who to Brian, looked more like butlers or gentlemen's gentlemen than shop assistants. As an act of deference, he took off his top hat.

'Good morning Miss. Let me guess.....your father's birthday?'

'That's right Mr Connolly. This is my friend, Brian. He's come to make sure I don't buy anything inappropriate.'

Mr Connolly looked Brian up and down and coughed to disguise the escape of a brief yelp of laughter.

'Very well Miss. Where shall we begin?'

They looked at toiletries. They looked at ties. They looked at cravats. They looked at a great number of things. Kate was totally absorbed in the task and Brian was impressed by the way that the staff of that venerable old establishment appeared to wait on her every whim. Brian naturally thought that everyone should treat her with that respect because he worshipped her but he was nevertheless surprised to see his reverence shared by these distinguished old men with their pinstriped trousers and silver hair. To his gratification, Kate seemed to include him in her quest. He hoped that this was a sign of acceptance or perhaps something more.

In fact Kate was simply being her normal agreeable self, returning friendship when it was offered. Brian had become her friend, but in the confused world of his dreams and desires he hoped and believed he had become something more. However, because he was Brian, he had no confidence about the matter.

Mr Connolly fondled the tape measure that he wore round his neck like a priest's stole.

'Has Sir seen anything he considers appropriate?'

'Not so far,' said Brian, aware of the old man's gentle mischief but anxious not to react badly in front of Kate.

'Perhaps Sir might like to purchase a new hat?'

'Now that's a thought,' said Kate.

'I think we should concentrate on your father's birthday present,' said Brian, trying to be statesman-like.

'Quite right,' said Kate. 'How about these?' She swooped upon a pair of cuff links.

'The very thing,' said Brian. 'I've got a pair like that at home.'

Kate woke from her shopper's frenzy with a peal of laughter.

'You twit,' she said as Mr Connolly wrapped the present.

'Now that's done, I'd be honoured if you'd let me buy you a cup of coffee,' said Brian.

'Why not?' said Kate.

'There you go Miss,' said Mr Connolly. 'Will I put that on your account?'

'No I better pay cash. I can't really charge it up to Dad can I?'

'No Miss,' said the old man, smiling and remembering occasions only a few years earlier when she used to do just that.

'Good bye Miss. Give my regards to your grandad.'

'Yes I will. To be sure.'

'Are you sure we couldn't interest the young gentleman in a new hat?'

Kate replied with a brief, mischievous chuckle. 'Another time perhaps. Bye!!'

'Good bye Miss .... and Sir.'

Then they were quickly back out in the noise and bustle of the street.

'Right then, where would you suggest?' said Kate as she put her father's gift in the car.

'How about the Bluebird,' suggested Brian as he gallantly put a shilling in the parking meter.

'The Bluebird it is,' said Kate. It was a walk of a couple of blocks down Jamieson Street to the more bohemian part of Town. Although it was still only early in the afternoon, the sun was already beginning to sink towards Mount Cameron and long, cold shadows were draping the shop fronts. But for all that, the streets were still busy. Wednesday was social services day and various pensioners and welfare recipients were queuing at government offices to receive their cheques.

A minor disturbance had broken out on the steps of the Social Welfare office where a number of middle aged and elderly pensioners were waiting to receive their cheques and cash them at the "Town and Country Hotel" across the street. Two young constables had broken up the fight and were moving them on. As they moved away, an old man with a striking head of silver hair turned and addressed the policemen. Brian couldn't catch what he said, but there was something about the old man's dignified contempt that impressed him. The very young policemen blushed and smiled sheepishly as they stood their ground. The old man wrapped himself in his old tweed overcoat and turned his back on them.

Kate noticed Brian's fascination.

'He's like King Lear,' she said as they went off to the Bluebird.

The coffee was always good at the Bluebird and, because Brian's studentship cheque had arrived before they left Ross, he was able to play the gracious host.

'You are obviously a regular at Cohen and Cutler's' he said after the waitress took their orders.

'The family has had an account there for years,' Kate said simply.

'And that old chap knows your grandfather.'

'Yes they were in the first world war together.'

The Bluebird sometimes featured folk singers in the evening and Brian noticed a poster for Mervan Mithras that evening.

'You wouldn't like to come and see him I suppose?' He asked tentatively.

'Any other time I might, but we are having Dad's birthday dinner tonight. That is if he can get away from work in time.'

'Where does he work?'

'He works for the Government' she replied a little evasively with a slightly puzzled expression. 'But I had better be going. Can I give you a lift anywhere?'

Brian paid for their coffees and they headed back to the car. The streets were still busy and another frosty night was settling on the City. They noticed a disturbance up ahead. Lester was standing at the next corner making pronouncements upon passersby to their general discomfit and embarrassment. Most people tried to ignore him but Lester was a hard man to ignore.

'I saw yer.' He bellowed at Kate. 'Sneakin into the women's' pisser.'

Completely unperturbed, Kate smiled at him.

'But I'm a woman.'

Lester rubbed his eyes as if really seeing her for the first time.

'Why so you are.' He doffed his trilby and swept the pavement with a gracious bow. 'And eminently suited to the task.'

'Charmed I'm sure,' said Kate laughing and nudging Brian in the ribs.

Brian's adoration increased.

Half an hour later, Brian thought that his luck had finally run out when Kate dropped him off in Gracechurch Street outside Hugh's flat.

'You're sure you won't come in for a cup of tea?' Kate actually thought about it for a moment but then declined.

'No I really should be going. I can give you a lift back to uni tomorrow though if you can be ready by eleven.'

'That'd be wonderful,' said Brian.

'Bye' said Kate and she was gone.

Hugh looked pale and apprehensive as he opened the door. Irrationally, he expected it to be Mrs Malleson but on finding Brian on the doorstep he was still uncomfortable.

He ushered his friend upstairs into his kitchen, where Jim was presiding over the dregs of the sherry.

'Brian this is a friend of mine....'

'Jim Lovegrove,' said Jim leaping to his feet and firmly grasping Brian's hand.

'Brian McInerney. How long have you known our Hugo?' Brian would have preferred Hugh to be on his own so he could talk about Kate, but he was a naturally friendly person and was curious about this stranger that Hugh had taken up with.

Hugh looked on in helpless frustration. His few social skills had been taxed to the limit by a very eventful day. Normally he would have been pleased to see Brian but the burden of introducing him to Jim without betraying the secret of the conspiracy was too much. To make matters worse, Jim and Brian seemed to take an instant liking to each other. His hopes of an early night and a bit of solitude were dashed as Jim produced a flask of rum from his coat pocket and poured out a measure for Brian in Maggie's glass.

'We've got to know Hugh quite well in the past few months,' said Jim who was a little the worse for wear after an afternoon at O'Brien's. 'How well can you keep a secret?'

Hugh shook his head in disbelief.

'Are you sure you want to talk about this?'

Jim stumbled and almost lost his footing as he turned to look at Hugh.

'I suppose not,' he said a little thickly. 'Anyway Brian here's your health.'

'And yours,' said Brian as he helped Jim back into his chair.

'Now what's this about a secret?'

'It's a bit too early to say,' said Jim. 'Have a talk to Hugh about it some time. This is a remarkable old house and it contains an amazing secret.'

'Curiouser and curiouser,' said Brian. 'It's a lovely old place and it has a very positive atmosphere. I've always felt very comfortable here. Have you met Mrs Malleson? She's a dear old thing.'

'Only the once,' said Jim.

The conversation trailed off into small talk and the secret, in spite of Brian's efforts, remained a secret. But, unfortunately for Hugh, the conversation did not show any signs of petering out altogether. Hugh was also feeling a bit the worse for wear after an afternoon at O'Brien's. He would have welcomed a quiet chat with Brian and in view of Jim's readiness to reveal the secret, he had no qualms now about revealing it himself when Jim wasn't there. Brian was bursting with his news about Kate and wanted to bring her into the conversation somehow, even in front of Jim. He told them about the incident with Lester and how Kate had dealt with him so competently.

'Haven't you seen Lester before?' said Jim. 'He's quite a celebrity. Not quite the full shilling, but apparently he's filthy rich. They say he was umpiring a cricket match and he was hit on the head by the ball. After that he was never the same. He has his quiet times and then he has his more public times. He used to be an actor apparently, and when he's in one of his exhibitionist phases, you just have to throw a rock on the roof of his house at night, and he'll come out and perform.'

Brian was fascinated.

'Do you know where he lives?'

'Yes it's in the posh end of town. It's better to wait till about eleven.'

Hugh cursed quietly to himself, but fortunately, the rum had run out. He politely declined their invitation to return to O'Brien's and ushered them out the door.

As he lay in bed waiting for sleep to come, he bemoaned the relentless intrusion of change. He had only been in the flat for eighteen months but in that time, with Maggie and Brian, he had accumulated a lifetime of treasured memories - a reinvented childhood in a house much grander than he had known as a child. He had more or less decided to make sure that Brian and Maggie did not meet his new acquaintances, but that had been taken out of his hands. He didn't know what to do. He was fed up with the whole situation and wished he could simply turn back the clock.

The next thing he knew, it was two twenty five and the phone was ringing. The phone was in the downstairs hall and Hugh shared the cost with Mrs Malleson.

'I'm sorry to trouble you Hugo but I'm in a spot of bother. Do you think you could come and rescue me from the police station.' Brian sounded very drunk.

'Where's Jim?' asked Hugh.

'I seem to have mislaid him. The fact is I'm broke and its better for you to come and get me in a taxi, than for me to walk all the way to Gracechurch Street and wake you at four o'clock in the morning. Time and motion.'

Half an hour later, Hugh arrived at Police Head Quarters. The constable on the front desk asked him to confirm Brian's identity and address and then made a brief phone call. A few minutes later Brian was released from the holding cell, given back the contents of his pockets and released into Hugh's care.

'You'll be summonsed in due course,' said the custody sergeant. 'The case will probably come up in a month's time. Try not to do anything silly in the mean time.' The sergeant gave Hugh a sympathetic smile. 'Just see that he gets his head down and doesn't get into any more mischief.'

'It's been a pleasure to know you constable. The whole thing was a simple misunderstanding. It'll all be sorted out.'

'See you in court,' said the Sergeant with a grim smile.

Under any other circumstances, Hugh would have enjoyed the night time drive through the sleeping suburbs. Although spring was already beginning to stir in suburban gardens, the River still wore its cold, misty winter shroud and parked cars in the streets were dusted in light frost. He looked nervously over his shoulder to where Brian had slumped across the back seat and begun to snore.

'I'm sorry about that,' he said to the driver.

'I don't mind so long as he doesn't bring his guts up,' said the driver. 'What's he been up to?'

'I don't know yet and I don't think I want to.'

At four thirty, after a number of strong black coffees, Brian still wasn't making a lot of sense and Hugh was unable to determine why he had been arrested. With a supreme effort, he was finally able to pack the young reprobate off to bed with a precautionary bucket on the floor beside him. Then Hugh made his bedtime ablutions and escaped to the security of his own bed. By five o'clock he and his guest were sound asleep and silence settled on the flat.

At about five twenty, Hugh was woken by a doleful wailing sound that frightened the life out of him. He scrambled out of bed, grabbed a broom for protection and tentatively went downstairs to trace the source of the sound. Gingerly he made his way out into the little courtyard. The sounds were coming from beneath the trap door. As he woke up and his head cleared he realised that it was Mrs Malleson's cat. He had probably followed them down into the cellar and gone mousing or just gone to sleep. In consternation Hugh wondered how he could unlock the door. Jim had the key.

It was a real dilemma. At that hour of the night he did not feel like going down into the cellar anyway, but he couldn't leave the cat there for Mrs Malleson to hear or, even worse, smell when she returned. He tried the handle of the door. It yielded. Jim must have forgotten to lock it.

'Come on puss.'

Puss obliged and bounded up the stairs. Hugh was about to close the door again when he noticed a faint silvery light. He ventured a little way down the steps and saw that the light seemed to be coming from the old lantern in the corner. That was enough. Terrified he raced back up the stairs, shut the door and retreated to his bed.

'No more,' he muttered to himself. 'No more!! I just want to sleep!!!'

At ten o'clock next morning, Hugh was dead to the world. Brian was also in a comatose state as his metabolism struggled to recover from the excesses it had suffered on the previous night. Hugh was in no hurry to wake up, he'd phoned in 'sick' yesterday and could do the same today.

Brian on the other hand, had an appointment to keep. From the murky depths of his drugged slumber, some tiny remnant of consciousness remembered that Kate was going to pick him up at eleven. He neither remembered nor cared about anything else that had troubled him in the previous twelve hours.

Those recollections began to filter through his aching brain on the journey back to Ross. He hadn't remembered Kate's car vibrating so much on the previous day. Nor did he recall its engine having such a deafening roar. Nevertheless, he still doggedly insisted to himself that Kate's car was perfect like everything else about her - an Angel's chariot - even if she did throw it into the corners on the winding highway with a little too much gusto.

'You're looking particularly green this morning young man.'

'Shit' thought Brian. 'She's noticed.'

'Yes,' he said, 'I did a little too much socialising last night.' The recollection of a few of the previous night's calamities began to come back to him.

'Shit' he thought to himself again, 'shit, shit shit!!!'

About half an hour before they reached Ross, Brian asked Kate to stop the car. There was a bridge over a creek. He wandered a little way along the watercourse until he was out of sight of the car. Then he did what he had to do. The nauseous pain in his stomach stopped almost immediately but a blinding headache began to throb behind his eyes. He drank a little water from the stream, cleaned himself up and staggered back to the car.

'You poor thing. Do you want to try and curl up on the back seat. I've got a blanket.'

Kate's compassion didn't stop the headache, but it definitely consoled him.

'I think I'd better stay upright,' he said. 'But a blanket would be nice.'

She tucked him up and, in time, the cold convulsions of shivering abated.

'I'll take things a bit slower too, if you like.'

'That would be nice,' he whispered, silently reverencing the young lady's concern. 'Not just an angel,' he thought, 'a ministering angel.'

'I think perhaps you should have come to Dad's birthday dinner.'

'If only,' thought Brian. 'If only. Did he like the cuff links?' he gasped.

'He loved them.'

When they arrived at Trinity, Kate escorted Brian to the door. A pair of crows flew by calling to each other as they passed overhead.

'Friends of yours?' asked Kate. Brian answered with the haggard ghost of a smile. Kate accompanied him upstairs to his room, which fortunately was reasonably tidy.

'You had better get yourself to bed.' She took her blanket back and folded it over her arm. 'You need looking after and no mistake.'

With that she took her leave, little realizing the wonderfully restorative effect her ministrations would have upon the young man. After a shower and some aspirin he went to bed. His stomach felt OK and his headache was no longer quite so intense. He weighed up what he could remember of the previous night against what he could remember of the previous day. Then he gave himself up to healing sleep, convinced that he was still in front.

5: A Change in the Wind

9 Gracechurch Street
Darlington
Tuesday 12 August

Dearest Maggie,

I hope this letter finds you well and that boarding school isn't being too much of a pain.

I am missing you terribly and I can't tell you how much I am looking forward to the September holidays when the three of us can get together again.

A lot has happened down here in the last few weeks and I haven't been free to talk about it. But I have made up my mind and I want to tell you everything, you and Brian.

These people turned up at the flat one night in July with an incredible story about the history of the Cumberlands. They reckon that there was a secret civilization living here before the convicts arrived. They claimed that this house was built by people from that secret society. We went down into a cellar in the courtyard and found a kind of old fashioned class room with children's' exercise books. Some contained writing in English and others were written in a language we can't identify.

Brian dropped in briefly the other day which was quite a surprise, but I haven't heard from him since. I assume he is still coming here for the holidays.

Spring is well underway in Darlington and there are daffodils everywhere. I bet you can't wait to get back into the garden down here.

It's no exaggeration to say that last summer was the happiest period of my life and I can't wait to see you again.

Please write back soon.
All my love
Hugh.

PS Mrs Malleson was asking after you the other day.

Prison
18/8/69

Dear Hugh

What's this I hear about Brian getting himself arrested? What on earth were you thinking of, letting him go off on a wild goose chase with a complete stranger. Who is this Jim Lovegrove character?

There's been a hell of a row here. The nuns were saying that they wouldn't release me into Brian's care for the holidays. We had to ring Mum and Dad in England and fortunately Dad was able to sort it out.

You better not write to me anymore this term. They are probably censoring all my mail. I've had to smuggle this letter out with one of the day girls.

I do think you could have taken better care of him than that.

The spring is stirring up here too and it's lovely.

Take care of yourself and more importantly don't let Brian do himself any more damage. I'll be on the Friday night bus to Darlington on the fifth.

Love always
Your Maggie

Hugh read Maggie's letter a couple of times. It took a while for him to get over the letter's initial rebuke and he resented being held responsible for Brian's peccadilloes. It also took him a while to focus on the letter's more positive and affectionate conclusion. But eventually he was able to do so. He poured himself a glass of sherry in Maggie's glass, drank her health, and stoked the fire. He was determined to reclaim the past and had put on his wizard's dressing gown for the first time in ages.

With Mrs Malleson's cat for company, he savoured the sherry and lazily watched the glowing embers of the fire. No one could take last summer from him. Furthermore in a few week's time, he and Maggie and, hopefully Brian too, would begin to celebrate the Spring and reclaim their golden age. He was lazily contemplating the sherry in Maggie's glass and wondering about one for the road when the cat suddenly pricked its ears, tensed and jumped off his lap. A few seconds later, his door bell rang.

'Who could that possibly be?'

Reluctantly, he got to his feet and followed the cat downstairs. It was Lucy.

'I haven't got you out of bed have I?'

'No, no I was just having a nightcap.'

Mrs Malleson came to her door in response to the cat's scratching.

'Is everything all right Hugh?'

'Yes it's ok,' Hugh responded, trying to shield Lucy from Mrs Malleson's view as he did so.

Back upstairs, Hugh gave Lucy a sherry in his own glass and refilled Maggie's glass for himself.

'Is anything wrong?' he asked, noticing yet again how much prettier she looked without her spectacles.

'I suppose not,' said Lucy. 'I was just wondering if you had heard anything from Jim lately. He's still got all the exercise books.'

'No' said Hugh. 'I haven't seen him since the day we went into the cellar.'

'He could be back at sea I guess. Sometimes he goes to ground and we don't see him for weeks.'

'Where does he live exactly?' said Hugh with private suspicions as to why Jim might be lying low.

'He keeps that very secret. He likes to just suddenly drop in on you from out of the blue. But he keeps his private life very private.'

'Well to be honest I've found all three of you a bit on the secretive side. You all just drop in on me from out of the blue. I don't know where any of you live.'

Lucy blushed and the effect was not lost on Hugh.

'Yes I'm sorry about that. Both Jim and Robert act like they are in the secret service sometimes. It's funny how we were drawn together by a common interest in our history and the secret of these old houses but we each seem to be driven by different things.

'Robert dreams of producing some boring old thesis that will rewrite the Cumberlands' history and make his name as a historian but I don't know what's going through Jim's mind half the time. I sometimes wonder if he wasn't lost at sea for a little too long when he was shipwrecked that time.'

'Drank a little bit too much salt water do you mean?'

They shared a laugh at Jim's expense.

'An experience like that would have to affect you,' said Hugh. 'But that photo in Mrs Malleson's bedroom seems to bear out his story about the chap that rescued him.'

'Maybe. I still think he's a bit loopy.'

'Speaking of which, what's the story with Robert? That first night you came round here, there was no shutting him up and the second time I met him, when we went to O'Brien's you could hardly get a word out of him.'

'Poor old Robert is a sad case. He has some kind of mental illness, I don't know what he's got exactly but he has periods of extreme enthusiasm and other periods of extreme depression. They try to even out his extremes with medication. It works most of the time but sometimes, when he's really high, he starts thinking he doesn't need it anymore and he stops using it. When that happens, they admit him to "Hollybank" and get him stabilized again.

'He ended up there the day after our first meeting with you. And don't take any notice of his so called doctoral thesis on Cumberlands history. He hasn't even started at uni, although he does pester the History Department relentlessly. The sad truth is that he stacks supermarket shelves for a living. It's the only job he can hold down.

'I've known him since we were kids. He has his sweet moments when he is really good company. I've always been fond of him but he can stretch the friendship when he's high. He needs all the friends he can get. Robert introduced me to Jim. I don't know how they met.'

'What about you?' said Hugh. 'You don't strike me as a nut case. What's in all of this for you?'

'It's pretty much like I told you on that first evening. I climbed the fence looking for my ball and it was like stepping back in time somehow. The people were like a different race and they had a kind of grace and charm.

'I guess I've wanted to be a part of it ever since. The little girl's mother was friendly enough but it was obvious that I wasn't really welcome. Ever since that day I've just wanted to know what the secret is and I guess I've also wanted to be accepted by them. I don't quite know why we've had to be so cloak and dagger about it with you though. I live quite close by - in Newton Street - number 7 and you're welcome to visit any time you like.'

Hugh ministered to their glasses.

'Why don't you come round for dinner on Sunday? Mum and Dad have an open house on Sundays. A baked dinner.' This seemed like a wonderful suggestion and Brian was about to accept the invitation when he remembered Maggie.

'I'll be tied up for the next couple of weeks but I'd love to do it some time.'

'Well like I said it's open house every Sunday - 7 Newton Street.'

As Lucy stood up and reached for her duffle coat, Hugh was suddenly and pleasantly aware of the soft beauty of her shape beneath her black cord jeans and polo neck jumper. It was amazing how little he had noticed her when she was with Jim and Robert. She looked up, met his gaze and blushed again.

'Tell me Lucy' Hugh blurted out. 'Why did you walk out when you saw me in the Museum that day?'

Lucy's colour deepened.

'I er - just panic I guess. Too much cloak and dagger stuff!! Anyway I'd better be going. Thanks for the sherry'. She put on her coat.

'That was my pleasure,' said Hugh.

'So we'll see you in a couple of weeks then?'

'If not before. Thanks for coming round.'

He escorted her down to the street and watched thoughtfully as she walked off into the darkness. Confusion reigned in his mind as he went back upstairs, made his ablutions and went to bed. He tried to focus his thoughts on Maggie and her letter but could only remember the rebuke in her opening remarks. And she didn't make any response to the secret he had begun to share with her. Sleep was a long time coming.

His emotional confusion was waiting for him when he awoke next morning and it accompanied him to work. It was going to be a busy day for him. It was pay week and he had to prepare the payroll for all the City Council cleaners and outdoor staff. The work wasn't complicated but it was laborious. Fortunately, the people on his payroll were creatures of habit and things didn't change much from one fortnight to the next. But the task was still very detailed and required a lot of concentration.

Hugh not only prepared the payrolls, he also got to hand the workers their pay envelopes. One of the cleaning ladies was in her eighties. She couldn't read or write but had learned to draw her signature. She had a calm, bright eyed serenity and humility that won the respect of everyone she met. Giving Mrs Moran her pay was probably the most satisfying part of Hugh's job.

For the rest of that day, he had to concentrate on getting the payroll done. This meant forgetting about Maggie and the holidays. It also meant forgetting about Lucy and the guilty pleasure he felt whenever he remembered her visit the previous evening. By five o'clock that afternoon, the pay sheets were completed, signed by his supervisor and countersigned by the Town Clerk.

Riding home that night on the trolley bus, Hugh felt contented. He had done a hard day's work, his cleaners would get their pay tomorrow, and he would get an early night and twelve hours sleep.

He got off the trolley bus and listened to its receding electric whine as he sauntered towards Gracechurch Street. A quick meal of baked beans on toast, a glass of sherry and then bed. Anything more complicated than that could wait til tomorrow. He turned the corner into Gracechurch Street and his heart sank. Jim was loitering outside the house. There was no escape. He had been seen.

'Long time no see!' he called as Hugh approached.

'Seen anything of Brian lately?' Hugh retorted unable to conceal his resentment.

'I want to talk to you about that. He's a madman.'

'It'd take one to know one' thought Hugh to himself. 'Look I've had a long, hard day and I desperately need an early night.'

'I was only being sociable.' Jim, produced a bottle of rum from his jacket pocket.

'Yo ho ho?'

He followed Hugh inside and up the stairs.

'We need to talk.'

'What about?'

'About our future, me, you, Robert and Lucy.'

'What do you mean?'

'I mean that we may not be looking for the same things. It might be time to part company.'

'I don't follow.'

'It's simple. Robert is just a would-be academic and his mental health isn't too stable. Lucy is interested in architecture and social customs. But what we are on to is much more than either of those things.'

'What are we on to?'

'We are looking at immortality.'

'Pardon?'

'There are gateways in and out of this world. Death is only one of them. When I was lost at sea that time, I was in no danger of drowning but I still came very close to leaving this world.'

Hugh set about preparing his baked beans, while Jim poured two measures of rum.

'No thanks. I don't like rum.'

'I bet you've never tried it. I think I'll have to educate you in the ways of the world. Now where was I? That's right ways of leaving the world. Have you ever read the Bhagavad Gita?'

'I've heard about it but I've never read it.'

'Well you should. There are passages in it that talk about ways and times for leaving this world. Leaving it mind you.....not necessarily dying. And have you heard about the Bermuda Triangle or do you confine your reading to fairy stories like Alice In Wonderland?"

Hugh looked up from preparing his food with a glare that would have severely chastened anyone with any sensitivity.

'I know about it, whether or not I believe all the stories is another matter though.'

He continued to prepare his meal, pointedly doing so without offering to feed his visitor.

'Well think about it,' Jim continued, 'obscure parts of the world where ships, even entire squadrons of fighter planes can go missing - just vanish.'

'But that's in the Caribbean.'

'There could be more than one place where that sort of thing happens. Why do you think it took so long for the Cumberlands to be discovered by Europeans?'

'Obscure and previously unknown ocean currents,' said Hugh, referring imprecisely and mechanically to what he could remember from school.

'There's more to it than that,' said Jim relentlessly drawing his prey into the conversation. 'There are all kinds of energy out there that science doesn't understand. Beings that are free to come and go; that don't belong here - that come from other worlds-other dimensions.'

Hugh doggedly buttered his toast and tried to retreat.

'Don't you see,' said Jim earnestly. 'The boat that rescued me - the Dandillion-it just appeared out of nowhere. It didn't appear on the horizon and sail towards me. It was just there. And Norian was no ordinary human being. That photo in Mrs Malleson's room was taken at least fifty years ago, but that's how young he looked when he rescued me a couple of years ago. And what about the money he gave me? It was in mint condition but it was at least fifty years old.'

Hugh poured his beans onto his toast and inadvertently picked up his glass of rum. It wasn't that bad apart from being a bit on the sickly side.

'So what exactly are you proposing?' he asked while he primed his fork with the first mouthful of his meal.

'Norian seems to be able to travel freely between our world and some other world. I believe that I was on the threshold between the two worlds when he rescued me. I want to go back to that gateway.'

Hugh abhorred the sight and sound of anyone talking with their mouth full and studiously avoided speaking until he had swallowed.

'How are you going to do that? Do you know the latitude and longitude of the place where he found you?'

'No obviously not,' said Jim getting annoyed. 'But I think there are ways of finding out. The answer is in those exercise books from down in the cellar.'

'Have you managed to translate them?'

'No of course not,' said Jim, becoming more irritated. 'The ones that were written in English.'

'Oh the kid's stuff,' said Hugh scornfully, still smarting from Jim's earlier disparaging reference to his tastes in literature.

'They all told the same story. People were being rescued in a white ship by someone called Norian. They were escaping this world.'

Hugh took another sip of rum.

'And I'll tell you something else. After I read those exercise books I went and checked out a few cemeteries around the City. You know the names of the pre convict families Robert talks about - Fairchild, Malleson, Meadows, Penruddock etcetera?'

'Yes.'

'I could count on two hands the number of graves I found where anyone of that name was buried.'

'Are you serious?'

'I was never more serious.'

'Perhaps members of those old families are buried on the private islands.'

'That might be so. But that wouldn't explain the secrecy surrounding them.'

'So what are you saying?'

'I'm saying that Norian takes them from this world on his ship. They don't die. And if we could stow away on his ship or follow it in another boat we could avoid death too. Remember what he said when he rescued me. "Well you're back. You very nearly crossed over but now you're back".'

'I thought that just meant you nearly drowned.'

'So did I at first, but now I'm not so sure.'

'When are you going to let the others see the exercise books again?'

'I'm not sure there's any need for them to see the books again. Robert might go showing them to people at the uni.'

'Well what's wrong with that? It may be possible to translate them.'

'I don't want to lose control of it. If it becomes public we'll lose control and besides people will want to know where we found them. Do you want to own up to the burglary?'

Hugh insisted that Lucy and Robert could be trusted to keep the secret. He even went so far as to insist that, unless Lucy and Robert remained part of the 'quest', he would withdraw and deny Jim any further access to the cellar. The conversation became heated as Hugh poured their fourth round of rum.

At about five minutes to midnight, Jim went home leaving Hugh with the empty rum bottle, a plate of cold baked beans and plenty of food for thought. Jim had finally relented and agreed to share the books with Lucy and Robert, on the understanding that the quest to find a gateway from the world would remain a secret between him and Hugh.

~~~§~~~

On the morning after their trip to the City, Kate was waiting for Brian as he walked into the English lecture theatre. She had been very concerned about him and was pleased to see that he had apparently recovered from his excesses. They were still engrossed in conversation when the lecturer arrived so they sat together for the lecture. From then on, Brian made a point of sitting with Kate at all their lectures and she did nothing to discourage him. On a couple of occasions they had gone for coffee in the refectory after the lecture and a warm friendship continued to grow between them. Brian also found himself being absorbed into Kate's broader circle of friends and they no longer seemed as intimidating.

The last English lecture of term was at nine o'clock on the morning of the third of September. Brian finished breakfast with a most enjoyable cup of tea before setting off to attend. It was his final lecture for the term, which meant that, from ten o'clock, he would be on holiday. Together with Maxwell Tynan he had joined the University Folk Club and they had agreed to spend the afternoon putting up posters for a folk concert to be held at Carlingford the following week.
~~~

Carlingford was the second city on Greater Cumberland, and it was where Maggie attended boarding school. Brian had already written to his sister suggesting that they should go to the concert with Hugh. He was nerving himself up to invite Kate during the lecture. As it happened, Kate was already planning to go to the concert with her cousin Mark Denham who was to be one of the performers. They were going with a party of folk club members on the down train.

'They want to see if they can drink the train dry in a single journey. I daresay you could make a contribution.'

'Now I wouldn't like you to think I go doing that sort of thing all the time,' said Brian.

'And I suppose you and the other Ineligible Bachelors only drink lemonade at Insect Corner.'

'How did you know about that?'

'I have my sources young man.'

Brian felt flattered that Kate had taken the trouble to gather information about him. It did a lot to allay his persistent fear that she might never give him a second thought when they weren't together.

'I'll have you know that I'm a reformed character,' he beamed at her.

'Does that mean that you won't be talking to crows anymore?'

'I've already told you that was a deeply spiritual experience.'

'Ah yes. The "thousand fires", I was forgetting.'

Doctor Spotswood's arrival ended the conversation.

Kate had two more lectures and a tutorial to attend so they parted company after the lecture. Brian sauntered back to Trinity College feeling very happy with his lot in life. He didn't give the police car a second thought as he bounded up the front steps.   But once, inside he encountered the Dean of the College, Father Wallace, in the company of a young constable.

'Ah Brian there's someone here to see you.'

'Brian James McInerney?' intoned the Policeman.

'That's right.'

'You have been summonsed to appear in the Darlington Court of Petty Sessions on Wednesday the Fifth of November.'

He handed Brian the summons, doffed his cap to Father Wallace and walked out into the bright spring sunshine.

'I think Brian,' said the priest, 'that perhaps you and I should have a little chat. Can you come to my office in about half an hour?'

'Yes Father' said the crestfallen young man as he read the fine print of the summons.

"Hereof fail not at your peril." it warned.   The morning had been too good to last.

<p style="text-align:center">~~~§~~~</p>

It was a subdued and thoughtful Brian who met Maxwell Tynan after lunch. The meeting with Father Wallace had been uncomfortable, not least because the priest had shown no sign of anger or recrimination. He had shown nothing but genuine concern, unlike Brian's father who had simply said it served him right and questioned whether it warranted the cost of a reverse charge phone call to the other side of the planet.

Brian had consoled himself with the thought that it was just a harmless prank. But Father Wallace pointed out that a conviction might place his Education Department studentship in jeopardy.   After all the

Department might not want to have convicted criminals teaching the country's school children.

Brian hadn't told Maxwell about his spot of bother and resolved not to, as they plastered the campus with posters. Maxwell had shown a tendency of late to be rather patronising when listening to Brian's accounts of his peccadilloes. He had also made it pretty clear that he was sick of hearing about Kate. Brian put that down to jealousy.

After they had done the campus, they turned their attention to the town. They visited all the pubs and, in the interests of good will, purchased the occasional drink in exchange for the right to put up posters. By the time they had reached Insect Corner in the Old Bohemian, Brian's melancholy was beginning to lift. The publican, Lionel Moriarty (uncle of the beautiful Angela Moriarty of the moonstone eyes-although he didn't share her ethereal beauty) feigned a reluctance to have the posters in his establishment.

'I don't want my customers gallivanting up to Carlingford next Thursday, when they could be here drinking my beer.'

'Most of the regulars will be away on vacation then anyway,' said the always practical Maxwell.

'All the more reason not to encourage any more of them to go away,' said the publican.

'Well, look at it this way,' said Brian. 'The posters are works of Art. They'll add to the atmosphere of the place. They could even become collectors' items. In a few years time Maxwell here will probably offer you a fiver for one of them.'

Moriarty poured them a beer each - on the house.

'I haven't seen you around lately young Brian. Some of the other insects said that there might be a woman in your life these days.'

'There might be,' said Brian, blushing in spite of himself.

'Young Jack Mahoney's granddaughter no less. And what about your mate here. He's not a regular insect is he?'

'Sorry - I should have introduced you,' said Brian still absorbing the Publican's last remark - 'Lionel Moriarty, Maxwell Tynan.'

'And what are you going to be when you grow up Maxwell?'

'I am studying engineering,' said Maxwell a little testily.

'Well I'll tell you one thing,' said the publican with a wink at Brian. 'I've never yet met an engineer who had the right idea about anything.'

Maxwell didn't try to hide his displeasure and put his unfinished beer back on the bar.

'Don't take it personal son. At least you plan to grow up sometime, unlike our young friend here. You aren't planning to grow up any time soon are you Brian?'

'Not if I can help it,' Brian replied as he put his empty glass on the bar. 'Drink up Max and I'll get you another.'

Maxwell complied but pointed out that they still had work to do.

'Put your posters up anywhere you like,' said Moriarty as he refilled their glasses and went off to the main bar.

'Don't mind him Max. He likes stirring people up but he's a good bloke really,' said Brian, feeling suddenly protective of his "sheltered" friend.

At the risk of getting his head bitten off, he tentatively brought Kate into the conversation as they walked back to college.

'What did Moriarty mean about Kate being young Jack Mahoney's granddaughter?'

Maxwell rolled his eyes in disbelief.

'You mean you didn't know?'

'No. The only thing I know about her family is that her Dad and I share the same taste in cufflinks.'

Here was food for thought. Meeting the family was something he thought might happen one day. But this could be a bit awkward, particularly with a court appearance hanging over his head. Life was certainly becoming complicated.

'Ah well, one day at a time I suppose,' he thought and gave himself up to contemplation of the bright spring afternoon. A cool and frosty night was coming but for the present there was a new and pleasant warmth in the sunshine.

'Did you see that policeman at lunch time?' asked Maxwell as they turned in at the College gates.

'Yes' said Brian. 'He had a summons for Father Wallace. Drunk and disorderly I think.'

6: A Number of Journeys

Hugh waited anxiously at the bus depot. Although Maggie was in his thoughts most of the time, it worried him that he couldn't visualise what she looked like when they were apart. The recent distractions in his life had made this even more difficult. Letters maintained a kind of contact as far as they went, but they quickly ran out of new and meaningful things to say. If anything, letters reinforced the distance between them. And then there was Lucy.

The eight o'clock bus was as good as its word and Hugh stood nervously as the passengers disembarked, waiting for the familiar sight of the blue school uniform. That was another thing that worried him. He felt like a cradle snatcher waiting in a public place to pick up a girl in school uniform. This was perhaps odd given last summer's commitment to perpetual childhood.

However, at a stop along the way, Maggie had changed out of her school uniform into jeans and sweater and black suede boots. She had let down and combed out her long red hair and replaced her regulation blue school beret with a black one and looked absolutely stunning. How could he have forgotten that beguiling masque of freckles across the bridge of her nose. She dropped her bag as they embraced. The last of Hugh's misgivings vanished as he tasted again the freshness of her mouth and felt her next to him.

'Where's Brian?' she asked as they waited for her case to be unloaded.

'I thought he'd be with you. Didn't he catch the bus at Ross?'

'Well obviously not.'

There was no point waiting around because there wasn't another bus until the next morning, so they caught a taxi home. Maggie was eager to get back to the flat and, in her excitement, Brian's absence was temporarily forgotten. Hugh paid off the taxi and they hurried inside and up the stairs.

Maggie made a pot of tea while Hugh stoked the fire and after twenty minutes of similar domestic activity they settled in each other's arms on the rug in the firelight. Hugh began to think that, in Brian's absence they could go straight to bed, but Maggie pointed out that what he had in mind would have to wait a couple of days.

After a little while they adjourned to the kitchen and Maggie made them an omelette using some of the herbs she had picked to dry in the summer. It was almost like old times except that there was no Brian. At about ten o'clock, Maggie suggested calling Trinity College. Hugh thought it was a bit late but acceded to her wishes.

Father Wallace answered and – no Brian wasn't in. He understood that the Folk Music Society was having an end of term celebration and that was probably where Brian was.

'Can I take a message?'

'Just let him know that Hugh called and ask him to call me?'

Maggie was annoyed with her brother and felt let down by him. However, in Brian's absence, Hugh became the target of that annoyance. At about one a.m. they were ready for bed and Hugh sought to dispel her mood by suggesting a torchlight inspection of the garden. To avoid disturbing Mrs Malleson they went down the old, wrought iron fire escape that led from the back of the kitchen. The unlikely suggestion worked and they enjoyed a magical interlude revisiting the scene of last summer's happiness, now magically transformed with daffodils, jonquils and eggs and bacon transfixed in a light dusting of frost.

Trees that had shaded them from the summer sun now held up bare, budding branches that shone with diamond droplets in the cold torchlight. Maggie knelt down to pick some of the blooms, eager to immerse her hands in the greenery. It reminded Hugh of a much earlier time in his life before he ever had cause to be afraid of the dark.

The night was magical and the starlit darkness was full of benign and joyful mystery. Eventually, however, the cold prevailed and they went back indoors past the herb garden. Hugh made cocoa and prepared hot water bottles while Maggie found a milk bottle to use as a vase for the flowers. They retired to their warm bed to drink their cocoa while the jonquils, woken by the warmth indoors, began to suffuse the air in the room with their fragrance.

'Thank you for a truly magical end to the day,' said Maggie as she turned out the light and settled down to sleep in Hugh's arms.

<div align="center">~~~§~~~</div>

At about that time, Kate was dropping Brian off at Trinity College.

'So I'll see you on the down train next Thursday,' she said as she watched him fumbling in the dark to undo his seat belt.

'That depends on whether I can get out of your car or not.'

She leaned over to get a better look at his efforts to extricate himself.

'You would have to be one of the most useless people I've ever met,' she laughed as she leant further across him to undo the seat belt. Looking up and seeing her face so close to his, Brian, took a chance and tried to kiss her cheek. Instinctively, Kate anticipated, turned and gave him a long, sweet kiss on the mouth.

Sometime later, Brian walked up the driveway to the college with a skip in his step, listening fondly to the sound of Kate's Mini fading away on the chill night air. It was while he was looking for his front door key that he suddenly remembered Hugh and Maggie. He was supposed to be in Darlington!!

'Oh well,' he shrugged. 'They'll survive. It'll do them good to have a night alone together.' He found the key, opened the front door, did a little tap dance and went inside. He considered waking Maxwell to tell him his news but fought back the impulse.

'Perhaps not at three in the morning.' He contented himself with an exuberant thump on his friend's door as he went past.

The message to ring Hugh was taped to his door. He was sorely tempted to ring straight away but again common sense prevailed. He brewed himself a cup of tea and took it to bed, remembering as he did so, to set the alarm for seven thirty. He'd try to catch the eight o'clock milk train to Darlington. Surprisingly, in spite of his state of high excitement, he had little trouble getting to sleep and pleasant dreams awaited him.

<div style="text-align:center">~~~§~~~</div>

The morning of Thursday the 11th dawned clear and mild. At nine o'clock Mervan Mithras, the voice of his nation's soul, shambled onto platform three of Darlington station, guitar case in hand. The down train was ready to board and the platform was crowded. There were the usual travellers but there was also a larger number than usual of students and bohemians. Emily Oldfield noted this through the office window with some concern. They should all have done their end of term travelling a week ago. She had hoped not to see any more of them for another fortnight.

Mervan also noted the makeup of the crowd and automatically assumed that the student population was going en-masse to witness his performance at Carlingford. For this reason, he quickly strode down to the guard van which contained a small passenger compartment. The seats weren't as comfortable but there was privacy and he felt that he needed to keep a distance between himself and his audience until it was time to perform for them.

The Carlingford concert was the shared brainchild of Mervan and an entrepreneurial friend, Nathan Watson. They had chosen Carlingford because of its central location and their publicity targeted every tertiary institution and upper secondary school on the Island. The dream was to one day establish a Cumberlands equivalent to the American campus circuit. With a series of concerts on each of the major islands.

Folk concerts in the past had tended to be democratic amateur gatherings, usually for charity, where upwards of two dozen acts performed three song brackets regardless of their ability. Mervan and Nathan were after something more polished - five of the best acts they could find, all paid a cut of the takings.

Nathan would look after the front of house, and organise people to manage the sound and the lighting. In fact he had gone to Carlingford the day before to commence setting up at the Town Hall. The various folk clubs around the Island provided enthusiastic volunteers to put up posters which were produced by students from the School of Art in Darlington.

Mervan's contribution to publicity was an article and photograph in the Cumberland Times and a radio interview with the Cumberland Broadcasting Commission. His bracket would be the finale of the concert and until then he would enhance his elusive star quality by keeping a low profile.

In B carriage, Brian, Maggie and Hugh made themselves comfortable. The prodigal Brian had quickly been forgiven upon his belated arrival at the flat in Gracechurch Street and the threesome had spent a reasonably enjoyable week. However some tensions had arisen in respect of the trip to Carlingford. Maggie and Brian excepted, Hugh felt inferior and uncomfortable in the company of students and wasn't looking forward to the trip. He also resented the way that the other two had organised the outing without consulting him.

Another complicating factor was that Brian had booked a fourth seat for Kate. Maggie was a little apprehensive about this. A cousin of Kate went to Maggie's school and she was an absolute bitch. She was concerned that Brian might be falling under the influence of the wrong sort of people.

The plan of the university Folk Music Society had been to book all the seats in B Carriage and as the Down Train pulled out of the Station, the carriage was already half full of concert goers. Kate's cousin Mark Denham was there with a group of associates and his guitar at the ready. Under Cumberlands licensing laws, alcohol couldn't be served on the train until ten o'clock which was when the train arrived at Ross and the rest of the university crowd would come aboard. Then the campaign to drink the train dry would get under way.

As the train travelled through the northern riverside suburbs of Darlington, the festive atmosphere in B Carriage flourished.

For the benefit of tourists, Emily Oldfield provided a running commentary on the public address system, describing items of scenic, historical and social interest concerning each town along the route. Most people who travelled regularly on the train knew the commentary off by heart. At Insect Corner there were Emily Oldfield recitation competitions. On this particular morning as Emily's narration began, most of B Carriage chanted in unison with her. Fortunately for Emily, she delivered her commentary from a booth at the back of the cafeteria and could not hear them.

By the time the train pulled into Ross, Mark Denham was leading the occupants of B Carriage in an impromptu concert. Emily Oldfield's time honoured description of Ross as "an Oxford or Cambridge in the southern seas" went unheard. Emily however was now painfully aware of the unprecedented carryings on and was dreading the opening of the bar.

Momentarily leaving his splendid isolation in the guard van to go to the toilet, Mervan Mithras also heard the festivities. He found the situation perplexing. As the voice of his Nation's soul, he should perhaps have been in there leading the chorus. However it was clear that Mark Denham was obviously doing that quite effectively - perhaps a bit too effectively. Mervan decided to remain hidden. His chance to shine would come later that night.

Kate boarded the train at Denistone, a village two stops after Ross. She seemed to stop and exchange pleasantries with everyone in the carriage as she made her way down the aisle. However, Brian's anxieties were eventually put to rest as she took her seat. Maggie appeared to take an instant shine to her and, although Hugh was feeling very ill at ease and out of his element, he was charmed by her and made an effort to be sociable.

Opportunities for conversation were limited to intervals in the singing which were few and far between to begin with. However as the journey progressed, the singing waned and the business of drinking continued in earnest. People began to move around the carriage. Mark Denham came up and talked to them on his way to the bar. He was very taken with Maggie and stopped to talk to her again on his way back from the bar. That fact was not lost upon Hugh who began to sink into melancholy.

An amorous and intoxicated young couple withdrew to the guard van to indulge their passion in private. They encountered the voice of their nation's soul staring pensively out the window but they chose to ignore him and were quickly lost in an intensive and thorough exploration of each other's charms. Occasionally as they rolled around on the seat they would catch sight of Mervan and burst out laughing. Eventually he left them to it and went to the bar.

The cafeteria and bar carriage contained a couple of small tables and seats where patrons wanting a change of scene could sit to eat and drink. Mervan ordered a scotch and retired to one of these seats but every time someone came in from B Carriage, sounds of the revelry followed them in. Thus it was that about twelve miles out from Carlingford, Mervan heard the standing ovation that Brian received as he returned brandishing the last can of ale from the cafeteria.

To drink the train dry in half a journey was no mean feat and discussions would rage for years about how great an achievement it was. There was a legendary occasion in 1962 when two students were supposed to have performed the feat on their own but that took the whole day's journey. The popular folklore was that they had since drunk themselves to death.

Brian had upwards of twenty accomplices, but the number of people able to bathe in the glory and the number of supportive witnesses below the legal drinking age cheering them on made it a very popular achievement. And not all of those below the legal drinking age had abstained.

In August 1968, the normally conservative Cumberland Parliament passed a law which lowered the legal drinking age to 18. It was a Private Member's Bill introduced by a member of the notoriously conservative upper house. His public reasoning was that it would make young Cumberlanders less likely to fall prey to the influence of pernicious drugs like marijuana, LSD and other products of the swinging 60's. Many people in the country suspected that the Honourable Member's real reasoning had more to do with the fact that he owned three licensed hotels - two in Darlington and one in Carlingford.

Mervan decided to disembark at Redwood, the last station before Carlingford. This would enable him to arrive at the Town Hall later and more discreetly than the crowd in B Carriage. It would also give him the chance to go to the monkey house, a famous enclosure in Redwood Park that housed a colony of macaque monkeys from

Japan. He made his way past a number of signs stressing that food must not be thrown to the monkeys, and arrived to find an assorted crowd of onlookers.

The monkeys were in an excited state and a number of altercations had broken out which provided a lot of entertainment. A beast that Mervan assumed was the dominant male had chased a young pretender to the end of a high branch and was giving it the rough edge of his tongue. Interest in this confrontation was just starting to wane when another outbreak of territorial primate behaviour erupted outside the enclosure.

A wildly primitive looking family (from one of the **really** Outer Islands as the saying went) had appeared out of nowhere and begun to throw heaps of bananas to the monkeys. An enraged, red faced groundsman stormed up to them and proceeded to give them the rough edge of **his** tongue.

The primitives responded with taunts and jeers that Mervan thought weren't as intelligible as the comments emanating from the enclosure. They stood their ground until their cargo of bananas had all been discharged and then suffered themselves to be ejected but not before one of them had grabbed the groundsman's peaked cap and thrown it into the enclosure with the monkeys. The Voice of his Nation's Soul smiled to himself and stored up this little parable for future reference, possibly even a song.

He was still laughing inwardly about the incident as he boarded a bus for the City.

'Where do you think you're going with that thing?' said the driver, another belligerent character who seemed to think his uniform and peaked cap gave him as much authority as a police officer.

'It's not a thing, it's a guitar.'

'Large items of luggage are not to be kept in the body of the bus. There's a place for storing large items just behind me,' said the driver, 'Can't you read?'

'There's hardly anybody on the bus,' protested an incredulous Mervan. 'It's not in anyone's way.'

'Rules are rules,' said the driver, coldly. 'By the time we reach the City, the bus could be packed. So do as you are told and put your banjo in the proper place.'

'It's not a banjo,' said Mervan becoming angry. 'It's a guitar. It's a Martin Guitar and I'm not letting it out of my reach.'

'I don't care if it's a fuckin' Stradivarius, you can't take it back there.'

'Well fuck you then, you cretin,' said Mervan exploding in rage and storming off the bus.

'And get a haircut you pansy,' said the driver with a smile of contemptuous satisfaction.

It was the angriest Mervan had been in a long time and he was still trembling with rage half an hour later as he walked towards the City. The whole experience had been humiliating and it threatened to ruin his composure for the concert that night. He decided to stop at the next pub that he passed and calm himself down with a scotch or two.

By six o'clock that evening, in the Green Dolphin, Mervan was calm, almost to the point of apathy. An old lady, had seen his guitar case as she went up to the bar to get another gin.

'Are you the chap who's playing at the concert tonight? I saw your picture in the paper.'

This was balm for Mervan's troubled soul.

'That's right,' he said and drifted into a pleasant conversation with her. She told him about her ability to play the spoons and produce music by tapping the side of her head and varying the volume of air held in her mouth. Apparently she used to perform in hotels and for talent nights during the war.

Mervan bought her next glass of gin and another after that. The conversation moved on to musical preferences. She asked if he played anything by George Formby. Mervan had to admit that he didn't, but added that he was considering learning some. The old lady said how much she had enjoyed Herman's Hermits' remakes of some of the old Formby songs. It was seven o'clock when it finally dawned on Mervan that the concert was due to start in an hour and he had not been in contact with his fellow entrepreneur Nathan Watson since two o'clock on the previous afternoon. He took his leave of the old lady and went in search of a taxi.

'Don't forget your guitar,' she called out to him.

Retracing his steps, the gentleman vagabond kissed the lady's hand, retrieved his guitar and then went out into the gathering dusk.

At seven thirty, a taxi deposited him at the rear of the town hall and he hurried inside. Nathan was frantic but relieved to see him. The hall was filling up nicely, mostly with students and other young people but there was also a significant number of older and more conservative looking patrons.

'But they're all paying so we should be in business. You've just got to give them their money's worth.'

'That won't be a problem,' said Mervan as he stumbled, tripped over his guitar case and fell at the feet of the lovely Angela Moriarty who had just walked in. 'Are you all right?' she asked with some concern as he struggled to his feet.

'Never better,' replied Mervan as he lurched away, 'Never better.'

Mervan had harbored a lingering affection for Miss Moriarty for some time, having seen and admired her at a number of her recent performances. Her apparent concern for his wellbeing, deeply moved him. Later on, if the opportunity arose, he would tell her so.

In the dressing rooms out the back, he heard Mark Denham tuning up. Mark just loved to play and he had hardly stopped since beginning that morning on the train. There had been a barbeque for the patrons of B Carriage at the Denham family home and the music had continued unabated, except for a few brief interludes in which he tried to endear himself to Maggie. He nodded to Mervan and continued to play and sing without stopping to exchange any further pleasantries.

Mervan found a small room where he could be alone and compose himself. Denham was sounding particularly good. As one of the entrepreneurs organising the concert, Mervan should have been pleased with that. However as a fellow performer he had difficulty suppressing feelings of jealous anxiety. He concentrated on tuning up and then went in search of a cup of coffee.

There was a little kitchen at the back of the hall where the other performers had already gathered. Angela Moriarty was being Mother, and Mervan gladly allowed her to wait on him. The night was chilly and Angela was rugged up in a weather beaten old camel coloured duffle coat. Mervan mentally noted this with some disappointment. He would have expected her to wear something a bit more elegant. 'But then again,' he mused. 'I suppose it is a folk concert.'

The show was to be opened by Horst, a German Landscape Painter who was hitch hiking around the world. His conversational English was at times a little awkward but he did an excellent line in songs by Leonard Cohen and Simon and Garfunkel. He added an international flavour to proceedings.

Second on the bill were Eve and Stephanie a duo from Carlingford. To keep the genders balanced, Mark Denham would be next, followed by Angela and then Mervan would provide the finale. Miss Moriarty made a very respectable cup of coffee, as instant coffee went, and a sense of camaraderie developed amongst the performers as they sipped their drinks and waited nervously for the curtain to go up.

Mervan left them briefly to check the stage and steal a glance at the crowd through a gap in the curtain. He noted an interesting mix with quite a few older people - that is to say people in their thirties and forties. With some concern, he witnessed the arrival of the unruly element that had been feeding bananas to the monkeys earlier that afternoon. They reminded him of the unpleasant incident with the bus driver. He began to feel unsettled and hoped they wouldn't cause any trouble. Nathan placed a hand on his shoulder.

'It's time to start.'

Except for a few squeals of feedback as the microphones were adjusted, Nathan's opening remarks were well received. Horst was duly introduced as a visiting overseas artist and, after a few halting comments of his own, he started proceedings with *That's no way to say goodbye.*

Mervan watched most of Horst's bracket and was pleased to see that the crowd loved it. Horst's language difficulties endeared him to the audience. Mervan thought that his own articulate and urbane rapport with the audience, when the time came, would benefit from the contrast. Reassured, he went back to his dressing room to check his tuning as Horst launched into *The Boxer.*

As Mervan listened to the rousing applause at the end of Horst's performance, he congratulated himself on his organisational skills. He mentally congratulated Nathan as well and genuinely believed that they had engineered a major cultural event in bringing all these people together.

However, to some extent the patrons of B Carriage, although very appreciative of the concert, regarded it as just one of a number of events that day that were made important by their presence - such as drinking the train dry and the party that was to be resumed later on at the Denham household. Mark's parents were away overseas and he had the place to himself.

The day was a major social event. For this reason Kate and Maggie felt quite comfortable about leaving the concert for a coffee at the little cafe across the street during the performance by Eve and Stephanie.

'Actually,' Kate was saying, 'I can take or leave folk music. It's just that a lot of my friends are involved. How about you?'

Maggie admitted to similar feelings and didn't share Brian's enthusiasm. She and Hugh mainly listened to the Moody Blues.

'Hugh actually feels very out of place here. I've never known him to be in such a dark mood before. I'm dreading The Party.'

'Well we don't need to go back there for long and we can go and stay with my grandfather. It's been a long day and that would be a peaceful way to end it.' To their mutual relief, the two girls had taken an immediate liking to one another. They wandered back to the hall in time for Mark's bracket. He was still in good voice and he dedicated a creditable version of *Dear Prudence* to his cousin. It was Kate's favourite song.

Some members of the audience, particularly the monkey feeders, were also in good, if somewhat inarticulate, voice but for the most part they confined their comments to the intervals between the songs. Eve and Stephanie had lacked the confidence to talk them down but the rest of the audience did that for them. Mark on the other hand was able to deal with them.

Near the end of his bracket, he announced a song for all the Maggies in the audience and launched into *Maggie May*. He had spotted where Kate and Maggie were sitting and aimed his performance at them. Hugh got up and left. Kate saw this and the effect it had on Maggie.

'Don't worry,' she said. 'I'll tell Mark to pull his head in.'

Hugh burst free from the hall and took a few deep breaths of fresh air. For a brief moment he looked about him and considered going back into the hall but his anger carried the day and he stormed off down the street. He had only been to Carlingford a couple of times and he didn't really know his way around, but in his anger, his paramount concern was to get as far away from the concert as possible. Half an hour later, the tide of anger had begun to subside and he had no idea where he was. He had wandered down near the river.

At about that time, Angela Moriarty was concluding an impressive performance. Prior to taking the stage she had slipped into a pair of high heels and shed her old duffle coat to reveal a short and slinky little black, silk dress all of which showed her long flaxen hair and her shapely black stockinged legs to their maximum advantage.

With the exception of a few ladies from the Folk Music Society who took a dim view of Angela's slinky little black number and thought frayed jeans and a poncho would have been more in keeping with the folk tradition, the crowd loved her. The unruly element supported her warmly and enthusiastically.

As she introduced her final number, *Codeine,* she told them not to be silly. The entire audience, primitive monkey feeders included, loved her all the more. She walked off to deafening applause and Mervan, waiting in the wings, patted her reassuringly on the shoulder and said, 'Don't worry. You were great.'

A bemused Angela walked off shaking her head.

'How dare he patronise me like that.'

During Mervan's bracket, Kate, Maggie and Brian went in search of Hugh. Brian had wanted to stay, but as Kate pointed out, if you had seen one of Mervan's performances you'd seen them all. They found Hugh retracing his steps and Kate apologised to him for her cousin's behaviour.

'I've already given him a piece of my mind. He gets a bit too full of himself sometimes.'

Hugh said he had been offended for Maggie more than himself, because the song *Maggie May* was so obviously about a prostitute.

'Anyway,' said Kate, as Hugh's mood began to lighten, 'I've had enough of the folk music scene for one day. Let's skip the party and go straight to Grandad's. He's expecting me to bring a few people.'

They had to go back to the hall to pick up their luggage. From the sound of things, the concert was ending in uproar. The monkey feeders were beginning to make requests, especially for *Green Green Grass of Home* and *Irene Goodnight*. In the middle of *Wheels on Fire*, a banana had been lobbed onto the stage.

Mervan kept his composure and launched into *Irene Goodnight*. At the first chorus, the entire audience, monkey feeders and their detractors alike, joined in and they raised the roof. Mervan milked the song for all it was worth and the rendition went on for about a quarter of an hour before the audience would let him stop and bring proceedings to a close.

It was a shaken but satisfied Mervan who took his final bow as the curtain came down. He'd got them all singing together. It may not have been a song he particularly wanted to sing but he had seized the moment and put the song to good use. The performers gathered in the dressing room for congratulations all round. Mark invited Mervan to the party and the Voice of his Nation's Soul accepted the invitation magnanimously.

As the party resumed, a taxi deposited Kate and her friends outside her grandfather's house. Brian felt a little apprehensive about meeting any of Kate's family but Kate reassured him that her grandad was a sweetie. Mr Mahoney's housekeeper greeted them at the door and showed them to the guest rooms, where they stowed their luggage. She then ushered them into a parlour where Young Jack Mahoney the former Prime Minister was sitting enjoying a pipe and listening to the music of Vaughan Williams.

The old man got to his feet, kissed his granddaughter fondly on the cheek and warmly welcomed the others. 'And is this the young chap that talks to crows?' he asked as he shook Brian's hand. Brian looked a little sheepish but was secretly gratified that Kate had obviously talked about him to her grandfather.

'Only during moments of deep mystical significance,' said Kate, blushing and eager to change the subject. 'By the way Grandad I've got a bone to pick with you. You know that song you used to sing to me when I was little.....“Jerusalem   Jerosalem   Jeree   Jeri   Jerosulem, whenever he blows his noselum he has to take his boots off?”'

'Well I was at a rugby club party the other night and I heard them singing a different set of words to that song. They called it *The Harlot of Jerusalem.*'

'Well my dear if you will go and associate with rugby players that's the kind of thing you have to expect. But of course I am blameless in the matter.'

The initial shyness and awkwardness that Brian and Maggie had felt quickly began to evaporate. Hugh was still a little subdued but he was grateful to Kate and her grandfather for providing this safe haven and he warmed to the charm that seemed to be a Mahoney family trait. He searched his mind desperately for something appropriate to contribute to the conversation about rugby or football in general. He had grown up in a family that was obsessed with football but for the life of him he couldn't think of anything to say.

'You are obviously a devotee of the only true game,' said Brian. The old man smiled and Hugh looked on in open mouthed exasperation. 'What did Brian know about football?'

Brian continued: 'What's your view on the origins of our game. Do you think it's stolen from Australian Rules or from Gaelic Football.'

'Ah well,' said Jack as he re-lit his pipe. 'I don't think it was necessarily stolen from either. I think our Irish forebears brought Gaelic Football here with them and the game in the Cumberlands remained virtually unchanged. It was back in Ireland that the game changed. In 1884, the Gaelic Athletics Association was concerned to differentiate their game from Rugby and they made a lot of changes. That was when they introduced goal nets and the round ball. We still use the oval ball here, but not because of Australian Rules. Gaelic football originally used the oval ball.'

Kate took Maggie to one side. 'Would you care to take a turn around the room Miss Bennett?' she said and took her off to look at some of the paintings. The room was elegantly and comfortably understated. The wood panelled walls, leather lounges, velvet curtains and oil paintings, made the room feel extremely comfortable rather than grand or imposing.

As well as the paintings, there were a great many framed photographs spanning a century of Mahoney family history.

'That's Grandad in France during the First World War.'

Maggie looked up to compare the young officer with the old man as he sat enjoying the lively conversation with her brother by the fire. In many ways Maggie thought he didn't look old enough to have been in the Great War.

Mrs Sullivan the housekeeper stuck her head round the door.

'Would anyone like a warm drink before I go to bed?'

A long, thin, black cat with an elegant white throat wove its way into the room around her ankles and called out to Kate who responded in kind.

'Thomas!! You must meet Thomas. Do you know he's older than I am. He's 20 years old.'

'Is that a no?' said Mrs Sullivan with feigned impatience.

'Make us some cocoa Alice, and I'll pour us all a little glass of something else while the milk boils,' said Jack. 'Although these young lads here may already have drunk their fill today. Would you believe it Alice? They helped drink the down train dry between Ross and Carlingford.'

'Nothing would surprise me these days.'

As Jack poured them all a glass of Irish Mist and they began to think about bed and sleep, the party in the Denham family home was reaching fever pitch. Around a rekindled barbecue fire, the inexhaustible Mark with his guitar was leading a rowdy drunken chorus of rugby songs.

In the kitchen, scrawny bearded men in woollen bush shirts were drinking mugs of hard cider and listening to a continuous tape of Jane Birkin's *Je t'aime*, leering very knowingly at one another all the while. Joints were passing from hand to hand all over the house and one enterprising couple was busy copulating in Mr and Mrs Denham's marital bed. Horst had drunk far more than was good for him (although he was not alone in that regard) and kept colliding with the furniture as he searched the house for ever new distractions.

In a separate little parlour away from the main crowd, Mervan Mithras, seated on the floor, in the lotus position was introducing a small circle of pupils to Indian meditation. Opposite Mervan in the circle and finding it difficult to reconcile her slinky little black dress with the lotus position, was Angela Moriarty. She had been the subject of Mervan's attentions all evening and was anxious to escape at the earliest opportunity. It may have been the incense. Then again it may have been pollen from the flowers in a vase on the table behind him. Whatever the cause, the Voice of his Nation's Soul had just begun chanting a mantra when he was convulsed by a loud and violent sneeze. Angela opened her eyes and looked down to find a glistening set of dentures - top and bottom - in her lap.

There followed an awkward silence that was charged with a number of conflicting emotions. Mervan, scarlet to the tips of his ears, not to mention his gums, stared in abject misery at his runaway teeth which smiled up at Angela from between her shapely and elegantly black-stockinged thighs. He could do nothing to retrieve them. Angela, reluctant to touch the dental intruders, got to her feet and let them clatter to the floor.

'Well' she said. 'I'm sure this is all very interesting but I think I need a drink.'

A few seconds later, Mervan and his teeth had the parlour to themselves. He re-assembled his smile and retreated to the barbecue area in search of something to drown his misery. Mark Denham met him there and offered him a drink.

'Have you heard Angela's news?'

Mervan wasn't sure what news he meant but Mark quickly went on to tell him that a producer from the Cumberland Broadcasting Commission had been at the concert and signed Angela to do a series of five minute spots before the seven p.m. news on Channel 2.

'Isn't that great?'

'Yes, it's terrific,' said a crestfallen Mervan, trying to force a smile.

At the earliest opportunity he drained his glass, picked up his trusty guitar and wandered out into the darkness where there was weeping and gnashing of dentures.

7: A Parting of the Ways

Friday morning dawned clear and mild. Kate got up early from the room she shared with Maggie to attend seven o'clock mass with her grandfather. He heard mass every day and his granddaughter always accompanied him when she came to stay.

An hour later, they were all sitting down to a breakfast of bacon and eggs in a sunny room which opened onto an expansive garden. Everyone felt well rested and very much at home. Hugh in particular was grateful for a good night's sleep in a comfortable bed. If he had been able to see the desolation blighting the Denham family home at that moment, his gratitude would have been even more heartfelt.

After they had helped Mrs Sullivan with the washing up, Mr Mahoney took Maggie for a tour of the garden with Thomas and Kate. Brian went to have a shower and Hugh occupied himself looking at the photographs and paintings in the lounge room where they had been the previous night.

The paintings were mainly pastoral landscapes, and there was a painting of Darlington as a village. It seemed to predate the painting in the museum. Almost without thinking, Hugh found himself looking for the two oak trees that Robert had talked about on that strange night that now seemed so long ago. He found the trees in front of the colonnaded structure that was now the museum, although it was a much smaller building at that time. He also noticed a number of other much larger oak trees nearby that had not survived to the present day.

His attention passed to the photographs. They spanned a century, ranging from recent portraits of Kate and her siblings and baby photographs, back to pictures from the two world wars and further back to Jack's youth and childhood. There was one picture of a very small Kate nursing a much younger Thomas.

In a corner of the room above a little writing desk there was a photograph of Jack's wedding and a favourite portrait of his wife as a young girl. A little to one side of it was a photograph of Jack and another young man in tennis clothes. Something about the other man caught Hugh's attention. He was reminded at once of the calm, affectionate and slightly amused face in the picture in Mrs Malleson's room. Then it dawned on him. It was the same man - the man Jim claimed had rescued him at sea.

The business of the three visitors and their strange tale had been pushed to the back of Hugh's mind in recent days. His efforts to tell the story to Maggie and Brian had met with only a lukewarm response. Brian, who didn't have a cynical bone in his body as a rule, seemed quite sceptical about the whole thing. Maggie had been outraged that Hugh had taken three strangers into Mrs Malleson's flat - into her bedroom even.

'I don't know what I'm going to do with you two - Brian getting himself arrested and you breaking and entering.'

Because Jim still had the exercise books, Hugh had no evidence to back up his story. He offered to take them down into the cellar, but Maggie declined.

'It would upset Mrs Malleson, if she found out and anyway it's none of our business.'

That had pretty much been the end of it. He was reluctant to raise the subject again but this photograph had to be followed up. If there was a family connection between Kate and the young man in the photograph it might be possible to solve the mystery. At that moment Kate came back into the room with Thomas. Her grandfather and Maggie had gone in search of cuttings.

'So you're checking out the rogues gallery are you?'

'I wouldn't call it that,' Hugh laughed nervously. 'I find old pictures very interesting. Tell me Kate. Who is the man in this photo with your grandfather?'

Kate looked intently.

'That's one of the Fairchilds. He was a poet or something like that. Grandad's got some of his books in the study.'

'Is he still a friend of your grandad?'

'I suppose so. He may be dead of course. That picture was taken a long time ago.'

'So you know the Fairchild family.'

'Not personally. Why do you ask?'

'It's just that I've seen another picture of the same man in Mrs Malleson's flat back home.'

'It's a small world. Is Brian still in the shower?'

'Yes I'm waiting for my turn.'

'Maggie was telling me last night about his spot of bother with the law. She's quite worried about him. But he doesn't seem the least bit concerned.'

'It'll sink in when he has to have his day in court.'

'Fortunately I might be able to help there. Or rather Dad might.'

The young man in question came into the room.

'OK Hugo. Your turn and don't be all day.'

'Would there be any chance of having a look at those books?' asked Hugh as he went to the door.

'I'll ask Grandad when he comes back inside,' said Kate. 'And as for you young Master McInerney, I've got a bone to pick with you. We might have just had a very long shower but we haven't quite come clean have we?'

Hugh left them to it. When he emerged from the bathroom twenty minutes later, he found the others in Jack's study.

'Here are those books you were asking about,' Kate said and pulled up a chair for him at her side. Jack handed the slim leather bound volumes to him across the desk.

'They are beautifully done. The paper is handmade and it's all in his own handwriting. He bound the volumes and did the artwork himself.'

Hugh looked at the frontispiece. There was a dedication "to Jack and Gwyneth from Norian" and it was dated October 1926. The conversation had moved on to Jack's political career but Hugh became completely absorbed in his reading. The first volume contained a number of short poems all in an elegant flowing script. He opened the second book. It was entitled "Dandillion The White Ship" and it contained one longer narrative poem which was divided into a number of sections or chapters. It only took a moment for Hugh to realise that it told the same story that the children had imitated in the exercise books in the cellar.

What would Jim, Lucy and Robert say when he told them. He felt that he now had something substantial to add to their quest. On that first night when they came to his flat, Robert had said "we already know quite a bit about you. But we're more interested in this house or rather in who owns it." Now he had made a significant discovery. He wondered wistfully if he might borrow the book but realised it would be too much to ask.

'You like poetry then do you?' Jack asked, noticing the excitement in Hugh's face.

Hugh nodded.

'I'm particularly interested in the poet. I was telling Kate that the old woman in the downstairs flat at home has a picture of him in her...in her flat.' He finished lamely as Maggie looked up sharply remembering his invasion of Mrs Malleson's bedroom.

'How well did you know him?' asked Hugh anxiously, mindful that this might be the only opportunity he would get to pursue this line of inquiry.

'He was a very dear friend but we drifted apart over time - no fault of his or mine. I haven't seen him for many years. He was a great sailor. I believe the "White Ship" is a kind of allegory of his own life. I don't think I ever fully understood what he was trying to say. He called his yacht 'Dandillion.' '

Brian looked up. He remembered enough of Hugh's earlier account of the three visitors and their strange tale, to realise that what Jack was saying seemed to bear it out.

'Do any of his family still live around here?' Hugh persisted.

'Oh yes there are still a few Fairchilds here and there, if you know where to look. But look at the time. If you young people are going to catch the Up Train we are going to have to move. I can't lend you the books because they are very precious to me and irreplaceable. But you are welcome to come here and read them at your leisure whenever you are back this way.'

'I would like that very much,' said Hugh gratefully. He was nonplussed by his own audacity. So were Maggie and Brian. This wasn't like old Hugo to go talking freely to grownups.

~~~§~~~

As Jack Mahoney made his farewells to his granddaughter and her friends outside the Carlingford Station, a few survivors from the party at the Denham family home, looking seedy, green and very much the worse for wear, were already on the platform, draped across benches, propped against walls and waiting for the up train. They were longing for the chance to sleep off their headaches and nausea in its plush and comfortable seats. It was highly unlikely that much drinking would happen on today's journey.

'Hullo Horst,' said Kate. 'I loved your performance last night. What's the matter? You look terrible.'

'Danke Kate,' groaned the cadaverous looking minstrel. 'I too much haf drunk unt I am overhung.'

In due course, the Up Train and the Down Train pulled into the station from opposite ends of the Island. The two crews swapped trains to make their homeward journeys. Emily Oldfield noticed the fragile plight of many of the patrons of B Carriage with grim satisfaction. Once their journey commenced, Kate resumed the discussion she had begun with Brian earlier that morning. This time she was able to draw on Maggie for moral support.

'If you'd just tell Dad what happened, I'm sure he would be able to help. He might even represent you.'

'How could I afford his fee?' said Brian, a bit on edge about being pinned down on such a delicate subject. What he really meant was, that this was no way to be introduced to the Father of one's beloved. But he couldn't say that. What if it turned out that Kate didn't actually regard herself as his beloved yet? What if she was just being her normal helpful, compassionate self?
~~~

'Don't be silly. He wouldn't charge for one of my friends.'

Maggie and Hugh lent their support to Kate and Brian felt himself being cornered.

'You have to let them help you,' Maggie was saying. 'If you get a conviction you can kiss goodbye to your teacher studentship.'

'And from what you tell me,' Kate continued. 'You're not the guilty party anyway. The damage was done before you arrived. You just happened to be in the wrong place at the wrong time.'

'But what's your Dad going to think of me? I don't want to make the wrong impression on him.'

'He'll be fine. Just leave him to me.'

'It's an offer you can't refuse.' Hugh chimed in. 'You couldn't afford to pay anybody else to defend you.'

'Well if you're sure it's not too much trouble.'

'Good lad,' said Kate beaming and rewarding him with an affectionate kiss. A bemused Brian thought to himself that he would have given in a lot quicker if he had known he'd get that response. He fervently hoped that they'd all drop the subject now and let him forget about it again.

'I suggest we spend the weekend at my place then,' said Kate. 'We might as well strike while the iron's hot.'

'That sounds like a good idea,' said Maggie. With their parents abroad and not a lot of use at the best of times, Maggie often looked on her wayward older brother as an errant child she had to mother and protect. Kate's proposal would ensure that something was done sooner rather than later.

However, this latter suggestion wasn't at all to the liking of the two young men. Brian thought he had put his legal worries out of reach for the foreseeable future. The fact that Kate meant to deal with them immediately meant meeting the parents of his beloved sooner rather than later. He didn't feel quite ready for that.

For his part, Hugh was very unhappy with the turn of events. He had already sacrificed two days of his holidays to go traipsing up to Carlingford with a whole heap of arrogant, smart arsed students. He was not prepared to spend the last weekend of his holidays staying in a strange household.

Charmed as he was by Kate and her grandfather, it would be too taxing to have to meet with her parents and spend more valuable free time away from his beloved apartment with all its memories of last summer. Surely Maggie would feel the same. But unfortunately for Hugh and Brian, the two young ladies were in complete agreement.

A little cloud of anxious gloom descended upon the two young gentlemen while their companions chatted away in contentment. After a while Brian ventured up to the bar for an ale. Emily Oldfield served him and remembered him from yesterday. It seemed remarkable to her that he was clearly not in the same plight as some of his other compatriots in B carriage.

'He must be even more depraved than the others,' she thought. 'What a shame. He has such a lovely smile.'

At that point Hugh joined him and ordered a glass of sherry. While Kate and Maggie made plans for the weekend, the two young men discussed ways to change their minds. Hugh was able to quickly convince Brian that he needed some time at home before returning to work on Monday morning.

'And we don't want to put Kate's family to too much trouble,' said Brian as they finished their drinks.

On the way back to B carriage, Horst stumbled past them in a desperate attempt to get to the toilet. It was engaged.

'Quick,' said Brian. 'Try the one in A carriage.'

Horst didn't dare open his mouth.

'That's too far. It'll have to be the guard van,' said Hugh. They bundled Horst through the buffet car and out the other end to the guard van. Then they slid the door back and held him down with his head over the side. After about ten minutes of hard work, Horst's stomach had achieved some kind of equilibrium and they hauled him back to his feet.

'Danke,' said the invalid. 'That feels better, though my mouth is as dry as a buzzard's crutch.'

Horst thought that some schnapps would improve the taste in his mouth and he promptly went to the buffet car and ordered three glasses from a strongly disapproving Miss Oldfield. Hugh and Brian, while doubting the wisdom of this, nevertheless joined him in a toast to the speedy return of good health.

Horst drained his glass in a single draft and promptly demanded another. His two companions declined the offer of a second glass. The German skulled his second, then a third and underwent a violent shuddering convulsion.

'There that should do the trick.'

He took a deep breath, drew himself up to his full height and made his way back to B Carriage. Maggie passed him in the doorway.

'What's been keeping you two reprobates?'

'It was an errand of mercy, sister dear,' said Brian as they followed her back to their seats. The two couples immediately began to discuss the coming weekend. To Hugh's relief, Kate was quick to see his point of view about wanting some time at home before he returned to work. Maggie wasn't as understanding.

'Brian and I will be back on Sunday night and we'll be spending all of next week with you.'

'Yes, but I'll be back at work then.'

'But we've got to get Brian sorted out. And Kate's father can do that for us.'

'But we don't need to be there. Kate and Brian can sort it out. And what about all the cuttings, Kate's grandad gave you. You'll need to get them planted as quickly as you can.'

Maggie did not need to be reminded at that moment, of the pathos of her taking cuttings from one end of the Island to the other, to plant in a garden she'd only ever see for a few brief weeks each year - a pretend garden owned by someone else or rather by someone else's landlord.

Brian's head began to ring with alarm bells. He recognised that his sister was in the early stages of a mood. The room temperature would soon plummet to icy depths while she herself would begin to smoulder with volcanic intensity. What was Hugo thinking? He could normally read the signs. He should have caved in long before this.

'What say you spend tonight with us Hugh, and catch the early train to Darlington in the morning,' ventured Kate sensing the need to pour oil on the waters. 'Dad might be able to give you some more information about the Fairchilds.'

'Don't start him on that bullshit again!!' snapped Maggie.

'Are you sure your parents won't mind putting us all up at such short notice?' Brian asked, realising that if silence was allowed to settle on this impasse, reconciliation might be difficult.

'Of course not. They like to meet the people I mix with. It reassures them. Although in your case.' Kate raised her eyebrows. But only Brian was laughing. 'Anyway,' she continued. 'There's plenty of time before we get to Denistone. The offer is there but you're under no pressure. Just think it over. Brian, would you like to buy me a drink?'

'But you're under age.'

She cocked him a glance, with her supremely articulate eyebrows, that was as good as a kick in the shins.

'Well get me a raspberry spider then you buffoon.'

Brian finally caught on and they retreated as discreetly and quickly as possible.

'Good thinking,' said Brian as they sat down in the buffet car. 'I was about to suggest something similar.' This time she did kick him in the shins.

'Things seem pretty grim in there,' said Kate. 'Perhaps we should drop the plan to stay at my place.'

'I think it's too late for that,' said Brian.

'You and I could always meet with Dad next term. When's your case due?'

'The fifth of November.'

'Remember remember,' Kate chanted in an endearing attempt at a bass voice.

Emily Oldfield came to the bar.

'Not that young man again,' she thought to herself with a frown. 'Can I get you something?'

'Yes thank you,' said Brian, ' a cup of coffee for me and a raspberry spider for my little friend.'

Even Emily had trouble keeping a straight face as she dutifully prepared and served the two drinks.

'I feel like I've caused them to fall out with my invitation,' said Kate solemnly, unaware of the ice cream moustache she had just acquired from her spider.

'No it's not your fault. They've been spoiling for a fight all week. Poor old Hugo lives in the past a bit. Last summer was a magical time, but Maggie is outgrowing that now. She's happy to meet new people and experience new things. But Hugo doesn't want anything to change. We'll give them a bit of time alone together and see if they come to their senses. There's not much else we can do.'

<div align="center">~~~§~~~</div>

Kate and Brian returned to find that the troubled young couple had not come to their senses and an ominous, oppressive gloom had now settled heavily upon that part of B Carriage. After a few faltering attempts to start a conversation, Kate admitted defeat and, at a glance from Brian, they quietly withdrew in the direction of the buffet car. Years later, opinions were still divided over whose decision it had been, but be that as it may, they passed quickly through the buffet car and ended up in the guard van where they quickly became lost in an intensely enjoyable and thorough exploration of each other's charms.

They lost all track of time and were startled to hear Emily Oldfield's voice on the public address system announcing that they were about to arrive at Denistone

Station.   With their eyes still shining and hurriedly straightening their clothes, they scrambled back to B Carriage to get their luggage.

Hugh and Maggie had turned to blocks of stone, but not before Maggie had retrieved her luggage from the rack in readiness to depart. Hugh and his luggage remained unmoved. Maggie was pale and, to the inexperienced eye, may have seemed on the verge of tears. Brian however, recognised her pallor as white heat. The tears would come later.

The train came to a halt. Maggie picked up her things without a word and left the carriage. Kate and Brian looked entreatingly at Hugh.

'You're sure you won't come, just for tonight?'

'No thanks Kate. I better go home,' said Hugh and he probably was fairly close to tears.

'See you then' said Brian with a helpless shrug, and he followed Kate off the train.

Both Hugh and Maggie felt in their hearts that they had taken an irreversible step and each could feel their sundered paths setting like concrete. At the last minute, Maggie turned around to watch the train as it pulled out of the station but Hugh did not look back.

'This looks serious,' thought Brian as he absently did up a button on Kate's blouse that she had missed in their earlier haste. There was an awkward silence.

'Well,' said Kate. 'We'd better see about a taxi. Are you ok Maggie?'

'I'll be all right,' she replied, with a slight tremor in her voice as she looked at the carefully wrapped cuttings that Jack had given her. She dropped them into a rubbish bin.

'Please don't tell your grandad Kate. It was so sweet of him.'

They went off to the taxi rank and were soon loaded up and on their way to meet Kate's parents.

'Mum goes on a bit sometimes just don't take her too seriously. Dad's a sweetie. He longs for the quiet life. Leave the matter of your legal trouble to me. I'll know the appropriate time to raise it.' Kate chattered nervously like that until the cab pulled up in the driveway, while Brian and Maggie silently pondered their respective concerns.

Madelaine Mahoney was like no other parent that Brian or Maggie had ever met before. Virtually everything she did was a tour de force. However, for all that she had imposed a regime of firm parental guidance and control on her three children, rumours about a bohemian past abounded in the family. Some said that she had even smoked hashish while working as a nurse in Egypt during the second world war.

She kept up a fairly constant flow of conversation whilst busily preparing the evening meal. But for all her domestic preoccupation, she didn't miss a trick and was able to ask a number of probing questions of her daughter and her guests. She instantly picked up on Maggie's distress and she suspected that Brian's awkward shyness was out of character. She was also aware of an unfamiliar colour in her daughter's cheeks.

'And how was the Concert?'

'It was great,' said Brian, anxious to get some conversational runs on the board.

'Do you play an instrument yourself?'

'No,' he admitted, feeling that he might have appeared in a more favourable light had he been able to answer otherwise.

'Well don't just stand there Katie. Make your guests comfortable. Put a kettle on and show them their rooms.'

Brian had never seen Kate so flustered before, but it only added to her appeal.

A few minutes later their luggage was stowed away and Mrs Mahoney sat down to share a cup of tea with them.

'Was the dreaded Boy there?'

'No Mum, and thank goodness for that.'

'What boy?' asked Brian.

'Boy Upson,' said Mother and Daughter in the same breath and with the same tone of aversion and distaste.

'He's a young man with far too much land and money and nowhere near enough common sense to put either of them to good use,' Mrs Mahoney went on. 'And if I have to listen to one more of his boring anecdotes as Foxtrot Tango Lima the great aviator, I won't be answerable for the consequences.

'Do you know what his latest proposal is Kate? He's proposing to buy a bull, some kind of Brahman-Zebu cross thing - you know, the ones with a hump and a droopy sort of baggy fold under their neck. It's because they look eastern.   It's the kind of animal you'd buy to run somewhere tropical like outback Australia, not in a cool temperate climate like the Cumberlands and on a sheep farm for goodness sake! Funnily enough we don't get a lot of tsetse fly in this part of the world. He's got more money than sense.'

'It's a wonder he wasn't at the concert come to think of it,' said Kate. 'He's quite an enthusiast.'

'And what about you Maggie? Are you a folk singer?'

'No. We.....I mean I only came along because Kate and Brian like it.'

'Are you feeling all right?'

'Yes. It's just a bit of a headache.'

'Perhaps you should have a lie down before dinner. Fix her up with some aspirin Kate.'

The two girls left the room and Madelaine was able to start work on Brian. By the time Kate came back, her Mother knew Brian's age, his star sign, what he was studying at uni, his career aspirations and his views about the Vietnam war. He was talking quite freely and marvelling at what an easy conversationalist the mother of his beloved was.

'And how long have you known our Kate?'

'Now then Mum,' said Kate coming back into the room, 'don't go giving him the third degree. We met at uni.'

Brian was a little crestfallen. He would have liked to share the story of the crows with Mrs Mahoney. She seemed to have a great sense of humour. Kate however, believed in making her Mother work hard to satisfy her voracious curiosity.

'How's Maggie?' said Madelaine, changing her tack. 'She seemed more upset than ill.'

'She's just split up with her boy friend,' said Brian, failing to notice the slight, cautionary shake of the head from Kate.

'Ah I thought there might have been someone else. I was talking to Jack on the phone a while ago. He said he had dropped four of you off at the station. Well that's unfortunate. It might only be puppy love like they say but it's still possible to break your heart even at Maggie's age.'

Brian wasn't sure what kind of impression he was making on Kate's Mum but he was very favourably impressed with her. Kate looked on with mild frustration.

'Typical Mum,' she thought. 'If Brian's not careful he'll say something he might regret.'

~~~§~~~

At about that time, the Up Train was making its way through the outer suburbs of Darlington. Hugh was numb. His anger had sustained him for about an hour after the train pulled out of Denistone Station. But then it had deserted him and a cold, bleak emptiness had taken its place. He was heading back to Darlington and the flat in Gracechurch Street, that was the centre of his universe. But it was only the centre of his universe because he had made it a shrine to Maggie. Her memory and her personality were enthroned there along with the bunches of dried herbs and the golden memories of last summer.

But that golden age appeared to be over and those reminders of Maggie were now waiting to torment him and impress upon him just how much he had lost. Hugh had needed his fanciful daydreams to sustain him as he coped with the demands of everyday life in the real world. That support was gone now. Work would be unbearable. The flat itself would be unbearable.

The train pulled into Darlington Central and Hugh picked up his bag and walked off into the gathering dusk. He wandered aimlessly past the taxi rank, through the pedestrian underpass and roundabout into the centre of the City, dreading the desolation that he felt sure was waiting for him at Gracechurch Street. Even though he had lived and worked in the City for more than a year, he realised now how foreign it all still was. Or rather, he realised that he was the foreigner. He wondered if a reconciliation with Maggie might be possible but could
~~~

only remember the cruel and hurtful comments that had passed between them after Kate and Brian had left.

He wandered aimlessly through the City, past the central business district and down towards the river. There was a point near the harbour where two flights of steps led to a pathway by the water's edge. At high tide the path was submerged. At the moment the waters were flush with the pathway and the occasional surge of turbulence from passing ferries would cause wavelets to lap up over the concrete. In happier times, Hugh had drawn great pleasure from this sight: dry land and the water at the point of merging, a still point or equilibrium poised between two worlds. It took on a deeper significance now as the thought entered his mind that he only needed to walk down onto the pathway and from there step into the water.

He had to face massive changes in his life. He didn't know if he could bear the pain of life without Maggie. A massive wave of aching regret surged inside him. If the rest of his life was going to feel like that, he couldn't cope with it. The flat would be unspeakably painful for him. Before he had time to reconsider, Hugh walked down the steps onto the damp pathway.

'Do this', he thought, 'and in a few minutes the pain will be over.' He had no idea how long it took to drown, but he thought he remembered someone telling him that it was supposed to be quite pleasant towards the end. For a split second, the faces of family and loved ones flashed before his mind's eye, but the last image he saw was Maggie's face turned to cold stone. He bent over to look at the water, stepped on a patch of oily, greasy residue on the concrete and slipped off the edge.

The first thing he was aware of was the bitter, icy cold of the river water. For a moment, it drove all other coherent thought out of his mind. He could see nothing as the initial wave of shock engulfed him. He had swallowed some of the briny bilge and thought he was going to be sick. Waves of nausea gripped him and then he felt a sudden impact.

His feet had touched the bottom. Then he trod on a discarded beer bottle which rolled beneath his feet causing him to fall over backwards and begin sinking towards the river bed. After a few more frantic, floundering minutes, he was upright again. He took a moment to settle and then realised that his head was above water. At almost the same time he realised that he definitely didn't want to die just yet.

Still trying to control the contents of his stomach, he began to half wade, half swim back to the path. What if he couldn't climb back out? He'd die of exposure and cold rather than drowning. Should he call for help? But then he didn't think he could cope with the embarrassment if anyone learned of his accidental plunge of despair into chest high water. He reached up to the edge of the path and, searching with his feet, found footholds in the bank. In about five minutes he was back on dry land.

There was no one in sight. Good. That meant there were no witnesses. His next problem was how to get back to the flat before he caught a chill and died. Given that he was soaked to the skin, public transport seemed out of the question. He found his bag where he had left it at the water's edge. That contained dry clothes. If he could find somewhere to hide, he could change and then catch a taxi.

He picked up his bag and wandered off in search of a secluded spot. Yes he would catch a taxi home. It was still his home, in spite of the split with Maggie. If nothing else, his nearly drowning had rearranged his priorities. Survival, warmth and shelter were of the utmost importance to him now, much more important than painful memories. There was nothing like a brush with death, no matter how farcical, to put things into perspective. The one thing that stayed with him and terrified him after that misadventure, was a sense of horror at how close he had almost come to ending his life.

He crossed the road from the waterfront and made for the park in the grounds in front of the Houses of Parliament. It might be possible to hide in the shrubbery while he got changed. He noticed the smell of a cigarette and looked anxiously around. Then he saw its red glow and the grizzled face of a grey haired old man in a tweed overcoat, under an oak tree.

'Changed your mind did you?' said the old man.

'Shit,' thought Hugh. 'He must have seen everything.'

'You'll need to change or you'll catch your death. Here take a swig of this.' He produced a bottle of whiskey from his pocket. 'You don't need to worry,' the old man went on, seeming to read Hugh's thoughts. 'It hasn't been opened yet.'

He heard the crack as the seal was broken.

'There, it'll warm you up. Now come with me. I know a place where you can get changed in private. Have you got anywhere to stay?'

Hugh was mesmerised by the unreality of it all. When he left home to come to the big city, his mother had warned him about hanging round certain areas after dark. Cathedral square, an old cemetery behind the Parliament that had been made into a park, had a sinister reputation.

Exactly what it was, his mother had been too shy to put into words. But she had warned him that it was frequented by undesirables, especially after dark. Now one of those undesirables appeared to be offering him friendship and shelter in Cathedral square.

Hugh knew him by sight. He was a well known figure about the town - a kind of elder statesman of the derelict classes. On their trip to town, Kate and Brian had seen him in an altercation with two young policemen. She had likened him to King Lear but he was generally known as Old Riley.

'That's right get it down you. You'll feel better. Come and I'll show where to change. It's a gardener's shed over there in the corner. The groundsman was in the army with me. He gave me my own key.'

Riley put his hand out for the bottle.

'My turn now.'

He wiped the mouth of the bottle with his sleeve.

'Nothing personal, but you might have the pox for all I know.' He smiled a surprisingly bright eyed and engaging smile that gave the lie to his otherwise derelict appearance, and then took a swig.

'Right in you go. Sing out when you're done.' He put the whiskey bottle back in his pocket and walked off rolling another cigarette.

Hugh waited a nervous moment to be sure that he was alone and then quickly stripped off his wet clothes, towelled himself down and got into something dry. He didn't want to leave without thanking the old man for his hospitality so he waited until presently he became aware of the smell of cigarette smoke again.

'All done?'

'Yes thanks,' said Hugh, speaking to him for the first time.

'And have you got somewhere to stay tonight?'

'Yes, yes thank you. I've got a flat in West Darlington.'

'Well you have a bit more of this to warm yourself up before you go back outside.'

The old man put the bottle on the dirt floor, rummaged around in a battered old suitcase for a pair of eight ounce beer glasses and filled them with whiskey.

'My name's Riley. What do they call you?'

'Hugh. Hugh Conroy.'

'Well then Hugh Conroy, here's your health.'

They drank.

'Something must have upset you pretty badly. Was it a woman?'

This perceptive question brought Hugh back to reality. He had been having trouble believing the turn his life had taken in the last hour or so. It was all so out of character and unprecedented in his experience.

'Yes,' he said with some surprise before coughing on the whiskey.

'It's usually a woman,' said Riley. 'I reckon if they didn't have cunts we'd stick 'em in cages and throw rocks at 'em wouldn't we?........Wouldn't we?'

'Er yes I suppose so,' said Hugh.

'Well anyway you're young enough to start again. There's plenty more fish in the sea, but you won't find one by drowning yourself.'

<div align="center">~~~§~~~</div>

As Hugh went in search of a taxi, dinner was being served in the Mahoney household. Maggie had emerged from her bed refreshed, although still pale, and maintained a fragile cheerfulness that didn't fool anybody but won the sympathy of all. Perhaps Brian had a selfish motive for wanting his sister to be at her best in front of the parents of his beloved. But for all that, he genuinely loved his sister although he was not blind to her shortcomings. He also loved Hugh, in a fraternal sort of way, for what the three of them had shared in the past. But he was convinced that those days had now been consigned to history and that Hugh would be the real loser in all of this.

'And what do your parents do?' Madelaine asked as they waited for Kate's father to take his seat at the table. He had been held up at work and was just quickly changing out of his work clothes and freshening up before he joined them.

'They're both teachers,' said Brian. 'Dad was missing the old country so they've both scored teaching jobs in England. They'll be away for a couple of years.'

'And they didn't take you with them?'

'Mum!!' said Kate.

'No,' said Brian. 'It's all right. They offered to take Maggie but she wanted to stay here.'

'Because of her boyfriend. What did you say his name was?'

If looks could kill, Kate would have well and truly slain her mother by this time, but Madelaine was quite confident that she could more than manage her daughter. At that moment, Mr Mahoney came into the room. Maggie and Brian were both taken by how much he resembled his father Jack and this put them at their ease.

'Matt, these are two charming friends of Kate - Brian and Maggie McInerney. Maggie's a little poorly because she's just split up with her boyfriend.' Madelaine carried on, blithely ignoring the bolts of lightning blazing from her daughter's eyes.

'I'm sorry to hear that Maggie,' said Mr Mahoney, a little embarrassed at being informed of such matters. 'Never mind. There's plenty more fish in the sea - just as long as you don't mind being seen walking out with a fish.' Maggie responded to his smile in kind and the awkward moment passed.

'How was work today Dad?' said Kate rather pointedly.

'Flat out now you come to mention it Kate. That's why I was late. Who would like a glass of wine with dinner?'

Brian and Maggie said yes and Madelaine went out to the kitchen to begin serving the meal.

'I'm sorry about Mum,' Kate muttered as her father went down to the cellar.

'Relax,' said Brian. 'It's OK.'

'Just be careful. She always wants to know everything. Only give her ten percent.'

'She seems charming,' said Brian.

'Maybe,' said Kate, 'but it can get a bit wearing after a while.'

'Can you give me a hand please Kathleen?' Her mother called from the kitchen.

Kate's father came back with a bottle of red gand a bottle of white and offered them a choice. Brian said he was no expert in such matters.

'You wouldn't have had any part in drinking the train dry yesterday then,' said Madelaine drily as she served the meal and Brian realised where Kate got her articulate eyebrows from.

'They only drank the train dry of beer,' said Brian a little sheepishly.

'Jack was most impressed,' said Madelaine laughing.

They settled on the red, which was a light and fruity wine, and began to enjoy their meal. At the same time, Kate and Madelaine began to relax. The process of initiating Brian and Maggie into the household seemed to have been successfully achieved. Madelaine's curiosity appeared to have been satisfied for the moment and Kate no longer felt that she had to be so protective and possessive.

Mother and daughter understood each other very well and without anything being said they both appreciated the significance of Brian being there. He was Kate's first serious young man. Although Kate would never have admitted it, she wanted her Mother to be impressed by him. The question of his needing the assistance of a solicitor would need to be kept secret just for now.

8: A Change of Season.

Hugh sat in a trolley bus. It was Friday and he was on his way home from work. It was a measure of how far he had progressed through a very difficult transition in his life, that he was actually looking forward to the weekend.

Daylight saving had started on the first Sunday in October and it was enjoyable being able to travel home from work in broad daylight. It had been a very pleasantly warm day which had seen many girls out in bright summer clothes. Hugh took more pleasure in the beauty of other women these days.   He also felt a new connectedness with the passing streetscape - the renovated fifties and sixties shop fronts at street level overlooked by the faded elegance of Edwardian, Victorian and Georgian upper storeys. He was beginning to feel that he belonged in Darlington and not just in the Gracechurch Street flat.

The rift with Maggie was final. Brian and Kate had dropped around to collect the last of Maggie's things. They were very sympathetic and had offered him their continued friendship. At that stage Hugh was still numb with grief. On the night of his plunge into the river, he had returned to the flat and collapsed straight into bed where he found blessed, if short lived relief in the deep sleep of exhaustion.

He had woken at about eleven o'clock the next morning and taken an hour or more to find the courage to get out of bed and face his new situation. Hunger made him think about breakfast and he concentrated on that to begin with. Expecting to be totally crushed by grief, he was a little surprised to find that the reality was not quite so overwhelming. True - he felt thoroughly miserable and close to tears, but he was able to shut out some of his pain by forcing himself to concentrate on simple domestic tasks.

The bunches of dried herbs and other reminders of Maggie's influence on his life were distressing if he dwelt on them as such. But it was easier than he would have thought to ignore them. The realization dawned upon him that the vast majority of the time he had spent in the flat had been time spent alone and he had been quite self sufficient. It had been his fantasies about Maggie more than her physical presence that had kept him company. To tell the truth he had been more than a little disappointed by the changes he had noticed in her. Last summer she had been a different person and they had been perfectly compatible. At least that's how he remembered it.

However, one of the first casualties of Hugh's grief had been his short term memory. He would pursue a particular train of thought that would leave him feeling independent and comforted in a bleak sort of way. But after a time, whether it was five minutes or half an hour, he would forget his carefully argued rationale, his sadness would ambush him again and he would have to relive the pain of separation. Then with a weary but stubborn resolve, he would try to reassert his independence. On one such occasion he took Maggie's sherry glass, and hurled it into the fireplace, smashing it to smithereens.

He didn't need her and besides, she had shown no interest at all in the quest he shared with Jim, Robert and Lucy. That was where his future lay. He could make other friends. He had already begun to do that. Why only yesterday he had met old Riley in the street. The old man had remembered him and offered him a cigarette. Hugh had made a dog's breakfast of trying to roll his own but they had laughed about it and then Riley showed him how it was done.

They spent the lunch hour on a bench in the park outside the Houses of Parliament. While they were sitting there, Hugh's boss had walked past with a look of disapproval on his face. Hugh had noted this with perverse satisfaction. He smiled at the memory as the trolley bus began to climb up into West Darlington.

As he walked towards Gracechurch street from the bus stop, the thought occurred to him that Jim might be waiting on his doorstep. This excited him. It was about time they contacted him again especially now that he had some real news to advance their quest. However, there was no one waiting on the doorstep.

This fact, combined with the sudden realisation that the source of his real news was out of reach in Jack Mahoney's study in Carlingford left him feeling totally crushed. He no longer looked forward to the weekend as he unlocked the front door and walked upstairs to his flat. He sat down in front of the fire place and saw the fragments of Maggie's sherry glass still lying among the cold ashes. For the first time in weeks, tears of remorse began to flow as he gathered up the tiny glass fragments and put them inside Maggie's tea cup. He placed the cup on the mantelpiece in his bedroom.

At about nine o'clock he had to venture out to O'Brien's to buy some more sherry. The barmaid remembered him.

'Your friend was in here earlier - the one with the motor bike.'

'How long ago?'

'He came in about half past four. The other chap, the one who's trying to grow a beard, turned up later and they left together about six o'clock.'

'He didn't say if he was coming back?'

'Nothing specific - just that he'd see me later. I haven't seen any of you about for a while.'

'He works on a fishing boat and his movements are a bit unpredictable,' said Hugh listening with mild interest to his cheerful, conversational tone.

Nobody would be able to guess what was going through his mind. Here he was making friendly conversation with a grown up from the outside world. It was no more than the natural good will she bore to all her regulars and to the world in general but it pleased Hugh to realize that he was entitled to a share of that good will. In the past he had held himself aloof on his visits to O'Brien's, purchasing his sherry with as few words as possible.

On his way back to the flat, he pondered the news about Jim and Robert, remembering his earlier premonition that Jim would be waiting for him when he got home from work. In the past he had shared a number of similar premonitions with Maggie and they had believed themselves to share a very close psychic bond. But perhaps Hugh was telepathic in a more general sense. The idea of simple coincidence never entered his head. He had a premonition about Jim and at that time Jim had been quite close by, at O'Brien's, enough said.

Saturday was spent doing housework. The place needed a good spring clean. In fact he hadn't realised before how much dust had gathered on those bunches of herbs. A little in awe of his own audacity, he began to pull them down. With a lump in his throat he put them in the fireplace and, swallowing hard, he set a match to them.

With a surprising sense of exhilaration he watched and enjoyed the flames. By mid afternoon his independence began to flag and he went to O'Brien's on the off chance that Jim might be there - no telepathy this time, just wishful thinking. There was no sign of Jim and Hugh had the lounge to himself as Madge the barmaid served him his glass of sherry. There were only a few patrons in the main bar and they were preoccupied with the races on the wireless.

Feeling bored, Madge engaged Hugh in small talk - his relative inexperience being more than compensated for by her garrulous nature. At one point she lowered her voice confidentially.

'Do you mind if I ask you something?'

'No,' said Hugh.

'What's a young feller like you doing drinking an old plonko's drink like sherry? Don't you like beer?'

Hugh as usual was too surprised to take offence immediately.

'Dad gave me some beer one Christmas when I was younger but I didn't like the taste. It wasn't what I had expected.   Then a few years after that, at my grandmother's wake, someone gave me a glass of sherry. That was more how I expected alcohol to taste. I guess I've just stuck with sherry since then.'

'Well I'll tell you what,' whispered Madge, 'When you finish what you've got, I'll give you a beer on the house. Your tastes might have changed. A young feller like you shouldn't be drinking sherry.'

With a reassuring wink, she went off to serve someone in the main bar leaving a somewhat bemused young man to finish his sherry. As good as her word, she came back a few minutes later with a half pint of ale.

'There you go love. See what you think of that.'

Even before he took a sip, Hugh's immediate quandary was how to think of something suitably diplomatic and complimentary to say about the taste of the drink. It had been years since he had tried that first sip of bottled lager after gorging himself with various sweet Christmas desserts and the taste had been awful. But this wasn't bottled lager, it was an expertly poured nutty, brown ale with a rich, creamy head.

'That's from a new keg,' said Madge as Hugh took the plunge. He needn't have worried about what to say. He was genuinely and very pleasantly surprised and told her so.

'Good lad,' said Madge as duty called her back to the bar. On her return, they continued chatting for another hour.

Hugh purchased two more half pints. On Madge's advice he took them slowly and thoroughly enjoyed them. He also found himself opening up to Madge's subtle and engaging questioning and revealing quite a bit about himself. She knew some Conroys from up Carlingford way but hadn't met any of the north-west branch of the family.

'Don't mind me I'm just a sticky beak,' she said at one point after he had told her about the break up with Maggie. 'My Dad used to say that behind the bar you're just a drunk's labourer and he was pretty right. Not that I'm calling you a drunk mind. I sometimes think I'd go up the wall in this job if it wasn't for the stories that people have to tell about themselves. But what you told me is as safe as the confessional. I wouldn't tell a soul.'

One of the old punters in the bar called out.

'If you can drag yourself away from your fancy man Miss O'Brien there are some very thirsty men out here.'

'I don't think you're in any danger of imminent dehydration,' said Madge as she went back to the bar.

The conversation hadn't been one way traffic and for his part Hugh had found out a few things about Madge. For one thing she wasn't just a barmaid. She was the licensee of O'Brien's. The pub had been in the O'Brien family for years and she inherited the licence on her father's death. She employed two staff to help behind the bar: Lyle, a retired boxer in his fifties and Edna a younger woman in her thirties.

Madge soon came back and lit a cigarette for herself and for Hugh.

'What about that girl that comes here with you and the other two fellers. I thought she might have been a girl friend to one of you. I do wish she'd get herself some nicer looking glasses. Those old dark frames she's got at the moment don't do her any favours.'

Hugh agreed and commented that Lucy looked much nicer without her glasses.

'Does she indeed? Well that's very gallant of you to notice.'

The next time she returned from the bar, Madge had a favour to ask.

'Would you mind conducting a small transaction at the betting shop for me? I don't want them in the bar to know.'

Hugh was nonplussed. He'd never been inside a betting shop before, but then again he'd never drunk a pint and a half of ale before either.

'What do I do?'

'When you walk in the door, you'll see three counters: one for the gallops, one for the trots and one for the dogs. Go to the gallops counter and say you want to put ten bob straight out on Nostromo in the last at Goodwood and they'll give you a ticket. Remember, the last at Goodwood, that's on Lesser Cumberland. You're an angel.'

It was pretty much as Madge said it would be and Hugh was able to make the wager with a minimum of awkwardness. He returned briefly to the pub to give Madge the ticket and then he made his goodbyes. As he sauntered back towards Gracechurch Street, he noted with some satisfaction that he hadn't been troubled by thoughts about Maggie for quite some time. He had been too busy doing new things.

Buoyed up by this sense of satisfaction, he began to think about how he might keep himself distracted on Sunday. Back in the flat, he decided to continue spring cleaning for a while before he cooked his dinner. It was then that he found a scrap of paper with an address on it - 7 Newton Street. He remembered back to the night of Lucy's visit.

"I live quite close by - in Newton Street - number 7, and you're welcome to visit any time you like. Why don't you come round for lunch on Sunday? Mum and Dad have an open house on Sundays. A baked dinner."

Through all the stress and pain of breaking up with Maggie, Hugh had never once thought of Lucy. Now, as he set about grilling some sausages, the thought of a baked dinner next day was very appealing. He tried to limit his expectations and think only in terms of a purely social visit, but he felt a thrill of excitement whenever he thought of Lucy, just a few streets away.

'Tom O'Rourke,' said a large, bearded man with a stentorian voice and a very firm handshake, who greeted Hugh at the front door of 7 Newton Street. 'Which of my off-spring has invited you for lunch?'

'Lucy,' said Hugh retrieving his crushed fingers.

'And your name is?'

'Hugh....Hugh Conroy.'

'Well come in Hugh and make yourself at home. Lucy you have a visitor,' he roared as he led the way through to the back of the House. 'Excuse the mess, I'm a perpetual renovator. I'm knocking out the wall between this parlour and the kitchen. That will make better use of the space. Both rooms are a bit too pokey. Are you a home owner?'

'No, I just rent.'

'Ah well you've got all this to look forward to one day.'

Lucy walked out from the kitchen, wiping her hands on a tea towel.

'Hugh!!' she said blushing scarlet with a mixture of confusion and surprised pleasure.

'You did invite him didn't you?' said her father.

'Yes Dad. I just wasn't sure if he was coming today. It was a standing invitation.'

'Oh well. He's here now so make him welcome. I'll be out the back setting the table.'

He left them together, but his voice could still be heard all over the house.

'Come through and meet Mum,' said Lucy. 'We're nearly ready to eat.'

Mrs O'Rourke was a quietly spoken and gentle soul. Hugh was impressed by her tranquillity. In fact he marvelled at it given how loud and extroverted her husband was.

She greeted him kindly with a shy smile.

'You're just in time. Do you like roast lamb?'

'Yes thank you. I love it.'

'You better come and meet the rest of them,' said Lucy. 'I'll be back in a minute Mum.'

She led him out to a covered area at the back of the house. It opened onto an extensive vegetable garden and one external wall consisted of a grape vine on a trellis. Seated on one side of a large pine table were Lucy's married sister Elizabeth and brother in law Ted. Facing them across the table were her two brothers - Luke the older, who was Lucy's twin, and Trevor the younger. Between the two brothers sat Luke's girlfriend Margaret, a girl of about Lucy's age. They all went out of their way to make him welcome except for Trevor, a taciturn twelve year old who saw Hugh as an extra mouth to feed, which meant that there would be fewer baked potatoes to go around.

Lucy had to leave Hugh to go and help her mother as her father poured him a glass of claret.

'So how do you spend your time Hugh? Are you a student nurse like our Lucy?'

'No I work for the City Council.'

'Ah City Hall. I'd better watch what I say then. I'm having a running battle with the Planning Department. They won't give me a permit to put in a bigger kiln.'

'I work in the pay office,' said Hugh failing to realise that he was meant to ask about the kiln.

'Yes. I'm allowed to earn my living as a potter with the kiln I've got because it started out as a hobby. But if I build a purpose built facility to expand my output and put it on a proper business footing I will be in contravention of the planning scheme - not a permitted use for an area zoned residential. Bureaucrats! I ask you.'

'Now then Dad you used to be a bureaucrat yourself before you were fully potty trained,' said Elizabeth with a wink at Hugh. 'He's not happy unless he's got something to gripe about. How did you meet Lucy?'

'She was interested in the design of the house I live in. She and two of her friends came around one night to ask some questions about it.'

'Ah yes,' said Mr O'Rourke, 'the famous Jim and Robert. What do you think of young Mr Lovegrove?'

'He's all right,' said Hugh guardedly.

'Nothing strikes you as odd about him?'

'Not especially.'

'Ever seen his motor bike?'

'Well no, now you come to mention it.'

'Neither has anyone else, now you come to mention it. He nearly always turns up here dressed in leathers, but I've never seen the bike - never even heard it in the distance.'

'I'm sure there's a perfectly logical explanation Dad,' said Elizabeth. 'Perhaps someone gives him a lift on a motor bike. There's nothing sinister about him.'

'I didn't say it was sinister,' boomed her father. 'Pathetic perhaps or affected but not sinister; and what about Robert?'

'What about him?'

'Did he have his straitjacket on?'

'Dad, that's not kind,' said Elizabeth.

'Well come on. He's obviously away with the Fairies most of the time. There always was a bit of a loopy streak in that family. His grandmother was barking mad.'

'He can't help his condition,' said Elizabeth 'and well you know it. This is Dad's idea of table talk.' she said to Hugh. 'He likes trying to stir the pot.'

'What do you think of the red, Ted?' said Mr O'Rourke, changing the subject. 'I'm a poet and I don't know it.' He made the same joke every week and Hugh noticed Luke and Trevor mouthing the words as he said them.

Mr O'Rourke's attention passed from Hugh leaving him free to continue chatting to Elizabeth until Lucy and her mother wheeled in the dinner on a trolley and began dishing up. Tom carved the lamb and the plates were passed around the table to him. He served the portions with a running commentary.

'Luke eats like a horse. Margaret is on a diet although God alone knows why. Trevor eats like several horses. Lucy has the appetite of a canary. Hugh looks like he needs feeding up. Elizabeth is eating for two and so is Ted.' He beamed at them both. 'And Mother is probably sick of the sight of all this food that she has prepared for us. Will you see to our glasses Ted? There's a good lad.'

Lucy sat next to Hugh and the meal commenced. The food was excellent and for a while everyone at the table concentrated on eating. After he had blunted the edge of his appetite, Mr O'Rourke found his voice again.

'Well then Lucy how long have you known Hugh and what's his claim to fame? You know that I want my children to find companions who can bring some significant competence or qualification to my table. Ted's a doctor. Margaret is on the way to becoming a journalist.

What use to me is someone who works at City Hall? Can he help resolve my running battle with the Planning Department?'

'I work in the pay office,' said Hugh uncomfortably.

'Aha,' boomed Mr O'Rourke. 'Well I suggest you start docking the amount of hard earned ratepayers' money that goes into the pay envelopes of those mindless idiots in the Planning Department, until they begin to see some sense about my kiln.'

'I'm afraid I only deal with the cleaners and outdoor staff payrolls . So I can't help you.'

'The man's no use to me Lucy. You'd better find someone else.'

'Now then Tom. That's enough,' said Mrs O'Rourke quietly. 'Your food's getting cold.'

'You can appeal against decisions by Council,' Hugh suggested. 'There's a planning appeals board.'

'Yes yes, I know all about that. But it's the principle of the thing. Why should I have to be beholden to some bureaucrat over a simple matter like feeding and housing my family? What possible harm could a pottery kiln cause to the amenity of the neighbourhood?'

Ted took the opportunity to top up Hugh's wine with a sympathetic private wink as he did so.

'For goodness sake Dad give it a rest. It's not Hugh's fault that you can't build your stupid bloody kiln,' said Lucy in exasperation.

'It's all right dear,' said Mrs O'Rourke. 'I think we've heard enough about the kiln Tom.'

'All right all right my dear I'll get back in my box. I'm sorry Hugh. But I get a bit touchy if my basic liberties are threatened.'

'You could always stand for Council yourself Dad,' said Elizabeth laughing. 'You know. If you can't beat em join em.'

'That'll be the day,' he snorted.

'I'd just like to say that if there's any baked potatoes left, I'd be more than happy to polish them off,' said Trevor.

'Oh no you don't,' said Elizabeth. 'We'll share them out.'

As the meal ran its course, Mr O'Rourke became quiet and thoughtful allowing others to make the conversation. After a time, Hugh became aware that Luke and Trevor were debating the rights and wrongs of war in general and the Vietnam war in particular. Luke argued as a socialist and a pacifist while Trevor adhered to the domino theory. It was clear from the expressions on the faces of the rest of the family that they had heard this debate many times before.

'Don't provoke your brother like that Luke,' said Mrs O'Rourke mildly as her youngest son took umbrage at being called "a fascist reptile and a tool of the imperialists".

'He wouldn't be free to protest and demonstrate if we had a communist government, would he Dad?' said Trevor.

'It doesn't bear thinking about,' his Father replied.

'Dad definitely wouldn't get his kiln, if Ho Chi Min was in charge,' said Elizabeth.

'I think we've heard enough about the kiln dear,' her mother interposed.

'Anyway,' said Trevor defiantly, 'when I'm old enough I'll be joining the army. I'd be glad to go to Vietnam.'

'That might be difficult,' said Luke with a grin. 'The Cumberlands don't have a military presence in Vietnam.'

'Precisely,' said Mr O'Rourke. 'We don't even have conscription. And that is why I think all your student demonstrations against the war in Vietnam are a complete and utter waste of time. As if Uncle Sam is going to take a blind bit of notice of a bunch of silly kids wagging school and waving placards at the arse end of the world.'

'If you use that sort of language at the table you won't get any dessert, Tom O'Rourke.'

'Forgive me Mother. I got carried away in the heat of debate.'

After dessert, Tom suggested to Lucy that Hugh might like to see the vegetable garden.

'Every vegetable eaten at this table is home grown and organic. The garden is a team effort.'

Lucy welcomed the opportunity to leave the table.

'I'm really sorry about Dad,' she said when they were out of earshot walking amongst the beautifully landscaped garden beds. 'He started on the red too early today. He doesn't mean any harm. He just doesn't realise how overbearing he becomes when he's had a few.'

'That's OK,' said Hugh. 'I thought he had it in for me to begin with.'

'Oh no. He was just trying to be funny. He'll have a nap after this and he'll settle down. He works very hard during the week and getting drunk on Sunday is his way of unwinding.

'Are you interested in gardening by the way? You've got a lot of dried herbs hanging in your kitchen haven't you.'

'Oh no. They were put there by a ....a previous resident. I liked the look of them as decorations to begin with, but I've burnt them all now. They were starting to gather dust.'

'I thought you might have been a gardener too. I find it very therapeutic, getting my hands dirty and making things grow,' said Lucy kneeling down to pluck some juvenile weeds from a bed of carrot seedlings as she spoke.

'I can see how it would be satisfying,' Hugh admitted. 'Perhaps one day when I've got some ground of my own.'

They made their way back inside to help with the washing up. Mr O'Rourke had nodded off in his chair at the dining table. Hugh joined Ted, Trevor and Luke with tea towels while the women did the washing.

'You did very well under trying circumstances,' Ted told him quietly. 'He's not normally so tetchy.'

When the washing up was done, Mrs O'Rourke made them all a cup of coffee. They stayed inside to avoid the tectonic snoring of the sleeping potter.

'Even when he's asleep he tries to dominate the conversation,' she said with a rueful smile. 'You mustn't mind him Hugh. He's harmless really.'

When they finished their coffee, Lucy suggested to Hugh that they take a walk. They took their leave of the family and set off.

'I'm really sorry about Dad. He's not normally like that - so belligerent.'

'Don't worry about it,' said Hugh. 'Let's just enjoy the walk. It's a lovely afternoon.'

It certainly was. The day was fine and mild. The few clouds they could see were mares' tails very high in an otherwise clear dome of blue. They wandered happily through the streets of West Darlington. Although they were both shy by nature, conversation flowed easily between them.

Lucy had lived all her life in the suburb at four different addresses and they retraced her story. Hugh was interested to find out as much as he could about her past and he asked her about the house that had backed on to Montrose Court, the cul-de-sac full of strange houses where she had seen the cellar.

They found the house and the cul-de-sac. The cluster of houses was virtually unchanged.

'Do you suppose the pre-convict families still live there?'

'Well you're the one that works for the City Council. You could check the rating records and find out who owns the place.'

'I suppose I could,' said Hugh and he resolved to do that next day.

By the time they returned to the O'Rourke household, the sun had set and the first stars had appeared. They were both reluctant to say good bye.

'Will you let me know what you find out from the rating records?'

'Certainly,' said Hugh. 'I'll come around after work.'

'I could always come to your place. You know what Dad's like. Two days in a row might be a bit much for you.'

'OK. I'll see you tomorrow then. What say we have dinner at Montini's first, at six o'clock. My shout.'

'That'd be lovely,' said Lucy. 'Til tomorrow then.'

As Hugh walked back to Gracechurch Street, there was an unfamiliar skip in his step. It seemed that life without Maggie could be enjoyable after all. And to think that he had almost ended it all in the river. He also felt confident that the information he had acquired about

Norian Fairchild at Jack Mahoney's place, would earn him considerable kudos with Jim and Robert as well as Lucy. But then he remembered that the Jack Mahoney line of inquiry involved Maggie and Brian or rather their friendship with Kate. He hadn't heard from them since the day Brian and Kate came round to collect the last of Maggie's things.

<div align="center">~~~§~~~</div>

The next evening, armed with the rating information about the houses in Montrose Court, Hugh walked with Lucy towards Montini's. Their conversation picked up seamlessly from where they had left it the previous evening and Hugh tentatively took her hand. To his great satisfaction and excitement she let him do it and responded with a firm squeeze and then left her hand resting comfortably in his. Hugh's pleasure and contentment were short lived however because at that moment he noticed Jim Lovegrove walking towards them.

'Long time no see,' he yelled as Hugh furtively released Lucy's hand. 'I was on my way round to see you. Where are you off to?'

'I'm taking Lucy out to Montini's for dinner,' said Hugh almost through clenched teeth, hoping against hope that Jim would take the hint.

'Great,' said Jim. 'My shout. I just got paid this morning.' He held the door open for Hugh and Lucy, oblivious to the looks of annoyance and frustration that passed between them.

As meals go, the food was excellent. The food at Montini's was always good. However as a social occasion the evening was a total disaster. To begin with, Hugh had reserved a table for two and that was the only free table.

Jim prevailed on Jack Montini to bring a spare chair from the kitchen.

Because neither Lucy nor Hugh wanted Jim to be there they were reluctant to contribute to any conversation. This gave Jim a free hand to dominate proceedings. He had to pick that night of all nights to remember the night of Brian's arrest. He also had to persist in referring to Brian as the brother of Hugh's girlfriend.

'Has he had his day in court yet?'

'I don't know,' said Hugh abruptly. 'I haven't seen him or his sister for months and she is not my girlfriend.'

'That's not what Brian says. He reckons you and his sister have been lovers for years - childhood sweethearts.'

'From what I can remember, Brian was extremely drunk the night you met him and I wouldn't believe anything he said in that condition.'

The meal went through its courses, Jack taking every possible opportunity to apologise for the cramped space.

'The young gentleman said he wanted a table just for two. This is a nice little corner for couples to enjoy each other's company. If I'd realised there were to be three of you I would have reserved a bigger table.'

'It's not your fault' said Hugh icily. 'I only meant there to be two of us.'

'Just a simple misunderstanding,' said Jim blandly. 'Nothing to worry about Signore Montini. Can we have another bottle of this excellent chianti?'

'We've had enough,' said Lucy pointedly.

Giacomo was no fool and his heart went out to the two lovers. But he had to be polite to all his customers.

'Perhaps a glass of port. On the house.'

For once, Jim took the hint. When port and coffee had been served to the troubled threesome, Giacomo left them and returned to a table where he had been engaged in a conversation with company that included Mervan Mithras.

In the days following the Carlingford Concert, Mervan had kept a fairly low profile. Although the concert itself had been an unqualified success, the incident with the runaway teeth had put a damper on things for the Voice of his Nation's Soul. However Nathan Watson, his fellow entrepreneur, had finally been able to coax him out of his melancholy isolation. There was someone he wanted Mervan to meet.

That someone had proceeded to dominate the conversation and could be heard all over the restaurant regaling his companions with stories of his experiences as a pilot. Referring to himself by his call sign of Foxtrot Tango Lima, he recalled endless examples of his witty repartee with air traffic controllers at control towers around the country. It was a repartee that left Mervan cold, but with a series of winks and nods, Nathan counselled patience.

Foxtrot Tango Lima was none other than Boy Upson, the wealthy, young landowner and pastoralist. He was part of the landed aristocracy of the Cumberlands and a regular patron of Montini's whenever he was in Town. He was also an avid fan of folk music. As such he was very pleased to meet Mervan.

However, although he appreciated Mervan's fame, he was also in no doubt about his own celebrity. He expected Mervan to be very pleased to meet him as well. For much of the evening he was at pains to extol his own exploits and accomplishments. Mervan quickly formed the opinion that the young squire was full of crap and he was at a loss to know why Nathan expected him to sit there and listen to it.

After another bottle of wine, Nathan was able to gently remind Boy what it was they had come to discuss - the use of the thousand acre Upson estate to stage an open air music festival - a Woodstock in the southern seas. Suddenly Mervan was all ears.

9: Remember Remember

Next morning at work, Hugh was still suffering enormous frustration and anxiety as a result of the fiasco at Montini's restaurant. Jim had tenaciously followed him and Lucy back to Newton Street and by the time they got there, Lucy was in no mood for asking anyone inside.

Hugh looked up Lucy's parents' number in the phone book but his nerve failed him every time he tried to ring her. To make matters worse, it was pay week and his utmost concentration was required if he was to get the payrolls for his cleaners finalised. Eventually, after a considerable effort, he got the pay sheets balanced, signed and off to the accounts department. Travelling home on the trolley bus that night, he decided to go straight to Lucy's place.

Lucy's father met him at the door.

'Ah it's young Hugh in his City Hall clothes. You would be wanting Lucy I suppose?'

'Yes. Is she in?'

'Well no, as a matter of fact. You've just missed her. She and the other two musketeers left about five minutes ago.'

'Musketeers?' said Hugh beginning to sicken.

'Jim and Robert. Yes. Young Robert seems to have completed his convalescence.'

'Did they say where they were going?'

'Oh no. It's all very hush hush when those three get together.'

'I see,' said Hugh, now quite crestfallen. 'Well thanks anyway.'

'Don't mention it. Will we see you for lunch this Sunday?'

'I'm not sure.'

Tom O'Rourke gave him a sympathetic smile. When he wasn't full of Sunday claret, he could be quite sensitive to what other people were feeling.

Hugh made his goodbyes and began to walk back to Gracechurch Street. It was a beautiful evening, and any other time he would have enjoyed the late sea breeze and the sight of the first few yachts of the season out on the river. But in his present frame of mind he took no comfort from any of those things. By the time he turned into Gracechurch Street he was feeling thoroughly fed up and quite disappointed in Lucy. How could she have gone off with Jim after he had been such a pain the night before?

These ruminations were cut short as he turned in his gateway and saw the three musketeers in conversation with Mrs Malleson on the doorstep.

'Ah here he is now. He must have just missed his bus. I'll leave you to him.'

Mrs Malleson turned and went back inside to her flat.

'Greetings,' said Jim. 'I've got some stuff here we all need to look at.'

He held up a small suitcase. 'Those exercise books. Do you want to look at them here or at O'Brien's'?'

Hugh looked searchingly at Lucy's face but she remained impassive and withdrawn. Thinking that it might be easier to disengage from Jim at the pub later on, he suggested that they go there.

'You go ahead and I'll be along in a minute when I've changed into something more comfortable.'

Half an hour later, Hugh found the threesome in the little saloon bar, caught up in an awkward silence. Jim and Robert were half way through pints and Lucy hadn't touched a lemon squash.

'A sherry for you Hugo?' said Jim sounding patronising as Madge came to the bar. This rankled with Hugh. Only Brian had been allowed to call him Hugo.

'Hallo Hugh,' said Madge with a smile.

'Hallo Madge.'

'The usual?' she said brandishing a pint mug.

'Yes thanks. How did Nostromo go?'

'Won by a short half head and paid very nicely thank you very much. But he was still underdone. In a week or two, when they bring him over from Lesser C for the Derby, they won't get near him.' Hugh nodded, trying to look as though he understood.

She poured Hugh's ale and then went back to the bar.

'Well,' said Jim as Hugh took his seat beside Lucy. 'Let's get down to business.'

He put the suitcase on the table and opened it. 'Help yourselves. I've read most of them but I would be interested to hear what you think.'

'That's big of you,' said Hugh under his breath and was gratified when Lucy flashed him a glance that suggested she shared his sentiments.

For a time there was silence as Robert, Lucy and Hugh studied the exercise books.

'Are these all the books we took?' asked Robert eventually.

'That's right,' said Jim.

'Well there doesn't seem to be anything here that we weren't able to glean that day in the cellar. Half of it is stuff written in English by small kids, all telling the same story. The rest is stuff written in an unintelligible language by older kids. Until we can find some way of interpreting the foreign language, we're just wasting our time.'

'Well what would you suggest?' asked Jim, beginning to sound defensive.

'Well obviously, we need to find some way of translating the foreign language. My guess is that the books written in that language are telling the same story in a more adult form. I'd like to take them home to study them in more detail.'

'Do you have any skill in languages?' asked Jim scornfully.

'Well I at least deserve the same chance as you had to become familiar with them. If only we could find a key to translate it.'

Hugh bit his tongue as he thought of the leather bound volume on Jack Mahoney's bookshelf in Carlingford.

'What do you think Lucy?' asked Jim 'You've been very quiet so far.' Hugh mentally kicked himself for not having said something similar himself.

'I think we all should have the same chance as you to study the exercise books. One of us might be lucky enough to spot something.'

'Exactly,' said Robert. 'And there are other things we should consider. We've only been in the cellar once and we didn't get into all the cupboards. The cellar was clearly used as a kind of school. The books we found were from opposite ends of a spectrum, the very junior and the very senior. If we were to go back to the cellar, we might find other books from the middle of that spectrum - books written in English by older kids who tell a more mature version of the story. We might even get lucky and find books that contain both languages like the Rosetta Stone.'

'What do you say to that Hugo? Are you prepared to carry out a second burglary?'

Hugh looked to Lucy for guidance as he considered Jim's question. She responded with an expression he couldn't interpret that seemed to be both inviting and non-committal.

'I suppose so.' He said eventually.

'I think it would be useful to make a bit of a study of Mrs Malleson's habits,' said Robert. 'Presumably she mixes with others of her kind.'

'You make her sound like some kind of zoological specimen,' said Lucy.

'Sorry,' said Robert. 'I meant to say she might mix with other people from the pre-convict families.'

'Well that would be Hugo's department,' said Jim. 'He lives under the same roof as her. Although I must admit she seemed much more friendly tonight than on our first meeting.'

'She is a nice old lady,' said Hugh. 'She means us no harm. And after all she's entitled to the privacy that you want to invade. We should never have gone into her room that day.'

'But if we hadn't done that, we would never have found the picture of Norian Fairchild.' said Jim, trying to sound reasonable. 'And what were the odds of finding an actual photograph of him?'

Again Hugh had to bite his tongue as he thought of the photo he had seen in Carlingford of Norian and Jack Mahoney in tennis clothes.

'Well what do you want me to do?' he said eventually.

'Just go out of your way to make a bit more conversation with her. Try and find out what she does during the day?'

'I know that she harvests stuff out of the garden for the Flower Room.'

'What's that?' asked Jim.

'It's a kind of co-operative run by a group of old ladies,' said Lucy. 'They've got a little upstairs shop in Falconer Street about two doors down from the Crystal Theatre. I often go there to buy bulbs and seeds. They sell these wonderful old varieties of tomato and pumpkin seed. None of this modern hybrid rubbish. You wouldn't believe the flavours. I'll take you there Hugh.'

'Perhaps we should all go,' said Jim.

'I don't think that'll be necessary,' said Lucy. 'If we all turn up like the Gestapo we'll attract unwanted attention.'

'Last drinks everyone.' said Madge.

'What'll it be?' said Hugh, glowing with Lucy's invitation. 'It's my shout.'

Jim and Robert opted for ales and Lucy asked for another lemon squash.

'Although I might like a sherry a bit later on.' She added with a smile for Hugh.

'But these are last drinks,' said Robert.

'Don't worry about it Robert,' said Lucy trying not to sound patronising.

Hugh felt heartened by this and in his elation, he took the initiative.

'All right. You want me to find an appropriate day for another visit to the cellar. And you also want me to pry into Mrs Malleson's private affairs to see if there is some continuing link with Norian Fairchild. Well before that can happen, a few things need to change. It seems to me that all the responsibility rests with me and the rest of you can just melt into the darkness if anything goes wrong. I don't mean you Lucy. You've had me to lunch at your parents' place, but Jim and Robert just turn up out of nowhere. If anything went wrong they could disappear just as easily and I'd be left holding the baby.

If we are to proceed with this venture, I want to know where you both live and your phone numbers. Those are my terms. If you don't meet them you'll get no further co-operation from me.'

Madge came in with their drinks, half way through Hugh's ultimatum.   Lucy, flushed in the general excitement, had taken her glasses off to clean them and Madge also noticed how much prettier she looked without them.

Robert was most apologetic.

'I didn't mean to be secretive about it. It's just that Jim usually rounds us up. I live with Mum and Dad at 29 Hawthorn Street in Mill Farm. The phone number is 343030.'

'And what about you Jim?'

Jim took a long while to light a cigarette.

'This is quite unnecessary. Lucy can vouch for both of us.'

'I don't know where you live Jim,' said Lucy 'I've never been there.'

'I live at 4 Cranwell Street in West Darlington,' said Jim at last.

'Why that's quite close to where I live,' said Hugh enjoying the situation. 'Are you on the phone?'

'344517, but I'm away from home a lot when the boats are out.'

Hugh wrote the details down in a little note book.

'Thanks, that's enough to be going on with.' He raised his glass to the company. 'Well as soon as I have any information to impart, I'll ring you up and tell you. Then we can arrange a suitable time to meet and make further plans.'

Then on an impulse, in the heat of the moment, Hugh decided to press his advantage.

'Oh! I almost forgot. So much has happened since then. A few weekends back, I spent the night at a house in Carlingford. It belonged to the grandfather of a friend of mine. In that house I saw another photo of Norian Fairchild. He was with my friend's grandfather and they were both in tennis clothes.

'I also saw a leather bound book in Norian Fairchild's handwriting. It was an English translation of the story the kids were writing about in the exercise books. Its title is "Dandillion - The White Ship." '

There was a stunned silence. They all looked at him in amazement.

'I don't believe you,' Jim said eventually. 'What was the address? Who is your friend's grandfather?'

'I'm not at liberty to say. I don't want you blundering up there and doing something heavy-handed.'

Not much more was said after that, as they finished their drinks. Robert apologised again for seeming to be so secretive, and Jim sank into a dark and bitter mood. Hugh and Lucy were the first to drain their glasses and, prompted by a glance from Lucy, they stood up and made their goodbyes while Jim and Robert were little more than half way through their pints.

They said goodnight to Madge and then burst out into the now chilly spring night of sparkling starlight.

'You were brilliant,' said Lucy. 'It's about time someone stood up to Jim like that. And what an amazing piece of news, I'm so proud of you.'

'Once I knew I had your support it was easy,' said Hugh.

He took her hand, but she pulled him to her, took him in her arms and kissed him, her mouth still sweet with lemon squash. They stood there for a moment firmly wrapped in each other's arms.

'After the disaster at Montini's last night, I never hoped that things would turn out like this,' said Hugh as he came up for air.

Lucy nestled up against him and smiled contentedly.

'What about that sherry?'

They made their way to Gracechurch Street and upstairs into Hugh's apartment, followed by Mrs Malleson's cat. Hugh turned on a radiator to take the chill off the air.

'I'm right out of firewood,' he said apologetically. 'I've got two fireplaces, one in the lounge and one in the bedroom. In the winter I keep them both burning when I'm at home.'

'My grandparents' farmhouse had fireplaces in the bedrooms,' said Lucy as she sat warming her hands over the radiator. 'In the winter, Nan would put hot coals in the fireplace for us to watch as we went to sleep.'

Hugh busied himself pouring two glasses of sherry.

'I wonder what thoughts are going through Jim's mind at the moment,' he said as he gave Lucy her glass.

'Who cares? I didn't come here to talk about him.'

For a while, they talked about the rating details for Montrose Court. It appeared that every dwelling in the cluster was owned by the estate of N Fairchild. Further enquiries to the Accounts Department revealed that, regardless of who was actually living in the cluster of houses, the rates and utilities were paid for in perpetuity by interest from the estate. There was no way of telling from the rating records who those occupants actually were.

Hugh then went on to tell Lucy a limited amount about his overnight stay at Jack Mahoney's home in Carlingford. Because of Jim's outburst at Montini's he didn't want to mention the fact that Maggie had also been there. He said that it was at the home of the grandfather of a friend of a friend. Although the old man said he was welcome to visit any time to read the document, he felt that his connection was too tentative at this stage to follow up the invitation.

As it happened, Lucy didn't press the matter and began to edge her chair closer to where Hugh was sitting.

'You really need a sofa in this place.'

After two more glasses of sherry and a lot more conversation, in the absence of a sofa, they adjourned to the bedroom; Lucy let Hugh undress her, he returned the compliment, and they climbed into bed. The bed was cold and Lucy trembled, in his arms.

Maggie and Hugh had surrendered their virginities to one another and she had been his only lover. They understood each other's needs very well and the most enjoyable ways of satisfying them. But Lucy was different. Suddenly it dawned on Hugh that she wasn't trembling from the cold. He suddenly felt very protective towards her and this in turn inspired him to pursue a more gentle course with her.

An hour later they lay, comfortably spent, in each other's arms. Lucy had gone to sleep and Hugh could feel the moist warm kiss of her breath against his neck. He drifted into a sweet dreamy sleep himself. They slumbered on like that together for some time, until Mrs Malleson's cat leapt onto Lucy's stomach and she woke with a scream, albeit a fairly sleepy, contented sort of scream.

'I'm going to have to go home,' she said, reluctantly forcing herself to wake up.

'I'll make us some coffee,' said Hugh beginning to throw some clothes on. I'd better let our alarm clock go back downstairs while I'm at it. Come on puss.'

At two in the morning, Hugh returned to Gracechurch Street, having seen Lucy safely home under a brilliant dome of stars. He climbed the stairs, undressed again and climbed into the bed which still had a little of Lucy's warmth and perfume for him to savour as he quickly drifted back to sleep.

~~~§~~~

Hugh and Lucy met at lunch time next day their hearts still pleasantly full of each other and the spell of the previous night's lovemaking. Lucy suggested they go to the Flower Room since she needed to buy some tomato relish for her mother.

'Like I was saying last night, it's a collective run by a group of old ladies. They bring their garden produce and craft work here to sell. Everything from daffodil bulbs and antique vegetable seeds in season to baby clothes and beautiful cream cakes, sauces and jams.'
~~~

'And flowers?'

'Of course. Hence the name.'

They came in off the street up a narrow flight of stairs to where the shop was spread across a small suite of rooms on the first floor.

'Could I have two jars of number 9 relish please?'

'You're in luck Dear. We were right out but the lady is just unpacking another delivery out the back.'

'What's the significance of number 9?' Hugh asked.

'It's for accounting purposes. Each provider has her own number and they keep their anonymity.'

At that moment, Mrs Malleson emerged from the back room with her empty basket.

'Hullo Hugh. It's a surprise seeing you here.'

'I'm with Lucy. She's buying some relish for her mum. Do you remember Lucy. You've met her at the door a few times.'

'Yes I remember. Hullo Lucy.'

'Hi Mrs Malleson. We are big fans of your relish at home. I've often wondered who number 9 was.'

'Well now you know.' She smiled and took her leave.

<div align="center">~~~§~~~</div>

At three o'clock that afternoon, an unusually subdued Brian made his way to the refectory for coffee with Kate. He had just been to see his lawyer. Discreet discussions with Kate's father had established that as the Solicitor General, and a crown employee, he wasn't free to represent Brian. Strictly speaking, he was on the other side. However he was able to recommend an associate - a very capable defence lawyer who owed him a favour.

Richard O'Shannessy was quite unlike anyone else that Brian had ever met. A tall, florid faced, balding, middle aged man, he sat behind an old oak desk making laborious notes in an exercise book with a pen that he clutched like a dagger. He smoked a huge cigar, which Brian automatically assumed must have come from Havana, and offered one to his young client.

As Brian sat there puffing away and answering the questions that were put to him, he began to warm to the task of being a defendant. The nagging fears about his day in court that had been trying to haunt him for several weeks began to evaporate. This seemed like fun - especially the cigar.

For a few minutes after the questioning stopped, Mr O'Shannessy continued to carve out notes in his exercise book, seemingly oblivious to Brian. That young man was beginning to find the cigar a little bit too strong for his taste and had just resolved not to inhale anymore because of a nauseous light headedness that had suddenly overtaken him. His discomfort was about to increase.

The lawyer put down his pen and fixed him with a severe gaze.

'Well young feller, you're in trouble and no mistake. How much do you know about Lester?'

'Only that he is a theatrical eccentric who er .... likes to put on performances.'

'And so you joined the throng of inconsiderate voyeurs who have been beating a path to his door in the middle of the night to throw a rock on his roof so that he will come out and disturb the peace and amenity of the neighbourhood. Did anything strike you about the area where Lester lives?'

'It's in the posh end of town.'

'That's right. Lester shares a street with some very powerful and influential people.

'Although he is something of a black sheep, he is still a part of the establishment and comes from a wealthy old family. He can't help the way he is and his neighbours are willing to turn a blind eye to his eccentricities because he is one of them, so long as he doesn't actually do anyone any harm.

'But that does not mean that they will sit idly by and let people like you invade his privacy and make a public spectacle of him. It's been happening far too often lately which is why the police were lying in wait the night you and your cronies were arrested. Some wealthy and influential people, including judges and peers of the realm, have been baying for blood. They want to make an example of someone and it looks like you're it.'

'But it's hardly a hanging matter.'

'In the normal run of things, perhaps not. But this is a special case, and significant people have become very angry about it. Do you know who is representing your accomplices?'

'Who?'

'The people who were arrested with you.'

'No,' said Brian blankly. 'I'd never seen them before.'

O'Shannessy chiselled out another laborious note and became lost in thought. He seemed to forget Brian's existence for a time. Then he recollected himself and shut the exercise book.

'Right, I'll see you in my office in Darlington at nine o'clock sharp on the 5th of November. You will also need to think of some people who would be prepared to give you a character reference. Leave a list for me here at the office tomorrow. And you'll have to get a decent haircut and some respectable clothes.'

With that, the consultation was over and the young felon, for probably the first time since his arrest, found himself unable to escape the fact that he was now very worried about his predicament. He went back to the uni Refectory to wait for Kate. He brightened momentarily when she arrived but his gloom soon returned as he recounted the interview to her.

'O'Shannessy is supposed to be very good. The best in fact. That's why I was so thrilled that Dad thought of getting him for you. It must mean that he likes you.'

'It might just be a measure of how hopeless he thinks my situation is.'

'Now come on. This isn't like you to be so glum. I mean it's not as if you robbed a bank or murdered anyone.'

'He seemed almost hostile. I mean I thought as a defence lawyer he was supposed to be on my side but he made me feel dirty, like a peeping tom or something. He seems to think they're going to throw the book at me.'

'I'm sure they won't,' said Kate as she began rummaging in her bag. 'Anyway here's something that might cheer you up.' She put a medical prescription form on the table.

'It's for the pill.'

If Kate had wanted to take Brian's mind off the court case she could not have found a better distraction.

'Are you sure? I mean what about your....your concerns?' It was a matter that had been the subject of earnest discussion between them for a number of weeks.

The contraceptive pill had only recently become available in the Cumberlands, which was a predominantly catholic country with a very conservative upper house of parliament. This conservatism extended to many of the older doctors and pharmacists in the archipelago who refused to prescribe or dispense it. Even condoms, which were only available at chemist shops, were not always easy to acquire, especially if it meant having to ask female staff for them. Hugh had always found it an ordeal.

Many girls felt that they couldn't trust their family doctor to maintain confidentiality, and not inform their parents. This was particularly the case with older doctors who may have treated generations of the same family, from infancy to adulthood.

Kate had done a bit of discreet doctor-shopping and found a young, female general practitioner near the university. Brian rushed around to Kate's side of the table and gave her an enormous bear hug.

'That's more like it,' she said gasping for breath.

'You there, that man, unhand that fair damsel,' bellowed Mark Denham from across the room. 'Have you heard the news?'

'Yes Kate's just told me,' said a still wildly distracted Brian.

'Shoosh,' said Kate, blushing scarlet and placing a finger on Brian's lips. 'No Mark. What news?'

'Boy Upson is organising a three day folk festival for the January long weekend. A Woodstock in the southern seas no less.'

'Whereabouts?'

'On the Upson family estate.'

'I suppose it was only a matter of time. Is he doing it off his own bat?'

'No I think Mervan Mithras and his cronies are involved. But it should be fun. There's talk of getting overseas acts and of course our Angela is a TV star now so she'll probably get special billing.'

Miss Moriarty's five to seven spots on television had been a great success. As a concession to the conservative tastes of the Cumberlands Broadcasting Commission, she had refrained from singing any songs about substance abuse. Instead, she had opted for traditional ballads of love both requited and unrequited. Songs like *Barbara Allen*, *As Sylvie was a Walking* and *Greensleeves*, had won her a whole new audience.

'Yes even Mum is impressed with her,' said Kate. 'And that's saying something. But I'm afraid anything that Boy Upson is involved in will be a disaster. He's more trouble than he's worth.'

'Now now Kate,' said Brian. 'That's a bit pessimistic. If the Carlingford concert was anything to go by, a three day festival should be really great - the next logical step.'

'Well you've certainly cheered up haven't you? Let's just hope you're not behind bars for the January long weekend.'

'Point taken,' muttered Brian with a rueful grin.

<div align="center">~~~§~~~</div>

Mervan Mithras emerged from his sleeping bag full of a new resolve. The three day festival project with Boy Upson had begun to revive his spirits. During his meditation class, after the triumph of the Carlingford concert, Mervan's self esteem had taken a buffeting. He had spent the following few weeks licking his wounds and experimenting with a range of dental adhesive powders. Because he didn't own a television set he was spared the sight of Angela Moriarty's five to seven spots on channel two, but it still rankled that the talent scout from the CBC hadn't seen fit to offer him any five to seven spots. It particularly stuck in his throat because he had done the interview on CBC radio promoting the concert. He *was* somebody.

But all such grievances were now a thing of the past. On the previous afternoon, he had received a telegram from the CBC asking him to contact an assistant producer at Channel Two. This was recognition at last. Some television exposure in the months leading up to the festival would do wonders for his profile.

He had arranged to record some of his own compositions on a tape recorder at a friend's flat. That project would keep him gainfully occupied for the day and then he would be armed with an impressive demo tape to present to the television people. He had the flat to himself for the day while his friends were at work.

He spent eight blissful hours working up and recording acceptable versions of his best half dozen songs, mindful as he did so of the time constraints that the five to seven spot would impose. This meant a bit of judicious editing here and there, which turned out to be a gratifying experience. Some of the songs seemed to benefit from being shortened a little.

In the middle of the afternoon, he went out into the garden for a breath of fresh air. It was the garden where he had encountered the young hawk in his moment of epiphany and for that reason it was holy ground. He went looking for the bird, inadvertently trampling and destroying some of his friends' young tomato plants in the process. This time, there were no apparitions to reward his endeavours although masses of blossom on the angelina plum trees provided some compensation. He took the memory of their beauty back into the flat and returned to his labour of love.

<div align="center">~~~§~~~</div>

At 4:15 on the morning of the fifth of November, Brian decided to get out of his bed where he had been restlessly tossing and turning for hours. He made himself a cup of coffee and lit a nervous cigarette. Kate had vetoed his plan to anaesthetise his fears at Insect Corner on the previous evening.

'There'll be time enough for a drink after you've had your day in court. The last thing you want to do is to turn up in the dock hung over.'

Kate was going to drive him down to Darlington and had arranged to pick him up from Trinity at seven o'clock. Left to his own devices, the risk of Brian not getting there in time was too great. Kate's father had an apartment in Darlington for when his work obliged him to stay in town. The plan was that Kate and Brian would stay there for the weekend in the City as a treat before exams began the next week.

At six o'clock he showered and put on a three piece suit belonging to one of Kate's brothers. At any other time he might have enjoyed the novelty of dressing up, but after a cursory glance in the mirror to comb his recently shorn locks, he gave himself up to more cigarettes and coffee. He wasn't feeling particularly elegant. Kate found him prowling nervously in the college driveway at twenty to seven.

'It's not like you to be early for an appointment young man,' she said getting out of the car.

'Now let's have a look at you.' She straightened him up and dusted him down.

'My word you scrub up very well. You look great.'

Brian responded with a wan smile.

'We'd better be going,' he said.

'Have you brought a change of clothes or are you planning on wearing my brother's suit all weekend?'

'Shit. I forgot to pack a bag. Just give me a few minutes. I'll go and pack.'

Because of College rules about ladies not being in the rooms between 10:00pm and 10:00am, Kate waited in her Mini. She was determined to put on a brave face for her young man but she was finding his uncharacteristic anxiety infectious.

At 7:20 the Mini revved up and they were on their way through the clearing mists of a pristine morning. The beauty of the morning was lost on Brian. He was rarely awake at that hour unless he was making his way home from a night's revels somewhere.

'We'll need to stop somewhere for smokes,' he said as he lit the last from the packet he had bought the night before.

'You really need to give those filthy things up. Offer it up as a prayer for an acquittal.'

'Do you think it would help?'

'It won't do any harm.'

Conversation petered out as Kate began to concentrate on driving. After half an hour she looked across and saw that Brian had fallen asleep.

'Best thing for the little man,' she thought with a maternal smile. Brian didn't wake until they had reached the outskirts of Darlington.

'Back from the land of Nod then are we?'

'I must have dozed off,' he said apologetically. 'Sorry for leaving you on your own.'

'That's all right,' she said with another quiet smile.

At nine o'clock they were seated in Richard O'Shannessy's waiting room. After a wait of a few minutes, they heard his door open and smelt his cigar.

'Ah Mr McInerney. I almost didn't recognize you. You have certainly achieved an impressive transformation with him Miss Mahoney.'

'It was all his own work I assure you,' said Kate.

'Really. Oh well come into my office and we'll discuss the lay of the land.' This time Brian declined the offer of a cigar as they took their seats.

'Well young man,' said O'Shannessy as he sent a cloud of cigar smoke across his desk, I have been busy since our last meeting, following up a line of enquiry that occurred to me in the course of our conversation. I'm pleased to see that you have taken my advice to heart and made an effort with your appearance.'

'Clothes don't maketh the man Mr O'Shannessy,' said Kate defensively, much to Brian's mingled gratification and alarm.

'No Miss Mahoney. But they do maketh a favourable impression on crusty old judges and jurors. Are you following your father into the law?'

'No,' said Kate, 'Education.'

'Ah I see. Pity, I sense that you've got the family gift. But I digress. Back to the matter in hand. We are here to discuss Mr McInerney, not Miss Mahoney. I see that you have provided some very impressive character references - Father Wallace and young Jack Mahoney no less, a former Prime Minister or perhaps a family friend - very impressive, very impressive indeed.

'Now as I said, I have been making inquiries and my efforts have been rewarded. Through their solicitors, I have made contact with the other defendants in your case. To cut a long story short, they have made it clear that they didn't know you from a bar of soap. The first time they ever saw you was when you stumbled upon the scene of the crime just after they had been arrested: i.e. after the crime had been committed. At my request, they have made that fact known to the police who, after due consideration have decided to drop the charges against you.'

Brian was speechless for a moment as the lawyer's statement sank in.

'How long have you known this?' asked Kate.

'For some little while now Miss Mahoney.'

'And you've just let him stew over it unnecessarily.'

'My dear, there are many demands on my time. I am a busy man, and sometimes my pro-bono work has to take a back seat.

'But I am sure that a little extra time to ponder the ramifications of his actions will have had a salutary effect on young Mr McInerney and the future decisions he makes in life. Wouldn't you agree Mr McInerney?'

Brian was too relieved to argue although Kate was still outraged on his behalf.

'Thanks Mr O'Shannessy.'

'Can I interest you in a celebratory cigar now young man?'

'No thank you. I've given up smoking.'

'Probably a healthy decision. Do I detect the influence of Miss Mahoney?'

'It was entirely his own decision Mr O'Shannessy. I assure you.'

'Well and good Miss Mahoney, well and good. I hope that Mr McInerney has also decided to refrain from any further unseasonal, nocturnal visits to Mulberry Avenue.'

'Most definitely,' said Brian as they took their leave, 'and thanks again.'

'It was my pleasure Mr McInerney. Give my regards to your father, Miss Mahoney.'

'That devious old bastard,' said Kate when they were back on the street. 'Does Lester live in Mulberry Avenue by any chance?'

'Yes he does,' said Brian.

'And so does O'Shannessy,' said Kate. 'He's been dishing out some rough justice of his own, leaving you to stew like that. He could have put your mind at ease the first day you met. The old bugger.'

But then she saw the funny side of it and the main thing was that Brian was in the clear. Then, as close to basso profundo as she could manage, she waved an imaginary cigar under Brian's nose and intoned

'I hope that Mr McInerney has also decided to refrain from unseasonal nocturnal visits to Mulberry Avenue as well..... You bloody goose! Let's celebrate.'

1970

10: *Another Year.*

January 1970 had been a month of glorious summer in the Cumberlands. The academic year would not get underway until the beginning of February but when it did, it would do so without Brian McInerney. With a credit and three fails in the previous year's exams, his studentship with the Education Department was suspended until such time as he successfully passed all his first year subjects at his own expense.

Spurred on by his elation at not becoming a convicted felon, an elation that was turned to terrified relief when the culprits all received 14 days hard labour, Brian had turned over a new leaf and was determined to spend the new year earning enough money to support himself independently in 1971 while he rescued his academic career.

During the Christmas break, which he and Maggie had spent with the Mahoney family in their shack on Green Island, Brian had decided the employment prospects were better for him in Darlington than in Ross. So it was that on Monday the fifth of January, he went to the government employment office in the capital. He was interviewed by a crafty old public servant with a warped sense of humour who subjected him to a technique which he sometimes used to assess first time applicants.

He went to a filing cabinet and removed two cards.

'These are the only two vacancies on my books at the moment. Lusted Brothers the undertakers need an assistant in their funeral parlour to wash down bodies and there is a vacancy for a cleaner at Hollybank, the mental hospital.'

Brian amazed and confounded the old bureaucrat by taking a coin out of his pocket and tossing it.

'Heads the undertakers, tails the madhouse.' It came up tails. 'The madhouse it is. I'll take that one thanks.'

Clearly this young man was in earnest about finding work.

In actual fact there hadn't been a vacancy at the funeral parlour but there was a casual vacancy at the hospital. One of the regular cleaners had been obliged to go on extended sick leave and a temporary replacement was required. The current temp had scored a better job somewhere else and had moved on.

'I advise you not to refer to it as the madhouse when you go there. It is no joking matter and you may find it a stressful and depressing place to work in. But if you mean business I'll give you the details.'

So Brian duly presented himself at the hospital and, after a brief and fairly casual interview, was given the job, starting then and there. He was issued with a pair of overalls but opted to work in his customary black jeans. On the last Friday of the month, he had finished his fourth full week at the asylum and was heading home to Gracechurch Street on the trolley bus.

He had moved in with Hugh and was happily re-kindling their friendship. Most weekends Kate would drive down from Ross to be with him. Hugh and Lucy were now pretty much an item. Lucy got on well with Brian and particularly well with Kate. Maggie, who was now about to commence her first year at uni, had more-or-less become involved with Kate's brother Tim, a third year law student, but things hadn't healed enough for her to resume her acquaintance with Hugh.

The secret quest with Jim and Robert continued but it had not expanded to include Brian. Hugh hadn't forgotten how dismissive the two McInerneys had been when he tried to share the secret with them. As it happened Jim was reluctant to meet Brian again and tended to keep his distance. It seems that he had bolted on the night of Brian's arrest and left him to face the music on his own.

Brian was pleased to see Kate's Mini parked outside the house in Gracechurch Street when he arrived home. He found Kate and Lucy enjoying a cup of tea and a chat while they waited for their menfolk to return from work. They were discussing the disastrous three day folk festival on Boy Upson's estate the previous weekend.

The opening concert on the Friday night had been a resounding success. Angela Moriarty, who was now based overseas in Melbourne, stole the show with a stunning performance. She had continued to broaden her repertoire with material by Joan Baez, Judy Collins and Buffy Sainte Marie. She had cleverly adapted her acerbic sense of humour to produce an engaging and hilarious rapport with her audience. She wore the slinky and very brief little black dress that had become her trade-mark. On that occasion her slender and shapely legs were clad in fishnet stockings. Her long, flaxen hair took on an ethereal shimmer in the glow of the stage lights.

Mervan Mithras had watched her performance, torn between admiration and jealousy. He had decided to keep his powder dry and save his first appearance for a more strategic time. Unfortunately for Mervan, shortly after Angela concluded the opening concert with two encores, the skies opened and the rain bucketed down for the next two days.   Mervan was devastated but Boy remained buoyant.

'Cheer up Mervan.   Remember it rained at Woodstock.'

Those patrons whose tents were substantial and waterproof, stayed the course, but as the rain continued to fall, many of the less well prepared, threw in the towel and went home.

In the early hours of Sunday morning, an hour before sunrise, the rain subsided and the clouds cleared momentarily, revealing the moon, a couple of days past the full.   A restless Mervan, grieving for his aborted festival, got up from his bed in Boy Upson's old Georgian farmhouse and went outside to survey the damage.   He still hoped that something might be salvaged if the weather continued to clear.

Wandering through the homestead paddocks he beheld a wondrous sight.   An exotic white animal, some kind of cow with a hump and a pronounced dewlap, had a field to itself and was apparently meditating in a corner, glimmering quietly to itself in the moonlight.   Memories of the "The Crystal Cave" and the cult of Mithras came flooding back.

Surely this could not be a common domestic farm animal.   Like the falcon in the brambles that day in West Darlington, this had to be a mystical apparition.   Perhaps the festival was of secondary importance.   Perhaps the reason he was really meant to be there at that time was to encounter and be blessed by this bovine deity.

Knowing little about farming, Mervan opened the gate and left it open behind him.   It was lucky for him that he did, because a few minutes later, after he cautiously crept up to the apparition and began tenderly stroking its flank, the creature woke in fright and gave chase. The lucky few campers (including Hugh and Lucy) who heard the thunder of hooves in time to get out of their tents, beheld the voice of their nation's soul, barefooted and screaming at the top of his lungs, his long hair streaming behind him in the moonlight, being hotly pursued by a ton and a half of indignant Brahman bull. The bull remained at large for some time and relations between Boy and Mervan became strained to say the least.

When Hugh got home from work and changed his clothes, the two couples went out for dinner at Montini's. Conspicuous among the patrons already there was Boy Upson. He was sharing a meal with Nathan Watson, the entrepreneurial partner of Mervan Mithras. As usual, Boy's booming voice could be heard all over the restaurant and the topic they were discussing was the unfortunate minstrel.

'I'm sorry he has taken the matter so badly Nathan. But I'm still bloody annoyed with him for letting my bull escape.'

'He takes setbacks pretty badly for a bit but I've never known him to be so down for so long before. He normally bounces back after a good night's sleep.'

Giacomo joined them.

'I'm very worried about him too. I took some food to that depressing little flat of his and he hardly touched it. I think he should see someone.'

'What! You mean a shrink?' bellowed the Boy, for the benefit of all the clientele.

'Yes. He was saying some strange things, scary things about his cosmic destiny.'

'He'll be all right Jack. Mervan's problem is that he just takes himself too seriously.'

'Well I'm worried about him,' said Nathan. 'I've never known him to be in such a black depression. He hasn't touched his guitar since the big washout and he's gone on the dole. He always vowed that he would never do that.'

'Curiouser and curiouser,' said Brian as Boy and Nathan paid up and left, leaving a relieved and much quieter room behind them 'Well fancy that.'

'The dreaded Boy Upson,' said Kate with a grimace, 'the most conceited and insensitive person on the planet.'

'Who is he?' Lucy wanted to know.

'He's a wealthy landowner. It was his place where they tried to hold the three day festival. He didn't get wealthy by virtue of any talent of his own. He was adopted as an infant into one of the wealthiest families in the country. When his adoptive parents died they left all their estate to him. The other branches of the Upson family despise him but he has the hide of a rhinoceros and continues on his merry way. Because he isn't a blood relative the family even considered marrying him off to one of his cousins to recapture the fortune but none of the Upson girls would touch him with a barge-pole. You've just seen why.'

Jack came and ministered to their glasses.

'No unwanted extras tonight then,' he smiled. 'Two happy couples, that's what I like to see.'

After Jack had gone, Lucy and Hugh explained about how Jim had gate crashed their first date.

'Ah Jim Lovegrove,' said Brian, 'I met him that night I had my brush with the law. We had been on a bit of a pub crawl and then went looking for old Lester's place. He disappeared just after I stumbled into the police ambush.'

'Are you sure it wasn't just before?' said Hugh. 'I bet you're relieved they dropped the charges against you. No one expected them to go to jail.'

'The Darlington establishment was out to make an example of them,' said Kate. 'Dad was telling me they dug up this archaic piece of law and charged them with "lurking within the curtilage of a dwelling," positively medieval and it carried a prison sentence. Just imagine, hard labour in this day and age. One of them was a law student too but he can kiss his law career goodbye now.

'Brian's lawyer is a part of the same exclusive club and he made Brian suffer weeks of needless worry and anxiety by not letting him know until the day of the trial that the charges against him had been dropped, the old bastard. But let's not dwell on it anymore. Come on Brian, tell us about life in the looney bin.'

'It's quite interesting really. My boss is very easy-going. He's a retired tradesman who couldn't handle being retired, so he re-invented himself as a foreman cleaner. Most of the other cleaners are a similar age except for two who are more my age. One of those is a regular bloke but the other one is some kind of innocent, an idiot savant perhaps. His name is Kevin. He has a lovely singing voice though. The other day, I was up a ladder cleaning a light fitting when he tapped me on the leg, clasped his hands and started singing *Barbara Allen,* all unaccompanied.'

'And this is just the people who work there,' said Kate laughing. 'You should blend in well.'

'Do you see much of the actual patients?' Lucy asked. 'I'll be going there for training soon.'

'Oh yes, most of them are free to come and go in the wards and in the grounds as well. When you're in a community where 80% of the population have a mental illness it ceases to be an issue. You know, "In the Kingdom of the Blind the one-armed man is probably blind as well," or something like that.'

Kate collapsed into helpless laughter.

'You twit, where on earth did that pearl of wisdom come from?'

'H.G Wells, wasn't it?'

'I very much doubt it. You're a ratbag.'

After the meal, Kate drove them down to the Bluebird Café where Horst, the German landscape painter, was booked to play in the absence of Mervan Mithras. Horst was in fine fettle and he had long since recovered from the excesses of the Carlingford excursion. During his performance Anne Williams, a naïve, hippie friend of Lucy came and sat with them. She was an earnest devotee of Mervan and believed him to be an evangelist and a prophet.

'Have you heard about Mervan Mithras?' she whispered. Lucy shook her head.

'I was at a friend's place last night and he was there. He was very drunk and he was sniffing eucalyptus oil to help him communicate with the trees in the garden.'

'Really!'

'Yes he clearly didn't know what he was doing because the trees weren't eucalypts. They were all conifers. Do you think he might have lost his way?'

'Very possibly,' whispered Lucy solemnly, only just managing to keep a straight face.

<div style="text-align:center">~~~§~~~</div>

On Monday morning, Kate left early because she had an eleven o'clock lecture in Ross. Brian gave her breakfast in bed and got back into bed to share it with her. She was showered, dressed and away by eight o'clock, leaving Brian with half an hour to get to the hospital. He made it in plenty of time. He was made welcome by his colleagues as he walked into the crib room and poured himself a cup of tea from the urn while Ray, the foreman handed out the jobs.

A few minutes later a very flustered Kevin came in. He was running late and had missed his breakfast. He began to hold an egg under the hot tap.

'What do you think you're doing Kevin?' Ray asked.

'I'm trying to boil this egg for my breakfast.'

The room erupted with laughter.

'Take it to the kitchen son and get them to boil it for you,' said Ray wiping tears from his eyes.

Ten minutes later, Kevin returned with an omelette on a paper plate. The kitchen staff had thrown in two more eggs for good measure.

'They were very kind to me,' said Kevin, very much humbled and gratified by their compassion.

'They certainly were. Well when you finish your banquet you can join Colin in ward 6, floors and toilets. You can come with me today Brian and we'll do the lights in ward 7.' On the dot of 8.45 the cleaners, minus Kevin, set out to perform their allotted tasks.

Ray proved to be a good companion. Although he was the boss, he was not a slave driver and he had a very relaxed attitude. Their task consisted of removing the plastic shades from around the fluorescent tubes, cleaning out all the cadavers of moths and other nocturnal insects, washing the shades in a solution of concentrated detergent and replacing any blown or blinking tubes. When they were dry, the shades were put back in place.

'It's all adults in this ward, men downstairs, women upstairs,' said Ray. The ward was divided into rooms containing four beds each. There was a bathroom, kitchenette and common room on each floor.

'Sometimes they'll be doing group therapy in the common room. When that happens a doctor or nurse will tell you if it's all right to carry on with your work and remember you don't make eye contact with the patients or talk to them.

'Morning Harry,' he said with a nod and a wink to a passing inmate. When the patient was out of earshot Ray added in an undertone, 'He was a very successful and well to do accountant but his wife turned out to have a better head for figures. She cleaned him out and ran off with someone else so poor old Harry hit the bottle. He's mainly here to dry out but he also understandably has a lot to be depressed about.'

'Yes Doctor,' thought Brian to himself with an inward smile.

<div align="center">~~~§~~~</div>

Later that afternoon, a still sorely afflicted Mervan Mithras emerged from the cocoon of his sleeping bag and made himself a cup of coffee. He paid no attention to his once beloved guitar which was sadly gathering dust in a corner. He was totally disillusioned. The closing months of 1969 had seen his dreams steadily dismantled and shattered by a succession of disappointments.

The audition with the CBC was a case in point. He had arrived at the TV studio, armed with his demo tape and plenty of optimism. However the producer put the tape to one side and showed no sign of wanting to play it any time soon. He talked instead about the Carlingford concert and the way that Mervan had succeeded in getting the entire audience singing along. He then produced a dilapidated straw hat, checked shirt and a pair of old, blue overalls. What he had in mind was a hillbilly singalong, to cheer people up in the five minute spot before the 7:00pm news.

Mervan was totally dumbstruck. He stared open-mouthed at the producer while shock, disbelief and incandescent anger competed in a race to be the first emotion to reach the surface and erupt.

'Is something the matter?' the producer asked, quite unaware of having given any offence.

'I am a professional artist,' Mervan was finally able to articulate in a venomous tone. 'I do not do gimmicks and stunts.'

'Well I'm sorry you feel that way but that's what we want you to do.'

Mervan was adamant, but the producer knew what he wanted.

'Well I'm sorry to have wasted your time. We have another couple of artists in mind so I won't detain you. Don't forget your tape,' he added as Mervan stalked towards the door. With his guitar case in one hand and his demo tape in the other, the Voice of his Nation's Soul was unable to slam the door behind him. With no word of farewell, he shook the dust from his feet and stormed out of the building.

After a couple of whiskeys at the pub across the street he made his way to Nathan Watson's place to tell his tale of woe. Nathan calmed his friend's troubled mind by putting things into perspective.

'So what, he's just some square at the CBC. Nobody needs to know about it. You stood up for your principles.

There's nothing to be ashamed of or embarrassed about. You need to focus all your energy and attention on the three day festival in January.'

This soothing advice had the desired effect and Mervan was able to put the unpleasant episode behind him. But he still felt an underlying unease. He didn't deal well with unbridled anger. If anything, it usually left him feeling tainted and guilty.

November had come and gone and plans for the three day festival began to take shape. However December had brought further setbacks to his self-esteem. The manager of the Bluebird Café had reduced his residency from three nights a week to one every fortnight. His clientele wanted covers, songs that they knew. Mervan had begun to perform his own work almost exclusively. It was the Manager's none too tactful opinion that a lot of it was a bit too heavy for popular consumption.

Mervan was quite capable of doing very competent covers of Dylan, Donovan and Gordon Lightfoot but he stubbornly resisted the proposal and Horst with his Simon and Garfunkel repertoire, interspersed with a sprinkling of Leonard Cohen and Tom Paxton numbers was waiting in the wings. He also did a very presentable rendition of *Wooden Heart* in his native tongue.

The Manager was quite firm in his decision, telling Mervan that he would only reconsider if he added more variety to his repertoire. Nathan had thought it was a reasonable request, but the Voice of his Nation's Soul was adamant. He still picked up gigs at some of the more esoteric folk clubs or "cellars" around the Island, like The Drinking Gourd, but they didn't pay as well.

It was in the closing days of November through to the lead up to Christmas that a minor sensation began to make headlines in the capital's newspapers. There were reported sightings of a grotesque hump-backed figure, dressed in rags and loping around the streets of the suburbs late at night. One woman claimed to have been chased the length of O'Halloran Crescent and only escaped by taking refuge in O'Brien's Hotel.

She didn't get a look at her pursuer's face but went to some lengths to describe its horrible, heavy breathing and the slap of its feet on the pavement. Other sightings took place in West Darlington, North Darlington, Mill Farm and the outskirts of the Central Business District. The so-called "hunchback of the suburbs" captured the public imagination. There was a proliferation of sightings and some copy-cat apparitions, including one idiot in a gorilla suit.

It just so happened that in the middle weeks of November, Mervan Mithras had become worried about his fitness levels. He decided that he needed to exercise and jogging was the cheapest option available. Not owning a tracksuit or running shorts, he wore his oldest pair of jeans. They were frayed, heavily patched and almost falling apart. Dressed in these, an old singlet and gym boots he began to pound the pavements under cover of darkness.

He rarely saw anyone on these outings but there was one evening in O'Halloran Crescent, just past the junction with Gracechurch Street, when he noticed a woman walking ahead of him. She was about 100 yards away. Gradually as Mervan began to gain on her, she began to quicken her stride. After a couple of nervous looks over her shoulder, she started running for her life.

Mervan was beginning to flag by this time and he lost sight of her.

It was on the night of Friday the 19th of December that he was stopped by police. Although he didn't look very much like an athlete, he was eventually able to convince them that he was just out jogging. They had to agree with him, that he wasn't breaking any law. When asked if he was aware of the media reports about the hairy hunchback haunting the suburbs, he pointed out that he didn't own a radio or television set and he didn't read newspapers. They suggested that if he bought himself some shorts and got a haircut, he would be less likely to frighten people.

This advice didn't impress Mervan and when they said he was free to go, he gave a snort of indignation and broke into a canter. But his heart wasn't really in it anymore. That was the last time he ever went jogging.

~~~§~~~

Over time, Brian began to make some nodding acquaintances of his own among the patients at Hollybank. There was a strange, secretive little Irishman called Tom who would appear out of nowhere when Brian was working alone and talk to him in confidence as though they both shared a deep and significant secret. On the first occasion, he tugged Brian's sleeve and drew him away to a secluded corner and asked him to hold up his left hand.

'Count the digits, thumb and all. That's right, now how many?'

'Five, counting the thumb.'

'Right. Now count the spaces between them. How many?'

'Four.'
~~~

'Five digits but only four spaces. You'll find it's the same with your other hand too. They didn't think I'd work it out. Just because they were here first doesn't mean they know everything.' He nodded significantly and scurried off.

There was also a very attractive girl about Brian's own age. She looked Greek or Italian and she said he looked like Cat Stevens. She flirted with him shamelessly but, for all her mysterious allure, she was no match, in Brian's eyes, for Kate. Kate was definitely the custodian of his heart.

Another patient who interested Brian more was old Riley. Sometimes he saw the old man at group therapy sessions, seated beside an old lady. At other times he sat outside smoking in the sunshine. On one such occasion, he struck up a conversation while Brian was cleaning windows.

'I notice you don't wear overalls like the other cleaners. If you're not careful you'll get mistaken for a patient.'

'That's already happened a couple of times. It's quite funny really.'

'What's a young feller like you doing working in this place?'

Brian duly explained his financial difficulties and academic aspirations.

'It's only a temporary position relieving for someone who's ill. It may only last a week or two more but it's a start.'

'Apple picking pays well. That'll start in a week or two, plenty of fresh air and open spaces. I'll be doing that when I get out of here. Why don't you try it? Free accommodation and electricity. Like I said, it pays well and there's plenty of overtime to be had working in the packing sheds at night. I usually go to Murphy's orchard. It's a big setup and it has a longer season than most because it has more of the later maturing varieties.'

Brian thanked him and said he would bear it in mind. Then it was time for him to pack up and move inside. As he made his way back to the crib room he wondered what Riley was doing in the hospital. He seemed to be perfectly lucid and rational. He made a mental note to ask Ray about him next time they were alone together.

Back in the crib room, Ray asked Brian to use the last half hour before knock off time to empty and clean the ashtrays and rubbish bins in the Ward 5 common room. He was engaged in that task when a disturbance broke out. A new patient had arrived accompanied by paramedics and he was boisterously shrugging off the attentions of the nursing staff.

He had been found near the railway line just the other side of Ross with half a carton of ale, waiting to throw himself under the Up Train. He was very drunk and in an excited state. Police and Paramedics were eventually able to sedate him and put him in an ambulance for the journey to Hollybank, but he insisted on bringing his ale with him.

He was still clutching the half-carton to his chest as they manoeuvred him into the common room. An assorted group of male and female patients of various ages and varying degrees of sedation, witnessed the spectacular entrance from chairs ranged around the room. He was bellowing at the top of his voice ranting and raving in a jovial sort of way, but not making much sense at all. It seemed that he wanted a party to celebrate his arrival. He was steered towards a chair where they were finally able to relieve him of the bottles of beer.

With his hands thus free, he took a cigarette lighter from his pocket, dropped his jeans, turned his back on his audience, bent over and lit an enormous fart which sent a huge tongue of purple flame surging out into the room. The patients said nothing but sat there, impassive and critically appraising the performance on a scale of one to ten.

The nurses took advantage of his exposed nether quarters to inject him with a powerful sedative. He quickly succumbed and silence reigned. Two hours later he began to stir in his chair and shat himself.

'Ay! oop' boomed a boisterous nurse (a robust scouse woman in her late fifties) 'We appear to have embrowned ourselves.' They led him out of the room to clean him up. He was blubbering and sobbing. In spite of his sedation, he was all too painfully aware of his pathetic and degraded state. Half an hour later, washed and scrubbed and further sedated, he was put to bed. At about eight o'clock that night, the Voice of his Nation's Soul slipped into oblivion.

The oblivion lasted for the best part of two days. Consciousness began to return in intermittent bursts but his memory of recent days was almost non-existent, except for occasional fleeting and disjointed flashbacks. He vaguely remembered something about catching the Up Train and in time the doctors began to pursue that line of thought to jog his memory.

On his third morning in the hospital he started to remember everything and he was mortified. There was no way he was going to tell any shrinks about that. He began to consider escaping but in his still sedated state, it was more comfortable to lapse into drugged slumber. He could keep a secret. His initial plan had been for Mervan Mithras to die under the stately grinding wheels of the Up Train. Having found himself alive again, he decided that the Mervan Mithras persona did not have to share in that resurrection. In the short term he would feign amnesia while he pondered the future of Mervyn Purvis.

On his fourth morning in the hospital, Mervyn was allowed out of bed. He got dressed and was taken to join his fellow patients back in the Ward 5 common room. A few remembered his spectacular arrival a few nights before but, in their sedated state, most had forgotten it. They sat for the most part in silence although some talked quietly together while others played board games like ludo and backgammon.

At regular intervals, individual patients would be taken for private consultations or therapy sessions. Mervyn persisted in his pretence of amnesia and remained anonymous. At midday he was interviewed privately by a psychiatrist who gave him a series of tests to complete. Some were multiple-choice questionnaires on general knowledge. Some were mathematical and geometrical aptitude tests. Some were interminable lists of yes/no questions about his thoughts and feelings. Occasionally, the doctor appeared to be impressed by the scope of some of his replies. At the end of the session, Mervyn asked if the results suggested a high IQ. The doctor would only say it was an IQ he could be rationally proud of.

Later that afternoon a small group of trainee nurses came into the ward. Among them was Lucy O'Rourke. As part of their training, they were regularly exposed to all the different types of nursing. This was Lucy's first session in Hollybank. The week before had been geriatric nursing which had shaken the confidence and challenged the resolve of more than one student.

Today they were being instructed by a senior psychiatrist, Dr Patterson, and a senior nurse, Nurse Pomfrit. Talking in undertones, they gave thumb-nail sketches of the case histories of some of the patients.

'One chap is of particular interest. He was admitted a few days ago after displaying suicidal tendencies. He claims to be suffering from amnesia but it is quite possible that he is just refusing to acknowledge or admit to who he really is. That's him sitting in the corner near the aspidistra.'

Lucy recognized him instantly. She had already learned of the Minstrel's admission from Brian.

'That's Mervan Mithras.'

'I beg your pardon?' said Dr Patterson.

'Mervan Mithras. He's quite a well known folk singer.'

'You know him then.'

'Not personally but he is quite well known in folk music circles.'

'That is very useful information Nurse.....?'

'O'Rourke.'

'Nurse O'Rourke. I want you to come to my office and tell me everything you know about him.'

Early the next day, armed with Lucy's information, Dr Patterson sat down beside Mervyn in the Common Room which, at that hour, they had to themselves. The Doctor tended to unnerve Mervyn because he reminded him of his father.

'Well young man, I understand that you're a bit of a crooner. Does the name Mervan Mithras ring any bells?'

Mervan was thunderstruck. The colour drained from his face and then returned in a vivid and violent blush.

'That's not my name.'

'Not your real name perhaps. Is it a stage name possibly?'

Reluctantly he replied.

'Yes, it was a stage name.'

'Well I suggest you tell us who you really are. For one thing, you're entitled to National Health benefits to cover the costs of your hospitalisation and treatment, and you can't access them if you remain anonymous. And what about your family and close friends? They must be worried sick about you. You were found in the act of attempting suicide. We have to find out what drove you to that point and do our level best to make sure you never find yourself in that situation ever again.'

Realizing that the game was up, Mervyn capitulated and began to answer the Doctor's probing questions. Doctor Patterson was a skilled interrogator and a very sympathetic listener. In time, Mervyn began to describe some of his innermost experiences; the appearance of the falcon in the brambles, the white bull and other manifestations of his cosmic destiny that he had never shared with anyone else.

However some inner voice still urged Mervyn to remain on his guard. He mentioned those phenomena but he didn't elaborate on their deeper mystical implications. Nevertheless, as a result of that conversation, Dr Patterson began to adjust his medication. Since the patient was now capable of coherent, if somewhat fanciful, thought and able to talk sensibly about his situation, the amount of sedation was drastically reduced and an anti-depressant was prescribed.

Eventually the Doctor was able to persuade Mervyn to name his next of kin. However the patient was adamant that they shouldn't be told about his hospitalisation. Living as they did on Trinity Island, the time and money spent in travelling to Darlington to be at his bedside would be an unnecessary burden on them. He would tell them in his own good time when he got himself straightened out. He might even go home for a while then.

He made one concession and gave Doctor Patterson Nathan Watson's phone number. Although he thought his career with Nathan was well and truly at an end, he could see wisdom in the Doctor's suggestion that he re-establish some contact with the outside world with a view to his own eventual return to it.

Now that he was communicating and co-operating, he was transferred to Ward 2 where the patients weren't so heavily medicated and social interaction was more likely to occur. As it happened, this was Riley's ward. He was sitting in the common room with a very frail, washed out ghost of a lady of a similar age to himself when Doctor Patterson introduced the erstwhile minstrel to his new companions.

Riley noted the new arrival with interest and nodded a greeting, as did most of the other patients and the two nurses who were present. The nurses had already been briefed about Mervyn's case and kept an eye on him, always ready to engage him in conversation if he showed signs of becoming withdrawn or isolated.

The next afternoon during visiting hours, Nathan arrived with a bag of grapes. To begin with, their conversation was stilted and awkward. Mervyn was embarrassed by his situation and inhibited by the fact that he had abandoned his musical career which was the only thing he ever had in common with Nathan. Nathan, on the other hand, regarded Mervyn as a friend first and foremost. He was genuinely concerned for his well being and understandably wanted to know how he had ended up in Hollybank. Unaware of the hardening of Mervyn's heart, Nathan mistakenly believed that the erstwhile minstrel's best option was to resurrect his musical career.

'So you've had some kind of nervous breakdown, you're not the first great artist to do that. It could add to your mystique. There's no such thing as bad publicity.'

'I tried to throw myself under a bloody train.'

'What! Suicide? Wow! I never realized. I mean I knew you were feeling down after the festival.'

'Don't talk to me about the fuckin' festival. I'm through with all that shit.'

'You just need a break from it – a holiday.'

'I'm doing that now, here in the funny farm.'

'Here have a grape. I didn't know what else to bring.'

'Thanks,' said Mervyn, sounding underwhelmed.

A nurse, hearing raised voices was hovering nearby and ready to intervene, but the heated moment passed.

By the end of visiting hours, most of the grapes had been eaten and the conversation began to falter.

'I appreciate you coming Nathan but I'm going through some pretty heavy shit at the moment. I'm not the best of company. I'm still trying to get my head together.'

'That's cool. Can I still come and visit.'

'Yeah of course, just don't talk to me about music.'

'OK that's a deal. Speaking of deals do you want me to score something for you?'

'Thanks but no thanks, I'm doped up to the eyeballs as it is.'

11: *The Outer Islands*

As Nathan made his way home from the hospital, Hugh received a summons from his boss. Fearing the worst, he made his way to the Manager's office but he was greeted cordially enough and invited to take a seat.

'This rather strange item arrived in the morning post. Our records staff open all incoming letters to register them before I send them to the appropriate departments for processing. But this particular item is very conspicuously marked private and confidential for your eyes only.'

He handed the letter across the desk.

'Whoever the correspondent is, could you tell them to direct any future mail to your home address. There's a good chap. That's all.'

Relieved but puzzled, Hugh went back to his desk with the letter. He didn't recognize the handwriting of the address. There was no letter inside, only a colour photograph of a white yacht. The name of the yacht was clearly visible on the bow, "Dandillion". There was nothing written on the back of the picture. He returned to the envelope. It was postmarked Whiteford. That was on one of the outer islands, but he wasn't quite sure which one. He attempted to concentrate on work for the remaining half hour before knock off and the time eventually passed.

Whilst on the trolley bus home, he decided to go the extra three stops to Lucy's place. The photograph and its implications were not something he felt comfortable discussing with Brian. Mr O'Rourke answered the door and greeted him with his customary bone-crushing hand-shake.

'Ah Hugh, you've timed it well. Lucy's just this minute got home from work. She's in the kitchen. You know the way.'

The Potter went back to his kiln and Hugh went inside where he found Lucy sitting down to a cup of tea.

'Hugo! This is a pleasant surprise,' she said, colouring. Hugh attributed her blushes to the self-consciousness she usually felt about him seeing her in her nurse's uniform. Hugh actually thought Lucy looked stunning in her uniform but, because of Brian's frequent, flippant teasing on the subject in her absence, he was self-conscious about sharing the fact with her. But there was an undefinable difference about how she looked that day and Hugh was very favourably impressed.

'To what do I owe this pleasure?'

'I received this unusual letter at work today. Do you recognize the handwriting?'

Lucy looked intently at the envelope.

'Nope it doesn't look familiar to me. Can I look inside?'

Hugh nodded and she took out the photo.

'Wow this is incredible!'

'Who could have sent it to me?'

'Well let's think about it. It is obviously someone who knows where you work but it is also someone who knows about your interest in Norian Fairchild and the "Dandillion". That narrows the field considerably. It has to be Jim. It's the sort of melodramatic thing he would do; "private and confidential for his eyes only," what a wanker.'

'That's not a word I ever expected to hear from your lips Lucy O'Rourke,' said Mrs O'Rourke quietly, coming in from the garden with a freshly harvested lettuce.

For a second time, the colour rushed to Lucy's cheeks and Hugh wondered what was different about her.

'Whatever must Hugh think of you, using such language? I was going to ask him to have dinner with us but he may be too scandalized,' Mrs O'Rourke added, with a wry, and ever so slightly, mischievous straight face.

'He's heard worse I'm sure Mum. Of course he'll stay for dinner. I'll just go upstairs and change out of this daggy uniform.'

With that, she was gone, as Mr O'Rourke came in from his kiln and took two cans of beer from the fridge.

'Will you join me in a drink young man, before dinner?'

Musing on how things had changed since their first encounter, Hugh accepted the offer gladly.

<div align="center">~~~§~~~</div>

As Hugh and Mr O'Rourke clinked their cans of beer, Mrs Lovegrove (Jim's mother) heard a ring on her front doorbell. She opened the door to find a fidgety, bespectacled young man restlessly pacing on the front porch. He was wearing a black beret and duffle-coat and trying to grow a beard.

'Excuse me, Mrs Lovegrove?......My name's Robert. I'm a friend of Jim's. I was wondering if he was home or is he out on the fishing boat?'

'Neither, I'm afraid Robert. He's on a canoeing trip among the outer islands. He's been gone three weeks so far. I'm expecting him home in a fortnight. I don't know what he thinks he'll find out there. Most of those islands are private property. I'm expecting any day now to hear he's been arrested for trespass.'

'I hope it doesn't come to that,' said Robert trying to sound re-assuring.

'It's out of all our hands Robert, I'm afraid. He generally rings me on Thursday nights, so I'll let him know you called.'

'If you would. I have some very important matters to discuss with him.'

'Is it anything I can help you with?'

'No thank you, that's quite all right. Sorry to have troubled you.'

With that, he was gone, striding off down Cranwell Street in a cloud of bustling self-importance.

<div align="center">~~~§~~~</div>

Around ten o'clock that evening, after a very enjoyable meal with Lucy and her family, Hugh returned to Gracechurch Street to find a bemused Brian digesting the contents of an eventful day along with the contents of a tin of baked beans. He had learnt that he would be finishing up at Hollybank at the end of the next week. The cleaner whose place he had taken was now fit to return to work.

The blow was softened by the fact that he would receive a fortnight's pay in lieu of notice. He was further consoled by the fact that, with Riley's help, he had secured a job picking apples on Murphy's orchard, starting in a week's time. He was therefore untroubled by these developments because he had a couple of months work lined up with generous options for over-time guaranteed. What had left him bemused and mentally exhausted was the fact that he had been harangued for a couple of hours by a very agitated person, whom he had never met before.

'While you were dining out, I've been accosted by a madman. Do you know someone called Robert?'

'Yes he's an acquaintance. Was he a bit agitated?'

'That's putting it very mildly. He was going on about Jim Lovegrove and some double cross he's involved in.'

'It sounds like he might have stopped taking his tablets again. What was he saying about Jim?'

'Apparently he's taken matters into his own hands; left you, him and Lucy in the lurch, something about a canoeing trip in the outer islands. Does that make any sense to you?'

'It does now actually.'

'Is this something to do with that Fairchild business that you and Maggie fell out over?'

'It has everything to do with it and you were pretty lukewarm about it yourself actually, when I first told you and Maggie.'

'It all sounded pretty far-fetched. Is it still going on?'

'The mystery is yet to be solved, if that's what you mean, and Jim has been making himself scarce - since you moved in with me as a matter of fact.'

'Why would he do that?'

'Because he turned tail and ran the night you got arrested. But I got this in the mail from him today at work.' He took out Jim's photograph of the Dandillion and handed it to Brian. 'It appears that Jim has made a significant breakthrough in the outer islands.'

By the time he went to bed that night, Brian was fully in the picture. Hugh had filled him in on everything he and Lucy had been able to find out; including Robert's theory of an alternative history of the Cumberlands, Jim's shipwreck and rescue by Norian Fairchild and finally the picture of Norian in Mrs Malleson's bedroom. Brian was impressed and readily admitted that there was more to it than he had first thought. He was surprised that they hadn't attempted a second visit to the cellar. Hugh replied that Jim had the keys.

'But didn't you say he forgot to lock it?'

Truth be told, the sight of the glowing lantern on the night of Brian's arrest had terrified Hugh and he was reluctant to go back down there. Apart from Lucy, he hadn't mentioned it to anybody but he now told Brian everything.

'Well clearly you've got to go back down there, in daylight preferably. There's less chance of being spooked then. At the very least, check and see if the door is still unlocked. Do it while you're bringing in the washing some time.'

Brian now had the bit between his teeth. 'And I'll get Kate to ask about having another look at that book of poetry. How big was it?'

'No more than twenty pages.'

<div align="center">~~~§~~~</div>

At work next day, the other cleaners learnt of Brian's imminent departure. They liked him and were sorry that he was going. They promised a farewell drink or two at Jamieson's Hotel, to send him off. In the meantime, his last days at Hollybank were quite eventful.

One person who didn't want Brian to go was Tom, the strange little patient who had taken him to his heart as a confidante. Over the weeks, he had shared a number of incomprehensible secrets. Sometimes his secrets took a theological turn like his assertion that kangaroos and other marsupials were free from original sin because they didn't suffer the pangs of childbirth; what with the foetuses leaving the uterus when still tiny and taking up refuge in their mother's pouch. Having so many mysteries to share in the little time remaining, he began to dog Brian's footsteps over the last few days.

Another thorn in Brian's side was the Mediterranean girl, whose name was Angela. She intensified her flirting, intent on seducing him before he finished up. If he hadn't been so much in love with Kate, she might very nearly have succeeded. It certainly wasn't for lack of trying on her part.

Ray came to Brian's rescue on his second last morning when Angela had him bailed up at the top of a ladder while he was cleaning a light fitting. She wouldn't let him down unless she got a kiss and she was waiting to embrace him as he climbed down with his bucket. Fortunately it was a high ladder, but she was still endeavouring to reach as much of his anatomy as she could. Where was a nurse or a doctor when you needed one?

'Come on Angela,' said Ray. 'Let him do his work.'

'That's exactly what I'm trying to do. Just one little kiss.'

'Well kiss me then,' said Ray flippantly but not with any expectation, purely by way of distracting Angela's attention. To his enormous surprise, Ray, who was not a big man, found himself woman-handled and pushed into a corner with a mouthful of Angela's tongue. Brian scurried down the ladder and made his escape, leaving his boss to his fate. After about twenty seconds, Angela released a bemused, agitated but undeniably exhilarated Ray, with a wicked smile, and ran away.

'Just wait 'til I tell your wife,' she said, laughing as she disappeared out the door.

Musing on the fact that there was a first time for everything, Ray quickly made his way to the crib room where he found Brian calming his nerves with a restorative cup of tea.

'I think I need one of those too. Not a word about this to anyone you understand! If any of the staff had walked in on that little episode I'd have been finishing up tomorrow too.'

'Why. What happened? I didn't hang around once I'd escaped.'

'Well put it this way. The Missus has never ever kissed me like that. I thought I was going to choke.'

'That's quite a compliment. She's less than half your age.'

'Probably young enough to get me put away for having sex with a minor.'

'I'm sure she's over eighteen and she's no innocent. Didn't you enjoy it just a little bit? It was quite an adventure for someone your age.'

'That's enough of your cheek. I don't want to hear another word about it. In the interests of making ourselves scarce, I've got a little job that I've been saving up that will keep us out of harm's way for the rest of the day.'

The job involved leaving the hospital precinct to clean a little hall out in the suburbs. There were a number of such places which were used for group counselling sessions for outpatients. Ray and Brian loaded up a van with equipment and headed for Mill Farm. They had to sweep, mop and polish the floor of the main hall and clean the toilets.

Brian had been involved in this kind of work a few times.   Usually it was in church halls which were predominantly Catholic, but this particular building was different. It lacked the crucifixes and pictures of Our Lady that one usually saw. Although it had lead-light windows they didn't appear to be religious and mainly featured daffodils in green fields.

'What denomination is this place?' Brian asked.

'It isn't a church hall. It was a bequest made to Hollybank by the 'Fairchild Trust'. There's a plaque on the wall over there under that portrait.'

Brian's ears pricked at the mention of the name. What's the 'Fairchild Trust' when it's at home?'

'That's a good question. Your guess is as good as mine. It seems to be something from the last century. The Fairchilds were an old family but I don't think there's any of them around these days. That's one of them in the portrait.'

Brian cursed the fact that he hadn't seen the photograph of Jack Mahoney and Norian Fairchild that Hugh had discovered in Carlingford. Nevertheless, he studied the portrait. It was of a young, fair-haired man with sea-grey eyes. His clothing was of a simple cut in a late nineteenth/early twentieth century style and he was sitting at a desk.

Through the window behind him, a white yacht could be seen at anchor in a sheltered bay. Brian tried to remember Jim's photograph of the Dandillion and mentally compare the two pictures. He was no expert but they seemed to be images of the same craft.

By 3:30, they had finished the polishing and loaded the equipment back into the van.

'Right oh Brian, you can have an early finish. You live in Gracechurch Street don't you.'

'Yep.'

'I thought so. Well I'll drop you off on my way home. We can unload the van tomorrow morning.'

The van headed off through the suburbs. Brian knew that it would probably be their last chance for a private conversation and fortunately Ray was in a chatty mood.

'This time tomorrow you'll be moving on young Brian. Have you got anything lined up?'

'I have as a matter of fact. Next Wednesday I'll be heading across to Lesser Cumberland to pick apples on Murphy's orchard.'

'That was quick work. How did you manage it?'

'Old Riley gave me the phone number and said to mention his name. It worked like a charm and I got a job. It only took a couple of minutes.'

'What do you make of Riley?'

'He's an interesting character. I was going to ask you about him. What's he doing at Hollybank? There doesn't seem to be much wrong with him.'

'Oh he's interesting all right. He's one of a kind. There's one rule for Riley and another rule for the rest of us. You're right though. I don't think there's anything wrong with him. Have you ever noticed that old woman he sits with?'

'She looks like a ghost.'

'Yes she does. Well she and Riley go back a long way. I don't know the full story but she turns up here from time to time and whenever she does, Riley is never far behind her. He seems to have an arrangement with the powers that be in this place. That's the sort of person he is. Lives like a tramp and looks like one but he has friends in high places.'

~~~§~~~

Come knock-off time on Friday afternoon, the cleaners adjourned to Jamieson's Hotel for Brian's farewell. Jamieson's was a comfortable old pub that had been rebuilt in the art-deco style in the late twenties. It was conveniently out of sight of Hollybank but that is not to say that the occasional inmate didn't turn up in the saloon bar from time to time.

Ray shouted Brian his first drink and he settled for a brown ale.

'Well young Brian it's been nice knowing you and here's to your future.'

The other cleaners joined in the toast and wished him well.

'Are you going to miss us then?' Asked Colin, a fellow cleaner who had once worked as a producer for the CBC, before suffering a series of nervous break-downs.

'Definitely it's been great fun.'

'Has little Tom told you his theory about the Anti-Christ?'

'No. I'm ashamed to say I studiously avoided him all day. What's his theory?'

'He's worked out the identity of the Anti-Christ. You'll never guess who it is.'

'Go on then surprise me.'

'It's Donald Duck.'

Brian choked on his drink.

'That's his best yet! How does he explain it?'

'He's studied the New Testament and he found it in the parable of the good and bad seed. The bad seed sown
~~~

by the devil was called Darnel and that's how Americans say Donald – Darnel Duck. It becomes obvious when you have it explained, doesn't it?'

'You learn something new every day. Come to think of it, I suppose the duck does have a bit of fire and brimstone about him.'

'Very tempestuous. What are you drinking?'

'The brown ale. Thanks.'

Brian watched as Colin went to the bar. It was the first conversation they had ever had. Colin had some mannerisms that made Brian think he was camp. For that reason he was glad that Kate would be coming to Jamieson's as soon as she arrived from Ross.

The saloon bar was starting to fill up and amongst the new-comers Brian noticed Riley. Their eyes met and he came over as Colin returned with Brian's drink.

'I thought I'd discharge myself and come to your send off.'

'Can you do that?'

'There are ways. Hullo Colin, are you keeping out of trouble?'

'Trying to. Can I get you a drink?'

'Whisky thanks, no ice. Is he a friend of yours?' he asked, as Colin returned to the bar.

'It's the first time we've ever spoken.'

'He's a pile-driver but he's a good bloke for all that. Queers can do whatever they like as far as I'm concerned so long as they don't try to stick anything up my arse.'

At that moment Kate arrived, looking radiant if a little dusty from the drive. She was wearing a little yellow singlet top, the green suede mini-skirt that Brian was so fond of and Indian sandals. She gave Brian a hug and a kiss.

'Kate this is Riley. He found me the apple picking job.'

Riley bowed and, taking Kate's hands in his, he kissed them.

'Ah Kate, Kate, ignore the blandishments of this man and run away with me.' Kate was charmed and beamed at him.

'How could I possibly refuse,' she said as Colin returned with the drinks.

'And this is Colin. He's one of the cleaners.'

Kate smiled and said 'hi'.

'Merciful heavens,' said Colin, feigning exasperation, 'And what will Kate have to drink?' He ignored Brian's protests and Kate asked for an apple cider. 'One apple cider coming up.'

'He seems friendly,' said Kate. 'Is he a bit camp?'

'More than a bit,' said Brian. 'Tonight's the first time he's ever spoken to me.'

'He's all right Kate' said Riley. 'Although, knowing him he'll expect the three of us to buy his next three drinks.'

By the time he returned with Kate's cider, Colin had re-arranged his priorities and accepted that there was no future in cultivating Brian's friendship. It was an adjustment he had often been forced to make. He gave Kate her drink and was utterly charming for the rest of the conversation.

'Can I get you a chair Kate or would you like us to find a table?'

'That's all right thanks Colin. I've been sitting behind the wheel all the way from Ross. I'll stretch my legs for a bit.'

Their attention returned to the rest of the group. They were urging Kevin, who never drank anything stronger than lemon squash, to sing them a song. Crimson with blushes he finally agreed, clasped his hands, cleared his throat and sang *Galway Bay*.

'He's sweet,' said Kate. 'So innocent. I hope they don't take advantage of him.'

'No. We look after him and he does have an incredible voice.'

Galway Bay was followed by *Danny Boy* which was greeted with patronising but genuine applause.

'Can I buy you a shandy Kevin?' said Ray after the applause had petered out. 'Singing must be thirsty work.'

'No thanks, just a lemon squash,' said Kevin who was still blushing but justifiably a little pleased with himself.

'How about *The Good Ship Venus*, a drinker who wasn't part of the party called out. Kevin blushed uncomfortably. He knew the song by reputation and was scandalised by the very thought of it.

'Leave him alone, he's given us two songs already. That's enough,' said Ray defensively.

'Sorry. I was just asking,' said the punter, sounding aggrieved.

At 6:30, people began to say their goodbyes. Kate made a point of buying a drink for Colin as Brian thanked everyone and announced that he had a dinner engagement.

'What's poor Kate going to do?' Colin wanted to know.

'She made the booking,' said Brian laughing.

Ray came over and shook hands.

'It's been good working with you young Brian. When the apples are done come and see me. We might be able to find another job for you at Hollybank.'

'Thanks Ray, that would be great,' said Brian as he and Kate took their leave to a general chorus of goodbyes and good wishes.

~~~§~~~

Back at Gracechurch Street Brian had a quick shower and changed into something a bit smarter. Then they headed off to Montini's where they found Hugh and Lucy waiting for them.

'Lucy!' said Kate. 'You're not wearing your glasses!'

'At last somebody has noticed' said Lucy, torn between relief and exasperation.

'I've been wearing contact lenses for more than a week now. Not even Mum and Dad noticed it. And Muggins over there was blissfully unaware.'

'That's what it is', said Hugh. 'I knew last Thursday there was something different about you, but I couldn't put my finger on it.'

'Said the Bishop to the Actress,' Brian chimed in and they began to study the menu.

After they had ordered, they were surprised to see the erstwhile Mervan Mithras dining alone at a corner table. His hair was much shorter and he had traded his denim jacket and jeans for a pair of brown slacks and a green woollen pullover. During the odd quiet moment, Giacomo would sit with him and chat. Because there was no Boy Upson at the table to telegraph the conversation at the top of his voice, what they said remained private.
~~~

Lucy had some sad news. Robert had been admitted to Hollybank to re-establish his medication and generally calm him down.

'He's been threatening to blow a fuse for weeks now. It was only a matter of time. Fortunately I was training at Hollybank today and I was able to help him a bit.'

'How long will they keep him in?'Brian asked.

'It generally takes a couple of weeks.'

'He came round to Gracechurch street last Thursday night, while Hugh was at your place. He read me the 'Riot Act' for a couple of hours. I thought he was barking mad. He was far from pleased with Jim Lovegrove.'

'Bloody Jim Lovegrove and his stupid cloak and dagger stuff. That's all it took to push Robert over the edge, the thought that he was missing out and losing control of his pet project. By the way Kate, Hugh has filled Brian in on the whole Norian Fairchild thing so you might as well know too.'

'Is that the chap whose books of verse interested you so much? I remember showing them to you up at Grandad's.'

'Is there any chance of getting another and longer look at them?' Hugh asked.

'Not for a couple of months. Grandad is overseas at the moment on a lecture tour and Mrs Sullivan has taken the opportunity to visit her relatives back in Ireland, so the house is locked up for the foreseeable future. When they get back from their travels I'll arrange it.'

'Who's looking after Thomas?'

'Mum and Dad. He always stays with us at Denistone if Jack goes away.'

During the first course of their meal Kate was told the whole story.

'Wow that was quite a tale and have you checked the cellar door again?'

'Yes' said Hugh. 'It's still unlocked but I haven't been back down yet.'

'He's spooked,' said Brian with a mischievous grin.

'It's not that,' said Hugh blushing. 'I just don't want to risk it while Mrs Malleson is on the premises. If she was to walk in on us while we were down there it would be an absolute disaster. The next time she goes away we'll do it. She gets me to feed her cat if she's away overnight.'

After a toast to apple-picking and the future in general, they paid up and went home, leaving the room to Giacomo and Mervyn who were still deep in earnest conversation.

12: *To Lesser Cumberland*

On the following Monday morning, Brian accompanied Kate to Ross. While she attended lectures, he spent the day on campus, catching up with Maggie and also with some of his old cronies from 'Insect Corner.' It seemed that Maggie wasn't seeing as much of Kate's brother Tim these days. It wasn't a complete break but they were both more concerned with their studies than with romance. Or at least that was how Maggie put it. Nevertheless, she was happy at university and infinitely preferred it to boarding school.

Strangely, for the first time since breaking up with him, she asked after Hugh.

'He's fine. As you know I've been living at Gracechurch Street this past couple of months. He's got another girl friend these days. They seem to be very happy together.'

'Oh! Who is she? What's her name?'

'Lucy. Lucy O'Rourke, she's a nurse.'

'A nurse! Is she living with him?'

'No she still lives at home with her parents. And don't look down your nose like that. There's nothing wrong with nursing.'

'What's she like......to look at I mean, or partly that.'

'Well she's not as stunning as you - sister mine, which is what you really want me to say. But she is a very attractive and agreeable girl and when she's got her nurse's uniform on she's something else.'

'Don't be sleazy,' Maggie snapped. 'Anyway, he can do what he likes as far as I'm concerned. I've got a lecture to go to. I've also been invited to Kate's parents for dinner tonight. So I'll see you a bit later.'

'Will Tim be there?'

'How should I know,' she snapped without looking back.

Although he couldn't see her face, Brian could read facial expressions on the back of his sister's head and knew that he had touched on a sore point.

$$\sim\sim\sim\S\sim\sim\sim$$

Early that same morning, Mervyn caught a suburban train out of the city as far as Ferndale. This was the last stop on the northern suburban line. It was a small rural town on the outskirts of sheep grazing country. Because of his shrinking finances, he intended to hitch-hike to Carlingford where he planned to catch a ferry to Lesser Cumberland.

Like Brian, he had been persuaded by Riley to try his hand at apple-picking. He had moved out of his flat and left all his stuff at Nathan Watson's place. He had wanted to sell his Martin guitar but Nathan had pleaded with him not to burn his bridges and so it had been spared. Nathan still hoped that his friend and hero would get back into music one day.

Mervyn bought a meat pie and a cup of tea at the only café in Ferndale before venturing out onto the highway. The morning was misty and overcast with a distinct chill in the air. However he was in luck. After twenty minutes and the passing of a dozen cars, an old black Rover pulled up.

'Where are you going?' the young driver asked.

'Carlingford.'

'Well fortunately for you, that's where I'm going. Let's put your pack in the boot. I have to make a few brief stops along the way but we'll still get to Carlingford in good time.'

They were soon on their way. Mervyn thought conversation would be a problem and hoped he wouldn't have to say much. He was still very sensitive about events in his recent past. Surprisingly he found that he was soon chatting freely and comfortably. His driver had a way about him that quickly put Mervyn at ease. Although they had never met before, the driver looked somehow familiar. He definitely reminded the erstwhile minstrel of someone he knew from somewhere but where?

'What's happening in Carlingford?'

'I have to catch the ferry to Lesser Cumberland. I'll be picking apples over there.'

'I've done a bit of that. Which orchard?'

'Murphy's.'

'That's a pretty big concern from what I remember.'

'I've been told they have a long season.'

'Yes. He's one of our biggest exporters. Have you ever picked before?'

'No. This is my first time.'

'It's a good life out in the open air. It's gets a bit hard on the fingers when the cold weather sets in though.'

For a while, the conversation petered out but there was nothing awkward about the silence. Mervyn felt unusually comfortable and at ease as if they'd known each other for years. Occasionally the driver would point out some part of the landscape either natural or architectural that he particularly liked. He seemed to have a good understanding of Cumberlands history and geography.

It was turning into a beautiful day. The morning mists had lifted and a sou'westerly wind was parading a cavalcade of magnificent cumulus clouds across the sky. The road passed through grazing land which lapped up against lightly wooded hills which in turn were overlooked by a distant mountain range and the Central Highlands.

Mervyn was content to let the charm of the scenery work its spell, aided by the driver's occasional gentle commentary. It was a beautiful island and he rarely travelled out of the City to experience it.

After about an hour, Mervyn was surprised to find that he had been asleep. They had pulled up in a picturesque little village of Georgian sandstone cottages.

'Have to see someone here but I won't be too long. You might want to stretch your legs and have a look around. There's a couple of lovely old churches down by the river.'

Mervyn took his advice and spent a restful half hour walking through the graveyards and grounds of the two churches. They were shaded by massive oaks, elms and other old deciduous trees, whose leaves were just beginning to change colour.

Mervyn couldn't remember ever feeling so tranquil. He had dabbled in drugs and was definitely no stranger to drink. During his time in Hollybank, he'd had a chance to dry out. However, at the same time he had been pumped full of a cocktail of various medications. He had been given a course of tablets to continue with when he was discharged but he chose not to take them, so his system was the cleanest it had been for years. There was no chemical explanation for the wonderful peace and joy in his heart.

He wandered back to the car and found the driver waiting for him.

'Have you been waiting long?'

'No I've only just got back myself. Ready for off?'

'Sure.'

'What did you think of the churchyards?'

'They were beautiful, very peaceful.'

'It's a pity it wasn't a bit later in the year. At the height of Autumn you can be knee deep in fallen leaves. So what was your line of work before you decided to pick apples?'

An hour later, much to his surprise and surprisingly to his enormous relief, Mervyn had unburdened himself to his driver in a way that Dr Patterson could only have dreamed of encouraging him to do. For all that the good doctor was an astute and sensitive interrogator, the doctor-patient relationship had still been sufficiently adversarial to keep Mervyn on the defensive. While he had told him of the falcon in the brambles and the white bull, he had tried to conceal the full depth of the intense yearning those symbols awoke in him.

This total stranger on the other hand, seemed to understand that yearning completely. Talking about them to him, the symbols seemed to be credible and he didn't feel embarrassed about them, the disastrous consequences of the encounter with the bull notwithstanding.

'Your initial vision of the white bull grazing in the moonlight **was** a mystical experience. You spoilt it by trying to get too close to it. The bull and the falcon reminded you of the book you read, but even if you hadn't read 'The Crystal Cave', those sights would still have moved you deeply for their own sake.'

'I thought they were signs of what I was destined to become.'

'I doubt that. They were probably just moments of insight. You became lost in the beauty of what you saw. You may even have briefly felt at one with that beauty and through that, with all creation.'

Mervyn pondered these ideas in silence for a while and then his driver surprised him.

'Are you sure about giving up music? It may not lead to super-stardom but you're very good at it.'

'How do you know that?'

'I've seen you at the Bluebird a few times. You've changed your appearance since then. That's why I didn't recognize you at first. I really like your interpretation of Donovan's songs.'

Mervyn was dumbfounded.

'I never saw you there.'

'You weren't looking for me and I tend not to draw attention to myself.'

The conversation was interrupted for another brief stop. Mervyn was both impressed and mystified by his companion. Who was it that he reminded him of. What was he and why was he making these stops? Was he a doctor? He certainly had a lot of the mannerisms of a man in the medical profession, a certain bedside manner if you will. Or was he some kind of clergyman? He spoke with the assurance and wisdom of someone much older although he looked to be barely out of his teens.

Then again he might just be an insurance salesman with the gift of the gab. Was that where this conversation was leading? Mervyn was inclined towards the medical or religious options. His driver seemed to have integrity, a quality he didn't associate with insurance salesmen. But he supposed a really slick salesman could create an impression of integrity when it suited him.

His musings were interrupted by his driver's return. He handed Mervyn a bundle of letters.

'Could you put these in the glove box for me? Thanks.'

'How long have you owned this old Rover?' Mervyn asked as he closed the glove box, attempting to reverse the flow of information between them.

'Bought it new....that is to say the family bought it new and it's been in the family ever since. It's a good old bus. Do you drive?'

'No I never learned. Cars are a mystery to me.'

'It's a handy skill. Why have you never learned?'

'I don't know. I've never been able to afford to buy a car so I guess I've never bothered to learn to drive.'

'But you were earning a living from your music.'

'Not enough to buy a car. Do you live in Carlingford?' Mervyn had noticed how with no apparent effort his driver had turned the conversation back on to him.

'No I don't live there but my yacht is there at the moment. It's on the slip for anti-fouling.'

Mervyn deduced that his companion must be a doctor if he owned a yacht. 'Do you live on board?'

'Sometimes but not all the time.'

They were now travelling through the outer suburbs of Carlingford.

'I'll drop you off at the ferry terminal. What time do you sail?'

'Eight o'clock tonight.'

'That's a long time to wait. Have you eaten today?'

'I had a meat pie just before you picked me up.'

'That's not much. What say we go somewhere for a meal. Don't worry it's my shout,' he added, seeming to read Mervyn's thoughts.

'OK but only if you're sure.'

'Definitely. I've enjoyed chatting with you.'

The feeling was mutual. Although he was mystified about this new acquaintance he was making, there was no denying the euphoria and peace the encounter had evoked in him.

At 7:45pm Mervyn was dropped off at the ferry terminal after an enjoyable meal in a little French restaurant. The meal was accompanied by an excellent bottle of red wine, the first alcohol he had tasted since his admission to Hollybank. They had drunk in moderation and his head was still perfectly clear. In fact he hadn't felt so clear headed and contented for years. As he walked up the gang plank onto the Ferry it suddenly dawned on him. The mysterious driver was the spitting image of the lovely Angela Moriarty. They could be brother and sister. Mervyn had only gleaned one piece of information about the identity of his host. The waiter in the restaurant had called him Mr Fairchild.

~~~§~~~

At eight o'clock next morning, as Mervyn's ferry steamed into Cork Harbour on Lesser Cumberland, Madelaine Mahoney and Brian were enjoying a cup of coffee and a chat after breakfast, prior to her driving him to Denistone Station to catch the Down Train to Carlingford. Thomas was curled up asleep on a cushion in front of the fire.

The previous evening's dinner had been a pleasant occasion. Kate's brother Tim had not been present. He
~~~

was playing cricket on an Intervarsity tour of New Zealand. A discreet silence about his absence was maintained in front of Maggie that was not lost on Brian. He resolved to see what Kate knew about it.

There was no opportunity to do this after dinner because they were sleeping in separate rooms. Madelaine had made it clear that, although she had no control over, or illusions about, what they got up to when they were away from home, when under her roof the proprieties would be observed.

'Typical Mum,' Kate observed later. 'I know for a fact that she was three months gone with Tim when she married Dad. The best man was a shotgun.'

As Madelaine and Brian drank their coffee, Kate and Maggie were on their way back to Ross and Mr Mahoney was heading to Darlington for a meeting. Conversation was easy and comfortable. Madelaine complimented Brian on his resolve to get back to uni next year. She knew from her daughter that he didn't drink nearly as much as he used to and he was scrupulously saving as much of his wages as possible. Madelaine liked Brian and she had a feeling in her bones that he and Kate would marry eventually. She was comfortable, even happy with the prospect.

After a brief, pause, she startled Brian by talking about Tim and Maggie.

'She's much too young for him and he goes about life like a bull at a gate. He's never kept a girl friend for any length of time. I think Maggie is having second thoughts about him and to be frank, I don't blame her. Perhaps I should have a word to her. Tim will be all right after a bit. He'll lick his wounds over in New Zealand and then bounce back as if nothing ever happened.'

Brian felt honoured that Madelaine should take him into her confidence like that but he could add very little to the discussion: other than to suggest tactfully that Tim was nothing like Maggie's previous boyfriend in temperament or anything else.

'She was saying to me yesterday that they were both more concerned with their studies than with romance.'

'That's very sensible of her although Tim mightn't see it quite like that.'

<div align="center">~~~§~~~</div>

In due course, Madelaine drove Brian to Denistone station to catch the 'Down Train' at 10:00 a.m.

'Well good luck on the next chapter of your adventure. It's a good life down in the apple country, from what I've heard. Just don't come back talking like a hillbilly.'

Madelaine for the first time ever gave him a peck on the cheek by way of farewell as he boarded the train.

Brian settled down in his plush window seat and heaved a sigh of contented anticipation as the train pulled out of the station. It was indeed the next chapter of an adventure. He'd never been to Lesser Cumberland before. Madelaine's reference to hillbillys was typical Cumberland banter. The lesser island had a provincial stigma in the eyes of residents of the more 'cosmopolitan' Greater Cumberland. It was all tongue in cheek except for the intense inter-island rivalry in matters of football, cricket, rowing and horse-racing.

Lesser Cumberland was a little over half the size of the bigger island with large tracts of rainforest and wilderness that remained unsettled. It was more mountainous and less populous but the considerably smaller population felt that it punched well above its weight in sporting contests with the 'City Slickers' of the bigger Island. This was as much as Brian knew about his destination and he was looking forward to experiencing it all at first hand.

He listened sleepily to Emily Oldfield's time honoured commentary on the passing landscape. When she did the rounds of the carriages, he ordered tea and mixed sandwiches. She thought there was something familiar about him. Perhaps it was the smile.

Unlike certain notorious journeys in the past that she remembered with dismay, Emily didn't have to deal with a train full of drunken students on this occasion. In fact she had only served four alcoholic drinks that day by the time the train pulled into Carlingford. A retired elderly military gentleman drank three whiskey and sodas and Brian bought a can of beer around midday.

Brian spent the journey dozing and browsing through text books for the resumption of his studies the following year. Between reading and sleeping, there was also the passing pastoral landscape to admire by way of further relaxation.

The Down Train pulled into Carlingford station at 1:15 p.m. Brian made his way to the Ferry Terminal and stored his luggage in a locker. Then he bought a newspaper to check what movies were showing in Carlingford that afternoon. He had a choice between 'The Wild Bunch' at the Alhambra and continuous screenings of 'Helga' at the Tatler. He'd already seen 'Helga' with Kate in Darlington and didn't feel that he needed to see some of the more graphic scenes again so soon. So he opted instead for 'The Wild Bunch' after a counter lunch at a pub near the theatre.

Later that afternoon, after the movie, he made his way back to the ferry terminal where the ship was now ready for boarding. It was a vehicular ferry and various cars and semi-trailers were already being loaded. Before boarding the ship, he found a phone box and called Kate. Madelaine answered and after wishing him bon-voyage again, handed the receiver to her daughter.

'Hi Brian. Thanks for calling. Are you ready for off?'

'Yep, just about to board. It'll be a while before I see you again.'

'You never know. I might get down to see you over Easter. Just let me know what your accommodation arrangements are when you get there.

'How did you get on with Mum this morning?'

'She was fine. She surprised me actually and started talking to me quite candidly about Maggie and Tim.'

'Typical Mum. She was just fishing to find out if you knew anything she didn't. Only give her ten percent.'

'I thought she was taking me into her confidence. I was quite flattered actually.'

'As you were meant to be. Just be careful.'

'I'm going to run out of coins any minute. I just wanted you to know that I love you. This trip will be an adventure but I'm not looking forward to being away from you for so long.'

'It will be hard for both of us but don't lose sight of your plan – to be back at uni next year. I love you too and I think you're doing splendidly. You're my personal court jester and life will be incredibly dull without you but it will be worth it in the end. I can hear the beeps so bye.'

'Bye.'

The line went dead. Brian heaved a sigh, collected his luggage and went aboard. He had never been on an overnight sea journey before and the novelty of ship–board travel, in his own personal cabin was eventually able to distract him from his melancholy.

He was back on deck to witness the ferry's departure as it turned out into the river and then swung around to face the open sea. It might have been the sea air but whatever the cause he had worked up an appetite and he went down to the restaurant. He thought he'd treat himself to a slap-up meal even though it meant a slight incursion into his savings. It was the first such incursion for some time.

He by-passed the buffet section where people helped themselves to a selection of food from a series of bain-marie and took a seat in the restaurant proper. After half an hour he had ordered a 'Beef Wellington' and was savouring a glass of red wine while he waited for the meal to arrive. He took the opportunity to survey the other diners.

There was an interesting assortment. Two nuns had a table to themselves as did a man in his 40's and a child of 10 or so who, presumably, was his daughter. This latter couple were playing cards until their meal was served. A man and a woman sat at a table across the room from Brian. He assumed that it was a married couple. They had ordered a meal and a bottle of white wine.

Suddenly another man, who had been dining alone, spotted them from across the room and called out to them. He invited himself to sit at their table and brought his bottle of red wine with him. He then proceeded to dominate the conversation. The woman made an attempt to be polite but her partner made no attempt to conceal his resentment. Even if he had wanted to say anything, the conversation was being totally monopolized by the interloper, apparently under the delusion that he was being the life and soul of the party.

The 'Beef Wellington' arrived in due course. The nuns retired after their meal, as did the man and his daughter. Brian ordered dessert as more guests arrived for meals. The troubled threesome that he had been watching with interest, broke up. The couple left the field to the interloper, who poured what was left of their white wine into what was left of his bottle of red before making his own exit.

After eating a delicious slice of cheese-cake, Brian went back to his cabin and was soon in bed and sound asleep.

13: *Apple Picking*

Hugh had the flat to himself. Brian had been gone for ten days and Lucy was on nightshift for a week. He had really enjoyed Brian's stay but he was now appreciating the chance to be alone with his thoughts. He had dined, washed up and was savouring a nightcap of sherry before having an early night. Work had been hectic that day and he was very pleasantly tired. The ring on his doorbell was the last thing he wanted to hear, it was gone 8.00. He went downstairs to the street door.

It took a moment to recognize the bearded figure at the door but it turned out to be Jim Lovegrove.

'Hugo! Long time no see. We need to talk.'

'Do we? What about?'

'Did you get my letter?'

'I received an envelope with a photograph in it. There was no letter with it.'

'You got it then.'

'Yes I did. Don't write to me at work. It becomes complicated.'

'You got it then. Well that's what we need to talk about.'

'Just to me, what about Lucy and Robert?'

'Robert is back in Hollybank and Lucy is on nightshift. Look are you going to ask me in or not?' Jim was becoming angry and Mrs Malleson opened her door upon hearing raised voices.

'Is everything all right Hugh?'

'Yes. It's nothing to worry about.'

Hugh invited Jim in with a jerk of his head.

'And keep your voice down,' he hissed as Mrs Malleson closed her door and Jim followed him up the stairs.

'I don't want to make a night of this so make it brief.'

They sat down, Hugh didn't offer his visitor a drink.

'OK. What do you want to say?'

'I have found stuff out in the outer islands, hence the photograph.'

'So?'

'You claim to have access to a book written by Norian Fairchild. I have found his yacht, the Dandillion and other related information. Between us we can solve the mystery but only if we share what we have. Show me the book and I'll tell you what I've found out.'

'I can't show you the book because I don't have direct access to it. The person who owns it is away overseas for the next couple of months.'

'That shouldn't be a problem. Where do they live?'

'There is no way I'm ever going to tell you that. We're talking about a close relative of a good friend of mine and I'll never give you the chance to invade their property or their privacy.'

'So we don't have a deal.'

'We most definitely do not have a deal. I'll see you out.'

Hugh showed Jim out onto the street and then shut the door behind him. Back upstairs he poured another glass of sherry and tried to regain his composure. There was something decidedly creepy about Jim. How did he know that Brian was gone, that Robert was in Hollybank and that Lucy was on nightshift?

Somehow or other he was spying on them all. Hugh was worried that Jim might somehow make the connection between Brian and Kate. When he originally told the conspirators about the book of Norian's verse that night in O'Brien's, he said he had seen it in Carlingford in the house of a friend's grandfather. It would be disastrous if Jim was to discover who Kate's grandfather was and burgle his house.

Hugh met Lucy for coffee when he finished work next day. Her shift didn't start until 6:00 p.m. He had worked himself into a state fretting about Jim's visit and Lucy told him as much.

'To use one of Dad's expressions, Jim Lovegrove is "full of piss and wind". Don't let him wind you up the way he does with Robert. He knew I was on nightshift because he rang me at home. I gave him a piece of my mind about Robert. That's how he knew he was back in Hollybank. See, nothing sinister. It was just a simple phone call.

'I must admit I also told him that Brian had moved out. I couldn't resist telling him he had no need to be frightened of visiting you anymore. So there you have it. It sounds like you sent him home with a flea in his ear last night, which is what I did when he rang me up. You did the right thing and we can forget about him.'

It may have been Lucy's nurse's uniform that gave her an additional air of authority but her counsel had a salutary effect on Hugh's morale. She combined a lot of her mother's gentle strength with occasional flashes of her father's belligerence and Hugh found himself wishing she didn't have to start work at the hospital in half an hour. Nevertheless it was with a much lighter heart that he held her in a long embrace and kissed her on the hospital steps.

'Let's hope matron didn't see that or I'll be in her bad books again,' Lucy said with a blushing smile. 'Now off home with you and no more fretting.'

'Yes ma'am. I mean no ma'am.'

'You've been seeing too much of Brian. Bye.'

And with that she was gone and Hugh sauntered home with a spring in his step that had been absent all that day.

~~~§~~~

Many miles and a whole world away, Brian was revelling in the rusticity and novelty of his new surroundings. Work at Hollybank had been made entertaining by the exotic environment but for the most part it had consisted of dull monotonous tasks often carried out alone or with one other cleaner. In the orchard on most days there were usually six or so men picking. Generally each man had a tree to himself although, in the case of some of the really large trees, more than one picker was required. Conversations begun at tea-breaks were often continued in the trees later as mostly the pickers remained well within hearing distance of each other. But it was still possible to be alone with your thoughts if the particular conversation didn't interest you.

The initial soreness in Brian's neck and shoulders, from the weight of the laden picker's bag, was all but gone and he had taken to his new life like a duck to water. He felt like he had travelled back in time to the turn of the century. He had a small timber picker's hut to himself. A quarter of a mile or so up the road, there was a little cluster of churches; a milk bar which sold newspapers, bread, milk and some groceries as well as petrol; and there was a post office run by an elderly couple, Mr and Mrs Townsend, in the front part of their home. There was a phonebox outside the post office.
~~~

Some of the locals were very rustic. Old Tom the orchard foreman was a case in point. He was the father-in-law of the boss. His main task was ferrying the laden bins of picked apples to the packing shed and bringing back new empty bins, using a fork lift attachment on the back of a tractor. He spoke with the accent of a bygone time.

There was an interesting mix of pickers: The oldest was Charley Flint, a veteran of both wars, who wore a battered, ancient felt hat and habitually had a roll your own cigarette suspended from his bottom lip, so blackened with tar that it looked more like a dental swab than a cigarette.

Then there were the Viney brothers, twins in their early forties, who divided their time between agricultural labour and working on fishing boats. It was widely suspected that the Viney family numbered criminal elements within its ranks but Dave and Bob preferred to think of themselves as lovable rogues and tried to create that impression.

Riley, Brian and Mervyn completed the line-up. They were a friendly group and the differences in age and background made for a lot of banter and lively conversation. The orchard was one of several properties owned by the Murphy family and it would take a couple of months for them to pick it clean.

Brian, being naturally gregarious, fitted in well with the group, but Mervyn was more reserved and shy. Interestingly, Old Riley took the erstwhile minstrel under his wing, teaching him the finer points of apple picking and orchard life in general, whilst at the same time trying to draw him out in conversation. Riley typically seemed to have his own unique status on the orchard as he did everywhere else. Even the boss on his few appearances treated him with a kind of deference that the other pickers didn't receive.

On Friday nights the pickers went to Woodfield, the nearest town of any size, to replenish groceries and enjoy a meal at the 'Golden Fleece' road house. The first time Brian ate there, he earned the nick-name 'the Baked Beans Kid' when he ordered beans on toast which is what most pickers, Brian included, ate every other night of the week. After the meal they generally adjourned to 'The Crown' which was the only pub in the town.

Friday night shopping was a social highlight in the life of the community and during the picking season, the mix of locals and exotic itinerants lent an added carnival atmosphere to proceedings. The two populations were like oil and water swirling around each other in mutual and amused condescension. The only place where any friction was possible was in the pub.

The locals tended to keep to themselves, mostly drinking six ounce beers, while the 'exotics' drank pints or schooners. Riley was equally at home in either camp and Brian and Mervyn became honorary locals whenever they drank with him. Some of the younger locals felt territorial and a certain amount of arena behaviour occurred.

For a couple of seasons now the number of 'long-haired hippies' among the itinerants had increased. Occasionally a brawl broke out but they were usually over quickly, particularly since some of the 'long-haired hippies' proved to be hard men who were more than capable of looking after themselves. Because Saturday was a working day most pickers didn't make a late night of Fridays. Saturday nights on the other hand were another matter.

Life on the orchard had a rhythm of its own unlike anything Brian had ever known before. At uni there was the schedule of lectures, tutorials, essay deadlines and hangovers. At Hollybank most of the work was done inside under fluorescent lights and the surroundings were clinical and sterile.

In the orchard, Brian was out in all weathers and exposed to the elements with their subtle shifts of light and shade, wind and rain. Although he had a watch, he began to measure the time by the position of the sun in the sky. But he also became aware of another slower, deeper cycle, deeper even than the change and turn of the seasons as the leaves continued to change colour all around him. With each day he felt himself becoming more deeply immersed in the life and consciousness of the earth itself.

Although he never discussed it with anyone, Mervyn was undergoing a similar experience. His life had been forever changed by the time he had spent with the mysterious driver of the old black Rover. He now saw the world around him with new eyes and new sensibilities. With gentle and sometimes not so gentle promptings from Riley, Mervyn found himself being drawn into the daily conversations of the other pickers. He also found himself belonging and beginning to empathise in a way he'd never done before and all of it free from the 'poisoned chalice' of his musical vocation.

At night in the packing shed, Brian and Mervyn worked making wooden crates for shipping the fruit and sometimes they helped the women who sorted and packed the fruit. They rarely had to work beyond 10:00pm and at night Brian slept like a log once he had gotten used to the quiet stillness and the complete darkness in the absence of street lighting.

~~~§~~~

Many miles away in Darlington, Jim Lovegrove was in his room in his mother's house, licking his wounds. He had spent too long away on his canoeing trip and lost his job on the fishing boat. He was cooling his heels at home while he waited for a vacancy on another boat to come up. His mother was trying her hardest to persuade him to look for a job on land but he stubbornly resisted.

As for the canoeing trip, that had only met with mixed results. True - he had located the Dandillion and it was definitely the yacht that had rescued him but there was no sign of its owner. He went on board but everything was securely locked, so he didn't learn anything new.

He questioned some of the locals but they were uncommunicative. It was a small, windswept island known as 'The Spit', with only a few cottages. These seemed to belong to fishing families. The men were all out on the water somewhere and the only people he saw were women and children.

At first, the most he could gather from them was that the gentleman who owned the yacht was away somewhere. Further questioning revealed that the gentleman wasn't on the island. He had gone back to the mainland on a motor launch and nobody knew when he would be back. People often brought their yachts there because mooring costs on the island were cheaper than anywhere else.

There was no pub on the Island and, although he had a tent in the canoe, Jim decided against camping and waiting for the fishermen to return. It was a bleak, lonely, desolate sort of place and he resolved to go back to the
~~~

nearest large Island, Green Island, and stay the night in the pub there. He contented himself with taking some pictures of the Dandillion. Then on a sudden impulse, he wrote a short letter.

"Dear Mr Fairchild

You may not remember me but my name is Jim Lovegrove. Three years ago you rescued me at sea, looked after me til I was recovered and then took me to Dark Tor, from where I was able to make my way back home.

I will be forever in your debt for your kindness and hospitality.

However I feel that I haven't really been able to thank you properly. I would appreciate it very much if you could make further contact with me so that I can do so. My address is 4 Cranwell Street, West Darlington and my phone number is 344517.

Hoping to hear from you soon.

Yours sincerely
Jim Lovegrove."

He went back on board and was eventually able to push the letter under the main cabin door. He felt he had at last done something tangible to further the quest. It was something to report to his fellow 'conspirators' next time they met. Feeling quite contented, he paddled his canoe the relatively short distance back to Green Island. Whiteford was the main town on the Island. It boasted two pubs, a cinema, a handful of churches and quite a few shops, including a photography shop where he was able to get his film developed.

That night in the pub, he struck up a few conversations and listened in on quite a few others but learnt nothing to further his quest. It seemed that nobody had heard of Norian Fairchild. Although one or two had seen the Dandillion in their travels, they knew nothing about its owner. Jim was running out of money, so the next day he returned the canoe and used the refunded bond to pay for a ferry back to the mainland. He posted a photo of the Dandillion to Hugh prior to embarking.

Now back in Darlington, he was taking stock of his situation and brooding about the state of affairs. He was concerned about Lucy and Hugh. They were both being rather cool towards him. He was at a loss to know why they had been so offhand and distant the night he shouted them both to dinner at Montini's. True there was a bit of a problem with seating and the size of the table but that was no big deal, particularly since he had paid for the meal.

Although he had never said as much to Lucy, Jim rather liked her and apart from his mother, she was his only close female acquaintance. He never did anything about it, but he did sometimes fantasize about a possible relationship with her. However she had clearly changed. He blamed Hugh for this, with his claim of having seen a book written by Norian Fairchild; although he couldn't actually produce it for people to see.

It was partly to outdo Hugh's claim that Jim had gone on the canoeing trip. It was quite an achievement to locate the Dandillion but it didn't really tell them anything new. He had tried to use the photo of the yacht as a bargaining chip in the hope of coaxing Hugh to produce the mysterious book but clearly it hadn't been enough.

Now they were giving him the cold shoulder. Lucy was far from friendly when he telephoned her and Hugh was very inhospitable the night he visited him at Gracechurch street. He was downright hostile in fact. After a bit more brooding contemplation he resolved to go to Hollybank next day to visit Robert.

~~~§~~~

'The life and world I now depart were neither of them worth a fart' chanted Riley to some old forgotten music hall tune. He would often burst into scraps of song as he worked, usually deliberately distorting the lyrics of old standards. 'Blue skies are going to clear up. Put on a happy face' was frequently aired.

It was April Fool's day and they had been picking for nearly a month. St Patrick's day and Easter had been and gone and the pickers were walking back to where they had left their drink bottles, for a tea break and a smoke. It was mid afternoon and the day had been pleasantly mild with shifting cloud cover and a cool breeze.

They sat around in a loose circle. Charlie and Tom had sandwiches made by their wives and thermos flasks of tea. Others like the Viney brothers just rolled a smoke. If they were thirsty they picked an apple and ate it.

As they had their break, Dave Viney brought the conversation around to sex, in order to try and get a rise out of Brian and possibly Mervyn.

'You're a lucky feller being at university. I've heard all about those birds from the uni. They go all night some of them. It's the drugs they take and of course they've got the pill these days so there's no stoppin' 'em.'

His brother Bob took up the theme.
~~~

'I was rootin' a girl from the uni the other night and she'd had too much to drink,' 'Every time she threw up I could feel her tighten.'

Not to be out done, Charley Flint joined in with one of his war memoirs.

'I remember once in Egypt there was this wall with a whole lot of peep-holes in it. If you paid a sheckel you could have a look inside. It was full of these naked women dancin' around in a circle. One of them came up to my window and took the cigarette out of my mouth and stuck it in her mickey. After she'd gone round a couple of times she came back to where I was and stuck the smoke back in my mouth.'

Brian looked on in distaste and thought the cigarette would have to have been more substantial than the ghastly blackened thing hanging from the old man's lip at that moment. Riley said nothing and didn't seem to have been listening. Mervyn had been listening but he gave no indication of what he was thinking. Old Tom, the orchard foreman, joined in.

'It's all well and good for you young fellers to talk. You're on and off like sparrers. When you get to my age all you can do is pat it and wish it well.'

Then Riley decided to change the subject.

'I've got a brother at the university,' he said. This caused some surprise and curiosity.

'What does he do?' Dave asked.

'Nothin' much. He's in a bottle. Third shelf down on your right as you walk in the door.' He got to his feet and put his picking bag back on, signalling the end of the break.

Just before knock off time Riley came to where Brian was working.

'Don't let 'em get to you son. They'll soon tire of it, especially if you don't take the bait.'

~~~§~~~

The weeks continued to roll by and the leaves continued to fall. At the height of the autumn, when the leaves were at their most golden brown, they had been picking 'sturmers' a russet brown cooking apple. All that week, Brian's dreams were saturated in tawny, autumnal colours and a mellow contentment that went some way to easing his longing to see Kate again.

She had not been able to come and see him at Easter. She could have shared his picker's hut and his bed but there was nowhere for her to shower and the long drop lavatory was crude in the extreme. And speaking of crudity, he didn't want her to encounter the coarse behaviour of the Viney brothers. In actual fact, had she met them, they would have behaved like perfect gentlemen. They had only been trying to get a rise out of Brian to begin with. Acting on Riley's advice Brian had kept his cool and the Vineys eventually let the subject drop.

By and large, the pickers got on well and there was no friction or tension among them, the occasional argument about politics notwithstanding. The Vineys had been promising for some time that they would organize a day on a tuna boat for anyone interested. The outing eventuated on Sunday the 19th of April. Brian had gone but hadn't enjoyed it. The sea was rough and he had been sea-sick. Also he had not enjoyed the slaughter. He had never seen a live tuna before. He was impressed by their size and beauty and he thought the contest between hunters and hunted was too one-sided.
~~~

Back on dry land, the Vineys had taken everyone back to the family home which was quite close to the sea. Ma Viney had prepared a meal of roast lamb and baked vegetables. This was a relief to Brian who would have choked on tuna. It was a welcome pleasure to eat a home-cooked meal after so long and he lapped it up, his sea-sick stomach having settled. There was beer in plenty and whiskey to drink.

After the meal Dave produced a guitar, it was an old Martin that had belonged to his grandfather. The Viney family, Dave, Bob, their mother and their younger sister Elsie entertained their guests with a selection of country songs, mostly by the Weavers and the Carter Family. The performance was excellent. Soon everyone was joining in on the choruses; even Charlie Flint, who had a surprisingly good voice.

Dave was a very competent guitarist and the family's vocal harmonies were superb. Elsie's rendition of *Wildwood Flower* was the highlight of the evening. The guests were favourably impressed. Even Mervyn showed his appreciation, but he kept his own musical past to himself. Brian watched his reaction with interest, while tactfully keeping the erstwhile minstrel's secret.

'Normally Dad plays fiddle,' said Bob but he has been unavoidably detained.'

'At her majesty's pleasure,' Dave added with a broad grin, earning a back-hander from Ma for his trouble.

'There was no need to mention that you ratbag. You just thank your lucky stars you're not in there with him you young good-for-nothing. See to everyone's glasses will you Elsie love. There's a good girl.'

At about ten o'clock the pickers all clambered aboard Bob Viney's old DeSoto ute for the journey back to the orchard. They were about ten miles along the gravelled road, when the ute made an ominous, grating sound and ground to a halt. Bob knew at once that it was the clutch and they were stranded miles from anywhere on a lonely and little used road.

Smokes were rolled and curses were cursed as they sat there in the dark, vainly straining for the sound of oncoming traffic. They were out of luck and a cold night wind off the sea began to blow. They shared a bottle or two of beer and bemoaned their fate. After a time Brian noticed a faint light twinkling in the distant trees. He and Dave went to investigate.

'I didn't think anyone lived in this part of the world,' Dave muttered as they searched by torchlight until they found a track leading off into the bushes. Eventually they came to a tumbledown old farmhouse nestled among the trees. The light in the window came from a kerosene lamp. They climbed onto the verandah, which was shaded by massive old tree ferns, and knocked on the door. Somewhere inside, a dog barked but it did not sound threatening. Presently an old man opened the door. He was holding a kerosene lantern and an inquisitive border collie was at his side.

'What can I do for you? Is something wrong?'

'We've done the clutch on our ute and we're stranded back there on the road,' said Dave. 'Could we use your phone?'

'We never saw the need for a telephone so we never got one. Where are you headed to?'

'Murphy's orchard.'

'That's too far to walk at this hour of the night. Is it just you two?'

'No there's five of us in all,' said Brian.

'Five. I can manage five but it will take a while to get ready. You'd better come inside out of the cold.'

He ushered them into a room where a log fire was burning in a massive old fireplace. An old woman was sitting by the fire knitting.

'It's just some stranded travellers Mother. Their ute has broken down. I'm going to give them a lift to Murphy's orchard.'

'At this hour? Surely we could put them up for the night and you could take them in the morning.'

'There's five of them in all so I'd better take them now. Would you make them a cup of tea love, while I get ready?'

The old woman swung an old black kettle on a hinged bracket out over the flames of the fire and went to the kitchen for cups and a teapot. In the stillness, they could hear the waves breaking outside.

Left to themselves Brian and Dave indulged their curiosity and examined the place. It was like no other room Brian had ever seen.

'There's no electricity. It's like the olden days.' He went up to the mantelpiece. It contained a collection of old letters with two polished stones as bookends. Brian's curiosity got the better of him and he flicked through them. In the dim light he couldn't read the postmarks, and he didn't recognize any of the monarchs on the stamps.

'These letters are ancient. Some of them must be 90 years old.'

Then, as his eyes became accustomed to the gloom, Brian noticed the framed picture hanging over the fireplace. It was identical to the one he'd seen with Ray in the hall in Darlington and now, having seen Jim's photo of the Dandillion again, Brian was sure that this was the same boat.

'You'd better come away,' said Dave. 'She'll be back in a minute.'

By this time the kettle was singing lustily.

'The others'll be wondering what's happened to us,' said Brian.

'That's the least of my worries,' said Dave 'I'm fair bursting for a piss.'

Presently the old lady came back into the room bearing a tray with a teapot, cups and saucers, a jug of milk, a sugar bowl and a plate of shortbread biscuits.

'Here we are then,' she said, putting the tray on a little table near the fire.

'You shouldn't have gone to all that trouble,' said Brian as she sat back in her chair, very capably swung the kettle away from the flames and filled the teapot.

'It's no bother.'

'Where is your lavatory?' Dave asked, his situation becoming desperate.

'That depends what you want to do. If it's only a stand up job just go outside, not too close to the house though.' She smiled a wry smile at Brian as Dave frantically made a dash for the front door.

'Where are you from son? You don't sound like a local.'

'I'm from Greater Cumberland although I was born in Ireland. My parents emigrated when I was little.'

'Ah the big Island. I've never been that far myself; let alone the old country! Are you just down for the apples?'

'That's right. I'm saving up to go to uni.....to university.'

'Ah a scholar. Well good on you son.'

'If you don't mind my asking, who is the chap in that picture over the fireplace?'

'That's young Norian, bless him. He never ages. He comes to see us occasionally on his boat. He moors her in the bay outside. He says he'll take us for a sail on her one day fairly soon. I only hope he lets us take the dog.'

The conversation was interrupted by Dave's return.

'More comfortable now?' their hostess inquired.

'Much, thank you.'

She poured the tea.

'Help yourself to milk and sugar and have a biscuit too if you want.'

'Your husband's taking a long time.' Dave was becoming anxious about the others back on the ute.

'He takes his time. Not much longer.'

'How big is your car?'

'At a pinch it holds seven people but it's a bit of a squeeze. It's an old Chev.'

'What year?'

'I don't remember. It gave up the ghost about twenty years ago. It's been rusting away under the pine trees out the back ever since.'

Dave and Brian were now totally mystified and a little concerned, the excellent shortbread notwithstanding. They didn't like to think of the others back at the ute, freezing and cursing, unless of course someone else had picked them up.

Any further speculation was cut short by the return of the old man.

'Right then, everything's ready. I'll just throw down a quick cup of tea Mother and then we'd better be off. The tea was still piping hot so he poured some into his saucer to cool.

'I suppose we should introduce ourselves. I'm Harry Penruddock and this is my dear wife Maude.'

'Dave Viney,' said Dave standing up and shaking hands.

'I think I knew your grandfather, an unforgettable character.'

'And I'm Brian McInerney.'

'He's from the big island but from old Erin originally,' said Maude. 'He's a scholar but he's picking apples for the moment.'

'Pleased to meet you Brian. We'd better be going. Your friends back on the road will be freezing to death. Norian you stay here and look after Mother while I'm gone. The dog went and sat at Maud's feet as Dave and Brian thanked her and made their goodbyes.

They followed Harry outside and found two sturdy, grey horses harnessed to an old cart that was lit by two kerosene lamps.

'You should have let us help,' said Dave.

'It was no trouble. Now get yourselves aboard and we'll get started.'

Back on the road, Bob, Mervyn, and Charley were crowded into the cabin of the ute for warmth. Although warm it had been a very cramped and uncomfortable experience for all except Mervyn. He was very pleasantly distracted by thoughts of Elsie Viney, her flawless voice, her long, red hair, striking green eyes, the light dusting of freckles on her milk-white skin, her old fashion 1930's dress and her unspoiled, rustic perfection. Ladies of the folk scene back on the big Island, even the wonderful

Angela Moriarty, paled into insignificance. Elsie truly was *the* wildwood flower.

Presently they saw the approaching lamps through a gathering fog that had settled on them.

'What on earth is that?' said Mervyn, coming back to the present moment.

Gradually, the horses materialised out of the misty gloom. Before long Harry had turned the cart around and they clambered aboard and availed themselves of the warm blankets he had provided for them.

'Gidyup' said the old man and the two horses broke into a brisk trot.

'Don't you use a whip?' asked Bob who was in a hurry.

'Never saw the need. They'll do their best. They're just hitting their stride. You'll see.'

The passengers were soon asleep, except for Brian. He was sitting beside Harry in the driving seat, savouring the old world enchantment of the ride.

'Why do you call your dog Norian?'

'It's the name of a friend of ours.'

'Who is he exactly?'

'That my young friend, is a very long story.'

14: Cats Among the Pigeons

In the orchard next morning, the previous day's adventures dominated the conversation. There had been no conversation to speak of during the cart ride. Most of them had fallen asleep except for Brian and old Harry. Riley had been interested in the story to begin with but he reacted strangely at the mention of the Penruddocks.

'You're pulling my leg aren't you? Harry and Maude Penruddock!'

'No' said Brian. 'That's the names they gave us.'

'They were old when I was your age. You didn't smoke any funny cigarettes last night by any chance?'

'No,' said Dave, trying to look like butter wouldn't melt. 'Scout's honour.'

In spite of everyone's protestations, Riley remained unconvinced and went off on his own to pick in solitude while the others exhausted the topic.

Mervyn had shared the journey on the cart and like the others, he was mystified by Riley's reaction to the story. As the day wore on, the subject was talked out and people became preoccupied with their own thoughts. Mervyn in particular, had plenty on his mind. He had regarded his sojourn in Hollybank as some kind of epiphany. He had originally intended to die under the wheels of the up train and even though that plan failed he was still sure that his life as a musician was dead and buried.

That conviction had been rock solid until the Viney family burst into song the previous evening. Now all bets were off and Mervyn didn't know what to think. Was it because he had seen for the first time what music really should be like? Or was it because for the first time he had seen and heard Elsie Viney?

The ferment in his brain bubbled and fretted all day like boiling porridge and he felt like his head was about to burst. The excitement and anxiety of it all was wildly exhilarating but exhausting and relentless. He realized he had to talk about it to someone else or he'd explode.

It obviously wouldn't do to start asking the Viney brothers about their little sister's availability. He had made a point of complimenting them on their music at the first tea-break. His compliments were enthusiastically endorsed by Brian, and well enough received by the Vineys in a matter of fact sort of way. The family had always been musical but not for any commercial gain. In that part of the world people made their own entertainment.

Mervyn decided to join Riley in his solitude. He very diffidently asked the old picker what he knew about the Viney family, in particular about Elsie.

'Have you got some kind of death wish? If anyone touched a hair of that girl's head, Dave and Bob would have their guts for garters and that would only be after Ma Viney had chewed them up and spat them out. She's a rare little creature and no mistake but for looking definitely not for touching.'

'I was thinking more about her voice…her singing,' said Mervyn defensively but not very convincingly.

'Pull the other one son. I've seen her. I'll grant you she can sing like an angel and looks like one but she's only to be admired from a distance.'

The threatened explosion in Mervyn's brain had been averted for the moment and replaced by an implosion of all his budding aspirations and newfound musical ambitions, into a depressing soup of gloom. Perhaps it would have been better to have jumped under the train after all.

The gloom persisted for the rest of the afternoon until towards knock off time, when he found himself sharing a tree with Brian. It may have been because of Brian's naturally cheerful company that Mervyn found his own mood lightening. With that lightening, the cauldron of his passions began to simmer again.

He walked back to the pickers' huts with Brian at the end of the day.

'That was certainly some day we had yesterday,' said the former minstrel. 'Who'd've thought the Vineys would be so musical?'

'They certainly were. It was authentic somehow; the real thing, what the folk scene on the mainland tries to imitate.'

Mervyn knew that Brian was working at Hollybank during his crisis. He also knew and appreciated the fact that Brian hadn't said anything about his musical past to anyone at the orchard. They hadn't said a word about it to each other but Mervyn seemed to know that Brian could be relied on to keep his secret.

'What about their sister.'

'She's lovely,' said Brian, secure in his love for Kate.

'I meant her singing.'

'She was great – world class.'

'How old do you think she is?'

'I assume she's at least eighteen. She had a few drinks. But then I suppose the Vineys mightn't necessarily adhere to national licensing laws in the privacy of their home. What's her age got to do with anything? Girls' voices don't break do they?   She'll always have her beautiful voice won't she?'

'I sincerely hope so.   It's funny that Riley didn't believe old Mr Penruddock drove us home with his horse drawn cart. He was adamant.'

'He certainly was,' said Brian. 'I've spent the whole day wondering if we imagined it all.'

'That would be one hell of an hallucination, to transport five people, in a horse drawn cart all those miles.'

'I know but Riley is generally pretty sharp and he was particularly emphatic about the Penruddocks.'

'That may be so but you and Dave went into their house and had a cup of tea with them. That wasn't an hallucination was it?'

'There was no electricity and there were letters on the mantelpiece at least ninety years old if not more!'

'So what are you saying?'

'I'm saying that something might have happened that was outside the realm of normal experience.'

'Spooky. At least they got us home in one piece.'

They parted company when they reached their huts. The light was beginning to fade and Brian trod on something in the gloom. There was a squish of something semi-solid that yielded to the weight of his boot. Closer inspection revealed it to be one of a large number of horse droppings.

'Well there's nothing supernatural about that, thank God,' said Brian as he went inside and prepared to dine on a most un-paranormal can of baked beans.

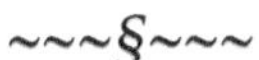

Jim's visit to Robert in Hollybank began awkwardly. Robert was very self conscious about his spells in hospital and usually his only visitors were his parents and Lucy. Jim had never visited him in hospital before and Robert suspected his motives. Rather than have their conversation overheard in the ward, he suggested they go for a walk in the grounds.

'Why have you come here? You never have before.'

'I was worried about you and wanted to see how you are getting on.'

'I'm all right.'

Lucy had been urging Robert to see less of Jim and not to be controlled by him. He had begun to see that Jim caused him a lot of stress, winding him up as he often did with his cloak and dagger behaviour. He had begun to see the wisdom in Lucy's advice and now, here he was, as large as life, in Hollybank of all places.

'My wellbeing has never concerned you before.'

'Robert, that is not a nice thing to say! I've always thought of you as a close and trusted friend. My friendship is constant and you can rely on me always. Unlike some people I could name.'

'What do you mean?'

'Well Lucy for example, she's changed; especially since Hugh came on the scene.'

'I've known Lucy since I was a little kid and I won't hear a word against her.'

'Fancy her, do you?'

'That's none of your business and anyway Lucy and Hugh are an item these days; so end of story.'

'Things started to go sour after Hugh arrived on the scene. I wish we'd never gone to see him.'

'But he has been very helpful;. What about the book by Norian Fairchild?'

'Have you seen the famous book?'

'No but he's explained that. When the book's owner gets back from overseas, Hugh will arrange for us to see it.'

'I wouldn't hold your breath.'

'I trust him. He's been quite up front about everything, unlike you sneaking off on your canoe trip without a word to anyone.'

'But I actually found the Dandillion and took photos of it. I left a letter to Norian Fairchild on board.'

'So you say. I haven't seen any photos.'

'Well what's this then?' Jim took a picture of the Dandillion out of his pocket and gave it to Robert.

'Lucy told me you sent a photo to Hugh.'

'And now I'm showing one to you.'

'You took your time. You're always playing games with us. I want you to go now.'

'But you and I were in this from the beginning. We should stick together. Bugger the other two.'

'Fuck off.'

Robert turned on his heel and stormed off across the grounds and back to his ward. Jim, for once, took the hint and headed home to Cranwell Street with his tail between his legs but Robert still had the picture of the Dandillion clutched in his hand.

<div align="center">~~~§~~~</div>

Later that week, Brian received a letter from Kate.

Denistone
April 20th

Hi Brian

We've had some sad news today. Thomas died sometime this afternoon. Mum found him on his favourite cushion in the bay window. She thought he was just asleep, which is what he did mostly, these last few years. When he missed his tea time, mum checked on him and he was cold. He was a dear old thing and I'm going to miss him terribly. All my life he's been there.

Tomorrow, Dad and I will take him up to Grandad's place in Carlingford and bury him in the garden. It's a pity he couldn't have held out just a bit longer, Grandad will be back from overseas in three weeks time. Mrs Sullivan gets back from Ireland tomorrow and she will soon be opening the place up.

Sorry for the sad tidings. I guess at his age it had to happen soon. At least he died peacefully in his sleep which is the best way to go. I'm glad you got to meet him.

I don't know if you've heard from Hugh and Lucy lately. Apparently their friend Robert will be coming home from Hollybank soon but Lucy is still worried about him.

This apple season seems to be taking forever. It's times like these that I really need you here with me. God alone knows why but I'm very deeply in love with you, my very own personal buffoon.

Remember
I'm always your
Kate xxx

Although he was saddened by the news about Thomas, Brian was obviously very much heartened by the conclusion of Kate's letter which contained her most explicit statement yet about her feelings towards him. He resolved to do some letter writing after dinner, firstly to Kate and then to Hugh.

~~~§~~~

A few days later when Brian's letter arrived at Gracechurch street it caused great excitement. Hugh found the letter when he arrived home from work. Without bothering to change out of his work clothes, he set out straight away for Lucy's place. She met him at the door and took him straight up to her room.

'This is amazing,' she said after reading the letter. 'It sounds like Brian's having a magical time down there.'

'And the old couple, the Penruddocks, actually know Norian Fairchild. He visits them, and moors his yacht in the bay behind their house. They've named their dog after him! I wish we could get down there.'

'That's not really possible at present but Brian says he's going to try and visit them again. He'll keep us posted.'

'Yes you're right we'll just have to leave matters in his hands for now.'

'And for now I've got you in **my** hands,' said Lucy as she caught Hugh in a fond embrace and knocked his feet out from under him. 'Together we stand - United we fall,' she said; as they collapsed onto Lucy's bed in a rough and tumble, playful embrace which eventually found Hugh flat on his back with a jubilant Lucy astride him sitting on his chest.
~~~

'We'd better leave it at that and go downstairs. Mum and Dad will be home soon with the groceries.'

They straightened their clothes and made their descent to find Lucy's youngest brother, Trevor sitting at the kitchen table eating a biscuit.

'Trevor,' said Lucy. 'I didn't hear you come in.'

'Obviously but don't worry about it.' He smirked. 'Your secret is safe with me as long as I get extra baked potatoes tonight.'

'You can go take a running jump. I won't be blackmailed, especially not by a little shrimp like you.'

The conversation was interrupted by the booming voice of their Father, Tom coming in from the garage with the groceries.

'Ah Hugh. Could you give us a hand getting these bags in from the car? There's a free dinner in it for you if you do. Robert is helping us too. He was knocking off for the day just as we were leaving the supermarket.'

It was the first time Hugh had seen Robert since he was discharged from Hollybank. They were both a little awkward to begin with but fortunately Tom dominated the conversation while the groceries were gathered in. Lucy put the kettle on for a cup of tea and then set about helping her mother to unpack the groceries and stow them away.

When everything was ship-shape, Mr O'Rourke went back to his kiln. He had a big order for a major client that was due the next day. The others sat down for a cup of tea around the kitchen table. Mrs O'Rourke didn't sit for long however as she had to finalize dinner which had been quietly baking away all afternoon.

Elizabeth, her now heavily pregnant eldest daughter, was coming with her husband Ted. Officially the baby was due four days ago and Elizabeth was feeling heartily sick of being pregnant. Her doctor husband was more philosophical about the delay but, as Elizabeth frequently pointed out to him, he was just an interested spectator.

Presently, Mrs O'Rourke asked Lucy to set up the table for the meal in the covered area at the back of the house. Given that there was a slight chill in the night air they would have to organize some heating. Lucy delegated Hugh and Robert to help her and they readily complied. There was a lot to talk about. When she first read Brian's letter, Lucy wondered what, if anything, Robert should be told. Would the news trigger another episode so soon after getting out of Hollybank? On the other hand if Robert was to find out later that they had kept the information from him, wouldn't that upset him even more? However the decision was taken out of her hands when Hugh, of his own volition showed him the letter.

'This is amazing. What with this letter, Jim's photo and the book at your friend's grandfather's place we are starting to build a clear picture. Thanks for sharing the letter with me Hugh.' He looked anxiously at Lucy. 'Please don't worry about me Lucy. I'm excited but I'm not getting high again.'

'Well just make sure you keep taking your tablets. Now come on! We have to get this meal set up. Dad would normally do it but he has a big pottery order to complete. We're having the roast dinner tonight because Dad is convinced that the baby will come before the weekend. I hope for Elizabeth's sake that it does. She's at the end of her tether.'

<p style="text-align:center">~~~§~~~</p>

By nine thirty the meal was over; Tom had excused himself and gone back to work, and Elizabeth and Ted had made their goodbyes. With these early departures, Trevor made a killing on the baked potatoes before he went to bed. But first he joined the others in helping his mother with the washing up. When it was all done they sat around the kitchen table with cups of tea. Robert only stayed long enough to drink his tea and then made his excuses.

'Mum and Dad will be starting to worry,' he said apologetically. 'Thanks for dinner.'

They all wished him a fond goodnight and then Luke, Lucy's twin brother who had come late to the meal went to bed.

'Robert is really a sweet boy,' said Mrs O'Rourke, 'when he's not unwell.'

'You're right Mum. As a kid he was quite normal. The problems only started when he reached adolescence. He just needs to keep away from people and things that cause him stress. People like Jim Lovegrove.'

'Now Jim *is* an odd boy, Lucy. I think basically he's just insecure and wants to impress people. He was very young when his father was lost at sea. I haven't seen him for a long time. Does he still dress up in motorbike gear?'

'He keeps to himself these days Mum. No one sees much of him.'

'He came round to my place one night a while back,' said Hugh. 'He was dressed in normal clothes then. He has grown a beard though.'

'Good grief!' said Lucy. 'The old man of the sea.'

'It might be something to hide behind dear.'

'No Mum. It'd be to draw attention to himself.'

'Don't be too hard on him Lucy. He is obviously troubled and looking for re-assurance. Perhaps boys like Robert and Jim are drawn to you because of your empathetic nature.'

'And what about Hugh then? Is he an emotional lame duck too?' Lucy laughed as her mum's cheeks coloured.

'You're getting more like your father every day. From what I've seen, I think you and Hugh are very good for each other. I'm sorry Hugh for Lucy trying to put me on the spot in front of you but I meant what I said. I think you are both very good for each other.'

<p style="text-align:center">~~~§~~~</p>

As he walked home from the O'Rourke's', Robert was struck by an idea. Their quest to find out more about Norian Fairchild was focused on access to the transcript of "Dandillion" when it became available, Jim's photo and Brian's encounter with the Penruddocks. Efforts to locate members of the pre-convict families had drawn a blank after Hugh's discovery that their municipal rates were all paid for by the estate of N. Fairchild. There was no record of the householders' names.

Robert decided to start reading the telephone directory, tracking down names that belonged to the pre-convict families and locating their addresses. Then he would do the same thing with the electoral rolls. This would keep him gainfully occupied and make a significant addition to their body of knowledge. He reminded himself to keep a cool head and stick to his medication regime. Even so there was a spring in his step on that walk home, that had been absent for quite some time. He whistled happily to himself.

~~~§~~~

Things were also moving again in Jim's life. He was no longer brooding at home under his mother's feet. He had finally secured a position on another boat. It was a much bigger vessel than he was used to. It stayed away at sea for much longer periods and specialised in deep sea fishing. Fortunately he knew a few of the crew members and they were able to help him learn the ropes. It still took him a while to find his way around the boat and familiarise himself with its layout.

Nevertheless he was happy to be back at sea. For a time, Norian Fairchild, Hugh, Lucy and Robert didn't cross his mind as he immersed himself in his new job with relief. Of course, back home, his mother would continue to worry about him the whole time he was away and the longer voyages would just add to her worries.

~~~§~~~

At about eleven thirty Hugh said his goodbyes. It had been an exciting day and a most enjoyable evening. As he walked home in the dark, he felt a deep contentment. He was secure in his love for Lucy and the place he now had in the O'Rourke family circle. He fondly remembered his tortuous initiation on that Sunday in October last year when he turned up unexpectedly for roast dinner.

It had been a baptism of fire but on further acquaintance and without an excess of Sunday claret Tom O'Rourke had proven to be a kind, generous and warm hearted man who was totally devoted to his family. His bark was definitely much worse than his bite. On the occasional Sundays when he did over-indulge he no longer seemed so fearsome.

As he turned into Gracechurch street, Hugh thought about replying to Brian's letter before he went to bed but decided against it. His day was replete, no need even for a bedtime sherry. He was ready for bed and all was well with his world.

<center>~~~§~~~</center>

Hugh's mellow contentment continued the next day. He met Lucy for lunch. She was on night shift for the rest of the week and they wouldn't see much of each other for that time. They were making plans for their holidays which they planned to take in the spring. Lucy was keen to meet Hugh's family. Hugh had told them about her in letters home and his mother was looking forward to meeting her. She had even hinted at coming down to Darlington for a visit. Back at work, Hugh's mind was very pleasantly occupied with these comfortable thoughts. His task for the afternoon mostly involved the filing of documents. It wasn't particularly mentally demanding and his mind was free to wander where it would.

When he got home from work that evening, he found that there was more mail waiting for him, in a large brown envelope. With a sickening shock he recognized Maggie's handwriting. He tore the envelope open and read the letter.

Madelaine College

Ross

25/4/1970

Dear Hugh

This letter will probably come as a shock to you but I hope it finds you well. I have been doing a lot of thinking lately, particularly about us. I've come to regret the way things ended between us - the fact that they ended at all.

We've known each other since we were little kids and we have so many memories and shared experiences. We gave each other our virginities and I think we have always really belonged together.

It's a real pity that things blew up the way they did that day on the train. We both said a lot of hurtful things that I'm sure we didn't mean. I realize now that I should have been more receptive when you tried to tell us about the Fairchilds, because it obviously means so much to you.

To try and make amends, I'm sending you this gift. I have taken a considerable risk in doing this - no less than two counts of breaking and entering. And you must keep it a secret. In particular Kate and the rest of the Mahoney family must never know about it. They have all been such wonderful friends to Brian and me.

I hope you find it useful. I found it an interesting read although the guy strikes me as being a bit self centred and full of self pity.

That's all I'll say for now. Do think about mending our differences. We still have so much to offer each other.

Much love

Still (hopefully)

your Maggie.

Almost numb with shock and confusion, Brian opened the parcel. It contained a school exercise book in Maggie's handwriting. It bore the title:

DANDILLION
THE WHITE SHIP
Norian Fairchild

Hugh tried to focus his thoughts. His immediate reaction was to read the document but after the first paragraph his conscience gained the upper hand. This situation was fraught with so many conflicted interests and loyalties. Firstly he was reading something sent to him by Maggie. He didn't know if Maggie knew about Lucy or not and was prepared to give her the benefit of the doubt. But here she was, at her most eloquent and persuasive, doing her level best to win him back at Lucy's expense.

Maggie had obviously broken into Jack Mahoney's house, removed the document, copied it and returned it to the house unnoticed. By asking Hugh to keep her secret from Kate and the rest of the Mahoney family, she was painting him into a corner. Brian and Kate had become interested in the whole Norian Fairchild saga. What was the use of Maggie's transcript if he couldn't share it with them and how could he show it to Lucy, given where it came from. On top of all that, Hugh knew from Kate, that her grandfather would be home from overseas in a couple of weeks and they could then make a legitimate copy of the document with his blessing.

Hugh paced around his flat, too restless and upset to sleep. He tried a couple of sherries as a tranquiliser. They were only partially effective. He knew he needed to go to bed and get some sleep but it was a bed he'd shared with Maggie as well as Lucy. He was not going to start comparing the two girls. He was too much of a gentleman. Lucy was a wonderful girl who had coaxed him out of his shell. She gave herself to him gently and freely and loved him unconditionally. There was no question of where his loyalty lay. Why then was he suddenly remembering the distinctive perfumes that Maggie always wore.

If only Lucy wasn't on nightshift. But then to his dismay he realized, or thought he realized, that this was something he had to sort out in his own head before he had any further contact with her or with Maggie for that matter. He banished himself to Brian's room and bed until he sorted things out to the satisfaction of his conscience.

<div align="center">~~~§~~~</div>

On Lesser Cumberland, the ferment in Mervyn's heart and mind continued unabated. He had trouble sleeping and in desperation he resorted to the medication he'd been given on his discharge from Hollybank. The tablets took the edge off his emotions but they also made him drowsy and his mouth was very dry all the time. At least he was able to concentrate on his work in the orchard. Gradually he began to confide in Brian who as ever was a sympathetic listener and a friendship began to grow between them.

It was not only matters of the heart that Mervyn wanted to talk about. The vexed question of music, in particular his aborted musical career, was a frequent topic of discussion.

Mervyn thanked Brian for keeping his musical past from the other pickers.

'It wasn't my place to go telling people about your past. Are you really sure you want to leave it in the past?'

'You know what it led to? I tried to kill myself by jumping under a train.'

'But booze and drugs had a lot to do with that didn't they?'

'They contributed to it and clouded my judgment but the desire to end it all was very real.'

Wow. I can't imagine ever feeling that desperate but you're over it now right?'

'I thought I was and that giving up music was the solution. Now I'm not so sure.'

'Not sure about what, music or suicide?'

'Oh not suicide, definitely not suicide but music. I feel like I want to write songs again.'

'About Elsie Viney?'

'Well yes but not with any view to musical stardom - just to celebrate what a beautiful creature she is.'

'You really have got it bad but it is entirely understandable. That's how I feel about Kate. But why shouldn't you write a song about her? You'd be doing it out of love, not to make money. I mean most of the great traditional love songs were written by ordinary men and women, not commercial song writers for profit. Did you bring your guitar with you? I haven't seen it.'

'No. I left it in Darlington. A friend of mine is minding it for me. He wouldn't let me sell it.'

'Well thank God for that. I suppose it's too fragile to have it freighted here.'

'As well as too valuable.'

'Well why not buy another one in Woodfield, a cheap one to tide you over. I saw some guitars in the general store last Friday.'

'I suppose I could couldn't I.'

'You bet you could.'

Discussions on these and other topics continued both in the orchard and at night in their huts. Riley often joined them in the orchard and learned a lot about his two colleagues in the process. He was happy to see the friendship developing between them. From the outset he had been worried about the erstwhile minstrel. He had learnt in Hollybank about the failed suicide attempt and he felt certain that friendship with Brian would do Mervyn the world of good.

Riley established the ritual of inviting the two young men to his hut on Saturday nights for drinks at the end of the working week. Brian had been surprised by the tidiness and cleanliness of the old man's hut. He had expected something more ramshackle given the man's derelict, bohemian reputation. But he was full of surprises and he was clearly a better housekeeper than Brian. Also, the hut was very well furnished for a picker's hut. There was a large chest of drawers, a fully stocked bookshelf and a couple of framed photographs on the walls.

One photograph in particular caught Brian's eye. The subject was a beautiful young woman. It was a head and shoulders portrait, vignetted in an oval frame. She had braided hair pinned up in an Edwardian style. She was looking back over her shoulder at the camera and smiling a radiant smile of pure happiness. Even in such an old black and white photograph, you could see the sparkle in her eyes, all these years later.

'Who is this lady? She is beautiful.'

'That's Edith. We go back a long way.'

Riley clearly didn't want to elaborate and quickly changed the subject.

One thing that was never discussed with Riley was their encounter with the Penruddocks. Brian was anxious to find out as much as he could about Harry and Maude and their dog Norian. Riley definitely knew something about them; as was evidenced by his singular reaction to their story that morning in the orchard. But it was clearly a sensitive topic with him. Brian was biding his time while he pondered the best way to broach the subject.

First and foremost Brian wanted to go back to the Penruddocks' house if it could be found. He began suggesting the idea to the Viney brothers as a possible project when the old ute was back in action. The Vineys were interested in the idea, Dave in particular because he had gone into their house with Brian, but it was not a high priority.

'Let's wait and see when we get the ute back,' was as much as Bob would commit to.

<p style="text-align:center">~~~§~~~</p>

As it happened, Brian didn't have long to wait. The DeSoto pulled up outside the packing shed two days later on the Saturday as the men were returning at day's end. Elsie was driving. She jumped out to greet her brothers. She was wearing jeans a shapeless old grey jumper and gym boots. Her hair was in a ponytail. Mervyn's heart began to hammer against his ribs.

'Here's your ute Bob. It handles like a tank but at least it has a working clutch again.'

'Thanks for that Elsie. I wasn't expecting it to be ready for a couple of days yet. Do you remember these blokes from dinner the other night?'

'I remember them but not their names.' She replied and blessed them with a bashful smile. 'I'm hopeless with names.'

Dave reintroduced Mervyn and Brian. 'Old Riley you know although he wasn't with us the other night.'

Riley swept the ground with a gracious bow.'

'Charmed Miss Viney.'

'So am I Mr Riley,' she replied with another blushing smile.

'Now I suppose you'll be wanting a lift back home,' said Bob.

'Yes and you can drive.'

'All right climb aboard are you coming Dave? We'll make a weekend of it and come back tomorrow night. Mum's a better cook than you.'

With that, the three Vineys made their goodbyes. The ute's engine fired and they were gone.

Mervyn's heart was still racing with wistful frustration. Riley put a hand on his shoulder.

'Come on son. You need a shot of whiskey. Coming Brian?'

15: Transcription

Back in Gracechurch street, Hugh had finally taken decisive action about Maggie's bombshell. It was now Friday night, Lucy's last night on nightshift and this was the fourth night of his ordeal. He had exiled himself to Brian's bed, in which he found a pair of Kate's knickers. Thinking they would look odd on the clothesline he made a mental note to include them in his next load of washing. He was too preoccupied with his dilemma to think about the potential comic possibilities of his discovery.

On Wednesday night it had come down to making an evenly weighted decision; would he stay with Lucy or go back to Maggie? He was disgusted with himself that it had come to that. On the bus home from work on Thursday night, in a moment of inspiration, he decided to go to O'Brien's and talk to Madge. She was the ideal impartial listening post. She was a straight talker with a wealth of experience and she had become a friend.

'What are you doing here in the lounge? You usually only drink here these days if you are with a lady. Are you expecting Lucy?'

'No she's on nightshift. I wanted to talk to you in private. I need your advice.'

'Oh! All right then but remember I'm only a drunk's labourer. I'm not a licensed head shrink so I'm not making any promises.'

What Hugh really needed at that time was to hear his thoughts spoken out loud. They had been revolving in his head ever since he read Maggie's letter. He didn't mention her transcription of "Dandillion" but he told Madge everything else. Between serving drinks out in the main bar, Madge listened to his story with great interest. When he had said his piece, she gave him a beer on the house and poured one for herself.

'That's it is it? You've told me everything?'

'Yes.'

'And were you listening to what you were saying?'

'Well…yes!'

'This Maggie must be something special if she can wrap you round her finger with a single letter after dropping you like a hot potato last September. I've watched you and Lucy these past few months and I've seen you coming out of your shell. Lucy has grown too. What's Maggie's big attraction? Is she better in bed or something? By what you say I gather she's a bit of a looker.'

This was cutting too close to the bone for Hugh's comfort.

'She's very beautiful and I've known her since we were kids but…'

'But what? Life isn't a beauty contest and anyway Lucy is a very attractive girl in her own right and you two are as thick as thieves. That's a fact and it sticks out like dog's balls.

'In twenty years time their beauty will be a thing of the past, it's what's left afterwards that matters. You're faced with a decision that only you can make. Only one thing is certain you can't have both of them and one of them will end up disappointed. If you mess this up you **could** lose both of them. Do they know about each other? Have they met?'

'Lucy knows I had a previous girlfriend but I don't think Maggie knows about Lucy.'

'If Maggie is Brian's sister as you say then you can be pretty sure that she does know about Lucy. Brian is an open book.'

Madge hadn't spoken angrily but she left Hugh in no doubt. He felt like he had received a kick in the pants.

'What you may have had with Maggie in the past is just memories Hugh. There's no future in memories. Believe me.'

Hugh took another sip of beer.

'Thanks Madge you've been a great help.'

'All part of the friendly service son,' she said as she went back to the bar smiling wistfully to herself about past memories of her own.

Hugh had walked back to Gracechurch Street through a chilly but bracing sprinkling of autumn rain. He felt that his priorities were now sorted out but he was mortified by how close he had come to choosing Maggie over Lucy. Madge's blunt home truths had left him feeling weak and ashamed. Perhaps unfairly, Maggie ended up on the receiving end of his mortification. He went upstairs to his flat and without a second glance put her letter and transcription of 'Dandillion' in the fireplace and set them alight. He drank a bedtime sherry while he watched the flames. Then, when the offending documents had been reduced to ashes, he went to sleep, back in his own bed.

<div align="center">~~~§~~~</div>

Friday had been a day of relative calm for Hugh but he was still nervous. That night he made a resolution to be waiting on the hospital steps when Lucy finished her night shift in the early hours of Saturday morning. Lucy was very pleasantly surprised to find Hugh waiting for her at 3am.

'Hugo! Couldn't you sleep?'

'No it's not that. I've missed you terribly this week of night shift and there's something I need to tell you about.'

'Nothing to worry about I hope.'

'No there's nothing for you to worry about although I've had a worrying few days. You know about Brian's sister Maggie and how we used to be together.'

'A little, yes.'

'Well you see I got this letter from her the other day and with it was a hand written copy of "Dandillion."……..

And so the whole story came out. Lucy listened intently with only a few interruptions seeking clarification of particular points.

'In the end I asked Madge for advice.'

'Madge!! Why on earth Madge?'

'She was a great help to me when Maggie and I split up. She's a straight talker and she knows what I'm like. I trust her. My thoughts had been racing around in my head for days and I had to talk to someone.'

'And what did she say?'

'She sent me home with a flea in my ear. She said you and I were made for each other and it sticks out like dog's balls.'

'Charming!! Well good old Madge. So I won.'

'Yes of course you did. I just needed to talk to someone about it.'

'Well since you've been such a brave, honest little man I'll come home with you to Gracechurch street and I'll wear my nurse's uniform in bed for you.' Hugh spluttered, unable to conceal his outrage.

'It's all right Hugh. Brian has told me about your little fetish. I think it's sweet.'

'Bloody Brian!! One of these days I'll wring that feller's neck. The fetish only exists in his lunatic head. It's a complete fantasy.'

'Well in that case you'll have to take my uniform off before you have your way with me.'

'Perhaps the uniform might be fun. Would that include the stockings?'

'They're panty-hose I'm afraid. So you'll have to improvise. Oh by the way Elizabeth had a baby girl in the early hours of Wednesday morning. Lucinda May. She's beautiful.'

<div style="text-align:center">~~~§~~~</div>

Later that morning, back at Gracechurch Street, Hugh and Lucy were sitting up in bed with tea and toast. Lucy had showered. It was 7am and she had to get home pretty soon or her parents would be starting to worry or perhaps suspect. Hugh offered to walk her home but then realized the flaw in his plan.

'I'll ring for a taxi for you.'

'That'd be great.'

They both began dressing.

'This uniform is looking very tired Hugh.'

'Tired but satisfied,' said Hugh 'and remember Brian must never hear of what transpired this morning.'

'Was it fun though?'

'It's always fun with you Lucy, with or without theatrical props.'

Hugh rang for a taxi. As they waited, Lucy asked a question.

'What did you do with Maggie's letter?'

'Same as her transcription of "Dandillion". I burnt it.'

'Are you going to reply to her?'

'I hadn't intended to.'

'I think you should. I know it's technically none of my business but you shouldn't leave her in suspense. That would be cruel. You should make an end with a gentle letter, because of what you had in the past.'

Hugh pondered this for a moment and quickly realized that Lucy was right.

'Of course. Thanks. That would have been very insensitive of me.'

Outside, they heard the horn of the taxi.

'I'd better go Hugo, before he toots again and disturbs Mrs Malleson. Thanks for a wonderful end to my working week. Come round later at a more respectable hour. Late in the afternoon when we've both had some more sleep. What say we go to Montini's?'

'Great idea. I'll book for six – o'clock not people.'

They went downstairs to the street, kissed and then she was gone. Hugh breathed a contented sigh and went back up to his flat.

9 Gracechurch St

May 2nd

Dear Maggie

Thank you for your letter which came as a shock. I thought our relationship ended forever that day on the train.

Thanks also for the transcription of "Dandillion" which you sent me. I can appreciate the risk and the trouble you took. Unfortunately by asking me to keep it secret from Kate and her family you have put me in an awkward situation. Kate and Brian have become very interested in the whole Norian Fairchild saga now. I can't share it with them without incriminating you and if I can't share it with them it isn't any use to me.

I decided the safest thing to do was burn the document so that nobody else finds out that you broke into Jack Mahoney's house to borrow and copy the original. Mr Mahoney will be back from overseas any day now and he has said that I'm welcome to examine the book at his place.

Unfortunately I have to say there is no chance of us getting back together. What we had in the past was lovely while it lasted but we've both moved on since then. You've got your uni career and I'm with someone else these days. What we had is just memories now and there's no future in memories.

I don't want to hurt you and I hope things will settle down in future so that we can be friends again - but only friends. I hope you find someone else soon. You're a beautiful girl and you'll soon find someone to make you happy.

Thanks for what we had in the past and all the best for the future.

Sincerely *(just)* your friend

Hugh."

Hugh was pleased with his day's work. It had taken the best part of six hours and several drafts to complete it and make a fair copy. He posted it on his way round to Lucy's place at five o'clock that afternoon.

~~~§~~~

Maggie received Hugh's letter on the following Tuesday. It took several readings for her to digest. The first conclusion she reached was that someone else had helped him to write it. There was an unfamiliar sense of authority and confidence in the way it was written that was not like the letters she was accustomed to receiving from him in the past.

She was upset to read that Hugh had burnt her transcription of "Dandillion" after the trouble, not to mention the risk, it had cost her. She was disappointed but not too disheartened. She still believed she could win Hugh back if she could meet him face to face without any third party there to put words in his mouth. She wanted him back and began to plan her next letter.

The fact was that, after the initial excitement of leaving school and starting uni, she was feeling a sense of anti-climax. When she broke up with Hugh that day on the train, she felt she was breaking free from the restrictions he was placing on her. But since the break - up, things had started to deteriorate.

The relationship with Kate's brother Tim, which started during the Christmas holidays, had seemed like a reassurance that life after Hugh would continue happily. The Christmas had been spent at the Mahoney family shack on Green Island. The whole family had been there and Brian as well. It had been great fun and Tim had been friendly and considerate as their friendship developed, but, because of Madelaine Mahoney's strict policy about sleeping arrangements, they were rarely if ever alone together.
~~~

They didn't really start getting to know each other until uni started. Tim wasn't deceitful or aggressive and his affection was genuine and generous but when they were alone together he couldn't keep his hands off her. These attentions were so frequent and heavy-handed that Maggie soon made the decision that she could never let him make love to her.

Their social life together was equally difficult. Tim mostly mixed with predominantly male sporting fraternities, with people much older than her. She began to feel that she was a trophy for him to show off to his friends. To begin with, she went to watch him playing cricket. Not many of the other players' girlfriends did this and the few who did were older than her. Some were jealous of her looks and gave her the cold shoulder.

As she sat through boring afternoons trying to look interested, she found herself pining for the idyllic afternoons spent with Hugh in Mrs Malleson's garden. How could she ever have thought of that relationship as constricting. After initially wanting to spread her wings, Maggie wanted to retreat back into the comfortable cocoon of Gracechurch street, but she was very much afraid that those days could never return.

She began to conceive the plan of copying "Dandillion" as a stratagem to get Hugh back again. The idea occurred when Tim gave his car keys to her to mind once when he went in to bat. She knew that Tim had a key to the back door of his grandfather's house. He first acquired it when he was at Boarding School in Carlingford.

Occasionally the opportunity would arise on Saturday afternoons to sneak away from school outings to help himself to the drinks cabinet when his grandfather and Mrs Sullivan were both away for the weekend. He had boasted about it and shown it to her once. It was a relatively simple task to take the key and get a copy cut. Returning the original to Tim's key ring was a little tricky but she managed it at another cricket match three weeks later.

In the meantime she had taken two day trips to Carlingford, one to borrow, the other to return the book. Although she had originally been outraged that Hugh had burnt her hard won handiwork she realised it was for the best. She would be mortified if the Mahoney family ever found out and she couldn't bear to lose their friendship. Thanks to Hugh, her secret was safe.

Since the break up with Hugh, Kate had become Maggie's confidante in most matters but the subject of Tim's 'caveman' behaviour couldn't be shared with Kate, or at least that's what Maggie thought. This meant that, for the moment, she was flying solo, trying to ease her way out of one relationship whilst rekindling another. All without offending or upsetting anyone. Hugh's mysterious new girlfriend was one possible casualty but she didn't really know her.

The truth of the matter was that Kate, her family and Brian were all watching on from the sidelines fully expecting Maggie and Tim to come to grief. Unbeknown to Maggie, they wouldn't have been in the least bit offended if she broke up with him. She would still retain her place in the family's affections. Everybody concerned was just treading too delicately to actually say anything and Maggie continued to fly solo.

<div align="center">~~~§~~~</div>

Back on Lesser Cumberland, Brian finally got the chance to go looking for the Penruddocks. It was Sunday the 10th of May. Bob Viney was nursing a fierce hangover and stayed behind. Dave drove the DeSoto and Mervyn came along too on the off-chance of catching a glimpse of Elsie. They had no trouble finding the spot where the breakdown happened. The problem was how to visualize in broad daylight, where they had seen the glimmer of the kerosene lantern in the dark that night.

They had followed a sandy track through the light scrubby bushland, that seemed to lead towards the distant light. But now, in broad daylight, there were any number of such tracks, made by animals, and leading in all directions. After an hour's fruitless scrub bashing, Brian was beginning to feel disheartened.

'I'm starting to think old Riley was right. Perhaps we imagined it all.'

'We both know better than that, don't we?' said Dave. Perhaps we're going about this the wrong way. Instead of trying to find the path we took to the house we should look for the way old Harry drove us back to the highway. There's no way you'd get a horse and cart down a pissant little track like this. We should look for where we came back onto the road that night.'

'There was a heavy fog by that time though, remember.'

'We could still see any side road wide enough for a horse and cart. There can't be too many in this God-forsaken place.'

They found two side-roads. In a hopeful sign, there were hoof prints and wheel ruts that looked recent on both of them. Dave followed one, Brian and Mervyn the other. They arranged to meet an hour later back on the main road. Dave's road had led to the sea. It must have been built in the past to service houses that were no longer there. All he found on the seashore was a ramshackle little hut and a dinghy secured under a tarpaulin.

Brian and Mervyn came back after an hour or so, with mixed results. The road they followed forked into two branches. One branch headed towards the beach. They followed that first and found two abandoned houses and not much else. Retracing their steps they then tried the second branch. This led up onto higher ground and the terrain seemed more like what Brian remembered. There were also plenty of hoof prints and occasional horse droppings.

They came out on top of a low flat hill and there it was, the old ramshackle farmhouse, surrounded by its verandah and almost hidden from view by the massive old tree ferns. The place looked deserted. There was no smoke from any of the chimneys and all the window blinds were drawn. They knocked on the front door but there was no answer, not even a bark from Norian the dog.

They went around to the back of the house where the barn and the stables were. There was no sign of the horses or the cart. The barn contained two large stacks of firewood and a substantial stack of hay bales. There were bins of oats and a large store of root vegetables. Outside was a stand of pine trees providing a windbreak for a paddock of pastureland. Under the pine trees, they found the rusting remains of the old brown Chev in the company of an old cart also derelict and much older than the one Harry had used to ferry them all back to the orchard.

All in all it was a very mixed outcome. Brian was in no doubt that they'd found the Penruddocks house but he couldn't shake off the very compelling feeling that it had been empty and deserted for many years.

'Oh well,' said Dave 'at least you found it. I don't think it's been deserted all that long though. The firewood and feed in the barn would have walked long before this. We can always try again later in the season. If it's still deserted then, I could get a good price for the firewood and the hay,' he added with a mischievous grin. Brian didn't know if he was joking or not as they piled into the ute and headed for the Vineys' place.

~~~§~~~

'Just wait here a minute,' said Dave as they pulled up outside the Viney farmhouse. 'I won't be a sec.'

He left Brian and Mervyn in the ute. While they were sitting waiting, Mervyn saw Elsie in the rearview mirror. She was walking up the driveway dressed in an old fashioned floral frock and a green cardigan. She was wearing a straw hat with a matching green ribbon and carrying a basket full of flowers.

She came up to them and Brian opened his window.

'Hullo. It's Brian isn't it? Sorry that's the only name I remember,' she said with a deprecating but very sweet smile for Mervyn. 'What are you waiting out here for? Didn't they ask you inside?'

'Dave said he'd only be a second,' said Brian.

'No Bob?'

'Bob's feeling a little poorly,' said Mervyn eager to get some conversational runs on the board.'

'Ah he's been on the grog again has he? He often comes unstuck on Saturday nights. He needs a wife to keep him on the straight and narrow. I'm sorry I still haven't remembered your name.'

'I'm Mervyn.'

'Mervyn. Right, I won't forget again.'
~~~

'Where ever did you get those flowers at this time of the year?' Mervyn asked.

'They're from the church. A lady grows them in a hothouse. She lets me bring home what's left over.'

I really enjoyed your singing the other night. You have a great talent.'

'Oh that,' she said,' blushing intensely. 'It's just a bit of fun. We all do it.'

'Well I thoroughly enjoyed it. I hope to hear you again some time.'

Elsie didn't get a chance to reply as Dave came back from the house.

'Hallo little sis. Back from Church then? I hope you said a prayer for me.'

'You need all the help you can get, you reprobate,' she said as she smiled goodbye to Mervyn and Brian and went into the house.

On the journey back to the orchard, Mervyn's mind was in overdrive digesting and reliving the conversation with Elsie. He blessed Brian for letting him take over the dialogue and treasured Elsie's every word, blush and smile. She was a perfect, unspoiled beauty. He regretted his choice of words when he complimented her singing. Saying she had a great talent made him sound like a talent scout. That was an echo of his Mervan Mithras persona. But overall it had been a pleasant and gentle exchange. In time his train of thought was distracted by Brian and Dave's' conversation.

'Where does Elsie work Dave?'

'She's still at school. This is her final year. She does have a part time job at Berechree's dairy up the road.'

'How long has she had her driver's licence?'

'She hasn't got her licence yet. She's only just turned 16 but she's been driving tractors and trucks round the farm for years. When she turns 17 she'll go for her licence and make it all legal. But Sergeant Harley, the local cop, is pretty easygoing. He knows Elsie is a good safe driver.'

'I thought you said your Dad was in jail.'

'That was down to fisheries inspectors from the big island. Harley nearly got busted too.'

A cold shadow subdued Mervyn's reverie. Only just sixteen!! Still at school!! He was seven years older than her.

<div align="center">~~~§~~~</div>

As expected, young Jack Mahoney arrived back in Carlingford on May 11th. The rest of the family gave him a few days to rest and get his bearings before catching up with him. Kate was busy with study commitments and completing a major essay so it was nearly a fortnight before she was able to spend a weekend with him. She found her grandfather well rested and content after a most enjoyable time away. The only disappointment in his homecoming had been the news about Thomas.

'When you get to my age Kate you become accustomed to losing dear friends but we haven't seen the last of Thomas. He's with your grandmother I don't doubt. Thank you for bringing him home. The spot where you buried him, under the magnolia was one of his favourite haunts.'

'Yes Mrs Sullivan told us where to put him.'

Jack and his granddaughter had a lot to catch up on. He had travelled extensively in France, England and Ireland, reconnecting with old comrades from the first world war and with family and friends, as well as giving a series of lectures on political theory. He was happy to share these experiences with Kate and also very keen to catch up on local family news.

'How is young Brian getting on? Is he keeping out of trouble?'

'He's a reformed character Grandad. He's hard at work picking apples down on lesser C at the moment. Before that he was a cleaner at Hollybank.'

'The mental hospital! That sounds like our Brian. Trust him to find exotic places to work in. There's no sign of him becoming dull and boring in his old age?'

'Not a chance in the world.'

'And little Maggie is she well?'

'I think she is finding Tim a bit overbearing.'

'Not surprising.

'Tim's a bit of a rough diamond. His heart's in the right place but he's a bit of a rogue. When he was at boarding school, he used to sneak into this place and help himself to the liquor cabinet whenever I was away at weekends. He thinks I don't know - must have gotten his own key cut somehow. He is too old for Maggie. Do you think I should have a word next time I see him?'

'I don't think that'll be necessary Grandad. 'I think their "relationship" is on its last legs.'

The old man and his granddaughter had a very enjoyable weekend. They did a lengthy tour of the gardens which were dormant in the impending winter cold. When the weather permitted, Jack would start preparations for the spring and do a bit of judicious winter pruning. For the moment, the ground was very wet under foot.

' The spring bulbs will be a little while yet but it won't be too long.'

It was on the Saturday afternoon that Kate broached the subject of "Dandillion."

'Of course,' said Jack. 'It interested that young chap who came here with you that time. What was his name?'

'Hugh Conroy.'

'That's right. He was very excited about it, wasn't he? Well the poem is only a couple of thousand words. Do you want to make a copy of it for him? A single exercise book would do it. I may even have one about the place that you could use.'

By Sunday afternoon the transcription was complete. Kate had neat and elegant handwriting and the finished product could be used as a template by any of the others who wanted to make their own copies. After dinner that night, Kate brought Norian Fairchild back into the conversation.

'Who was he exactly Grandad?'

'He was a very interesting character. I met him in my university days. The Fairchilds were a very old family and very reclusive. I was more aware of them through the trail of legal documentation generated by their property interests than any social contact, until Norian and I became friends. I knew a few of his cousins through work before I got into politics but not in a social way.

'In many ways, Norian seemed old beyond his years and yet he retained a child like quality an innocence if you will. He looked very young, like a teenager. His company was very enjoyable and lighthearted, but there was an underlying, wistful sadness about him.'

'Did he have many other friends?'

'He was universally popular and a welcome member of my general circle of friends. Most of the girls I knew were very taken with him. I think they wanted to mother him as well as get into bed with him.'

'Grandad! That's a bit risqué for your vintage.'

'Kate my dear. Things were swinging long before the swinging sixties,' the old man laughed. 'They might have been more discreet about it in those days but not always. Human nature never changes, nothing new under the sun as they say.'

'I guess you're right. Mum and Dad were a shotgun job weren't they?'

Jack smiled. 'That was much later. But getting back to what I was saying, you must understand Kate, that the so called 'Great War', I never did like that term, was an horrific disaster which wiped out most of my generation and left those of us who survived, mentally scarred and traumatised. Going to university in the early twenties was a time of escape and trying to recapture our innocence.'

'Was Norian in the war too?'

'Not as a soldier but he drove ambulances. I didn't meet him until after the war but he told me about it later.'

'Did he study law like you?'

'No, Classics.'

'And what do you make of his poem?'

'To be honest I still don't know what to make of it. I get it down and read it every now and then. I assume it is autobiographical in some way. He called his yacht "Dandillion".

'But if it is autobiographical, the symbolism and imagery are too deep for me to understand. The poem remains a complete mystery to me.'

'It makes for an interesting read,' said Kate. 'Although all that stuff about faerie kings and immortal elves smacks of 'Lord of the Rings.'

'It does rather but "Dandillion" was written in the early 1920s, if not before. 'The Hobbit' wasn't published til 1937 and 'Lord of the Rings' came out in the 1950s. As far as I know, Norian knew nothing of Tolkien and his poem is completely original. What it really means however is anybody's guess.'

'Did you ever discuss it with him?'

'The opportunity didn't arise. I never saw him again after the day he gave it to me. I realized later that it was his farewell gift. He is probably dead and buried by now, 1926 was a long time ago. Unless of course he *is* immortal, which I very much doubt. Anyway I hope your copy will satisfy Hugh's curiosity. He was saying that there was a picture of Norian in his landlady's house. Is she someone of my age?'

'A similar age, yes.'

'She might be one of his old flames. He had a couple of favourites I remember and I know of at least two who bore his children. They must have been heartbroken when he disappeared.'

~~~§~~~

On Monday morning after mass and breakfast with her grandfather, Kate drove back to Denistone armed with her copy of "Dandillion" and Jack's reminiscences about Norian Fairchild. She decided that the best way to generate copies of the poem was to type it and use the 'Gestetner' machine in the uni Library. Four copies should be enough, one each for Hugh and Lucy, one for Brian and one for Robert. If by any chance more copies were needed she could run them off. By Wednesday afternoon the task was done. Brian's copy was in the mail with a covering
~~~

letter and she would deliver the others to Gracechurch street on the weekend.

16 : Dandillion the White Ship

I am a lonely mariner
An exile and a prisoner.
The ocean is my prison
And my cell a white ship.

What crime have I committed?
What sentence do I serve?
My children are my lasting crime.
My sentence is my endless life.

The ocean is my prison
And my cell a white ship

I MY CHILDHOOD

My Father is a Faerie King.
He journeyed to this world of men
With his closest family and friends
To learn the ways of humankind.

In four great ships with carven prow
They crossed the intervening seas
Sailed up the river Parfentine
And for a time they settled there.

They journeyed from the Deathless
Realm
Where long our kind have made their
home.
And whence in time we must return
When summoned by the ones who
rule.

I was born here in this world of men
The only world I've ever known.
All I knew of the Deathless Realm
Was nursery rhyme and children's tales.

At first I was a lonely child
And six long years elapsed before
Another faerie child was born.
So I looked elsewhere for company.

II DANIEL

Daniel was my childhood friend
A mortal child, a miller's son.
We rambled through our childhood days
Through woodland glades and meadow
lands.

Sometimes we played with little boats
Or helped his father in the mill.

We rode the wains at harvest time
Each day brought new things to explore.

One day against my father's will
I sailed my skiff on the Parfentine
A rolling river broad and deep,
And prone to sudden squalling winds.

That day my skiff was overturned.
Poor Daniel saw it from the shore.
He braved the River Parfentine
And swam to try and rescue me.

In time I brought my skiff to rights
And only then saw Daniel's plight.
I sailed towards him with all speed
But all my efforts were in vain.

I dragged him from the roiling stream
And sadly brought him back to land.
Like myself just ten years old,
My closest, dearest friend lay dead.

Up 'til then I'd not seen death,
Complacent in my deathlessness
But now I saw its consequence
In Daniel's family's cruel distress.

My Father took me to their home
To share their grief and mourn with them
To see their tearful suffering
And with these words to ease their pain.

'Beyond the islands of the Moon
We know your son is living still.
In time you will re-join him there
And never part from him again.'

'These things you see with elvish eyes'
The grieving Miller answered him.
'But death alone can reunite us
With the son that we have lost.

'Your elven eyes can see beyond.
But we miss Daniel here and now.
We ache to see him in our grief.
Such grief is pain beyond your ken.'

To my Father I then spoke.
'Father, gift them with our sight.
Show them Daniel living still
Beyond the Islands of the Moon.'

'Norian you are asking much.'
My Father said, 'For though we share

A common maker with mankind
Our feet are set on different paths.

'Death is the burden they must bear
While we must bear with deathlessness.
For a given time our paths may cross
But the Maker alone knows to what end.

'Mankind has grown from mud and mist
And strives through life and death for
light.
We must grow from air and light
Becoming one with all that is.

'Men can learn from what we teach
But understanding grows within.
It can't be bought it must be earned.
It can't be given as a gift.'

'But surely Father,' I exclaimed
'By giving up his life for mine
Daniel earned the gift of light
For those who love and grieve for him.'

'My son there is light in what you say
And much that I must contemplate.
For this brief time I will grant your wish.
And the Millers will find peace in sleep.'

We gathered then round Daniel's bed.
And father sang an ancient song
Transporting their enchanted minds
Through realms of sleep and waking
dream.

And they beheld the Outer Isles
The elusive Islands of the Moon
From whence no Mortal can return
That most men only see in death.

And they saw Daniel in the care
Of family who had gone before.
He waved and smiled as through a veil
Which only love could penetrate.

Long hours they stood in conversation
Elders and descendants both
Under the Outer Islands' Spell
While starlit waves around them broke.

At last my Father called them back,
The Miller's little family
And they slept easy in their beds
In sweetened grief suffused with joy.

Daniel's love slept with them all
And with them woke to face the dawn

And all the days that lay ahead,
A gentle hero to us all.

III THE COVENANT OF NONESUCH

When another seven days had passed
My Father, Mother and myself
Journeyed to the Miller's house
With healing words and other gifts.

We took the makings of a meal
And for that time they were our guests.
A gentle happy meal was shared
And then my Father spoke these words.

'On the day that Daniel died,
At my son's request I granted you
A glimpse of Daniel beyond death
An instance of our elven sight.

'This was to ease your sorrowing.
Daniel died for my son's sake.
And we are chastened by your grief.
It is a burden we must share.

'That night I said that our two kinds
Have separate paths that they must
 tread.

But our two families have been joined
By Daniel's selfless sacrifice.

'We are forever in your debt
A debt we'll struggle to repay.
But I now see how it can be done
If you will hear me and agree.

'I have decided, should you wish
To gift your family with our sight
At all times and in all things
Beyond the scope of humankind.

'This must be done in secrecy
Lest stress and tension should arise
Among others jealous of your gift
And the bond our families share.

'The gift once given must be used
In secrecy to serve mankind
And to rescue children cast away
By cruelty and abandonment.

'To do this you must first remove
Your loved ones quietly from here
To settle in a secret place
And build another village there.'

The miller's daughter was dismayed.
'Must we then leave all our friends?'
Her father shared her sad concern.
'This gift seems more like punishment.'

'Hear him out' my mother said.
'Our folk will keep you company.
And you may bring your living kin
And closest friends if they so choose.

'Not all at once but by degrees
In secrecy they can withdraw
From here beside the Parfentine
To share your new life far away.'

The Miller and his family
Were unpersuaded by these words
And with anxious glances they displayed
Uncertainty and deep concern.

Then Dan the Miller spoke again
'Your gift is exile from our kind.
That is how it seems to us.
How can exile heal our pain?'

'Think back to the night of Daniel's
 death,'
My Father said, 'and what you shared

With him and all your parted kin,
Those hours of sweet communal bliss.

'Accept the gift of Elven sight
And that communion will be yours
At all times and beyond all days
Death shall divide you never more.

'In both worlds shall you live at once,
Like Elvenkind and, should you wish,
You need not suffer mortal death
But choose your final crossing time.

'To journey to the Outer Isles
When your earthly duties are complete.
Bodily to journey forth
Unto the Islands of the Moon.'

They sat in silence for a time
In wonderment and deep amaze
Considering my Father's words
Deeply in their inmost hearts.

Then raptured glances were exchanged
And suddenly their thoughts found voice
In a babble of excited words.
They understood my Father's gift.

Then my Father spoke again.
'Of all the gifts I can bestow
This is the greatest I can give
To mend your grief and heal your hearts.

'Only mortal bodies die
But men can't see beyond that death.
In grief they must rely on faith
And hope that souls continue on.

'To you I give that certainty
You will become half-elven kind.
This bond our families can share
As Daniel's lasting legacy.

'All your descendants from this day
By right of birth shall also share
This blessing that I here bestow
Upon you all if you agree.

'To children that you take in care
Abandoned, orphaned or abused,
From anywhere around the world,
The gift is yours to freely give.'

The miller clasped my Father's hands.
'We accept your gracious gift

For the kinship of our families
And the many blessings it will bring.

'We will found a settlement
To ratify our covenant
Like no other will it be
And so 'Nonesuch' shall be its name.'

IV MY YOUTH

In time my childhood days went by
Yet no one took poor Daniel's place.
I showed my family full respect
But spent more time with mortal folk.

I shared their labour and their toil.
The farming life appealed to me.
I learned their lore of husbandry
Of raising crops and tending stock.

I found that I had healing skills
That mortal men did not possess.
Men and beasts and plants alike
I cured their ills and helped them thrive.

In my sixteenth year I met a girl
Sweet Madelaine of fourteen years.
Our hearts and souls and bodies woke
And melding we became one being.

At last I was alone no more
In her I found myself complete
My every yearning satisfied
All that I am I gave to her.

We farmed a little piece of land.
It was her father's wedding gift.
My parents looked on in dismay
For what our destinies would be.

Two healthy sons were born to us
The image of their mother's kin.
And then two daughters elven fair
Sweet echoes of the Deathless Realm.

We nurtured them and watched them grow.
They founded families of their own.
We treasured every newborn soul,
My dearest Madelaine and I.

We were together sixty years
And in that time I saw her fade
Her fragile beauty withering
But ageless was the love she gave.

At last I lost her to the grave
And a sickness that I could not cure.

Our mortal children mourned with me
And her sweet loss I still endure.

V EXILE

I am a lonely mariner
An exile and a prisoner.
The ocean is my prison
And my cell a white ship.

Why must I journey far and wide?
Why is it I can never rest?
Why is no place home to me?
How has this become my fate?

I am a prince in endless exile.
I loved a girl of other kind,
A mortal girl of fleeting grace.
And we conceived a mortal child.

My deathless family was dismayed
They feared a partly mortal child
Could never claim my heritage
Being in part her mother's kin.

They bade me cleave to my own kin
To make the voyage our kind must make
To our ancient home beyond the bounds
Of earth and time of space and death.

I cursed that homeland as a place
I had neither seen nor wished to see.
My curse was met with banishment
Despite my father's earnest pleas.

In time my family left this world
When I was only five years wed.
'Twas then my banishment bit hard
And ever since, my heart has bled.

They live now in the Deathless Realm
And earthbound here I still remain
With all my earthly flesh and blood
While generations fall like leaves.

Centuries passed and their numbers grew
Spreading around this mortal globe.
A second exile then I chose
And hid from them my agelessness.

The generations come and go
And still I watch them all unseen.
They bud and bloom then wither and fall
Earthward and begin anew.

I wish that I could also die
And thus escape my deathlessness.

But my life and I are from elsewhere
I'm destined for a different fate.

VI AMNESTY

Long years elapsed and centuries
And very little change occurred
'Til finally an offer came
Which saw my circumstances shift.

An overture was made to me
Through visitations in my sleep.
The banishment remained in force
But mercy of a kind was shown.

Counsel visited my dreams,
An understanding of my past.
The clear responsibility
Of actions for their consequence.

My exile had been self-imposed
By things I'd done and words I'd said.
It was I who cursed the Deathless Realm
And I who wed a mortal wife.

Neither had been done before
By any person of my kind.
I alone of all my blood
Had dared to curse the Deathless Realm.

I alone had sired a race
Of mortal kind with elven seed.
My blood line spreads around the world
And to these children I am bound.

Long years I hid myself from them,
Hid from them my agelessness.
But now in dreams I was compelled
To show myself by claiming kin.

The Nonesuch Charter would expand
To my descendants if they wished
To share the gifts of elven sight
And access to the Outer Isles.

I was commanded to construct
Dandillion the white ship
To ferry any of my kin,
Who so desired, to the Outer Isles.

Embarking at the 'Cypress Gate'
In secrecy to make our way
From rivulet to open sea,
To that sea beyond the light of day.

Where the Outer Islands lie
In mystic mist and lambent light

Mid the sparkling foam of starlit seas
Where Madelaine forever waits.

Though I can take them to those Isles
I myself can't go ashore
Where Madelaine, made young again,
Welcomes our descendants home.

I can but fondly wave to her
And she can do no more for me.
While the banishment remains in force
And ever earthbound I remain.

My heart and Madelaine's are one
But never can our bodies touch
'Til the banishment has been revoked
And I am free to leave this world.

The ocean is my prison
And my cell a white ship.

17: Cards on the Table

It was lunch time on the last Friday in May, Brian went along to the post office on the off chance of mail.

'Hullo Brian,' said Mrs Townsend, 'there's a parcel for you. Not just a letter this time.'

'Thanks Mrs T,' said Brian, smiling as he recognized Kate's handwriting.

'You're on the last lap now with the apples. A few more weeks will see it done for another year. Make the most of this lovely mild day. There won't be many more of them this side of Spring time.'

'No I guess not. Old Riley has been warning me what to expect.'

'I suppose you'll be off back to the big Island as soon as you can, what with a young lady waiting for you.'

'That's right. I've loved it down here but I am really missing Kate.'

'Only a few more weeks son, Cheerio for now.'

'Bye Mrs T.'

Walking back along the road, Brian opened the parcel. There was a brief note from Kate saying she would write more soon and then there was the transcript. He started reading as he walked along. He had no idea what to expect and he approached it with an open mind, quickly becoming absorbed in the rhythmic language and the imagery.

He couldn't immediately see what relevance it had to Jim being rescued at sea by Norian Fairchild; to Robert's alternative history of the Cumberlands; or Harry and Maude Penruddock and their dog named Norian. He just treated it as a piece of literature and was favourably impressed. Reluctantly, he left the document on his bed and made himself a substantial cheese sandwich (his lunch) which he ate as he walked back to work in the orchard.

<p style="text-align:center">~~~§~~~</p>

As Brian pulled on his picker's bag, Kate was driving out of Ross, bound for Darlington. She had read her copy of "Dandillion" a few times but had to put it aside and return to her studies. She was a relative newcomer to the quest being pursued by Hugh, Lucy and Robert and she didn't know what they hoped to learn from the transcript.

As she read the poem, she tried to reconcile the character of the poet with her grandfather's description of the Norian Fairchild that he knew personally. There was no humour of any kind in the writing but there was plenty to explain the underlying wistful sadness her grandfather had spoken of.

She felt that she had gained a kind of stereoscopic sense of the man and his pain; the university student of the 1920's and his figurative representation in the poem. She dismissed the talk of immortality as promptly as her grandfather had. It was just poetic licence but she thought it was an effective poetic device to capture the pain of lifelong grief and separation. She looked forward with interest to hearing the impressions and responses of the others in Darlington.

<p style="text-align:center">~~~§~~~</p>

Most of that Friday evening at Gracechurch Street was spent reading and re-reading the poem. Lucy cooked up some "spag bol" to sustain them. The only preconceptions she had to inform her reading were the accounts of the small children in the exercise books from the cellar.

'One of the kids in the exercise books referred to the Cypress gate and a stream,' she said as they sat down to eat the meal she had prepared.

'What are your first impressions?' asked Kate as she primed her fork with spaghetti.

'Confusion,' said Hugh. 'I suppose I got myself into the habit of expecting "Dandillion" to answer all our questions about Norian Fairchild. But this poem poses more questions than it answers. It's not what I expected at all. All that stuff about fairies and immortal elves is a bit rich in this day and age.'

'Yes,' said Kate. 'I said to Grandad that it smacked of "Lord of the Rings" but, as he pointed out, "Dandillion" was written in the early 1920's, if not before, and "Lord of the Rings" came out in the 50's. Even "The Hobbit" didn't come out till the early 30's. Grandad is sure that Norian knew nothing about Tolkien or his work.'

'I envy your grandad,' said Lucy, having actually met Norian Fairchild and gone to uni with him. Although come to mention it, I suppose Jim Lovegrove has met him as well.'

'Speaking of Jim, said Hugh, 'I've just remembered something extraordinary that he told me in August last year. It was the first thing about him that made me wonder if perhaps he wasn't all there. He turned up here at the flat one night and started spouting all this stuff about gateways out of this world.

'He went looking in graveyards and comparing the number of pre - convict family names on the headstones with the number of convict family graves. He reckoned there were hardly any graves of pre - convict families. I said perhaps they were buried on the private islands but he reckoned that they weren't actually dead. Norian took them from this world on his boat and they avoided death. If you could stow away on his boat or follow it in another boat you could avoid death too.

'I thought he'd gone barking mad. When I asked him where he got the idea from he said the exercise books from the cellar. I still thought he was crazy but now I've read "Dandillion" that section "The Covenant of Nonesuch" seems to be saying something very similar.' He thumbed through his copy. 'This bit. "You need not suffer mortal death but choose your final crossing time………Bodily to journey forth unto the Islands of the Moon." However did Jim cotton on to a such an exotic concept of his own accord? And the poem seems to bear out his outlandish theory.

'And another thing I've just remembered from that night. Apparently, when he rescued Jim, one of the first things Norian Fairchild said to him was "Well you're back. You very nearly crossed over but now you're back". At the time I thought it just meant Jim had nearly died. Jim thought that too, to begin with but then he began to think differently-obviously.'

'How come you've never mentioned any of this before?' Lucy asked.

'To tell you the truth, I'd forgotten all about it 'til now and anyway, Jim swore me to secrecy at the time.'

'That'd be right. Knowing Jim, he probably hasn't shared all the exercise books with us. He could be sitting on books which contain more of the story. That'd be typical.'

'There's a bit here in "Amnesty" said Kate. " The Nonesuch Covenant would expand to my descendants if they wished, to share the gift of Elven sight and access to the Outer Isles." Some old timers refer to the Cumberlands as the Outer Islands. I've heard Grandad use the expression.'

'In the poem, the terms "Outer Islands" and "Islands of the Moon" seem to be interchangeable,' said Lucy as she began to wash up the dishes.

'Are we meant to take the poem literally or is it allegorical?' Kate wondered as she picked up a tea towel. 'I can't really accept all that stuff about immortals and avoiding death.'

By 10.30 Kate's eyes were starting to close by themselves.

'I'm going to have to go to bed. The drive from Ross always tires me out. I'll see you in the morning.'

She left Hugh and Lucy still poring over the poem and went into Brian's room. The bed had been freshly made up and there was a note and a small parcel on the pillow. The note was composed of letters cut from a variety of different publications.

Miss Mahoney

Your Secret Is safe With us.

Kate opened the package to find her knickers, which Hugh had discovered during his moment of crisis, all freshly laundered and smelling of honeysuckle from a little cake of scented soap that they were wrapped around. She smiled.

'I wondered where they had got to.'

~~~§~~~

By the following Tuesday, Robert had read his copy of "Dandillion". Lucy had dropped it around to his parents' place on Sunday evening on her way home from Gracechurch Street. Robert's reaction had been one of disappointment and frustration. He didn't have a romantic bone in his body and thought the poem was a heap of soppy, sentimental crap. He wanted tangible forensic evidence to quantify and substantiate his theories.

He had received a phone call from Hugh, inviting him to come to O'Brien's the next evening to compare their thoughts about the poem. He welcomed this opportunity to exchange ideas. It would give him a chance to share a few discoveries of his own. He had persevered with his telephone directory and electoral roll searches and had enjoyed some success.

Wednesday night came around and Madge poured their drinks with the slightest of winks at Hugh that only he picked up and he blushed.

'OK Robert,' said Lucy as soon as they were seated. 'What did you think of it?'

'I was pretty bloody disappointed Lucy, to be honest. It was just a load of soppy poetry.'

'Now don't go off half cocked. You knew all along that it was going to be a poem. How many times did you read it? Please say it was more than once.'

'No actually. Once was enough.'
~~~

'You did go off half cocked. Look Robert, it's a substantial document we know to have been written by Norian Fairchild. He wrote it to communicate something. It was a gift for Kate's grandfather. But even though they were good friends, he can't make head or tail of it.

'We have to try and work out what Norian was trying to say and also pick up on any clues or references that might help us in our quest.'

'But all that stuff about immortality gives me the creeps.' Robert had received the standard Cumberland education in a catholic school. Its religious instruction about life and death, Heaven and Hell had terrified him then and it still did. He conquered his fear by adopting a shield of scepticism. It served him well enough as long as he didn't look too closely at what he was being sceptical about.

'But Robert, you know there's something about Norian that is out of the ordinary. Remember when he rescued Jim and the money he gave him. All of it was brand new and yet it pre-dated 1920 and then there was that painting of Dandillion winning a race at the Cork Regatta in 1837, skippered by N. Fairchild. And don't forget Kate's Grandfather was at uni with him in the 1920's.'

'That could have been **his** grandfather at uni and the guy at the regatta **his** great great grandfather or something. And anyway, we only know that the bloke at the regatta was N. Fairchild. It mightn't have been Norian. It could have been Nigel or Nicholas or Noddy for all we know.'

Alarm bells began ringing for Lucy. She didn't like the belligerent tone creeping into Robert's voice.

'Remember the exercise books from the cellar, Robert. We think the poem is the story that the kids were trying to tell. The true meaning of the poem could answer all our questions and that meaning is hidden somewhere in the text of the poem.'

'Oh you mean like a code,' said Robert, beginning to sound both mollified and interested.

'Yes a code if you like,' said Lucy, relieved that the crisis seemed to have passed. 'So have another look and see if you can find anything.'

Fortuitously, speaking for the first time, Hugh calmed the situation further.

'You were saying on the phone the other night that you'd had some luck with your own research.'

'Oh yes. I thought of a way of tracking down where the pre-convict families live, blindingly simple really. Remember Hugh when you checked the rating records of some of the cul-de-sacs, the rates were all paid by the estate of N Fairchild.'

'I only checked for the cluster at Montrose Court that Lucy visited when she was little.'

'No matter. I realized peoples' names and addresses would all be published in phone books and on the electoral roll. So I started checking them out for pre-convict names.

'They were in the minority. The bulk of surnames were of Irish and therefore convict extraction. However in the wake of the two world wars there was an influx of immigrants, again mainly Irish but also English, Scots, Welsh, Greek and Italian.

'The pre-convict families tend to be thinly spread throughout the whole community but I found a small but significant number of pre-convict clusters, mainly in

White Thorn, Mill Farm and West Darlington. I walked to the addresses and almost all of them were in cul-de-sac clusters. The next step is to find out the age and occupation of the people living there. I'm still working out the best ways of doing this.'

'Well to start with,' said Lucy, 'does the supermarket where you work do home deliveries?'

'Yes mainly for customers with special needs, the elderly, frail and the disabled.'

'Well there's a starting point, see if there's anyone like that receiving deliveries in the cul-de-sacs.'

'That's a great idea Lucy. I might see if I can go on the actual delivery rounds.'

'That could earn you some browny points with your boss.'

'That wouldn't do any harm. So far I've only looked in the Greater Darlington area. I've still got to do Carlingford and the Northwest Coast.'

'You're not likely to find any of that sort of architecture outside Darlington. The art teacher who originally sparked my interest in the subject said it was mostly confined to Darlington.'

'It would still be good to check phone books and electoral rolls for up north and the other Islands too,' said Hugh. 'Do you need a hand?'

'I'll let you know,' said Robert, now sounding much more relaxed and cheerful. They finished up their drinks and went home.

Hugh walked Lucy to her door.

'That was touch and go there for a while with Robert. You could see him working up to an explosion. Thank God you got him to think of the poem as a code.'

'That was God's work more than mine, definitely divine providence. He'll forget it's a poem now and examine it forensically syllable by syllable. He'll probably even plot the punctuation marks on a graph.'

'Well at least that'll keep him out of trouble.'

'Will you come in for a cup of tea?'

'No it's a bit late. You're more than welcome to come back to my place.....for a cup of tea.'

'That was downright mischievous. We've both got work tomorrow. Off home with you, you wicked, wicked man!!'

~~~§~~~

Next day, while Robert sought to inveigle his way onto the grocery delivery rounds, Brian and Mervyn were given an interesting assignment. While the rest of the pickers continued to pick in the main orchards, old Tom took them some miles away to a small and ancient little orchard near an old cemetery. They had become used to riding on the tractor with the wind in their hair, hanging on for dear life on unsealed back roads. It was part of the charm of the rustic life that particularly appealed to Brian.

The old orchard was like nothing they'd ever seen before. The trees were ancient, gnarled and huge. They hadn't been pruned for decades. The apples were old varieties that hadn't been commercially harvested for more than fifty years. Some of them were huge, looking more like small pumpkins than apples. All of them had been afflicted by an aphid infection which old Tom called "wooly aphis".

This would normally render them unsellable but the Boss had found a market. They could be sold for juicing. For some reason, the aphids, which appeared as little,
~~~

white, wispy fibres, did not preclude them from juicing. Brian theorised that the aphids might have been a valuable source of extra protein.

Be that as it may, the orchard was being harvested for the first time in half a century. The place had the air of an old church or museum and both Brian and Mervyn felt a reverence for the venerable old trees.

'It's only for juice boys, so just rip 'em off any old how, the quicker the better,' Tom had said before he drove off but they ignored him and picked respectfully.

They worked steadily and, partly because of the size of the fruit, the bin began to fill up quickly. By 10 a.m. it was full and after about a quarter of an hour they could hear old Tom's tractor in the distance. They spent the interval exploring the orchard and its surrounds. The cemetery came up to its southern boundary. Judging by the look of the moss covered headstones the graveyard was at least as old as the orchard if not older.

'That would be worth a bit of an explore later, if we get the chance,' said Brian. He was young, in love and had everything to live for. Therefore he didn't share Robert's morbid fears of death and mortality, nor did he need the shield of cynicism. It would be hard to find a less cynical person than Brian. The picturesque old graveyard thrilled and charmed him with its ancient gothic beauty in the same way that the old orchard deeply moved him. It all made for a fascinating change of scenery, the chilly wind and frosty morning notwithstanding.

In due course, Tom arrived with two empty bins and loaded up the bin which was full of the morning's work.

'It was a bloody nightmare bringing two bins together but they'll keep you busy 'til afternoon tea time.

Gettin' the full bin home safe on these roads won't be any bloody picnic either. I'll see youse later.'

They worked through 'til midday and then they stopped for lunch.

'Tom's going to have to get a move on, said Mervyn. 'We're onto the second bin already.' He looked across to the cemetery and saw someone bending over one of the graves. It was a fairly recent grave and the dirt hadn't fully subsided. The person stood up to straighten her back and Mervyn recognized the long red hair of Elsie Viney. She appeared to be talking to the grave or presumably to its occupant as she gathered up the withered flowers and did a bit of judicious weeding. Beside her on the ground was a basket full of fresh blooms.

'I'll be back in a minute,' Mervyn said to Brian and he headed for the cemetery.

'Be careful,' said Brian who had now seen Elsie.

As Mervyn walked through the cemetery gate, he heard a ferocious barking. From out of nowhere, two enormous black German shepherds appeared and set up a menacing growl, while displaying a fearsome selection of fangs. Elsie looked around and saw the situation.

'It's all right Brutus. Fang come here. Sorry about that Mervyn. They won't hurt you, at least not unless I tell them to. What are you doing here?'

'We're picking the old orchard for juice.'

'It'll be full of wooly aphis.'

'Apparently that doesn't matter for juice. Is this someone close to you?' he asked, indicating the grave.

'Yeah. My Uncle Terry, my mum's little brother. He was always very kind to me. He died in a car crash back in January. He owned Brutus and Fang, so I've adopted them.

I look in on him when I can just so he doesn't get lonely. I always used to tell him my troubles when he was alive. I don't see why I have to stop just because he's dead.'

'So you believe in life after death?'

'Of course. Don't you?' Mervyn was silent for a moment as he considered his response and Elsie started selecting and arranging the fresh flowers for the grave. She was back in her blue jeans and gym boots with the shapeless old grey jumper which nevertheless didn't completely conceal her lissome, slender shape as she moved, almost in a lounging way, about the grave, reaching over and across it to tidy it up. It looked for all the world like tucking someone up in bed.

'Well,' she said gently, 'do you or don't you?'

'I'm not sure,' he finally ventured.

'Does that mean you're an atheist?'

'Oh no. I'm pretty sure I believe in God. My problem is that for a little while I thought I was the man himself.'

Elsie burst out laughing.

'You thought you were God! Come off it. Seriously?!'

'I used to be a bit full of myself,' said Mervyn sheepishly. 'Delusions of grandeur I think it's called.'

'Sounds like it, thinking you were God. I never heard the like. He'd have a bit to say about that, I reckon.'

'I think he'd find it funny, just like you did.'

'I don't think he'd hold it against you afterwards though, especially if he got a laugh out of it.'

'How old was your uncle?' Mervyn was eager to change the subject.

'He was a couple of years younger than Dave and Bob. He was a surprise baby like I was.'

'What do you mean?'

'He happened when grandma thought her childbearing days were over.'

'And did that happen with you?'

'Yep. Ma reckons I must have come out in the bathwater.'

'Pardon?'

'Living in the country on tank water, particularly in the summer, people tend to share the same bathwater. After I came along, Ma always made sure she got first go in the bath before Dad had a chance to muddy the waters so to speak. I don't think you can conceive that way though.

'My guess is they got drunk one night and had a tumble which they didn't remember next morning. I always use the shower. They had that put in when I was born. What are you going to do after the apples are picked?'

'No idea, head back to the big Island I guess although it is very nice here. I'll miss you.' Mervyn immediately mentally kicked himself and wished he could unsay it. Elsie's face coloured.

'That's a strange thing to say. You barely know me.'

'I meant your music, your singing.'

'Oh that.' She was still blushing. 'It's just a bit of fun. Anyway it's time we were gone. Come on boys.' Brutus and Fang got to their feet, and looked Mervyn up and down suspiciously as Elsie gathered up the spent flowers in her basket. 'Bye Uncle Tez, bye Mervyn. I've enjoyed our chat.'

She gave Mervyn an uncertain, puzzled 'almost' smile and then she was gone. Mervyn wasn't sure whose conversation she had enjoyed, his or Uncle Terry's. There was a car parked on the road close by and within a few minutes Elsie had loaded up the dogs and driven away.

As he walked back to the old orchard, Mervyn wished there was a train he could throw himself under. His body language made it abundantly clear that now was not the time for conversation. Nothing was said for the rest of the day. Mervyn smouldered painfully and morosely in isolation. Brian compassionately trod on eggshells, making sure he never approached the bins while Mervyn was there.

When both bins were full, Mervyn slumped under a tree and rolled a rare cigarette. From a discreet distance, Brian could see that he was crying. With his own heart wrung for his new comrade he ventured a few steps towards him. But with a gentle shake of his head, Mervyn warned him away. There was still no sign of Tom so Brian went over to check out the cemetery.

The oldest headstones were half a dozen dated 1782. Their inscriptions read, 'Unknown sailor, death by shipwreck.' It took a while to discern the old writing because of the moss. These burials had obviously taken place long before the wreck of the Dryad. This would be news for everyone back home. None of the other graves were older than 1810 and the names were mostly Irish. He kept a keen eye out for the name Penruddock, but no one of that name was buried there.

18: Another Winter

The month of June was a week old and, in the orchard, winter had started to bite. Most mornings, the pickers woke to find the ground blanketed in a heavy frost. The river which formed the boundary to the orchard flowed eastward into the Tasman Sea. During the winter months, fog gathered in the river valley over night. If the morning winds allowed, the fog would follow the watercourse and be funnelled out to sea.

If the wind was in the east, the fog would be trapped and pushed back up the valley and the orchard would be blanketed in cold, dank, dripping mist for much of the day. For the benefit of the pickers, there were fire pots placed strategically around the orchard to warm their hands and dry out their canvas picking bags. This had to be done often because the cold and the damp were relentless.

At about this time every season, Riley questioned why he bothered to pick apples but, as he told a disillusioned Brian and Mervyn, another three weeks would see it done and they could go back home. This was incentive enough for Brian who had Kate to look forward to. Mervyn's future was less certain. There was no woman waiting for him back on the Big Island and no future to speak of. He had wondered about trying to find more work on Lesser Cumberland. Learning to prune the apple trees was suggested but that would mean continuing to work through the winter in the icy weather. However after the encounter with Elsie in the cemetery, he just wanted to get home as soon as he could.

Riley was complacent. He'd resume where he left off, living in the gardener's hut in Cathedral Square. He had secure tenure of a kind there for as long as his old war comrade remained in the employ of the Darlington City Council. As always he'd find some way of landing on his feet. Unlike Brian and Mervyn he didn't have a long future to look forward to.

He had come to terms with death and dying in the trenches on the Western Front. He'd lost good friends there, where life was cheap and the stench of death was everywhere. Many of his comrades relied on prayer to begin with. This remained enough for some but others quickly became disillusioned by the barbarity they witnessed at first hand, a barbarity they were often obliged to practise themselves.

Riley had been born into a devout catholic family, in fact his younger brother was a priest and his older sister was a nun. To begin with, as a child, he believed everything he was taught. Later, with the onset of puberty, his body began to prompt him to follow a contrary path and there was some parting of the ways from Catholicism. But there were little fragments of insight from his religious childhood that stayed with him, elusive and intangible fragments that couldn't be put into words and that other people wouldn't understand.

Like Hugh, Brian and Maggie, Riley had spent his childhood in Middleton, on the north west coast of Greater Cumberland. The sight of the three peaks of Trinity Island had also captured his young imagination. Early in his childhood they became the three ships sailing by in the Christmas Carol. One of his most enduring memories was the sight of the parish women after mass, clustered, gossiping outside the little red brick church, while across the bay behind them, the three peaks of Trinity shone blue in the morning sunlight. All these years later, he still derived peace and a sense of belonging from that comfortable memory.

There was also a recurring dream that had visited his sleep countless times throughout his life, from early childhood to the present day and particularly during the war. In the dream he was burrowing up through a tangled undergrowth of briars and brambles from out of some underground place of confinement. It was in the early pre-dawn. There above him, caught in the brambles was a torn fragment of white cloth that seemed to glow in the darkness; a fragment torn from the clothing or wrappings of someone who had passed that way a few minutes before him. That dream convinced him, at a very early age, that Christ's resurrection was an historical fact. In the trenches, the dream also somehow reassured him that he would survive the war.

These convictions he kept to himself during a long and often difficult life. Although he frequently felt alienated by areas of catholic teaching, he still retained a certain catholic sensibility and a love of the essential, ancient mysteries of his childhood faith. However, he did not wear his heart on his sleeve in such matters. To casual observers and even close friends and associates he gave not the slightest hint of these inner sensitivities.

It was time for the morning tea break and he walked back to the nearest firepot, wiping his hands and fingers on his old tweed overcoat prior to rolling a cigarette.

'This is the coldest bloody winter I can remember,' said Charlie Flint.

'You say that every year Charlie,' said Riley. 'That's not to say it isn't true though. We might be heading for another ice age.'

'Headin' for! It's fuckin here already. It's cold enough to freeze the balls on a billiard table.' Charlie spat what was left of his blackened cigarette into the fire pot and opened his thermos flask for some hot tea.

'At least you've got a missus to go home to and keep you warm at night,' said Riley.

'She's like a block of ice, always has been.'

'Now that's hardly romantic Charlie,' said Dave Viney as he bit into an apple. 'Surely a hot blooded young stallion like you can bring her to the boil.'

'What goes on in my fuckin bedroom is no business of yours you smart alec.'

'Ah so it is a 'fuckin' bedroom then. Not just for sleeping in?'

'Ah piss off!'

Charlie turned his back on Dave and concentrated on drinking his tea. No one was in a hurry to leave the fire pot and start picking again but as usual Riley was the first to put on his picking bag and head back to work. The sun began to break through and the mist began to clear a little.

'Thank God for that,' Brian said as he joined Riley for the first time that day and they shared a tree.

'Yeah if only it would last. Have you got any work lined up for when you go back?'

'Nothing definite. Ray at Hollybank said to come and see him on the off chance so I'll do that. What have you got planned?'

'Back to being a gentleman of leisure. Keep in touch when we get back. I enjoy our conversations. What do you reckon Mervyn will do?'

'I don't know. He's still got it bad for Elsie Viney but he realizes he's too old for her. She's still at school.'

'Yes he's been a bit down in the dumps these last few days.'

'He did talk about going back to Trinity Island to be with his family for a bit and he's getting back into music since he bought that guitar in Woodfield a couple of weeks ago.'

'Ah yes music. Can you make much money being a crooner?'

'He did quite well for a while but he got into booze and drugs and went off the rails.'

'Will you keep in touch with him when you go back?'

'I dunno. I quite like him now that I've got to know him. It's up to him I guess.'

The mist began to thicken again and the brief gleam of sunlight was gone. With the return of the gloom, Riley and Brian withdrew into their private thoughts for a while until Brian broke the silence again about ten minutes later.

'How long have you picked apples for?'

'I've picked on this orchard every season since 1940. So this year is my thirtieth.'

'That's a long time. What's the connection with this place?'

'Well back then, the orchard was owned by the current Mr Murphy's father and his uncle. I was in the army with his uncle and we were good mates. He's dead now but my connection with the family still goes on.'

'Is that why Mervyn and I were able to get a job here, on your say so?'

'Probably. I'm a bit of a fixture here. I've had the same picker's hut every year. It's my second home. All the cooking gear and blankets have been there since 1940 and a lot of my books.

'Back then, the second world war was just getting started. I was only 43 at the time so I probably could have lied about my age and enlisted with the Australians, like Charlie did, but I'd had enough of war in the first show. Back in 1914 everyone was mad keen to go for the adventure. It was a free trip to see 'Mother England' and Europe. People really thought it would all be over by Christmas but it wasn't. It turned out to be a fuckin bloodbath that virtually wiped out a whole generation of young men from all around the world. For some reason, the Cumberland casualties in World War I were exceptionally high. Hardly any of us came back.'

'Things were different the second time. Young Jack Mahoney was the Prime Minister then. He reckoned that the country's population hadn't recovered enough to send its army abroad again in 1940 and I reckon he was right. This time, with the Japs on the march, there was a real possibility that the Cumberlands could be invaded. Of course the bloody Tories attacked Mahoney at the time, saying the empire needed us, but he stuck to his guns and kept our armed forces at home for self defence.

'Mahoney put the Cumberlands onto a full war footing; blackouts, rationing, the lot. Petrol became very scarce. The country's agriculture and industries were used for supporting our allies. He didn't stop individuals like Charlie who enlisted in the Australian army but he made it very clear that the Cumberland armed forces were staying put. He also formed a home guard, a sort of part time territorial army made up of veterans like me to support our regular troops.'

Brian and his parents had arrived in the Cumberlands in 1951 as immigrants from Ireland. He was two years old at the time and now he was keen to learn at first-hand what the war years were like in the archipelago.

'Was there ever really any risk of a Japanese invasion?'

'Bloody oath there was. The Japs meant business. They already had special bank notes printed for when they planned to take over Australia. So the risk was bloody real all right. But fortunately, by the middle of 1942, they were held up. The Yanks were involved by then and there were a couple of big sea battles in the Pacific that went our way. They started to slowly push the Nips back after that and an invasion didn't look likely any more.'

'I never realized that it came that close. I mean the Cumberland Archipelago is miles from anywhere.'

' The world can feel like a pretty small place when trouble comes lookin' for you. Fortunately it didn't come any closer to us. But no one could really rest easy til the whole thing was finally over. But just like the first war, it didn't end all wars. It's still going on. Look at Vietnam.'

'So was Jack Mahoney a successful prime minister?'

'I think he was and he was a very popular one which amounts to the same thing. Him and his father before him, Old Jack Mahoney, they were our most successful Labour Leaders. They were both clever, highly educated men but they had the common touch.'

'Yes Young Jack is a terrific bloke. He's Kate's grandfather I've met him a few times, stayed at his house once.'

'Really! He's young Kate's grandfather! Well bugger me, it's a small world.'

By this time Riley's bag was full and he moved away.

'All right young Brian, I'll leave that last branch to you and head off in search of pastures new.' He came to the bin where Charlie was emptying his bag and still complaining about the cold. He made a mechanical response to Charlie's grumbling but didn't stay to chat. He found a medium size tree that he could handle comfortably on his own, settled down and once more became immersed in his thoughts.

The morning gradually passed and lunch time drew near. One by one the pickers made their way back to the bin. Mervyn and Brian were chatting as Riley walked up. The bin was full and they were waiting for old Tom to bring another empty bin out from the packing shed. The sun had broken through again and the mist was showing signs of lifting. Tom's tractor could be heard in the distance as they leant their laden picking bags against the side of the bin to ease their backs.

<div align="center">~~~§~~~</div>

It was Wednesday night again. Robert had had a week to re-appraise "Dandillion" and he was back at O'Brien's with Hugh and Lucy. The weather was bitterly cold and, since Madge hadn't gotten around to setting a fire in the lounge, they were sitting at a table in the Bar. Madge had waived her long standing rule about ladies in the bar a few times lately, for reasons of convenience. Lucy was now pretty much a regular in her own right and as Brian had once suggested to Madge "who said she was a Lady anyway?" The cold had kept a lot of the regulars away on that particular night so things were pretty quiet.

'Well Robert,' said Lucy when their drinks had been served, 'What have your investigations revealed?'

'No clear answers at this stage Lucy but a few things to follow up. This business about mortals and immortals could just be class distinction, you know middle class versus working class. It's all sounds a bit snobbish if you ask me. Or it could be the difference between pre-convict and convict.'

'I gave a lot of thought to places and place names in the poem. There aren't many. First there's the 'Deathless Realm' and I've no idea what that's meant to be or where it is. Then there's the place the four so-called 'Fairy Ships' sailed to on the river Parfentine, which seems to be the principal setting of the poem.

Then there's 'Nonesuch' which is somewhere away from where the poem is set - far away from the settlement on 'The Parfentine'. Then there are the 'Islands of the Moon' which seem to be interchangeable with 'The Outer Islands'. They can only be reached after you die. But you've said that Kate reckons 'Outer Islands' is just an old fashioned name for the Cumberlands which only adds to the confusion.

'Now this is all just symbols in a poem which could contain a coded meaning or message, but I don't think I know how to dig that meaning or message out of poetic language. You blokes'll have to do that. What I intend to do is work on the two tangible geographic entities, a river called the 'Parfentine' and some place called 'The Cypress Gate' which has access to a rivulet. 'Parfentine' could be an old name for 'The River'. It's funny that our city's river didn't get a more imaginative name than just 'The River.' If I could find either of those two places somewhere here in the real world, I might start to think the poem was believable.'

'Well Robert,' said Lucy as he paused for breath and a sip of beer, 'You certainly have been busy. You deserve a special stamp for good work and a gold star for effort. But you seem to be steering away from the possibility of anything magical or mystical in all of this.'

'I can't prove or quantify anything like that. That's your department and possibly Jim's. Perhaps we should show him "Dandillion" and see what he makes of it. He still doesn't really believe that Hugh found the original. That's why he started acting strange.'

'He's always been strange Robert.'

'Stranger then. And he was in it from the very beginning.'

'What do you think Hugh? Should we bury the hatchet?'

'Probably. I'm still very curious to find out how he got that notion of leaving the world without dying, before ever we got hold of "Dandillion". Was it something he learnt while he was on the boat with Norian Fairchild? We can only find that out by talking to him.'

'OK' said Lucy. 'I'll ask Kate to run off another copy.'

They rugged up and ventured out into the cold.

'It's probably snowing down on Lesser C,' said Hugh as they headed into the icy blast.

<div align="center">~~~§~~~</div>

Madelaine College
Ross
8/6/70

Dear Hugh

Thanks for your last letter. Although you said there is no purpose to be served by us meeting any time in the immediate future, I beg to differ. If you are serious about ending what we had, the least you can do is say it to my face.

I firmly believe we have what it takes as a couple and I deserve another chance to prove it to you.

I have booked a table for two at Montini's for 7.PM on Saturday 13th. In spite of your last two letters saying you won't meet with me, I urge you to be there for both our sakes.

Please be there.

Always your

Maggie.

This letter was waiting for Hugh when he got home from work on Thursday night. His last two letters to Maggie had been emphatic and explicit. The second letter was bordering on brutal. Lucy knew about the exchange of correspondence but kept out of it, other than urging Hugh to be 'firm but kind'. Reluctantly in desperation, Hugh decided that his only option was to simply not show up. Next day he sent her a telegram saying simply, 'I won't be there.' That was as much as he could do.

Maggie arrived at the restaurant twenty minutes early. Giacomo thought it odd that she had brought a bulky overnight bag with her but said nothing as he showed her to her table. It was a busy night and he had plenty of other guests to attend to. By 7.30, Hugh hadn't arrived and Maggie was starting to look pale and fragile. Giacomo asked if she wanted to order for herself but she opted to wait a little longer.

By 8.30 a lot of the guests had paid up and left but Hugh still hadn't arrived. Giacomo was starting to worry. Boy Upson arrived at 9.00 and his booming voice put paid to the awkward silence that had begun to grow. Boy and Maggie were the only two guests by now and Maggie was sobbing quietly in a broken, distraught way.

'She has been stood up by her date,' Giacomo whispered to Boy with a finger to his lips.

'Stood up!' said Boy, miraculously in an undertone. 'Well we can't have that. Whoever stood her up must have rocks in his head. Look at her! She's so pretty. Leave this to me.' He went over to Maggie's table. 'Excuse me Miss, we both seem to be without dinner partners and I was wondering if you'd be my guest.'

Maggie looked up, surprised and unsure. Embarrassed by her teary state, she started to rub her eyes with the back of her hand.

'No don't do that,' said Boy, handing her a clean, folded handkerchief. 'Your table or mine? I assure you my intentions are entirely honourable. Jack here can vouch for my character.'

Giacomo smiled. 'This gentleman is a very good friend of mine Miss. He will cheer you up.'

Maggie looked into Boy's eyes for the first time and saw only genuine concern, a kind of innocence in fact.

'OK,' she said in a shaky voice, 'your table.'

'Excellent, let me escort you,' he almost boomed, taking her elbow and guiding her to her seat.

Maggie's mind was racing. In some ways what was happening seemed so unbelievably corny, like a B-grade movie even down to the clean hanky. But in another way it was just what she needed at that time. It wasn't Cary Grant or Roger Moore who was playing mine host. It was a slightly balding, slightly overweight youngish gentleman. He was well dressed in a conservative, countrified sort of way. He had a very respectful manner and periwinkle blue eyes. She didn't realize how out of character it was for him to speak so gently and quietly.

Maggie had no intention of taking advantage of the fact, but it was patently clear that he was fascinated by her. By the time they ordered their meal, her tears had gone along with the tremor in her voice. At the same time her common sense began to warn her that this might be a set up but Giacomo was a famously well respected man and she didn't think he would be party to anything of that sort. The fact that she didn't have anywhere to sleep that night was a problem, but she would deal with that later. There was always the YWCA.

'And now,' said Boy. 'Tell me all about yourself.'

'Only if you reciprocate.'

'All right. But I asked first. How did you come to be here tonight in such unhappy circumstances?'

Bit by bit, without naming any names, Maggie told him about Hugh and the failed relationship, about heavy handed Tim and the absentee parents in England who weren't a lot of use at the best of times.

Out in the kitchen, Giacomo and his kitchen staff were doing the washing up and marvelling at the fact that they couldn't hear a word that Boy was saying. They took it in turns to sneak glances through the screen to see what was going on. He was definitely talking but, 'wonder of wonders', he was doing it quietly!

Back at the table it was now Boy's turn.

'I'm a bit like you in the absentee parents department. I'm an orphan.'

'Oh I'm sorry,' said Maggie.

'It's all right, I landed on my feet. I was adopted by a childless couple who raised me as their own. I was 20 before I finally found out, so I've never really felt adopted.

When they died they left everything to me. It's a very large property. The rest of the family don't like me very much but that's alright. I don't like them very much.'

A couple of 'Gyro Gearloose light bulbs' lit up in Maggie's mind. Out in the kitchen the wonder and speculation continued.

'Is he drinking?' whispered Giacomo to the current look out.

'Yes,' she whispered back. 'They've started on the bottle of red.'

'I'll serve the soup,' said Giacomo. 'How long before the main course?'

'15 minutes max' said the Chef.

'Yes it was my place where we tried to hold the three day festival,' Boy was saying as Giacomo arrived with the soup.

'Here we are. No more tears? That's what I like to see.' The colour had definitely returned to Maggie's cheeks and she was starting to enjoy herself She had also realised that her host was none other than the 'dreaded' Boy Upson but he was contradicting everything she'd ever heard about him. Hugh was completely forgotten. She wasn't falling for Boy, not by any means. She was just enjoying the unexpected turn of events.

'And the wine is to your satisfaction?'

'As always Jack. As always,' Boy positively purred.

The little Italian shook his head as he walked back to the kitchen to update the others. The meal ran its course. Boy insisted on dessert and gelati was ordered. He also insisted on paying the bill (which was just as well) then he looked at his watch. It was 11.15.

'I've got an early start tomorrow. Can I give you a lift anywhere?' Maggie hesitated. 'You have got somewhere to stay. You didn't come down here without a plan B!'

'I thought I'd stay at the Y,' she said, dreading an invitation back to his place.

'**The Y!**' Boy roared and then collected himself. Someone in the kitchen dropped a saucepan. 'That won't do at all. I'll book you into a good hotel and don't panic it's not the one I'm staying at. Jack can I use your phone?' He called out in a moderate bellow.

'Sure sure. Use the one in the office.'

Half an hour later, Maggie was sitting on a bed in a very expensive hotel room trying to take in what she had just experienced. Boy had left her at reception, saying he would pick her up at 8.30 in the morning and fly her back to Ross. She would be back at Madelaine College by 10.30. She made herself a cup of coffee and took it to bed. She drank her coffee and then, still incredulous but very weary, she fell asleep.

<p style="text-align:center">~~~§~~~</p>

By 8.00 a.m. after a good night's sleep, a shower and a continental breakfast, Maggie was ready and waiting for Boy's arrival. He turned up on the dot of 8:30, wearing tan riding boots, moleskin trousers, pale blue shirt and tweed sports coat, looking every inch the landed gentleman.

'You slept well?'

'Very well thanks and thank you for a wonderful evening last night.'

'My pleasure. I'll pay your bill and we'll be on our way.'

They were soon on the highway, heading out of the city, over 'The River' and on their way to the airfield. It was a small facility across the highway from Darlington's main international airport. It was a base for the aero club, some small charter airlines and two flying schools. Maggie had never flown before and she felt a nervous, excited anticipation as they got out of the car. At that precise moment an Air New Zealand DC9 took off from the main airport and roared its way into the sky, further adding to her excitement.

It was a fine day and the sky was clear.

'We'll get a good view up there today. I'll take us east to the sea, follow the coast up north and then cut back across to my place which isn't far from Ross. Have you flown before?'

'Nope. This'll be my first flight.'

'Well you've got a lovely day for it. It'll be a bit noisy but you'll soon get used to it. There might be a bit of turbulence at times but it's no different to a small boat bobbing up and down on the water.'

They walked past a line of small light planes 'til they came to a trim little Cessna with blue and white livery.

'This is us. I refuelled on Thursday when I arrived so we can take off as soon as I get clearance from the Tower across the road at the main airport.'

While Maggie got settled in her seat and fastened her seat belt, Boy did an external check of the flaps and rudder and removed the chocks and the wires that tethered the plane to the ground.

With all this done, he climbed aboard, belted up and started the engine. It was a deafening roar.

'A bit noisy indeed!' thought Maggie as Boy did an instrument check and began talking to the control tower.

'Foxtrot Tango Lima to Darlington Control.'

Maggie couldn't hear the Tower's responses but after a few exchanges, the plane began to taxi out onto the runway. They reached the runway's end and turned to face into the wind. A few more exchanges with the tower and then Boy opened the throttle. The whole aircraft shook as it gathered speed and began hurtling down the runway. Suddenly the ground fell away beneath them as the plane rose into the air and began climbing.

Maggie was captivated. Soon the plane levelled out and the roar of the engine softened a little. Boy looked across and smiled. He was in his element and in this situation he was obliged to shout at the top of his voice to make himself heard. The world seemed to creep below them at a snail's pace and yet they passed through some wisps of low cloud that sped by giving an indication of the plane's actual speed.

Once over the sea, Boy pointed out sharks and giant rays in the clear waters below. Then the plane banked to the left and they headed north. Away to their left was the rugged east coast of Greater Cumberland. Maggie recognized beaches where she and Brian had swum: all magically transformed and miniaturised.

It was an enchanted time that Maggie never forgot and all so totally unexpected. When she got out of bed the day before at Madelaine College the most she had hoped for was a reconciliation with Hugh. She had not countenanced failing to do so, nor had she looked beyond that eventuality. And now here she was being flown home in a private plane by a complete stranger, reputed to be a crashing boor, who had been charm personified, treated her to a slap up meal and paid for her accommodation in a classy hotel; all without making a single demand on her person.

They banked to the left again and headed back over land. There was a little turbulence as they crossed the coast but nothing to speak of. In time they were flying over pastoral land and losing altitude.

'We're flying over my place now,' Boy shouted, as he circled around a large field that was marked out as a runway. He throttled back and gently, the plane descended until suddenly they were back on the ground again. Boy taxied into a hangar and turned the engine off. The silence was deafening. Back outside, Maggie looked up at the sky and found it hard to believe that she had actually just been up there, hundreds of feet above the ground.

'Well how did you like your first flight?'

'It was wonderful. Thank you.'

'Yes it's great fun. I never get tired of it. Now would you like a cup of tea before I drive you back to Ross? I'll get my housekeeper to brew one.'

For a second Maggie wondered if this was when he would demand something of her but the mention of a housekeeper partially allayed her concerns. She was also beginning to feel that Boy could be trusted.

'It'll have to be a quick cuppa I'm afraid. I've got to be somewhere else after I drop you off at the uni.' As they walked towards the old Georgian homestead he pointed out various items of interest.

'That's where we had the stage for the festival, pity it got washed out. And that's my Brahman bull. For a little while I thought of diversifying into beef but I've thought better of it. I just keep him as a pet now. I call him Mervan.'

'And come and have a look at Nostromo, the derby winner. He's the wonder horse from Lesser C. I'm a co-owner. We're spelling him here until he starts his spring preparation. He could be off to New Zealand or possibly Australia. There's talk of a Cox Plate campaign.'

He whistled and a handsome black thoroughbred with a white blaze on his forehead ambled up to the fence.

'He's quite tame.' The horse nuzzled up against his face. 'You try.' Maggie, who had always loved horses took her turn. As well as a nuzzle she received a complimentary lick of her face. 'He must really like you.'

Inside, the kitchen of the house looked like it hadn't changed in a hundred years. The wall was exposed sandstone and the ancient pipes of the plumbing were in full view.

'Mrs Morgan. Mrs Morgan?' There was no answer. 'She must be at Mass, which reminds me I'll have to go to the vigil mass at six thirty. Just have a seat. I'll be mother. How do you have your tea?'

'White and no sugar.'

It was a very passable cup of tea which was consumed pleasantly, without incident and they were soon speeding away in Boy's burgundy coloured Jaguar, headed for Ross and the university.

19: Riley

While Maggie was being entertained by Boy at Montini's, many miles away in Riley's hut on Lesser Cumberland, Mervyn was finally unburdening himself to Riley and Brian. It seemed that the encounter with Elsie in the cemetery had sapped his morale completely.

I'm worried that Elsie will tell her brothers,' said Mervyn.

'I think that would be highly unlikely son,' said Riley. 'You worry too much and Elsie has probably forgotten all about the whole conversation and never given it another thought.'

'You didn't see the look on her face, the sudden change,' said Mervyn. 'We had been having a lovely conversation and then, when I put my foot in it, she just packed up and left.'

'So how did you put your foot in it exactly?' Brian asked.

'I said I'd miss her when I went back to the big island and she said "That's a strange thing to say. You barely know me." '

'Did you qualify your remark?'

'I tried to. I said I meant I'd miss her music.'

'Well that sounds reasonable.'

'But she just up and left.'

'Had she finished tidying up her Uncle's grave?'

'I dunno. I guess so.'

'Well there you are then. You probably haven't upset her at all. You're worrying too much about nothing.

'And anyway, I thought you had accepted the fact that she is too young for you.'

'Yes I have I suppose, but that doesn't make it any easier. She has such a profound effect on me. You can't just turn that emotional attachment off like a light switch. She's a fascinating person. Her conversation is almost childlike in a way and then she can stop you in your tracks with something quite profound or wise in the ways of the world. I just couldn't bear it if I'd gone down in her estimation.'

Riley became impatient at that point. He wasn't unsympathetic but he thought Mervyn was starting to wallow in self pity.

'I'm getting a bit tired of this conversation. For God's sake man pull yourself together. If you keep working yourself up like this, you'll end up back in fuckin Hollybank. Now have another drink and forget about her. Either that or go into Woodfield, find a whore and shag yourself stupid.'

This outburst proved to be an effective circuit breaker as Riley intended. Mervyn opted for another drink and Riley softened his tone.

'You're not the first man to get tied up in knots over a woman who is out of reach, but the first time it happens to you, it feels like you are.'

Brian looked across at the picture of Edith on the wall.

'Will you tell us about her now?'

The old man let out a long sighing breath.

'All right, since it seems to be a night for this sort of thing. Apart from Edith's sister in law, I haven't spoken to anyone about this in years and it's to go no further. Understood?'

Brian and Mervyn nodded.

'Edith's family and mine were neighbours when we were kids and she and I were always pretty sweet on each other right from the start. When we were little, we were just good mates but as we got older and she started looking like that,' he nodded at her picture, 'the friendship became more grown up and physical. No one seemed to object. My parents liked her and I got on well with her parents. It was taken for granted that we'd end up married when we were a bit older.

'Then the first world war happened and I enlisted. There was no doubt in Edith's mind. She was going to wait for me. We would have married before I went away but our parents said wait 'til I got back. You see back then people thought it wouldn't be a long war but they were wrong.

'Now while I was away, Edith's old man had money troubles. He owned a hardware store which started to go broke, on top of which he was a gambler. By early 1917, he was looking at ruin until this bloke offered him a way out; a proper cunt of a man, Les Keogh. He was a little spiv who didn't enlist but stayed at home and got rich while us mugs went away and got shot up. He had always fancied Edith.

'He offered Edith's Dad a lifeline on the one condition, that he got Edith. Her Dad was already up to his neck in debt to Keogh so he caved in and agreed to his terms. Of course Edie fought against it for as long as she could but the family put a lot of pressure on her, making her feel responsible for saving the business and her father's self respect.

'In spite of all their pressure she resisted until one night, Keogh raped her. When he'd finished, he said "now your precious soldier boy won't touch you with a bargepole." After that she was never the same. The light and the fire went out of her. She felt defiled, which of course she was. She also felt unfit for me, which of course she most definitely wasn't. I would still have married her but the marriage to Keogh went ahead before I got back.

'And she's still married to him but she's been in and out of institutions for years. She never recovered from the rape and for years he used to knock her about. And so one night as he was coming out of his favourite pub I did for the cunt. I thrashed the livin' daylights out of him; blinded him in one eye ruptured his spleen, ruined one of his kidneys and broke a few ribs for good measure.

'I got seven years for grievous bodily harm and malicious assault. I was also charged with attempted murder which was fair enough but for some reason the jury acquitted me of that. I think a lot of people wanted to see Keogh brought down. Perhaps a few of the jurors did too.'

Riley hadn't raised his voice during this account. The two young men looked at him in awe. Mervyn felt his worries pale into insignificance.

'Did you ever see Edith again?' Brian asked.

'The only times I get to see her are when she gets admitted to Hollybank.'

For both Brian and Mervyn, the penny dropped.

'The old woman you always sit with is Edith!'

Riley nodded.

<div align="center">~~~§~~~</div>

On the morning after her flight with Boy Upson, Maggie met Kate for a coffee in the Refectory between lectures.

'Where did you get to on Saturday Maggie? I looked in a couple of times at Madelaine but you weren't there. Mum wanted to ask you around for dinner.'

'I was in Darlington,' said Maggie with a blush.

'You're not still trying to get Hugh back, 'cause if you are you haven't got a hope.'

'I was but I'm not anymore. I wrote to him last night and apologized for being such a pain.'

'So what happened to change your mind?'

'I had written to him a couple of times' – another blush - 'asking, or rather demanding' –more blushes – 'that he meet me at Montini's on Saturday night. I'd never been there before but I understood from you that it was a bit of a haunt of his these days. He sent me a telegram saying he wouldn't be there but I went anyway, hoping he would change his mind. I thought if I could just see him face to face I could get him back.'

'What did you do when he didn't show up?'

'I sat there feeling sorry for myself for a couple of hours until I was rescued by a knight in shining armour. And on that subject, I've got a bone to pick with you Miss Mahoney!'

'What do you mean?' said Kate, wondering where this was heading.

'Well! Said knight saw that I was upset. We were the only customers left by that stage. He gave me a clean folded handkerchief to dry my tears,' - yet another blush - 'invited me over to his table, was utterly charming all evening and paid for the meal. Then, when he discovered I didn't have anywhere to stay, he booked me into a very comfortable hotel.'

'Oh Maggie you didn't!'

'It's all right. He spent the night in a different hotel. Now we come to the bone. You have always led me to believe that this man was a crashing boor; an odious, self centred, egotistical and loudmouthed boor. I found him to be gentle, considerate and sweet in a shy kind of way. He only raised his voice once in the restaurant when I said I was planning to stay at the YWCA. And of course, flying home in his plane yesterday, he had to shout to make himself heard.'

Kate was flabbergasted 'Maggie, Maggie, Maggie! Please don't tell me you've fallen for Boy Upson!!!'

'Well his behaviour towards me contradicted everything you and your mum have ever said to me about him. But no I haven't fallen for him. I'll always be very fond of him because of his kindness to me. He paid for the hotel room too by the way, which is just as well because I couldn't have afforded it. He is obviously filthy rich but he is also too old for me.'

'He is the same age as Tim.'

'Exactly! Too old for me and I wouldn't take advantage of him.'

'So you've got Tim out of your system.'

'I did that ages ago – no offence. I just hope he has got me out of his system.'

'I think he has. He met someone in New Zealand.'

'Well I hope they'll be very happy together. I'm over romance for the moment and I'll concentrate on my degree.'

'Probably for the best. You were taking a risk with Boy.'

'I don't think so. Mr Montini didn't seem overly worried and from what I hear, he is regarded as a good egg.'

'He is universally regarded as a good egg. But Maggie please be very careful. You took a great risk.'

'I'm no expert Kate. But I wouldn't be surprised if Boy is still a virgin.'

'Yes you're right. He probably is still a virgin. All that noise he makes is just over-compensation.'

'I still think he's sweet, in his own **quiet** way.'

Kate shook her head. 'Are you sure he didn't just have laryngitis?'

'That's enough about him,' said Maggie, pointedly changing the subject, 'How's that idiot brother of mine getting along on Lesser C? Is he managing to keep out of mischief? He hasn't fallen for some hillbilly chick down there among the apples has he?'

'Nope. He's having the time of his life but he is keen to come home. Only another couple of weeks to wait. I've really missed him and he is not an idiot by the way. He's more of a buffoon and he's the funniest person I've ever met. Even when we make love he makes me laugh. You know he's got pet names for my boobs?'

Maggie shook her head in disbelief.

'Good grief. I'm almost afraid to ask. Please don't say Pinky and Perky.'

'Shit no. More exotic than that. Promise you won't let on that I told you. Maggie nodded and braced herself.

'My left boob is Simon.'

'And your right boob is Garfunkel,' said Maggie collapsing in laughter. 'What a silly twisted boy.'

~~~§~~~

The season was nearly over. June was half over. The winter cold was becoming increasingly bitter and the apples were nearly all picked. Brian was in his hut,
~~~

putting the finishing touches to his appraisal of "Dandillion". He had already written a covering letter to Kate. Through the thin wall of his hut, he could hear Mervyn next door, playing and singing his heart out. It didn't sound happy. Rather, it was heartfelt and wistful but musically very strong and different to Mervyn's usual style.

With Mervyn's music in the background, Brian decided to read his appraisal one more time before he went to bed.

Dandillion The White Ship

Dandillion is a collection of six poems:
(I) My Childhood,
(II) Daniel,
(III) The Covenant of Nonesuch,
(IV) My Youth,
(V) Exile,
(VI) Amnesty.

The poems connect to form an autobiographical narrative.

The narrator, Norian Fairchild, feels guilty and responsible for the death of his childhood friend Daniel. Daniel drowned trying to rescue Norian whose skiff had capsized on the turbulent river Parfentine. The grief of Daniel's family asks the eternal human question: Is there life after death? Norian's father "shows" them that this is the case.

As Norian reaches adolescence, he finally finds a friend to take Daniel's place. He falls in love with Madelaine. They marry and raise a family. After 60 years of marriage, Madelaine dies, leaving Norian responsible for their children and subsequent descendants.

Again Norian has lost his closest companion to death. Death and separation is the dominant theme of the whole narrative. Norian feels guilt for Daniel's death and in some way his grief for Madelaine seems to be tinged with guilt. Is this because he is 'immortal' and Madelaine isn't?

This brings us to the parallel theme of immortals and mortals. In the poems they appear to be living side by side until Norian's 'immortal' family leaves to return to the 'Deathless Realm'. Who are these immortals and mortals? Are they people who believe in immortality as opposed to people who don't; i.e. Religious v Secular; Spiritual v Materialist? Whatever they are, Norian appears to be caught between the two.

Because Daniel died for Norian's sake, Norian's father feels an obligation to Daniel's family. This results in him conferring a semi-immortal status on them and they go to live secretly in a village called 'Nonesuch'. This agreement is called the 'Covenant of Nonesuch'. From their new home in Nonesuch they are obliged to work in 'the secret service of mankind and to rescue children cast away by cruelty and abandonment.'

Children that they rescue and adopt will automatically become semi-immortal or 'half-elven' as the poem says. I won't get into the 'Elven' 'Tolkien' thing. Kate's grandad is adamant that Norian Fairchild knew nothing of Tolkien and anyway 'Dandillion' predates Lord of the Rings by a quarter of a century at least.

The poems 'Exile' and 'Amnesty' deal with Norian's life after his 'immortal' family leaves. He has also exiled himself from his descendants, apparently to hide his 'agelessness' from them. Then by way of dreams he realises and accepts responsibility for those of his actions that led to his banishment from the 'Deathless Realm.'

Although that banishment remains in force, he is ordered to re-establish contact with his 'mortal' descendants, build the ship 'Dandillion' and convey those of his descendants who so wish, to 'The Outer Isles', where his late wife Madelaine waits for them. In essence, the 'Covenant of Nonesuch' is expanded to include Norian's mortal descendants. But although he can take his children to the 'Outer Islands', he himself cannot go ashore and be reunited with his wife, until his banishment is ended.

In conclusion, 'Dandillion' describes pretty accurately the human condition. The use of two distinct races to explore the question of life after death could symbolize any number of things, but you can get lost in symbols and go looking for deep hidden meanings until the cows come home.

The whole poem is written beautifully and simply. I don't think it is meant to be complex and I don't think there is any complex concealed message in it. Norian probably knew when he gave it to Kate's grandad that it would not be understood because Jack Mahoney wouldn't take it at face value. He'd look for hidden meanings the way we have. But nevertheless, Norian wanted to leave a record of his life's story in his own words, anyway.

After many readings I have decided that the easiest way to make sense of the poem is to take it literally. Norian Fairchild is some kind of 'immortal', living among us today. When I asked Mrs Penruddock about the picture of Norian in their house, she said "That's young Norian, bless him. He never ages."

The mysterious village of Nonesuch could well have been the 'pre-convict' population already living in the Cumberlands when the Dryad was shipwrecked here in 1807 or whenever.

'And now it's past my bedtime,' he scrawled at the bottom.

'Sweet dreams.'

PS I was wandering around in an old cemetery near one of the orchards and found six graves of anonymous shipwrecked sailors. They were dated 1782 which is a long time before the wreck of the Dryad.

PPS We're all being very secretive about this. Is it OK to talk about it to other people? Old Riley knows a lot and he's been around for a long time. He clearly knows something about the Penruddocks. And now I really must get to bed. No more questions please!!!

~~~§~~~

Next morning was very cold but also blessedly clear. The pickers watched last night's fog obediently flowing down the river and out to sea. They gathered around the firepot for a minute before starting work and chatted while the smokers among them smoked.

'Merv,' said Dave. 'I had no idea you were a musician. I could hear a guitar last night. I wasn't sure if it was coming from your hut or Brian's so I snuck up and did a bit of eavesdropping. You should have said, that night back at Mum's, and joined in. There might still be time to get together for a bit of a jam before the picking's finished.'

'Our Mervyn is a man of hidden talents,' said Riley as the former minstrel breathed a sigh of relief that Dave was
~~~

being so friendly. Clearly Elsie hadn't said anything about the cemetery episode. Maybe Riley was right. Perhaps she had never given the incident a second thought.

'That'd be great Dave,' he said. 'I'd like that very much.'

They headed off among the trees and Brian kept close to Riley to strike up a conversation.

'Not many more sleeps now before we can all go home.'

The old man smiled.

'I reckon next week will see it done son. You'll be keen to see Kate again.'

'You bet. How will you get back?'

'A mate of mine operates a little freighter that runs between the two main islands. He lets me travel free.'

'You've got friends everywhere.'

'Must be my personal charm.'

'Can I ask you something?'

'Sure.'

'That morning we told you about meeting the Penruddocks, you were sure we imagined it. You almost had me convinced until after work that night, when I trod in the shit that one of the carthorses left outside my door.'

'I suppose I did speak a bit sharpish. It was just a shock, suddenly hearing their names again after so many years.'

'So you knew the Penruddocks.'

'Years ago I did.'

'A few weeks ago, Dave and Mervyn and I went looking for their house. We found it eventually but it looked like it had been deserted for years.'

'That doesn't surprise me.'

'But out the back in the barn there were supplies of firewood and hay and stuff that all looked pretty recent.'

'That doesn't surprise me either.'

'And there was nothing imaginary about the cup of tea and the shortbread.'

'Maude is justly proud of her shortbread or at least she was when I knew her.'

'There was a picture on the wall of Norian Fairchild and the Penruddocks called their dog Norian. Does the name mean anything to you?'

'I've certainly heard it before. It sounds to me like you've been doing a bit of detective work. In the normal run of things I don't think you would have noticed any of those things if you hadn't been looking for them.'

'I have I guess. It's more some friends of mine back on the Big Island. They've got this theory that there were people already living in the Cumberlands before the wreck of the Dryad back in 1807 or whenever it was. I think they've been too secretive about their investigation.' Then he took a deep breath before continuing. 'What would you say if I told you I have a copy of a poem purportedly written by Norian Fairchild? He gave it to young Jack Mahoney when they were at uni together in the 1920s.'

'I'd be very interested indeed but look out, here comes Charlie Flint. He's probably after cigarette papers. I've got to be somewhere tonight. Bring the poem round to my hut tomorrow after work and I'll tell you as much as I know.'

Brian's bag was full by that stage and he left the two old men rolling smokes. It had all been so incredibly easy. He decided to keep this new information to himself until he got home and looked forward to tomorrow night. At the bin, Bob, Dave and Mervyn were happily discussing the respective merits of Hank Williams and Woody Guthrie and they were getting on like a house on fire.

~~~§~~~

At lunch time, Brian walked up to the post office to post his letter and appraisal of "Dandillion" to Kate. He wasn't expecting any mail himself but Mr Townsend asked him if he would pass on a letter to Riley. Walking back to the orchard he noticed with interest that Riley's Christian name was 'Liam'. Being a sticky beak he looked on the back of the envelope and saw that the sender was a Nancy Keogh.

Riley looked shocked and anxious as he took the letter and retired to a secluded place to read it. After that, he kept to himself for the rest of the afternoon. On the odd occasions when they met at the bin, Brian thought he looked worried and preoccupied so he didn't try to restart their earlier conversation. He would wait til tomorrow night when, hopefully, all would be revealed.

After work that night, Dave and Bob joined Mervyn in his hut and took it in turns to play songs. Mervyn found himself wishing it could all have happened much earlier in the season. The Vineys played him some songs that were locally written and unique to the folklore of Lesser Cumberland. While some were bawdy and crude in the extreme, others were well crafted with a distinctive and haunting style and sound.

Mervyn did his best to write down chords and lyrics and commit melodies to memory. The Vineys were also impressed by some of his more gentle Donavanesque compositions. He did not share his tribute to Elsie which was still taking shape. Meanwhile, back in his hut, Brian
~~~

listened to the music through the wall and went to sleep thinking about what Riley would have to tell him next day.

The next day was Friday and the clear, fine weather continued. Mervyn and the Vineys were as thick as thieves, Charlie was still complaining about the cold and Riley was still keeping to himself. At about 11.a.m., Tom came back from the packing shed with a new bin and a message for Riley. A telegram had been phoned through.

As soon as he heard the message, Riley emptied his half full picking bag. Without another word, he left the orchard and went back to his hut. He didn't come back and the curiosity and speculation among the pickers steadily increased. They pestered Tom but he wouldn't be drawn. He's had some very bad news in a telegram and telegrams are private.'

At knock off time the pickers went into the packing shed to see if there was any news. Apparently Riley had caught the shuttle-bus into Westfield at lunch time. He didn't have any luggage with him so it was assumed that he would be back later in the day. Brian and Mervyn suspected that Riley's telegram had something to do with Edith but they kept their suspicions to themselves.

<div align="center">~~~§~~~</div>

In the small township of Buckton, about 54 miles north of Woodfield in the mountainous centre of Lesser Cumberland, the local parish priest was just finishing his dinner. He had said the Saturday evening vigil mass and was looking forward to an early night in preparation for the gruelling round of masses tomorrow, in various little churches scattered through his rather disparate parish. He was letting the fire go out. The ring of the doorbell wasn't a welcome sound but it was all part of the job. It took a while to recognize his visitor in the dark, while he groped for the light switch.

'I've come to make my Easter Duty.'

'Liam!'

'Confession and communion between Ash Wednesday and Trinity Sunday? Is it still a mortal sin if you don't do that?'

'Liam! I was beginning to think I'd never see you again. Come in out of the cold.'

The priest ushered his visitor into the parlour and poured two glasses of whiskey. Have you eaten?'

'Yeah. I had something at the pub.'

'Well sit down and make yourself comfortable.' He put some more wood on the fire. This looked like turning into a long night after all. 'What can I do for you? Something serious must have happened to flush you out of isolation.'

'Bad news I'm afraid.'

'Edith?'

'Yeah. She died yesterday about 9.30 in the morning. I got a letter from Nancy on Thursday telling me she'd had a couple of strokes and was badly paralysed. And then yesterday I got a telegram saying she'd gone.'

'That poor woman, what a terrible life she had. I remember what a beautiful girl she was when we were all growing up together.'

'Men in your line of work aren't supposed to notice that sort of thing little brother. But you're right. Of all people, I'm the one that best knows how beautiful she was, how happy and spirited, until that cunt got his hands on her. She should have been my wife. She wanted to be my wife!'

'Yes she did and she was betrayed by her family while you were overseas fighting for your country. But unfortunately in the eyes of the law and the Church, she was Keogh's wife.'

'Don't give me that bullshit. Just because a wedding ceremony ticks all the right bureaucratic boxes doesn't mean that God meant it to happen. God didn't join Edie to fuckin Keogh. Edie's old man and the priest did that and they were both in Keogh's pocket. He thought his money could get him anything he wanted. It couldn't buy him a new eye or kidney though.'

'Liam what you did to Keogh was entirely understandable but I hope you're not still savouring your revenge. Apart from some momentary satisfaction, what did it achieve?'

'Absolutely fuckin nuthin. I got seven years, and I soon learnt from Nancy that he started to knock Edie around more than ever after I thrashed him. Smashing the bastard up was the worst thing I could have done and every day that passes I regret it more than ever.

'What I should've done was take Edie away from him and skipped the country; made a fresh start in Australia or New Zealand.'

'Although you could never have legally married her if you did that, I still think that it would have been preferable to what happened. Don't tell the Bishop I said this, but I think God would have blessed the union between you and Edith regardless. What happened with her and Keogh was in no way sacramental.

'The sacrament of marriage is conferred by the couple on each other as an act of mutual love. The priest is just a witness. Edith certainly didn't confer any kind of love on Keogh and he just wanted to possess her.'

'It means a lot to me to hear you say that Jim.'

'Well unlike most of the situations that arise in my job, where I have to interpret Church law, I had inside information about you and Edith. I saw the love grow between you and the way it lit the pair of you up. It was the real thing and no mistake.'

'Why did you choose a life where you couldn't experience love like that for yourself?'

'I just felt I had a vocation.'

'Did you ever question that vocation after you were ordained?'

'Yes, now and then. It hasn't always been easy. I'd be lying if I said otherwise. I'm not blind to female beauty but I've never met a woman with an attraction for me that comes anywhere near what existed between you and Edith.

'Some of my younger colleagues were hoping that Vatican II would allow priests to marry but it doesn't look like happening now. But all of that aside Liam, I value my vocation and I believe in what I do.'

'The thing I could never accept about the priesthood is the vow of obedience. What if your Bishop says one thing and your conscience says another?'

'I'm always guided by my conscience first and foremost Liam, on any issue of real importance. What the Bishop doesn't know can't hurt him.'

'Fair enough I suppose. How's the rest of the family?'

'Well apart from us two there's only Paddy's family and Annie left. Annie is getting very frail now. She's in the Mother House in Darlington. She'd dearly love to see you again. We've all missed you.'

'And what's Paddy up to? Has he still got the boat?'

'Yep. His grandkids crew for him these days, even young Jasmine. She's an enchanting child, an old head on young shoulders. But you haven't met her or any of her siblings have you? They're a delightful family.'

'They wouldn't want anything to do with an old jailbird like me.'

'Nonsense! Every one of Paddy's kids and grandkids knows about you and Edith and what you've both suffered. They'd treat you like a hero.'

'D'you reckon?'

The two brothers talked until midnight, when the priest reluctantly insisted that he had to get to bed.

'I've got four masses tomorrow and about 100 miles of driving. You're welcome to come with me or stay here and take it easy. I don't think you should be alone at a time like this though. I think your grief has made you numb and the full impact hasn't hit you yet. I deal with grieving families most weeks of the year and I know the signs.'

'You're probably right. The whiskey has helped though.'

'There's a bed made up in the guest room. I'll show you. Make yourself at home. And one last thing, were you serious about confession and communion?'

<center>~~~§~~~</center>

Jim was out of bed, showered and dressed by 7.30. He looked in on the guest room and to his dismay and disappointment, found that his brother had left during the night. There was a note.

Dear Jim

Thanks for your hospitality. It was good to talk. If you need to contact me I'm at Murphy's orchard down Woodfield way.

Give my regards to the rest of the family,

Ever yours

Liam.

PS You forgot to give me a penance or don't they bother with that since Vatican II?

20: *Homeward Bound*

Tuesday June 23rd dawned cold and clear. This would be the last day of the season and it would be short. There clearly wasn't a full day's picking left. The mood among the men was festive, Riley's absence notwithstanding. It was clear that the old man had received bad news of some kind but he was a self sufficient and resilient character and everyone fully expected him to bounce back when he was over it. The police had been notified as a precaution, but there wasn't a lot they could do. It was a free country and Riley was a responsible adult. There was no suspicion of foul play.

The Vineys had organized a farewell get-together for the pickers at their mother's place for Thursday night. It was a positive sign that Mervyn was looking forward to it. However, Brian wasn't at all sure that the former minstrel was over Elsie and he was keeping his fingers crossed. Mervyn wasn't over Elsie exactly but he was resigned to the fact that she was permanently out of reach. He just wanted to leave her with a good impression and give the musical performance of his life. His song about her hadn't materialised. He had a melody he was happy with but the lyrics he had written didn't do her justice.

The last piece of orchard they had to pick was new and the trees were young and small. No ladders were needed and the picking was easy. As they homed in on the last couple of trees, Brian found himself stalling and watching the other pickers. He had one apple left on his tree and he was determined to make it the last apple picked for the season. He succeeded but then realised that Old Tom had been trying to do the same thing.

It was all over by lunch time, so the pickers climbed aboard the DeSoto and headed into Woodfield for a meal and a drink at the pub. While they were in town, Brian and Mervyn booked tickets for the Friday night sailing of the ferry to Carlingford and Brian sent Kate a telegram telling her to expect him on Saturday morning. Most of the other orchards had finished up a week ago and the exotic, itinerant pickers had already gone home.

This meant they had the place to themselves to begin with. The barmaid was monopolising the juke box which contained mostly country music. Local country singer Tex Buchanan was clearly a favourite with her and the pickers heard quite a lot of Tex to begin with. Mervyn scanned the few non country songs and selected Norman Greenbaum's *'Spirit in the Sky'*, but it was a long time coming.

They played some pool and discussed their various plans for the future. Surprisingly, Mervyn turned out to be the most competent pool player. His father on Trinity Island owned a table and Mervyn had grown up playing the game. Dave was the only one who could give him a run for his money.

Like gardening, chess and cryptic crosswords, pool was one of the things Brian liked the idea of but lacked the perseverance to ever master. He had his own technique in such situations. He called it 'buggaring up the profile'. On the pool table, this meant smashing up any clusters of balls that tried to gather and hoping that somewhere a ball would be flung into a pocket. The trick to this technique was trusting to luck and plenty of bravado. 'Aha! You've fallen into my little trap,' was something he often said when an opponent was clearly running rings around him. To most people, pool was a game of skill. To

Brian it was a game of pure chaos and chance. He was thoroughly enjoying himself and the ferry ticket in his pocket was his passport back to Kate. The only discordant note or notes to cast a shadow on festivities came from Tex Buchanan on the juke box.

'Put on your prettiest dress Mary Jane
Pack up your little valise.
Your daddy's on the run from a ball and chain
Your Mummy's been taken by the police.'

...was the frequently repeated chorus of one morbid epic that seemed to go on forever. It bored its way into Brian's subconscious and took months to erase. Eventually, Norman Greenbaum took over from Tex Buchanan and they all welcomed the change. However, when Mervyn tried to play '*Spirit in the Sky*' a second time he accidently selected '*Everything is Beautiful*' by Ray Stevens to the bemusement of everyone except the barmaid who seemed to be happy with the selection and gave Mervyn the thumbs up.

~~~§~~~

Two days later while Ma Viney and Elsie were finalising preparations for the end of season "do", Hugh sat in the Gracechurch St flat reading a copy of Brian's assessment of "Dandillion". It had arrived in the post that day, from Kate. Hugh hadn't reached any conclusions of his own about "Dandillion" as yet and he read Brian's interpretation with interest. It was no surprise to him that Brian would reach a totally opposite conclusion to the unsentimental pragmatism of Robert.

Hugh looked forward to sharing it with Lucy on the down train the next day. It was a long weekend for the Queen's birthday and they had both taken an extra day's
~~~

leave for Friday. They were going to stay with his family in Middleton on the North-West Coast, returning on the up train on Monday. Lucy was working 'til 10:00 p.m. and would meet him at the station in the morning. This meant that Brian and Kate would have the flat to themselves for Brian's first weekend back home.

As Hugh sat reading Brian's handiwork, that young gentleman was riding in the DeSoto with Dave and Mervyn on his way to the "Do". Brian was full of excitement and exhilaration. This time tomorrow he would be in Cork with Mervyn waiting to board the ferry.

The smell of roast lamb greeted them on the verandah as Dave led them into the house. Elsie and Ma Viney were still hastily putting the finishing touches to the meal and Ma was getting a little flustered in the process.

'Make yourself at home boys,' she said over her shoulder. 'Bob will you get them something to drink and introduce yourself? They know where you've been so don't be shy.'

'I'm Bob senior' said an older version of Bob and Dave as he furnished them with glasses of ale.

'We'll have some fiddle tonight' said Elsie with a smile as she walked past with a handful of cutlery to set the table. She hadn't yet changed for dinner and was wearing jeans and an old green sweater with 'Bugs Bunny' on the front.

'I'll probably be a bit rusty Pet,' her father said as he sat down and shared a drink with his young guests. 'So what do you think of our little Island?'

'It's great,' said Mervyn. 'I've really enjoyed it here.'

'Me too,' Brian added.

'I've just been on the big island for 6 months,' said Mr Viney, 'but not in the most salubrious of circumstances. Let's just say I'm pleased to be back.'

'Here's to being back home again,' said Brian raising his glass.

'Amen to that son. Amen to that.'

At 7:30 p.m. they sat down to eat. Bob junior had been out working on a fishing boat for the day and they had waited for him. Elsie in the meantime had changed into a navy blue 1930s party dress with a silvery floral pattern. It was a dress her mother had worn when she was her daughter's age and it suited Elsie perfectly. The effect was not lost on Mervyn or Brian but, much to Brian's relief, the former minstrel seemed to be quite composed. He was conversing easily with everyone and giving the performance of his life. He was determined not to put a foot wrong.

It was a strange thing, given the environment and company he had been working in for the last couple of months, but Mervyn seemed to have developed some social graces that hadn't been part of the Mervan Mithras repertoire. He had grown or matured somehow, especially since the encounter with Elsie in the cemetery.

'Can I make a request for "*Wildwood Flower*" a bit later Elsie?'

'Sure. I hear from Dave that you're a bit of a musician yourself. You kept that hidden didn't you!'

'I had lost interest in music before I came here so I left my guitar back on the big island but when I heard you all playing here, it revived my interest; so I bought another instrument at the general store in Woodfield.'

'You'll be able to give us a song then.'

'He picks with his fingers,' said Dave. 'I want him to teach me.'

'The only thing you've ever picked with your fingers is your nose,' said Ma Viney.

'And apples Mum,' said Bob junior. 'He also picks apples.'

'Hopefully not at the same time,' quipped Ma with a wink at Mervyn.

In time the roast dinner was consumed, to universal satisfaction. The Viney brothers cleared away the dishes while their mother and sister served the pudding, a Rhubarb and Apple crumble that Elsie had made. It was her specialty and it was served with fresh cream from Berechree's dairy. The menfolk did the washing up and Mervyn and Brian were issued with tea-towels.

When everything was made shipshape, drinks were refurbished, musical instruments were tuned and the music began. The Viney family combined to sing *Sweet Fern* with Elsie singing the lead, the menfolk joining in the chorus and Ma Viney providing some yodelling. Mervyn was content just to listen to the first song but after that, Dave insisted that he 'get stuck in' and so he complied.

After joining in for *Diamonds in the Rough* and *Grave on the Green Hillside*, Mervyn was asked for a song. He obliged with Donovan's *Catch the Wind* which went down very well.

'That was beautiful,' Elsie said. 'As good as the original.'

Mervyn responded with a smile and then played *Don't Think Twice*.

'I've got to learn how to pick like that,' Dave enthused, and the session began to warm up.

At one point, Elsie took the guitar from Dave. She was still learning and wasn't yet as proficient as her brother. The old 'Martin' had a very high action and thick strings which Elsie found difficult to play. It was a heaven sent opportunity and Mervyn made the most of it. 'Try my guitar Elsie. It's got a lower action and lighter strings.'

She accepted the invitation with immediate results.

'This is much easier to play, the strings are like silk,' she beamed as she joined in on the next two songs. Mervyn's heart swelled as he watched her revelling in the experience of playing his guitar. Without being prompted she soon gave the instrument back to him.

'OK Mervyn, give us another one.'

That session was easily the most satisfying musical experience of the former minstrel's life. Brian watched his friend with feelings of admiration and relief. He was playing it perfectly; he wasn't hogging the limelight and his added accompaniments to the Vineys' songs were restrained, tasteful and enthusiastically received.

At about 10pm, Brutus and Fang started barking out in the yard and there was a knock on the front door. Bob junior went to answer it.

'Well, look what the cat dragged in,' he said as he returned a few minutes later with Riley.

'I couldn't let the season end without saying goodbye,' he said as he took a bottle of whiskey from the pocket of his overcoat. Everyone was very glad to see him. Brian studied his face closely. He looked happy enough but Riley played with his cards close to his chest. Any questions about his whereabouts over the past few days were played with a straight bat.

'Just some family stuff,' was as much as he would say.

He answered Brian's questioning glances with the briefest of winks and an equally brief and slightly conspiratorial smile. He said he had already eaten but graciously and enthusiastically accepted some rhubarb and apple crumble from Elsie. While he was eating, the music continued. Bob senior tuned up his fiddle and played some Irish airs and then a few square dance tunes. When Riley had finished his crumble he enthusiastically joined in the chorus singing. Around 11.00pm, he took centre stage and sang *The Parting Glass*. Then he looked at his watch. 'I have to love you and leave you I'm afraid – somewhere to be. Brian and Mervyn, I'll see you back on the big island. Thanks for the crumble Elsie – one of your best. Goodnight everyone.'

When he had gone, the session faltered for a second or two but then Ma Viney started singing *Will the Circle be Unbroken* and they were all soon singing their hearts out again. It was almost as if Riley had never been there. Towards the end of proceedings, Elsie sang *Wildwood Flower*. There was a look almost of surprise on the girl's face as her flawless voice soared effortlessly up to the high notes in the refrain. It was a sound of pure delight. She finished the song to universal acclaim and a special thank you from Mervyn.

Because they had a big day ahead of them next day, Brian and Mervyn had booked a taxi for midnight to take them back to the orchard. As that hour drew nigh they began to make their goodbyes. Then Mervyn played a spur of the moment masterstroke. He picked up his guitar but instead of putting it in its case he gave it to Elsie. The Vineys were incredulous.

'You're not serious' said Elsie in amazement.

'Elsie, this is a nice little instrument but my guitar back on the mainland is nearly ten times its value. You keep this one until you're ready to upgrade to something better and whatever you do, don't stop playing and singing. You and your family have got something special. Don't ever give it up.'

While the rest of her family looked on, Elsie gave Mervyn an enormous bear hug and kissed him on the cheek, her green eyes were sparkling. 'Thank you so much.' Then they heard the horn of the Taxi.

'That'll be Ted Maloney,' said Bob senior, he won't appreciate you calling him out at this hour.'

'We've already thought of that,' said Brian, 'we're going to give him a ten quid tip.'

'Shit a tenner! That ought to perk him up. Well you better not keep him waiting. I wonder if we'll ever see you two boys again.'

'I certainly hope so,' said Brian. 'My girlfriend Kate would love it down here.'

'I'd like to come back sometime for the music,' said Mervyn.

'Any time mate,' said Dave. 'You've still got to teach me finger picking.'

Ted Maloney gave another, louder blast on the horn.'

'You'd better go,' said Elsie 'and thanks again Mervyn.'

Then he and Brian left to a chorus of goodbyes and some added vocal support from Brutus and Fang who had been woken again by the taxi.

Ted Maloney dropped them off at the orchard at 12.30. Not much was said during the journey. Ted was taciturn. Under his overcoat he was in his pyjamas. Mervyn and Brian had plenty to talk about but they were saving it for when they got back. Brian was looking out for the place where old Harry Penruddock had taken them back to the highway on the night the DeSoto broke down. As they passed that spot he looked intently for where he thought their old farm house should be. He was rewarded by a distant gleam of light flickering amongst the trees.

They reached the orchard and paid the fare. Ted's eyes lit up with a benevolent sparkle when he saw the ten quid tip, and he found voice.

'Thank you very much for that boys. That's very decent of you. See you next season.'

He drove off and they adjourned to Brian's hut for a cup of tea and a post mortem of a most eventful evening. They noticed that Old Riley's hut was in darkness.

'Congratulations Mervyn you handled the whole evening perfectly. That was a master stroke giving your guitar to Elsie.'

'Yes I think it was, even if I do say so myself. The idea just came out of the blue. I can take comfort from the fact that, wherever I end up, Elsie will think well of me. My God she's a beautiful creature.'

'She certainly is and after tonight she will always think of you as a dear friend. Well done, and what about Old Riley turning up out of the blue?'

'It was quite a surprise but it was great to see him again.'

'He seemed almost like an apparition. How did he get there and where did he come from? I didn't hear a car.

And where could he have gone afterwards at that hour, on foot?'

'We were singing so loud we wouldn't have heard a car. And don't forget, there's a bit of a village up by the jetty where the fishing boats are moored. He could have gone there.'

'I suppose so. Did he have anything to drink?'

'I think so. He brought a bottle of whiskey - and he ate all the rhubarb crumble that Elsie gave him – every last crumb. I don't think ghostly apparitions eat rhubarb crumble. And anyway he said he'd see us both back on the big island.'

'Yeah you're right. I guess there's nothing to worry about.'

'Of course there isn't. Are you all packed and ready for tomorrow?'

'Yep. Just got to wash up these mugs and pack them. We can have breakfast at the Golden Fleece in the morning.'

~~~§~~~

While Brian and Mervyn were eating their breakfast at the Golden Fleece next morning, Hugh and Lucy were making themselves comfortable on the down train as it pulled out of Darlington Central on the dot of 9.30. Lucy was looking forward to meeting Hugh's family and he was looking forward to showing her off to them. It would be his first trip home since Christmas.

He also had other good news to surprise and impress his parents with. He had recently successfully applied for a promotion in the pay office from base grade clerk to a level 3 position. He had Lucy to thank for the necessary coaching and motivation and he would start
~~~

work in the new post on Tuesday, after they got back from their trip. It would mean an appreciable pay rise which was another reason for the contented satisfaction he was feeling at that time.

At 10.30, Emily Oldfield began taking orders for morning tea and Hugh showed Lucy Brian's appraisal of "Dandillion".

'Wow' she said, when she had read it. 'That is very well written and, for Brian, remarkably sensible.'

'Yes,' said Hugh 'and diametrically opposed to Robert's opinion.'

'It's very appealing, the idea that there is something wonderful and magical behind it all.'

'What do you make of his comment about us being too secretive?'

'It's a fair point I suppose. I guess I inherited that from Jim and Robert to begin with. Yet in some ways the whole thing seemed so farfetched I would have been too embarrassed to talk about it to grownups. Dad would have been merciless.

'It was almost like a game of let's pretend or make believe. But there were these tantalizing little bits of evidence that occasionally turned up to keep us hooked. I don't know what Robert or Jim would say about opening it up to other people.'

'Speaking of which have you heard back from Jim?'

'Not yet. I took a copy of "Dandillion" round to his place and met his mother. She seems nice. She said Jim was out on a boat and expected back in about three weeks time.'

Kate was eagerly waiting at the ferry terminal at Carlingford on Saturday morning as the ferry steamed up the river. She had driven up from Denistone the day before and stayed with her grandfather overnight. It was a bitterly cold morning with an icy wind coming off the river. As luck would have it, she was dressed in the same outfit that she was wearing in the sports car that day almost a year ago when she and Brian first met. Blue denim jeans with just the right degree of weather-beaten fade, a cream camisole which showed just the right amount of cleavage, an exotic looking embroidered astrakhan jacket and riding boots. She smiled as she remembered the silly antics of her beloved that day.

The ship was made fast and eventually passengers began to disembark. Then the three month wait was over. Mervyn waited at a discreet distance while they threw themselves into each other's arms in a long embrace. In time they both came up for air and Kate held Brian at arm's length and looked him up and down.

'My word country life must agree with you, you're looking great.'

'You're looking pretty fantastic yourself.' Then Brian remembered his fellow apple picker.

'Kate this is Mervyn – Mervyn, Kate.'

Kate shook the erstwhile minstrel's hand and thought to herself how much his appearance had changed.

'Pleased to meet you Kate.'

'Likewise. How did you like picking apples?'

'It was wonderful, a completely different world.'

They offered Mervyn a lift back to Darlington but he declined, saying a friend would be picking him up later. There was no such friend but Mervyn wasn't going to be a gooseberry. He would buy a ticket for the up train and he looked forward to sleeping all the way back to Darlington.

'So that's the famous Mervan Mithras,' said Kate. 'Not like his stage persona.'

'No. He's left all that behind him. I've gotten to know him and I've watched him changing. He's a good bloke actually.'

'I've always thought he was a bit up himself - more than a bit actually.'

'He'd probably agree with you….that he used to be.'

'Well what next? Do you need to eat or will we hit the frog and toad?'

'The 'frog and toad' sounds good, back to Denistone?'

'No fear! Darlington. I want you all to myself. 'Hugh and Lucy are out of town for the long weekend and Hugh has given us the run of the flat while they're away. The family can wait a few more days to see you. I've packed some sandwiches and a thermos of tea. We can have a picnic somewhere on the way. God it's good to have you back.'

<div align="center">~~~§~~~</div>

As Kate's Mini sped out of Carlingford, Hugh was showing Lucy the sights of Middleton. So far, the trip home had been a great success. Hugh's parents were very taken with Lucy and she was favourably impressed by them, and very relaxed in their company. Hugh's mum had been a nurse so they had that in common.

Mr and Mrs Conroy were very happy, not just with Lucy but with the changes they saw in their son. The decision to abruptly uproot him and transplant him in Darlington had been quite a gamble. His mother had been against it but his father thought it was the only way to jolt him out of his cocoon of fanciful introversion.

A friend of Hugh's father was able to pull strings to secure the job at the City Council. The Gracechurch Street flat was advertised as fully furnished. Mr Conroy accompanied his son to Darlington to see him settled in and then left him to sink or swim, blissfully unaware that Gracechurch Street was the centre of a mystery as far-fetched as any of Hugh's fanciful daydreams at home had been.

But in exploring this new mystery Hugh had begun to develop some social skills and make new friends. His only childhood friends had been Brian and Maggie. While Brian got on well with Hugh's parents, Mrs Conroy thought Maggie was a little miss who was far too aware of how pretty she was. The young McInerneys moved to Green Island when their parents were posted to the school there at the end of 1958. Hugh didn't make new friends in Middleton after they left. He kept in touch with Brian and Maggie by letter and hardly ever left the house.

Now here he was, back home for the long weekend with a lovely girlfriend, a promotion at work and a self-assurance that had been totally absent before he went away. Even his 12 year old sister Annie was impressed. Lucy had to share a room with her and they happily chatted away about Hugh's foibles and follies until Mrs Conroy called out telling Annie to let Lucy get some sleep. It was a small house and sound carried.

Out in the bracing morning air, Hugh had taken Lucy on one of his favourite walks; up Roberts Street to the top of the hill overlooking the town. From there he was able to point out various landmarks: the convent school in the grounds of the church; the sawmill across the river whose siren 'the Mill Whistle' marked the phases of the working day and served as a time piece for the whole town; the wharf on the river, from which converted schooners carried timber products to various centers around the archipelago. Their eyes followed the river out to its estuary, beyond which the three peaks of Trinity Island could be seen like mysterious blue pyramids on the horizon.

<div align="center">~~~§~~~</div>

Back on the 'frog and toad' Kate and Brian were having the time of their life filling in details of the past three months that hadn't made it into letters. Brian heard about Maggie's thwarted attempts to lure Hugh back and the interlude with Boy Upson.

'And have they seen any more of each other since?'

'He sent her a card for her birthday.'

'Shit! I'd forgotten all about her birthday. I'll have to do a bit of grovelling next time I see her.'

'I'll enjoy seeing you grovel. Fancy!! Forgetting your own sister's birthday!!'

'All right! Since you're being so sanctimonious, when is Maggie's birthday?'

'Well it's... er.'

'Come on smart arse, when is it?'

'Well it's ....sometime in June?'

'You're lucky you're driving. I shall be demanding satisfaction later so consider yourself under sentence.'

'We'll see about that. I could always make you get out and walk.'

'That'd be cutting off your nose to spite your face.'

'Huh!! The conceit of the man.'

They continued on in similar fashion all the way to Darlington with one stop mid-afternoon for a picnic lunch at a road-side reserve at the highest point on the highway. There was a small group of crows high in the leafless branches of the old deciduous trees. Brian thought it was only courteous to say a few well chosen words in 'crow'. Kate joined him enthusiastically but it was to no avail.

After a few minutes the crows took flight. Being highly intelligent birds, they correctly deduced that the two humans were taking the piss. A similar conclusion, although differently expressed, was reached by an elderly couple, whose caravan the lovers hadn't noticed nestled behind some evergreen bushes and shrubs.

Sunday morning in Darlington dawned foggy and cold. However, all was cozy in the flat at Gracechurch street thanks to open fireplaces and the ample supply of firewood provided by Hugh. Kate, in just her knickers, went to the kitchen to make a cup of tea. She had left Brian fast asleep with a smile on his face. She poured a cup for herself and stood with it at the kitchen sink staring out the window, lost in thought and waiting for her tea to cool a little.

Kate had inherited a number of traits from her mother, in particular the art of tea-making. Both ladies were renowned for the scalding temperatures they conjured up in teapots. This was the furthest thing from Brian's mind as he quietly crept into the kitchen and saw a chance to surprise the love of his life.

More than once in the past it had been happily received by Kate when he crept up behind her and gently clasped 'Simon and Garfunkel' to her in a tender embrace.

Not this morning however; not with a scalding hot cup of tea in the vicinity. Kate had no idea he was in the room. She was completely lost in a happy reverie recalling some of the pleasures of the night before.

When Brian made contact, Kate screamed, her hands flew up and the scalding tea went all over 'Simon and Garfunkel', who began to blister immediately. Kate was beside herself with the pain.

'What can I do?' said Brian in a desperate panic. The lesions and blisters were looking angrier by the second. His immediate impulse was to hold Kate in a comforting embrace but of course that was out of the question in this situation. 'If only Lucy was here, she'd know what to do. Don't they rub butter on burns?'

'That was in the dark ages. I need to get to 'Out Patients' at the hospital. But not dressed like this and I can't drive!'

They decided a taxi was out of the question for reasons of modesty.

'It will have to be an ambulance then,' said Brian. 'You poor thing.'

In due course an ambulance arrived and Kate, in a loose fitting bathrobe, with a mortified Brian for company, was taken to the hospital. Once there, relief was blissful and swift. A nurse lavishly applied a cooling, soothing antiseptic cream that was also an anaesthetic and the pain was soon over. Then the annointed area was covered in a protective bandage.

'You'll have to come in tomorrow to have the dressing changed and again the day after. Then we'll give you some cream that you can use at home,' said the nurse.

'I could do that for…..' but the words died on Brian's lips. The nurse who was a girl of a similar age, laughed out loud at the menacing thunderbolts in Kate's eyes.

'What makes you think I'd give you the satisfaction? You can consider yourself on probation.' But Kate was so relieved about the pain having stopped that she couldn't keep a straight face.

'Can't I at least kiss them better?' was the last remark the nurse heard from Brian as they left the room to ring for a taxi home. They were both laughing again.

21: *After Apple Picking.*

Early on the morning after the Queen's birthday holiday, Brian went out to Hollybank where Ray and the other cleaners were gathered in the crib room before starting the day's work. They were pleased to see him again and he joined them in a cup of tea. Unfortunately there was a full complement of cleaners at that time but Ray knew of a vacancy in the hospital laundry. He introduced Brian to the laundry manager, a taciturn red haired man in his early fifties who was rumoured to be a member of the Cumberland Communist Party.

Brian was employed on the spot. The laundry was a big operation and took in work from other health facilities in and around the city. This included laundry from operating theatres in Darlington's two major hospitals. Huge bags of the soiled linen were dumped on a loading bay at the back of the laundry. It was one of Brian's duties to open these bags and empty the contents into large mobile carts ready to be washed by the women at the far end of the building.

The soiled linen from operating theatres could be confronting and Brian had to tell the boss if there was anything too confronting for the women to see. It was generally soaked in blood that had begun to congeal. There were often little shreds of material which Brian assumed were human flesh and bone fragments – shavings if you will. Most of the other dirty laundry stank of urine. Brian didn't have much of an appetite when he got home to Gracechurch street that night.

There was no companionship to be had with the other laundry staff. The women kept to themselves. Apart from the boss, who was distinctly unchatty, the only other male on the staff was a morose, slightly overweight young man called Simon. His only topic of conversation was deadly venom. He had an encyclopaedic knowledge of all the world's deadliest snakes, spiders, scorpions, amphibians and marine creatures.

With no prompting he would regale Brian with detailed descriptions of these deadly creatures: the nature of their poison, the toxicity of same, how long it took to kill a human being, and a vivid description of the symptoms the victims would display and the agonies they would endure in the process. Simon delivered these gruesome litanies with a poker face. But in spite of the deadpan delivery, his relentless obsession with the subject suggested that he found it stimulating.

Brian felt a painful homesick longing for the orchard on Lesser C. If only he could be back there, up on a ladder, in a tall tree with the wind in his face, listening to the distant chatter and laughter of the other pickers and the gentle rumble of apples being emptied into the bin. He felt that whatever career his university studies eventually equipped him for, apple picking would always be his favourite kind of work. The only respites in his working day at the laundry were morning tea, lunch and afternoon tea breaks. These he spent with the cleaners in their crib room. Fortunately it was quite close to the laundry.

'What do you think of Simon?' Ray had asked him. 'He's a right little ray of sunshine isn't he?'

Brian just grimaced and shuddered.

'I think he has all the makings of a serial killer,' said Colin. 'It stands to reason.'

As Brian struggled through his first day in the laundry, a Cumberland Airways Fokker Friendship flew out of Darlington Airport. It would do a circuit of the main islands of the archipelago. It was part of a twice daily passenger service, anti-clockwise in the morning and clockwise in the afternoon. The first stop would be Trinity Island. Mervyn was onboard and his Martin Guitar, its case festooned with "fragile" stickers, was safely stowed in the luggage compartment.

This would be Mervyn's first trip home in a long time. As yet his family knew nothing of his suicide attempt and his subsequent spell in Hollybank. He had decided they didn't need to know about it. He had kept in contact with his mother by monthly letters so they knew he'd been apple picking. Doubtless they would have wondered and speculated about this career change. He had also told them to expect him home soon. This was a departure from his normal practice. In the past he used to just lob up unannounced, usually in some kind of crisis.

His parents, particularly his mother, wondered about these little signs of change. She had also noticed subtle differences in the letters he wrote, especially those from the orchard. They seemed to be less self-absorbed. He asked how things were with the family on Trinity as if he really wanted to know. His letters also contained descriptions of some of the characters on the orchard, including the Vineys and their music. Any references to Elsie were guarded but he mentioned her a few times, in particular the unspoiled purity of her voice. Mrs Purvis's motherly intuition did a bit of reading between the lines. Letters in the past had been about his own musical attributes not those of others.

It was midday when the plane touched down at Trinity airport. Mervan waited to collect his guitar and suitcase and then he took a taxi home to Willow Bend, the small village where his parents lived. He felt a thrill of pleasant excitement as the taxi took him through the landscape of his childhood. The family home, a modest little three bedroom bungalow, came into view. It was unchanged from the days of his early childhood, a welcoming haven and a place of security.

Over the years, as the star of Mervan Mithras rose and fell, his visits home had seemed unreal. He had been caught up in his fantasies and living his delusional legend. This time as he walked up the old familiar side path with its row of geraniums, he was really coming home. He had trodden that path countless times throughout his childhood. He saw the little hole in the concrete where he and his father had played an improvised game that was part soccer and part billiards, trying to pot a marble using only their feet. They had invented it on the day of his grandmother's funeral.

His father answered the door.

'Well, well, well, the prodigal returns. It's good to see you son and you're just in time for dinner. Your room is ready and waiting so stow your stuff in there and freshen up. Mum's just setting the table.'

'No fear' his mother called from the kitchen. 'Not before I get a kiss.'

Pretty soon the three of them were sat around the table in the bright sunny kitchen eating shepherd's pie made from the minced up remains of the Sunday roast. The kitchen hadn't changed. The old black combustion stove still held court in the fireplace. It was used for cooking, heating and powering the hot water cylinder which stood close by, enclosed in an airing cabinet.

An old black kettle stood on the hob singing softly and only needed moving onto the stove-top for a few minutes to come to the boil when required to make a cup of tea. From the old wireless in its black bakelite shell, the reassuring tones of the CBC Country Hour gently intoned chronicles of rainfall averages and stock prices as it had done for as long as Mervyn could remember.

One of the things about Elsie that had appealed to Mervyn, in addition to her beauty and her gentle charm, was the way she belonged where she lived. She was enshrined in the love of her family but more than that she was immersed in the very being of the orchard community, the cemetery where her uncle was buried, her school and Berechree's dairy. She belonged and when she sang she gave a voice to where she belonged.

Now, sitting in this comfortably unchanged kitchen, Mervyn felt a sense of his own belonging and realized he had been trying to escape it for most of his life. He heaved a deep and heartfelt sigh and surrendered to it. After a dessert of tinned peaches and cream, Mr Purvis excused himself and went back to work. Mervyn picked up a tea towel and helped his mother with the washing up.

~~~§~~~

That week's Wednesday night gathering at O'Brien's included Brian and Kate. Kate's burns had required additional dressing changes at the hospital and she would not return to her studies in Ross until Monday. Brian regarded this as a bonus to compensate for his unhappiness about working at the hospital laundry. But
~~~

he was still wracked with guilt about the pain he had inflicted on poor Kate.

They were both looking forward to seeing Lucy for the first time since her return from the trip to Middleton. She arrived with Hugh and Robert at 7.30 and drinks were ordered.

Madge had finally abolished her old prohibition of ladies in the bar. It was Kate's first time at O'Brien's and Brian introduced her to Madge as he bought the first round of drinks. He also introduced her to Robert who rather bashfully shook her hand. Robert was a little wary but Kate's smile was in no way threatening and he was also reassured by the fact that she got on so well with Lucy.

'Well then,' said Hugh after the introductions and pleasantries were completed. 'Let's get down to business. We've got a lot to discuss. We've all had a chance to read Brian's appraisal of "Dandillion". To be honest, I still haven't made up my mind about the poem yet. Brian's opinion that it should be taken literally is very tempting. It would mean that Norian Fairchild is some kind of magical or mystical being. I've always liked the idea of other worlds or realms co-existing with the world we live in.'

'Does that mean you believe in fairies?' asked Robert with, for him, gentle sarcasm.

'I'd like to think that they exist,' said Hugh 'and folk tales about them occur in many cultures. But I admit in the mid twentieth century it is a bit hard to believe that there is an immortal being living amongst us century after century and never ageing.'

'Precisely,' said Robert. 'It's the century after century bit that is the basic weakness of the poem as a reliable text.'   He thumbed through his copy of "Dandillion". 'Listen to this. "And earthbound here I still remain with all my earthly flesh and blood while generations fall like leaves. Centuries passed and their numbers grew, spreading around this mortal globe."

'Just do the arithmetic. Over centuries you're talking about thousands of descendants. He'd need a ship the size of the Titanic to carry them all. It'd be a full time job. I'm sorry Brian but when you look at the numbers it just isn't believable.'

'That was the other way of looking at it of course,' said a smiling, affable Brian who was quite unperturbed. 'When you put it like that Robert, it's hard to contradict you. I guess I was treating "Dandillion" as a piece of art or literature. He may have just been using exaggerated poetic language to paint a picture of the burden of responsibility that he felt he had to cope with.'

Robert was relieved that Brian had taken his rebuttal without any animosity or resentment.

'I'm no expert with poetry and stuff like that Brian. I just read it with an eye for what I could quantify; and after centuries, how much paternity could Norian Fairchild claim. If we were able to trace our ancestry back over several centuries we'd find that we are descended from hundreds of people but that descent would be heavily diluted. Perhaps there is something more in the poetry that you haven't spotted yet.'

'That's a good point Robert,' said Kate. 'In the poem Norian talks about the descendants as if they were his sons and daughters – immediate descendants. What if he's not talking about the descendants of the children that he sired with his wife (supposedly) hundreds of years ago, but children he has fathered with other women over the years since his wife died? Grandad was telling me that he knew of at least two women who had babies by him in their university days back in the Twenties.'

'So not only is he an immortal he's a randy old bugger as well,' said Brian.

'I can hardly believe I'm having this conversation.' Kate shook her head. 'Do any of us really believe that Norian Fairchild is hundreds of years old?'

Lucy explained to Kate about Jim's rescue at sea by Norian, the 1920's bank notes in mint condition, the picture of Norian in Mrs Malleson's flat, the fact that Kate's grandad had been at uni with him in the 1920's and the painting of Dandillion winning a race at the Cork Regatta of 1837 skippered by N. Fairchild.

'That's all well and good Lucy,' said Robert, 'but like I've said before, there are plausible alternative explanations. The person who rescued Jim at sea could be the grandson of the man Kate's grandfather knew at uni and the winner of the boat race in 1837 could be his great great grandfather or something. I know which I find easier to believe.'

Then Brian recounted what old Mrs Penruddock had told him about the picture of Norian on her wall.

"That's young Norian, bless him. He never ages. He comes to see us occasionally on his boat. He moors her in the bay outside. He says he'll take us for a sail on her one day fairly soon. I only hope he lets us take the dog."

'Now Mrs Penruddock is an old lady and she has known Norian all her life. Apparently in that time he hasn't aged.

'When the DeSoto was repaired a few of us went looking for the Penruddock place in daylight. We found it but it was all locked up and deserted. The blinds were all drawn and nobody answered our knocking. Although the barn was full of hay and stuff there was no sign of the horses. It felt very much as if the place had been deserted for years.

'When we first told Riley about our encounter with the Penruddocks, he didn't believe us. It made him angry. However when I raised the subject with him again a few weeks later, he was a little bit more forthcoming. He said he had been shocked and surprised because he hadn't heard the Penruddocks' names for so long.

Then I asked him about Norian Fairchild and mentioned "Dandillion". He had heard of Norian but he hadn't heard of his poem. He was busy that night but he said to bring it to his hut the following night and we could discuss it further. I'm sure he knows something about it all but unfortunately, because of a family bereavement, he left the orchard suddenly next day and we never had the chance to talk about it again.

'I'm hoping he'll turn up again in Darlington soon but Riley moves in mysterious ways his wonders to conceal or whatever.' Brian always qualified his quotations and proverbs these days if Kate was present. Her eyes sparkled and she smiled a mischievous smile that promised consequences but for the moment let it pass without comment.

'And the last bit of information I have about the Penruddocks is not exactly hard, cold fact but I'll tell you anyway. On the last night on Lesser C we'd been to a party. We caught a taxi back to the orchard around midnight. It drove past the spot where the DeSoto had broken down. I was keeping my eyes peeled and saw a glimmering light amongst the trees. As on the night of the breakdown it was the only visible light for miles. So perhaps the Penruddocks are back home again.'

'That's another point I want to follow up,' said Hugh. 'This sailing trip that Norian was going to take with the Penruddocks reminds me of that bit in the poem about him taking his descendents to the 'Outer Isles' on his boat and thus avoiding death. That stuff that Jim was talking about.'

'Well,' said Lucy, 'We'll just have to wait a couple of weeks 'til Jim gets back to shore and you can ask him all about it.'

~~~§~~~

Back on Trinity Island, Mervyn continued to reconnect with his roots. Mrs Purvis was pleasantly surprised when he expressed an interest in resurrecting the little vegetable garden he had cultivated as a child. He had spent many happy hours in that patch on the western side of the quarter acre block.

He remembered a particular spring when all that part of the yard had been covered in self-sown marshmallow plants some of which grew five feet and more in height. They had been infested by peculiar red and black beetles whose offspring were connected to their rear end and followed them everywhere, walking backwards. Mervyn had never seen such creatures before and was fascinated by them. His mother had called them bee-beetles.

In time, Mr Purvis had cleared the yard of the marshmallow trees, put in a garden and encouraged Mervyn to cultivate a small plot of his own. Because of a rheumatic back, Mr Purvis's gardening days were long over and the land lay fallow except for Mrs Purvis's flower
~~~

beds. Even they were dormant now in the winter cold although the daphne would soon be flowering.

Mervyn loved the scent of daphne. It filled him with an intense nostalgic yearning which for some reason reminded him vividly of Greek mythology. It was many years later, when he read Ovid's 'Metamorphosis', that he realised the connection and began to wonder about himself. Then he had read 'The Crystal Cave' and his trouble had started. But he was over all that now and he just wanted to reconnect with the little boy who planted broad beans, lettuces, cabbages and carrots in that holy ground so long ago.

Mervyn's parents, particularly his father, were anxious that he should soon think about finding another job but they were also aware that their youngest son was undergoing some kind of significant transformation and they didn't want to put him under any pressure. Surprisingly, Mervyn himself raised the question of finding a job, one night when he and his father were playing pool.

His rheumatic back notwithstanding, Mr Purvis was still a lethal opponent in a game of pool and a hard man to beat but his concentration wavered when his son started talking about finding work on the Island, perhaps an office job. They called it quits at two games all and continued the conversation over a beer in the kitchen.

Mr Purvis held a senior management position at the Trinity Island Butter Factory but there were no clerical vacancies at the factory at that time. He remembered Mervyn's flat refusal to even consider working in a sawmill in the past, and saw it as progress that he was now prepared to look at other options. They resolved to pick up a copy of the Cumberland Government Gazette next day to see if there were any Government jobs going on the Island.

For the next few days, Mervyn kept himself occupied chopping and splitting firewood to keep the old combustion stove and hot water system fully supplied. One of his older brothers who still lived on the Island normally did this to spare Mr Purvis's ailing back. Mervyn also gave his old garden bed a rough digging over as a first step in bringing it back to life. He went on a lot of walks revisiting favourite places from his rather solitary childhood, this included long beach walks.

The long, thin shape of Trinity Island was such that the sea was visible from every part of its landmass. On Greater and Lesser Cumberland this wasn't the case. Both there and on his travels abroad, Mervyn found that he missed being able to see the ocean and felt stifled and confined by the fact. This was particularly the case in parts of mainland Australia. Being back on the Island of his birth he drew great comfort from the nearness of the sea and the sound of the waves breaking. He could hear it from his bedroom at night and he now realized that it had been the soundtrack to his early life.

He wasn't blind to the danger and cruelty the sea was capable of. Two boys his own age had drowned at a parish picnic one year. Fishermen were occasionally lost at sea and the coastline was littered with shipwrecks from previous centuries. After the drownings at the picnic he never swam in the sea again.

He was content to wander on the beach exploring what the receding waves had left behind; scraps of seaweed, driftwood, busy little crabs on the glistening sand, cadavers of larger creatures that would soon be devoured by scavengers and return to the elements, the plaintive cries of the soaring gulls and behind it all the endless procession of the waves. Images of beach, seaside and seagulls featured in many of Donovan's songs. Mervyn had written songs in that style but in doing so he didn't draw on his own experience of the sea, rather he simply imitated Donovan.

In all his efforts at song writing, Mervyn had tried to write the sorts of songs that were fashionable at the time. For a while this meant protest songs: anti-war songs, particularly with the Vietnam War in mind, anti-atom bomb songs and apocalyptic songs like Barry Mc Guire's *Eve of Destruction*, which afforded the artist an opportunity to revel in the fact that everything was fucked.

Then there were songs about escape through drug culture. Mervyn had used speed and grass but he drew the line at L.S.D, so his attempts at psychedelia were the result of imitation not hallucination. All this slavish imitation was aimed at earning him stardom and fame. The idea of drawing on his own experience and the beauty of the Island where he was born and raised never occurred to him, at least not until now.

Neither of his parents had fully understood Mervyn's craving for stardom and how intense that craving was. He had never really shared his music with them. He had retreated to his room to develop his skills as a guitarist and a songwriter and he would spend hours playing and singing his heart out. Through the walls they could sense the emotional intensity of his passion and were baffled as well as unnerved by it.

When Mervyn had returned from his unsuccessful assault on Australia and New Zealand his parents had hoped he had gotten it all out of his system. However the twin experiences of reading 'The Crystal Cave' and then seeing the hawk among the brambles in the garden in North Darlington had rekindled and fanned the original craving into a raging conflagration. He was the 'Voice of His Nation's Soul.' Greatness and stardom could be achieved at home in The Cumberlands.

Now at last the fire was extinguished. Seeing the enjoyment and satisfaction the Vineys got out of their music caused the scales to fall from Mervyn's eyes. His desire to write a song about Elsie was the first genuine creative impulse he had ever been visited by. Stardom was irrelevant. He just wanted to pay a beautiful compliment to a beautiful girl whose friendship meant the world to him. He might just write a song about the long beaches of Trinity Island while he was about it.

<div align="center">~~~§~~~</div>

While Mervyn was re-discovering himself on Trinity Island, Angela Moriarty (of the moonstone eyes) was reconnecting with her family back in Darlington. Her musical career in Australia had shown a lot of promise to begin with but things had stalled. She was a very competent guitarist and she was blessed with a beautiful, some would say angelic, voice. She knew that her looks and wardrobe were a great asset where at least half her audience was concerned. But she was a realist. She only did covers of other peoples' songs or songs from the traditional repertoire. She did not write songs of her own and she saw that as a distinct disadvantage.

Beyond the folk scene, she scored a couple of TV spots and a couple of people had offered to 'manage' her with a view to breaking into the 'Big Time' of show business. It quickly became clear that her fame and fortune could 'apparently' progress in leaps and bounds if she let sleazy impresarios take her to bed. The few moth-eaten hopefuls who had dared to proposition her had been promptly sent packing with a flea in their ear. Angela had a very clear sense of her own worth. While she had enjoyed being a folksinger for a while, she wasn't willing to prostitute herself to advance in that profession. Truth be told she was getting a bit bored with the whole business and wanted to resume her medical studies.

As luck would have it, she received a letter from the CBC offering her a contract to record ten more songs for the 5 to 7 spot on Channel 2 before the evening news. Furthermore they would pay her airfare from Melbourne. This was a perfect opportunity to get home free of charge and take stock of her situation. She had packed all her stuff from the little bed-sit in Northcote where she had been living and shipped it off to Darlington, all with no regrets.

Angela's mother was a doctor with her own general practice in Mill Farm. She was pleased to have her daughter back home again for a while. With her greying black hair and sapphire blue eyes, she was unlike her daughter in looks but they were very similar in temperament. Happily, as well as being mother and daughter, they were also the best of friends. Angela never knew her father. 'It's just us little one' was how her mother always answered her daughter's questions until she eventually stopped asking. There were no photographs of him anywhere in the house. When she was still quite small, Angela realized that 'Moriarty' was her mother's maiden name.

Doctor Moriarty hadn't been overly concerned about her daughter's foray into the folk music scene.

Angela wasn't the type of girl to get stars in her eyes. From an early age it had been clear that she would follow her mother into the medical profession and she wasn't star-struck about that either.

<div align="center">~~~§~~~</div>

As the month of July drew to a close, Hugh began to feel comfortable in his new position in City Hall. He now had to manage the payrolls of administrative and technical officers and keep records of their leave entitlements and their daily time sheets. Unlike the cleaners he had looked after in his old position, administrative and technical officers were covered by complicated awards which involved meal and travel allowances and made for a lot of tortuous and intricate variations among employees. This meant that he had more responsibilities but his immediate supervisor was a friendly and easygoing type who nevertheless kept a close eye on things and was always ready with helpful advice when needed.

On Trinity Island Mervyn had applied for three jobs advertised in the Government Gazette. He had received acknowledgements and was waiting to see if he would be granted an interview. In the meantime his garden bed had been thoroughly dug over. He had planted peas, broad beans and carrots and would soon be planting lettuce. He continued to take long walks on the beaches near his home and occasionally played his guitar at night in his room.

On Lesser C, Dave and Bob Viney were helping Old Tom with the winter pruning on Murphy's orchard along with Charlie Flint who was still complaining about the cold. Elsie continued to revel in the sound of her new guitar and she was growing in confidence and competence as a guitarist.   Her affectionate gratitude to Mervyn continued to grow, in a purely platonic and little sisterly way.

On the last Friday of July as Brian made his reluctant way from the cleaners' crib room to the laundry, Colin took him to one side.

'Keep this to yourself Brian,' he whispered. 'There will be a new vacancy for a cleaner coming up very soon.' With a wink and a pat on the bottom he went back to the crib room. Brian dared to hope as he nerved himself to face another smelly, boring and venomous day in the laundry.

22: *Jim*

By early August there was still no word from Jim. The copy of 'Dandillion' Lucy left with Mrs Lovegrove, had included a conciliatory letter apologizing for any past unpleasantness and inviting him to come to the Wednesday night gatherings at the pub and share his reaction to the poem.

Opinions varied within the group as to why Jim hadn't responded. Lucy was disappointed and took a negative view. She had written the conciliatory letter and made a considerable effort to swallow her past resentment of Jim's behaviour in order to make a fresh start. She now began to regard his silence as a snub. 'Leopards don't change their spots,' she said more than once.

Brian was more open minded and willing to be patient.

'He probably needs time to study the poem thoroughly. Remember we've been doing that since May. It's worth waiting a bit longer. You never know, he may come up with a completely new perspective.'

'He can't have seen it yet,' said Robert. 'If Jim had read his copy of 'Dandillion' even once he would have been round here like a shot. That's the sort of person he is.'

Little did they realize that Lucy's letter and the copy of 'Dandillion' remained unopened in their package at the foot of Jim's bed where Mrs Lovegrove had put them. Jim was lying in a coma in the Intensive Care Unit of Darlington hospital. He had been there since July 7th. He had slipped and fallen down a companion way in the still unfamiliar, bigger fishing boat and plunged several feet into darkness landing heavily, and suffering severe head injuries.

In the sunny kitchen of the Purvis home on Trinity, Mervyn had heard a brief report on the 'Shipping News' that an injured crewman had been rushed to Dark Tor and flown to Darlington by air ambulance after an accident at sea. No names were mentioned and the story didn't rate a mention in any other news bulletin.

At work, Lucy had heard about a serious case of head injuries arriving by air from Dark Tor but she didn't make the connection. It was only after a couple of weeks when she met Mrs Lovegrove arriving at the hospital that she realized. In her distracted state the anxious mother, took a while to recognize Lucy in her nurse's uniform.

'I'm afraid he hasn't seen the package you left for him dear. They brought him straight to the hospital. Hopefully when he comes home.'

Jim's mother was facing this latest catastrophe with her usual stoic fortitude. Her husband had died at sea and her son seemed hell bent on following him - first the shipwreck and now this. 'Please God' she thought, 'if he lives he'll look for a job on land.'

She had no extended family to look to for support during this crisis. She and her husband had married against the wishes of their respective families. He belonged to an obscure Bretheren sect and her family was part of a breakaway, dissenting sect which held 'heretical' opinions as to the true identity of their 'Elect Vessel'. Both families had completely ostracised the loving couple when they married (a forlorn, lonely affair in a registry office).

A childhood and adolescence spent in such a confining and stunting environment had left the newlyweds ill-equipped for making new friends and social contacts in the wider community of the Cumberlands. They had been brought up to regard such people as infidels who were damned to Hellfire. This meant that Mrs Lovegrove had few friends and Jim was the only family she had left in all the world. Hence the stoicism she had developed to cope with the pain of life.

Her son remained in a coma. The outlook was grim but where there was life there was still some faint vestige of hope. The staff were very kind to her and did their best to keep her informed, not that there was much change in her son's condition. She was amazed and deeply moved by the kindness of all these strangers, none of whom would have been welcome to break bread with her family. But infidels or not, they gave her the only real care and compassion that she had known since her husband's death.

They continued to monitor everything the multitude of instruments with all their tubes, wires and sensors could tell them about Jim's vital signs but they could only watch from the outside. There was no way of knowing if any part of his consciousness was still functioning.

Was all his awareness extinct or had his soul already begun its transition into death? Was he already following one of the pathways out of this world that he talked of to Hugh in the Gracechurch Street flat nearly a year ago? Now, for all anybody knew, he might be travelling through unimaginable vistas and landscapes of the soul. Or was he no longer aware of anything – brain dead? If, against all the odds, he woke up and made a full recovery, there was no guarantee that he would remember anything his soul experienced during the coma, or was there?

<div align="center">~~~§~~~</div>

When Lucy shared the news about Jim with the others they were genuinely concerned. They hadn't always seen eye to eye with him but he was still one of them. To hear that he was near death was shocking. Equally shocking was the possibility of him surviving with brain damage, or even in a vegetative state. Lucy felt ashamed of herself for her original negative reaction when Jim didn't show up at O'Brien's. She was also deeply moved by the tranquil fortitude of Mrs Lovegrove.

Lucy shared her concerns with her mother who told her as much as she knew of Mrs Lovegrove's story. 'It's a cruel and unnatural thing. Parents, brothers, sisters and cousins: people they'd known all their lives just cut them dead and had no further contact. It was as if they had ceased to exist.'

'I never realized - and all because of their religion? Well it's a bloody cruel religion if you ask me.'

'And then on top of all that, Mr Lovegrove drowned at sea when Jim was just a baby.'

'Given that background I can understand why Jim turned out so strange.'

'Yes. Poor things, it can't have been easy for either of them.'

Lucy was on nightshift that week and Mrs O'Rourke made a casserole for her to take to Jim's Mum next day.

'Lucy dear, come in?' She ushered Lucy into the spotless kitchen and put the kettle on for a cup of tea. 'You're not at work today?'

'I'm on nightshift this week. Mum made this casserole for you. You're probably too busy to be bothered with cooking at a time like this.'

'Thank your mother very much for me it was a kind thing to do. I've been at the hospital all morning. They performed an operation last night to relieve pressure on Jim's brain. It's frightening to even think of such a thing but it's amazing what they can do these days. I don't know how it went though. The surgeon won't be back until this afternoon to tell me.'

'From what I heard last night, it went very well and the surgeon was happy with how it turned out.'

'Well thank God for that.'

<div align="center">~~~§~~~</div>

At the Hollybank Laundry, after six weeks in the job, Hugh's morale had reached a very low ebb. Everything about the place was oppressive. Nothing he did seemed good enough for the manager and Simon's company was becoming steadily more toxic. It wasn't in Brian's nature to be intentionally unkind to anyone, particularly anyone as 'troubled' as Simon appeared to be. Where the Viney brothers or Riley would have just told him to shut up or piss off, he felt that he had to at least appear interested.

He made the mistake of trying to catch Simon out by asking questions about a particular deadly creature on different days to see if he contradicted himself. He never did and what's more he took Brian's questions as a sign of genuine interest. Believing he had found a convert, he began bringing books and magazines about venomous creatures to share with Brian during tea and lunch breaks thus depriving him of his brief moments of respite in the cleaners' crib room.

Things took an alarming turn one Tuesday night in August. He had gone to bed early because he was emotionally exhausted and extremely depressed, after a particularly gruelling day in the laundry. Sleep came to him blissfully soon. To begin with, it seemed that his unconscious mind was trying to soothe him with deeply lyrical amorous fantasies from the very core of his romantic soul.

He found himself in a blissful dream. He was in an ancient, mystical English forest. It might have been in Camelot. It might just as easily have been Sherwood Forest. Everything was sparkling and dew fresh in the swaddling mist of early dawn. Somewhere a throstle sang. He came upon a little clearing surrounded by flowering Horse Chestnut trees. In the centre of the clearing a lady was lying on a couch. As he drew closer he saw that it was Kate. She was dressed in a long, sapphire blue, pre-Raphaelite gown. Her feet were bare and her long strawberry blonde hair was bedecked in spring flowers. Her hands were folded on her breast.

Was she sleeping or had she been bewitched or enchanted? Brian hurried to her side. He had forgotten how lovely she was. He reverently kissed her lips and then held his breath. After a few seconds her eyelids fluttered and then her beautiful hazel eyes opened. She saw him and sat up smiling. Brian took her hands in his and kissed her again. She opened her mouth to speak but something dreadful had happened to her. She spoke but not with her own voice. It was the voice of Simon.

'The world's most dangerous spider is the Sydney Funnel-Web. This species of venomous mygalomorph spider is usually found within a 60 mile radius of Sydney, Australia. It can range in length from half an inch to two inches.

'Funnel-webs can be found in suburban gardens as well as in bushland and are extremely aggressive. They have larger fangs than some species of snake and are capable of biting through human fingernails and toenails.

The bite of the Funnel-Web is extremely toxic and can kill a human being in just 15 minutes.

'To begin with you will experience tingling around your mouth. Your tongue will twitch uncontrollably. Your mouth will fill up with saliva. Your eyes will fill with tears. You will experience profuse sweating and chronic painful muscle spasms. Your blood pressure and heartbeat will increase dramatically before your respiratory system painfully shuts down and you die.'

'No No No!!!! Please God no more.'

Hugh woke to the sound of Brian's desperate cries and hurried to his friend's bedside.

'Hey calm down. Whatever's the matter?' Brian was sitting bolt upright but he still wasn't awake.

'No more fucking funnel-web spiders. Bloody Simon. I've got to get out of that place. It's killing me.'

Hugh put his arm around his friend's shoulders and held him in a comforting embrace.

'You've obviously had some kind of nightmare. You just need to wake up. Everything's all right,' he said in a soothing, gentle tone.

Brian shuddered then took a deep breath.

'It was the grandmother of all nightmares.'

'Come out to the lounge. I'll stoke up the fire and get you a sherry.'

The two friends sat in front of the fire and Brian, calmed by the sherry, described his dream to Hugh.

'It started out so beautifully. It was just like Prince Charming and Snow White. Kate was looking so radiant and sweet and then when she opened her mouth she turned into bloody Simon and started talking about spiders. Honestly Hugh, I don't know how much longer I can stick it at the laundry. Is your old position at the City Council still vacant?'

'No it's been filled. I'm training my replacement at the moment.'

<div align="center">~~~§~~~</div>

Next evening they met with Robert at O'Brien's.' They had been quickly assimilated into the fraternity of regulars in the bar. There were ten or so who were there most days, mostly retired and elderly who listened to the races on the wireless and patronised the betting shop next door. They had welcomed Madge's change of policy about ladies in the Bar and had been charmed by Lucy and Kate from their first meeting. The bar boasted two curiosities: a Back Pool table and a dartboard with a peculiar swelling growth, half the size of a tennis ball at the 25 past position.

Alf Prentice, a retired carpenter had been the first to extend a hand of welcome. He and his mate Vern Talbot were there most days. In retirement, their wives had subtly trained them into a comfortable routine to ensure that they weren't under their feet all day at home. Both men were also keen gardeners who more than earned their keep with a bountiful, year-round supply of vegetables.

'No Lucy tonight?' Alf enquired.

'No she's on nightshift this week,' said Hugh.

'That's right I was forgetting. She's a nurse isn't she, a little Florence Nightingale.'

'Yes, and you should see her in her nurse's uniform,' said Brian. 'She looks absolutely stunning. Doesn't she Hugh?'

'Shut up Brian.'

'I can well believe that,' said Alf.

They bought their beers and adjourned to a table leaving Alf and Vern to their game of crib. Hugh gave Robert the latest news about Jim. He also told them what Lucy had learnt from her mother about Mrs Lovegrove's life and the way she had been ostracised by her family when she married.'

'What's ostracised?' Robert wanted to know.

'That's when they bury your head in the sand.'

'Shut up Brian.'

Apart from the news about Jim there was nothing further to discuss which had any bearing on their 'quest'. Alf and Vern had finished playing crib. Vern went home and Alf who was sitting on a pint of stout came over to their table.

'How long have you been a regular at O'Brien's Alf?'

'Years and years Brian. I remember when Madge was knee-high to a gooseberry bush. In fact I was in here the night she was born. When he got the news, Madge's Dad shouted everyone in the bar a drink to wet her head. In my apprentice days we used to come here for a beer every night after work, me and Liam Riley. We were apprenticed to the same master carpenter. I've still got all of my tools and I do the odd job here and there to keep my hand in.'

Riley was a carpenter!'

'He was until the first world war. He had a lot of bad luck during the war and when he came home - ended up in jail but he was highly skilled in his trade. I hoped he would go back to it when he got out of prison but he couldn't stick at anything much after that. At heart he's a very good man. He was just dealt a bad hand.'

'I first met him when I was working as a cleaner at Hollybank,' said Brian.

'Ah he must have been there looking after Edith. She died recently. That's a sad story - two beautiful young people who had the world at their feet until the bloody war and then Keogh broke both their hearts forever. He deserved the thrashing Liam gave him.'

'I picked apples with him this year at Murphy's orchard on Lesser C. He got the job for me actually. Just said to mention his name.'

'Yeah he was a great mate of Billy Murphy. They were in the army together. I still catch up with Liam now and then at the 'Town and Country' on pension day but I haven't seen him for quite a while now. Fancy you knowing him but then I suppose he knows just about everybody. He's quite a character.'

'He certainly is,' said Brian as Madge called time.

'That's your lot for tonight boys. See you tomorrow. Any word on Jim, Hugh?'

'Still unconscious Madge. I'll let you know if there's any change.'

'Thanks. It's rotten luck for the poor kid.'

<div align="center">~~~§~~~</div>

While Madge was getting ready for bed, Lucy was quietly enjoying her tea break in the hospital canteen. A friend of hers from ICU stuck her head round the door.

'Hey Lucy. Your friend's waking up. Come quick. He might recognize you.'

With her heart in her mouth Lucy sculled what was left of her tea and hurried after her friend. They both hastily scrubbed up, donned masks and gowns and went to Jim's bedside. He was still wired up and connected by tubes to various devices and most of his head was swathed in bandages but his eyes were open and he was looking around him in quiet confusion.

'Jim. Thank God you're awake.'

He looked at her. Because of her gown and mask and his heavily medicated state he didn't know Lucy but when she spoke, something about his eyes suggested that he responded to the sound of her voice. His mouth worked but he wasn't capable of speech.

'Don't try to speak. Just take it easy 'til you get your strength back.'

He looked at her and tried to smile. It was the sweet bewildered smile of a small child. Lucy kissed his hand and fought back tears. I've got to get back to work but I'll see you tomorrow. I'll tell your mum.'

<p style="text-align:center">~~~§~~~</p>

On the following Monday a resolution came to Brian's laundry ordeal. Just before morning tea time he was able to surreptitiously absent himself from the laundry and escape to the cleaners' crib room before Simon could corner him.

'It's a while since you've joined us,' said Ray. 'We were beginning to think you had given us away.'

'No fear. It's bloody Simon. Every chance he gets he bails me up to talk about poisonous animals. I'm literally having nightmares because of it.'

'Fear not,' said Colin. 'Relief is at hand.'

'Yes,' said Ray. 'I was coming round to see you later today. It seems our Colin is going back to the CBC to work, so in a week's time we'll have a vacancy. If you give notice at the laundry today you can start with us again next week.

The laundry manager was unimpressed when Brian gave notice but he seemed to be unimpressed about everything Brian did so that was no matter. He expected Simon to be sorry to see him go. He probably was but he took Brian's giving notice as a betrayal and never said another word to him. Brian took the snub with a grain of salt and looked forward to Friday and freedom.

<div align="center">~~~§~~~</div>

Friday morning dawned cold and misty on Trinity Island. Mervyn was taking a long beach walk before breakfast. He enjoyed the solitude at that time. Away to the East he could see the sun rising over the mountains of Greater Cumberland in the crimson distance of the horizon. Mervan Mithras had never been awake and out of doors at such an early hour to see the sun keeping its daily covenant. To Mervyn, it felt like a personal pact between himself and our nearest star as it rose clear of the horizon igniting the new day with all its promise.

It was a deeply spiritual experience and he was on a 'high'. As he continued his walk, he noticed a figure in the distance. It gradually came into focus as someone walking a greyhound. In his exalted state, Mervyn didn't mind this intrusion on his intimate dialogue with the cosmos. He resolved to greet whoever it was with a cheery 'good morrow.' This cheery greeting withered unspoken however as the approaching figure spoke first.

'Well, if it isn't Merv the Purve! I heard you were back.'

It was someone from his school days using the hated nickname unheard for so long. Sometimes nicknames are bestowed with cheerful, if mischievous goodwill among friends. More often, to Mervyn's mind, they were designed to humiliate, injure and degrade. They were a hostile brand imposed by society.

His spiritual 'high' evaporated instantly and he was plunged back into the schoolyard pain he had spent years trying to escape. He said nothing and kept walking. The other man shook his head, wondered if it was something he'd said but then shrugged it off.

'The Purve was never quite right in the head.'

With his beautiful morning in tatters, Mervyn left the beach and walked home by road. For the first time he wondered if he'd made the right decision coming home to Trinity. He loved the island itself and his family but he held most of the people he'd grown up with in contempt.

He also hated his name. The surname couldn't be helped, he supposed and he knew that being named after his much loved uncle Mervyn, the champion axeman, was meant as a compliment: but in conjunction the two words Mervyn and Purvis were a recipe for disaster. Perhaps he should use his middle name, 'David.'

Mrs Purvis noticed that her son seemed out of sorts when he sat down for breakfast.

'How was your walk son?'

'All right.'

'Did you see anyone you know?'

'Nuh.'

She didn't press the matter but for a moment she worried that her son was lapsing back into the moody withdrawal of earlier days. When Mr Purvis joined them at the table a moment later, he was full of Friday morning exuberance and the joy of the imminent weekend. His contented pleasure was infectious and Mervyn's mood began to lighten as they shared a hearty breakfast of porridge followed by eggs and bacon and a cup of tea.

After breakfast they took up their respective tasks: Mr Purvis went off to the butter factory, his wife to the laundry and Mervyn to his garden. He was planting out lettuce seedlings which he'd raised under glass. The peas, broad beans and carrots he had sown a few weeks earlier had all sprouted and were well established. A lot of judicious weeding was required to eliminate competition for his emerging crop.

Snails and slugs were beginning to pose a problem as the weather started to warm up. Like his father, Mervyn didn't share the ruthless hostility that many gardeners harboured where these creatures were concerned.

'They were here long before we were son and they have as much right to a square meal as we have.'

Like his father before him, Mervyn would go out at night with a torch and a plastic bucket, gather all the gastropods he could find and take them a long way off to start life anew in pastureland on one of the many dairy farms in the area. He thought they were beautiful creatures.

When he finished in the garden Mervyn spent about half an hour chopping and stacking some more firewood. Around ten o'clock he heard the postman's whistle. Shortly afterwards his mum came to the door.

'Time for a cup of tea son. There's some mail for you. The postman had delivered him an acceptance letter from the Post Master General's Department inviting him to start work the following Monday at the PMG office in Hampshire, the main town on Trinity.

There were probably no more than twelve hundred permanent residents on the Island, but they had the same postal and telephonic needs as people on the larger, more populous Islands. Because there were forty miles of ocean between Trinity and Greater Cumberland, the smaller Island had to have its own PMG workforce and infrastructure.

Mervyn would be working in a three person office with the senior clerk and a female typist and telephonist. The senior clerk had conducted the interview. He was a kindly man in his mid fifties and a friend of Mervyn's Dad. The interview had been a relaxed affair and Mervyn was the only applicant granted an interview, although he didn't realize that at the time.

There were two other applicants, one from Lesser C, the other from Green Island. The expense and logistics of organizing interviews with these two candidates were considered to be unwarranted. The applicants weren't public servants so there was no obligation to grant interviews and nothing in their applications suggested that they were any more suited to the position than Mervyn.

There was a second letter in a lavender envelope with a beautiful handwritten address and a faint scent of perfume.

'What lovely handwriting,' his mother said as she handed the letter to him. She had already looked on the back of the envelope to learn that the sender was Elsie Viney. She kept a straight face and studied her son's reaction. He didn't recognize the handwriting either and like his mother, he checked the back for the sender's name. A smile of delighted surprise momentarily lit up his face and for a second he blushed scarlet. His mother chose that moment to go and fill the teapot.

Viney's Farm
20 Old Coast Road
Woodfield South
Lesser Cumberland.
13/8/70

Dear Mervyn

I took the liberty of getting your forwarding address from the orchard, I hope you don't mind.

I just had to write and thank you again for giving me your guitar. It's a beautiful instrument. It sounds great and it's so easy to play. I can even do barre chords now. Dave and I are trying to teach ourselves to pick with our fingers like you do. There's a long way to go but it's not sounding too bad.

Dave and Bob have been helping old Tom and Charlie Flint with the winter pruning on Murphy's orchard. Do you reckon you'll be back for picking next year?

There's still no sign of Riley. We think he must have gone back to the big island without telling anyone.

I've passed the half way mark at school for this year. I'm not sure what I'll do next year. There is some talk of me going to Cork to do a course at Business College – typing, shorthand and book-keeping. I'm not sure if I want to though. I don't like the idea of leaving home. I'm quite happy here on the farm.

Do you see anything of Brian? He's such a funny, happy go lucky sort of person. It would be nice to have you both back down here next season.

Anyway Mervyn that's about all my news for the moment. I hope you'll write back and let me know how you're getting on. Everyone here sends their love.

Ever yours
Elsie.

PS Brutus and Fang got out last week and chased the postman. They didn't do any *real* damage. He wasn't happy though and the dogs are in disgrace at the moment. It looks like I am too for forgetting to secure the gate properly. Ho hum.
Elsie. xx'

Mervyn's heart was full to overflowing and the joy of the morning's sunrise returned. All was well with the world. What a lovely letter.

'Well Son tell me about Elsie. She has a lovely singing voice by all accounts.'

'Who told you that?'

'You did you goose! You mentioned her more than once in your letters from the orchard. Tell me all about her?'

Several cups of tea later Mervyn had poured out his heart. His mum had been a most attentive listener. 'She sounds lovely. Do you think she feels the same about you?'

'I'd like to think so but I doubt it. I think we're just friends especially since I gave her the guitar. Anyway Mum I'm too old for her. She's only sixteen and I'm twenty three – seven years older.'

'Sweet sixteen and never been kissed. Did it never occur to you that your Dad is twelve years older than me?'

~~~§~~~

Back on the Big Island, there was a joint celebration at Jamieson's on the Friday night to farewell Colin and welcome Brian back to the fold. Kate turned up from Ross at about 5.30.

'Ah' said Colin. 'It's Joan of Arc. I understand this cruel man tried to burn you at the stake recently. But he didn't go into details.'

'It was more a case of being boiled alive but we can both be grateful he didn't go into details. I hear you'll be going back to the CBC. That's exciting.'

'Yes it is rather. Not 'News' again but 'Light Entertainment', much less stressful. First up I'll be producing a series of 5 to 7 songs featuring Angela Moriarty. Not in the studio this time but in scenic locations around the archipelago.'

'The angelic Miss Moriarty,' said Brian.

'Yes I understand she is quite desirable if you like that sort of thing.'

'I thought she was based in Australia these days.'

'She was, but she's back home for a while. I was talking to her on the phone. It seems she's a bit disillusioned with showbiz and people wanting to manage her. So she's managing herself and considering her options. That's not uncommon. Showbiz is full of people who handle themselves.'

There was a call for hush while Kevin sang *Mother Machree.*

'You should sign Kevin up,' Kate whispered.

'That's not as silly as it sounds.'

'I was being serious!'
~~~

'Is there any more news about Jim?' Kate asked after the applause for Kevin.

'Continuing to improve but it will take a while. He's out of Intensive Care and all the wires and tubes have been removed. He finds speech difficult apparently and he's still not really with it. Only his mum and Lucy are allowed to visit him at this stage. He only woke up ten days ago so he's still got a long way to go.'

<div align="center">~~~§~~~</div>

3 Farm Lane
Willow Bend
Trinity Island.
29/8/70

Dear Elsie

Thank you so much for your letter. It was a lovely surprise hearing from you. I often think about you all on Lesser C and wonder how you're getting on.

I'm very happy to hear that the guitar is giving you satisfaction. I would love to hear how you and Dave are sounding with finger picking. I just picked it up from watching other people on TV: Peter Paul and Mary mostly and then there was that Canadian show 'Let's Sing Out.'

Just work out simple patterns with your thumb on the bass strings and with your fingers on the treble strings two at a time: downwards with the thumb and upwards with the fingers.

Sorry. You've probably worked that out for yourselves. I used to have a good book about it, with plenty of good diagrams and pictures. I'll see if I can find it and send it down to you. I look forward to hearing you both next time I'm on Lesser C.

Unfortunately that won't be next apple season. I've just started work with the PMG here on Trinity. It's an office job and I'll be stuck on the Island for a year 'til I build up some annual leave. I'll definitely come down then for a while. In the mean time I'm slowly getting used to wearing a collar and tie again!

Are you sure about Business College? It would be handy to have a qualification. I can understand your reluctance to leave the farm. You really seem to belong down there somehow. Perhaps you could go home for weekends. I suppose it would be too much, travelling to Cork and back five days a week.

I've been reconnecting with my childhood memories here on Trinity. I've even replanted the little vegetable garden I had when I was a kid. I go for lots of long beach walks and play music some nights. It would be great having someone to jam with, like Dave has with you.

Anyway Elsie that's about all my news. I haven't seen Brian since we got back to the Big Island. He hopes to be back at uni next year. There's a girl he's pretty sweet on.

Bye for now. Say hallo to everyone and I'll look forward to your next letter.

Yours sincerely

Mervyn

PS are Brutus and Fang keeping out of trouble?

23: *Another Spring*

In time, the bitter cold of winter gave way to the gentle temperate fragrance of Spring. Daylight saving came in and the general mood of people began to lighten. Nevertheless Kate and Maggie continued to concentrate on their studies as the business end of the academic year drew inexorably closer.

Kate's burns had healed beautifully without any scarring or disfigurement much to her relief and that of Brian who took every opportunity to examine and soothe the injured parties. He was content that their ever so slightly asymmetrical perfection had been fully restored. In fact they looked even better if it was possible to improve on perfection.

Maggie was doing well, with her studies, much better than her brother had done in his first year. But, through no intention of her own, in the vernal awakening that was astir in the Cumberland Archipelago at that time, she had yet again become a person of interest. Mark Denham had been quite taken with her the first time they met on the Down Train, the day of the Carlingford concert. Kate had warned him off on that occasion because of Hugh but he was pretty sure that Maggie was now unattached.

He made a point of sharing her table if he ever saw her in the ref even if other people were sitting with her. He was a pleasant and personable enough young man but Maggie wasn't at all smitten. As she had told Kate, she wanted to concentrate on her studies. She'd had enough of romance for the time being. She also suspected that Mark was a bit of a man's man and one of the boys. If he viewed her as no more than a potential conquest, which was entirely possible, she had no desire to become another notch on his bedpost or a trophy he could show off to his friends.

The sap was also continuing to rise in Boy Upson. After the encounter with Maggie at Montini's and the flight back to Ross next day, he had tried to forget about her. He thought himself too old and staid whereas she was so young and vibrant. He didn't think he was weakening in his resolve by sending her a birthday card for June 20th. They had shared star signs and birthdates that night in the restaurant. Maggie had sent a pretty little card thanking him for his card and his past kindness. In spite of all his carefully argued rationale, Boy now found that he couldn't stop thinking about her.

The only thing on Maggie's mind at that time was her end of year exams. It was now mid October and her first exam was less than four weeks away. She was determined to excel and show Brian how it was done. There had always been a little bit of sibling rivalry, at least on Maggie's part and unlike Brian, she was fiercely competitive. She looked forward to being one year ahead of him when (hopefully) he resumed his studies next year.

Brian was still diligently saving as much money as he could. He needed enough to pay his university fees, a year's accommodation at Trinity College and then general living expenses. He blithely believed if he just kept at it he would save the required amount. Kate was more practical and not so confident. Every now and then she would urge him to do the sums. What was the actual cost of a year at Trinity? What was the cost of a year's university fees? These matters were normally handled by the Education Department which administered and paid for Teacher studentships.

Kate had confided her concerns to her parents. They agreed that the wage Brian earned at Hollybank mightn't be sufficient to meet his objective. Mrs Mahoney said that if need be he could live with them in Denistone for a year. Kate pondered her mother's offer. Although she wasn't sure how practical it would be for Brian and herself being together under the parental roof, she was gratified nonetheless that her parents were so kindly disposed towards him.

However, Kate's Dad pointed out that care would need to be taken with regard to Brian's self esteem.

'It would have to be managed tactfully Kate. We can't have your young Galahad feeling like a kept man. It wouldn't do to have the love of your life feeling emasculated – not at his time of life.'

'Matthew Mahoney I hope you're not implying that living under my roof would have an emasculating effect on anyone!!'

'Madelaine, Madelaine, pearl of my heart's desire, the thought never crossed my mind.'

Kate struggled to keep a straight face. Only her dad would dare to tease her mum like that. Only he could get away with it.

'What Brian needs is some kind of permanent part time job in Ross that leaves plenty of time for study. Leave it with me. I don't want to get anybody's hopes up but I've just had an idea.'

He went off to his study to make a phone call. Left to themselves, Madelaine muttered to Kate.

'If that man isn't very careful, there'll be a lot more pepper in his beef stroganoff tonight than he bargained for.'

~~~§~~~
~~~

In the meantime, Brian had been back in his old cleaning job for a couple of months. While it would never be as enjoyable an occupation as apple picking it was infinitely preferable to working in the laundry.

To begin with he was disappointed to notice that some of the more interesting patients had been discharged. Little Tom with his mysterious secrets was a case in point. But Brian realized it was selfish not to be grateful that the strangely engaging little man was deemed well enough to go home. The more he had gotten to know Tom, the more uproarious and hilarious his company had become. It had quickly gotten to the stage where he had to be studiously avoided or no work would ever get done.

The one possible cloud on his horizon had been the wayward and wilful Angela. He was relieved to learn that she had spectacularly discharged herself by eloping with one of the male nurses. Some token efforts had been made to track down the two miscreants but the authorities were actually glad to see the back of them.

Life at Gracechurch Street continued as usual, although Lucy didn't spend as much time there now. Most of her spare time was taken up helping Jim's slow recovery and supporting Mrs Lovegrove. The Wednesday night meetings with Robert at O'Brien's continued.

In the few remaining weekends before exams, Kate had chosen not to come to Darlington. Brian was able to be philosophical about this and kept himself amused to the best of his ability. He actually used those weekends and a lot of his week nights to start re-reading the novels and textbooks he hoped to be studying again next year. In this way he could be with Kate in spirit and earning some brownie points as well.

At this time, Robert's contributions to the quest were becoming rather esoteric. He was quite disillusioned with "Dandillion", since none of his colleagues had managed to glean anything useful from its poetic imagery. On the surface it was just a fairytale.

Because of the connection between Kate's grandfather and Norian Fairchild they were all assuming or hoping that the poem was set in the Cumberland Archipelago. Robert had begun to think that was just wishful thinking. However in the middle of his doubt and disillusion an idea occurred to him. If he could locate one of the places named in "Dandillion" somewhere in the Cumberlands, it would be a credible sign that there was some factual basis to the poem.

The most realistic sounding names were the Cypress Gate, with its nearby stream, and the River Parfentine. He bought maps of the Darlington area from the Lands Department and spent hours studying its rivers and creeks but he did so aimlessly without any method or system: vainly hoping he would chance upon something that would make everything suddenly come clear. When this didn't happen immediately, he became disheartened.

But there was something of the terrier about Robert and he found that he couldn't let the matter drop. In a moment of inspiration he made a decision. The principal river in the Darlington area was called 'the River'. The principal river in "Dandillion" was the Parfentine. If there was any factual basis to the poem then the Parfentine and the River would probably be one and the same. All he had to do was look for some tributary to the River that was large enough to be navigable by an ocean going vessel, which presumably Dandillion (the white ship) would have to be. This was something systematic and structured and Robert's spirits rose.

Most of the tributaries sprang and flowed from the heights of Mount Cameron. They fanned out from the mountain flowing through various suburbs of the City to enter the River from the west. Whenever it rained heavily, all the Mountain streams would suddenly explode into raging torrents which rushed down into Darlington sometimes causing flash flooding in city streets. At such times, Hugh liked to think, the primitive force of nature which the Mountain held at bay, would break free and show the city and all its inhabitants who was really in charge.

Unfortunately Robert could not verify the width or depth of the tributaries from the maps. He traipsed around the City and its surrounds to inspect as many of the rivulets as he could find. Some had long since been covered over by the City and now formed part of its storm water drainage system. Those rivulets that weren't covered didn't look deep enough or wide enough to carry ocean going vessels. In the end he had to admit defeat.

<div align="center">~~~§~~~</div>

While all his friends and acquaintances were going about their lives, Jim was still slowly emerging from wherever his mind had been since his accident. He was now familiar with the company of his mother and Lucy, not as the people he had known before but as kind strangers he had come to know since he regained consciousness. They meant no more to him than the nurses and doctors who looked after him.

He had no memory of anything before he woke up. He knew some of the words that people spoke to him but they didn't always make sense. Everyone was very kind to him and he responded in kind with a gentle and confused benevolence. Eventually he took Mrs Lovegrove's word for it that she was his mother, though what that meant exactly wasn't always clear.

Gradually he found himself able to form words of his own and he attempted to respond to peoples' questions but it was hard work. Lucy was a confusing figure because sometimes she was dressed like the other nurses and other times she wasn't. Gradually he learnt her name. One thing that distinguished Lucy and his mother from the hospital staff was their anxious sadness. They spoke brightly and cheerfully like the others but their anxiety still showed through.

On a Wednesday evening in late October, Lucy brought Hugh to visit. Although he'd been warned what to expect, Hugh was deeply shocked and saddened by Jim's condition. There was a faint glimmer of recognition in the patient's eyes as he smiled an innocent bland smile. To Hugh it was like looking down into deep wells. It took an age for anything to penetrate down to Jim's awareness and even longer for any response to return. Everything was so slowed down but there was a kind of benevolent light in his eyes. Occasionally it would cloud over and contact would be lost for a time.

'Jim this is Hugh. Do you remember him?'

Jim's reply astounded them all. 'Montini's!' He smiled broadly and then the smile was replaced by a look of anxious regret and sadness. 'Montini's. Sorry.'

Jim's confusion and momentary sadness were confounded by Lucy's reaction.

'That's brilliant Jim! Well done. That's the first thing you've remembered.'

'Montini's?' Jim repeated again hopefully.

'I've got to tell your mum.'

Lucy didn't have long to wait to pass on her news because Mrs Lovegrove arrived at that moment. She greeted her son with her customary kiss which he accepted with his customary complacency.

'Mrs Lovegrove this is Hugh, he's another friend of Jim's.'

'Hullo Hugh. I'm finally getting to meet some of Jim's friends at last. It's very kind of you to come and visit him.'

'We've all been very worried about him.'

'Yes it's been a long struggle but I think he's slowly turning the corner at last, aren't you son? If it's a fine day tomorrow they're going to let him up to go outside in a wheelchair for some fresh air and sunshine. His broken bones are healing nicely and the plaster will be coming off soon so that's more good news.'

Lucy told her about Jim's memory of Montini's and she responded with the most brilliant and radiant smile that Lucy had seen from her. It was a little used expression and it's warmth and happiness were not lost on Jim either. They had stirred another, much older memory than the fiasco at Montini's – a deep, foundational recollection of maternal reassurance and nurture from his earliest infancy.

Lucy and Hugh made their goodbyes and headed for O'Brien's. Although he was happy about the first tentative return of Jim's memory, Hugh was visibly shaken and deeply upset by the extent of his injuries.

'I suppose you must deal with that sort of damage on a daily basis.'

'Not always that severe, but the job of nursing is about mending damaged people and it takes a lot of getting used to. You have to put on a bright and positive face for the sake of the patients and their families.

'Jim is the first close acquaintance I've had to care for. The first time I saw him, when his eyes had just opened and I saw how badly smashed up he was, it knocked me for six. Fortunately he was still in ICU at that stage and I didn't have to care for him. They just called me in as someone who knew him. I thought I was going to lose it entirely but when I got back to my own work I settled down again pretty quickly.'

'I don't know how you do it,' said Hugh and he gathered her up in a huge embrace as much for his own reassurance as anything else. 'You're bloody amazing.'

'You realize we're in broad daylight. The punters in O'Brien's are probably ogling us as we speak.'

'Who cares!'

Lucy was correct in her assumption. They walked into the bar to a standing ovation. Brian had spotted them and alerted all the regulars. A year ago Hugh would not have coped at all well in such a predicament but he'd learnt a lot in recent months and acquired some poise.

'Thanks everyone. Drinks are on Brian for being such a smart arse.'

People seemed to think that was a good idea and empty glasses were being lined up on the bar – ten in all. It was Brian's turn to squirm. As it happened, the ten punters were just about to leave for a darts tournament across town at the Waggon and Horses but they hung around for a few minutes just to add to Brian's discomfort.

After the darts team had gone with cries of 'next time,' Lucy and Hugh joined Robert at their table, pointedly leaving it to Brian to at least get their drinks.

'Have you been causing a disturbance in my public house Master McInerney?'

'Not really Madge just a little harmless fun.'

'You're a young harum-scarum. These are on the house.'

Madge had been pleasantly surprised by the impact the young 'conspirators' had made on her older regulars. It had always been a comfortable bar but now it seemed to be a brighter happier place as well. It had also become a much more interesting place to work in. Some of the other younger regulars started bringing their girl friends too: before and after dates, and they all wanted something to drink.

'You just can't help yourself can you?' said Hugh as Brian returned with their drinks.

'Just keeping you on your toes.'

'Well don't sleep too soundly tonight. There may be a reckoning. We wouldn't pull the same stunt you did tonight because Kate's too nice a person. But when you're on your own, you're fair game. There's a target on your back.'

'Can we get down to business?' said Robert. He hadn't been impressed by Brian's stunt because it could have embarrassed Lucy. 'What's the news about Jim?'

Hugh told him what they had just seen at the hospital. 'He's badly smashed up. Even with Lucy's warnings I wasn't prepared for it. In the old days he was so sharp and articulate. You never knew what he was up to. Now he just seems childlike. He can barely put two words together and his reactions are so slowed down.'

'That was the first time you had seen him Hugh. I'm there most days and I've seen the progress he's making,' said Lucy. 'He may never recover completely but he could still get a lot of his old acuity back.   Remembering Montini's tonight was a major achievement.'

'I don't think I'd like to see him in his present condition,' said Robert.   'Perhaps later on when he's getting a bit better.'

Lucy agreed. 'I think it would be too upsetting for you at this point.'

Alf came past on his way to the bar.

'What's on the agenda tonight then? You're always very businesslike when you get your heads together.'

'Just stuff,' said Robert. 'It wouldn't interest you.'

'You never know son, it might.' Alf hadn't taken offence, because Brian had given him a placatory nod and wink. Alf surmised that he'd soon be in the picture and Brian had resolved then and there to enlighten him at the first available opportunity. Alf went back to where his mates were listening to the night trots on the wireless. In between races there was music by various artists. Brian was alarmed to notice that Tex Buchanan was now starting to get some airplay on the Big Island.

The 'conspirators' got down to business.

'Has anyone had any more success with "Dandillion"?' Hugh wanted to know.

'I've been giving a lot of thought to Kate's theory,' said Brian.

'What theory?'

'About which of his descendants Norian transports on Dandillion. Remember she drew a distinction between the descendants of Norian and his wife and those children he sired over the centuries with other women. It might only be those later descendants that qualify.'

'I don't see why,' said Robert 'and either way it would still amount to thousands of people over the years.'

'That's not necessarily the case. I think it may be a case of individual women here and there. He might have taken other partners over the years and maintained a monogamous relationship with each of them until they died.'

'But remember,' said Lucy, 'Kate's grandad reckoned he had two women on the go when he was at uni back in the twenties – at least two.'

'Were they his exact words?'

'I can't remember precisely. We'll have to check with Kate after her exams are finished. When will that be?'

'Her last exam is on the morning of November 16th – Political Science.'

'I'm still not persuaded by any of this immortal fairy stuff,' said Robert. 'It all sounds too make-believe. I think our only objective is to prove that there were, normal, ordinary, flesh and blood people living here before the wreck of the 'Dryad.''

'Well what about the old gravestones I found on Lesser C,' said Brian.

'What gravestones?'

'Near this ancient orchard we had to pick, there was an old cemetery. Although most of the headstones were dated from after the wreck of the 'Dryad' to the present day, there were six old gravestones in a line, dated 1782. I mentioned it in my appraisal of Dandillion, towards the end.'

'I didn't read right to the end. I'd seen enough to get the gist of what you were trying to say,' said Robert and Brian rolled his eyes.

'I also mentioned that I thought the village of Nonesuch might have been the settlement that pre-dated the arrival of the convicts. Did any of you read it right through?'

Hugh and Lucy confirmed that they had.

'Thank you,' said Brian, sounding as close to exasperated as he ever got. 'Well what do you think?'

'What was written on the old headstones?' asked Hugh.

'Unknown sailor death by shipwreck.'

'That doesn't prove there was already a community living here before the wreck of the 'Dryad. They might have been buried by their shipmates.'

'Their shipmates would have known their names and anyway the old headstones are proof that at least somebody was on Lesser C prior to 1807.'

'That's Lesser C,' said Lucy. 'I thought we were assuming that 'Dandillion' was set on Greater Cumberland?'

'We have to be open to all possibilities but the old headstones are tangible evidence of something. Don't you think so Robert?'

'Yes I do. They are of more value than the poem, if you ask me.'

<center>~~~§~~~</center>

Giacomo Montini was worried about Boy Upson. Since that extraordinary evening back in June when he had 'rescued' Maggie, Boy had changed dramatically. Gone was the boisterous, loud-mouthed persona he'd been known for. He had become withdrawn and diffident. He hardly ever raised his voice these days and he appeared to be wasting away.

Finally, one night in the restaurant after the other patrons had gone, Boy had poured out his heart. A fortnight after receiving Maggie's thank you for the birthday card, he'd written suggesting meeting for a cup of coffee in Ross sometime. She replied that it would be nice to catch up but could he wait til her exams were over on November 17th. He took heart from the fact that she had named a date when they could meet. It wasn't a brush off. However it didn't ease his emotional turmoil. He was actually losing weight and it was starting to show.

Boy had been loved and cherished by his adoptive parents, and he had become used to getting anything he wanted in life. Now for the first time, he had encountered something or rather someone, utterly desirable, that he lacked the competence, experience and understanding to acquire. He'd never felt inadequate before.

Girls had never appealed to him because the only girls he had known were his cousins. They had always treated him with contempt because he stood to inherit his adoptive parents' fortune at their expense. He dismissed them all as a pack of ghastly harpies and promptly lost all interest in the fairer sex. He had good friends, almost exclusively male, and was quite content with his lot until the night he met Maggie.

She had looked so vulnerable and fragile and so beautiful, unlike the Upson harpies in every possible way. When Giacomo had told him she had been stood up, Boy's characteristic bravado had carried the day. It had swept him up and Maggie as well, but in doing so it had swept him out into unfamiliar territory. The adrenalin charged euphoria of the encounter sustained him until he dropped Maggie off at Madelaine next day. Then, as he drove away to keep his next appointment, the euphoria evaporated and he realized that his world had changed. He was in a situation where his abilities as a successful pastoralist and businessman counted for nothing.

Giacomo listened to Boy's concerns with his customary compassion and alert interest. Truth be told, he'd often wondered about Boy's sexual orientation.

'How old are you Boy? If you don't mind my asking.'

'Twenty five.'

'And Maggie, how old is she?'

'I don't know. She's at uni though.'

'She must be at least 17 then. And is this the first time you've felt this way about a girl?'

'It's the first time I've felt this way about anyone.'

'Then you've got it all in front of you and a lot to learn. The first time it happens is always the hardest I guess. For what it's worth, I think you've behaved in a gentlemanly fashion and you've probably made a good impression but you must give it time. Give her time to get to know you better. Just concentrate on being a good friend. From what you've told me you didn't force your intentions on her physically.'

'Shit no. I should think not.'

Giacomo looked at Boy with gentle shock and amazement, suddenly seeing him for the first time as the absolute 'innocent' that he actually was.

'If she agrees to a coffee after the exams that's good but it might be no more than a casual act of friendship. If she doesn't agree to a coffee, that's too bad. I think she would owe you a debt of gratitude though, for your kindness here that night and flying her home next day. But that might be the full extent of her feelings for you.

Just be patient and try not to get your hopes up. You've got a lot to learn yet before you get romantically entangled with anyone. She is very beautiful but you hardly know her. For all you know, she might snore or have bad breath.'

Boy didn't realize that Giacomo was joking and looked embarrassed and confused. He remembered liking the scent of Maggie's perfume. It was lovely, like everything else about her and that had been enough.

24: The End of 1970

November came and with it the end of the academic year. The morning after Maggie's final exam, Boy rang her at Madelaine and arranged to meet her that afternoon at the antique 'Old Cumberland Tea Rooms' in the main street of Ross. It was an enjoyable meeting and Maggie was happy to share her end of year celebration with him. He was able to relax in the presence of his obsession and enjoy her conversation. It was only when they were apart that he got agitated. For Maggie, the longer Boy went without 'making a move' on her, the more comfortable she felt about a nice, platonic friendship between them – with no strings attached.

Mark Denham hadn't gone away and he still pestered her for a date but Maggie was always able to put him off without bending the truth too much. She had come to believe that the 'first love' she had shared with Hugh would probably never be equalled with any other partner. Perhaps they had committed themselves too much when they were too young but it had been such an adventure, so deliciously daring, given that they were still children. No subsequent relationship could achieve that same exquisite and novel intensity.

When she accepted defeat in her quest to recapture Hugh she had called it a day. At that time at least, she had no desire to submit her body to anyone else's sexual appetite. She thought it must be possible to live a full and contented life being single and there was something romantic in the idea of Hugh being her only lover. All of this boded well for the friendship with Boy if he continued to show such shy reserve.

~~~§~~~

On the last Friday in November, exam results were published. Kate scored three distinctions and a credit and Maggie achieved two credits a distinction and a high distinction. Both girls were very happy with their marks and relieved that it was all over til next year.

Kate treated herself to a short holiday in Gracechurch street with Brian and set out that afternoon. She arrived around 5.30 and found Brian just home from work and checking the letter box. He had mail from O'Shannessy.

'What does he want with me now. Don't tell me he's decided to send me a bill after all this time.'

'No he wouldn't do that. He was repaying a favour from Dad.'

It turned out to be a letter advising Brian that he would learn something to his advantage if he attended chambers in Darlington at 10.30 a.m. on Tuesday November 31st.

After a happy weekend at Gracechurch street, Brian and Kate duly turned up at the appointed time on Tuesday morning and sat with mounting curiosity in the waiting room.   They could hear O'Shannessy's voice loudly declaiming on the telephone and smell his cigar from behind his closed door. Presently, the lawyer put down the phone and came out to the waiting room.

'Ah Mr McInerney and Miss Mahoney as well, an added delight. Come in. Come in! It's time for elevenses. Can I interest either of you in tea and scones?'

He pressed a button on his intercom and left instructions with his secretary.   Presently they were comfortably settled in deep armchairs around an antique
~~~

table and enjoying a Devonshire tea. O'Shannessy was being mother.

'Now you must be wondering why I've asked you here so I'll get straight to the point. Mr McInerney I understand that you are currently working as a cleaner at Hollybank Psychiatric Hospital, with a view to resuming your studies at university next year.'

'That's right. I have to successfully complete a year's study at my own expense before my studentship can be re-instated.'

'Just so. That's what I'd been led to believe.

'Well young man I'm in the happy position of being able to do you a substantial favour. You will remember from our first meeting, that I have chambers in Ross as well as here in Darlington, not as large an establishment: just four offices, a typing pool, meeting room, kitchen and bathroom. The elderly lady who has been responsible for cleaning the premises wishes to retire at the end of the year. I'm therefore offering you the position on a salary of 800 pounds a year.

'The work for a young able-bodied man like yourself should take little more than an hour to an hour and a half a day If your work proves satisfactory and the foreman cleaner at Hollybank assures me that it will, the job is yours not only next year but for as long as you want it, even beyond the re-instatement of your teacher studentship. It would be, if I may say so, a useful little earner. Are you interested Mr McInerney?'

'Is the Pope a Catholic?' said Brian. 'That would be great Mr O'Shannessy.'

'My pleasure,' said the lawyer as he went to the drinks cabinet for the sherry to seal the arrangement.

'And Miss Mahoney would you now consider the ledger to be squared between us?'

Kate rushed over and gave him a hug and a kiss on the cheek. 'You're a Baa-lamb!'

'Hush! Be still my beating heart,' purred, the blushing solicitor as he poured three glasses of sherry and they toasted their agreement. The little celebratory meal lasted about twenty minutes until Mr O'Shannessy's next appointment.

'You can start in the position in February. That will allow you to keep working at Hollybank in the interim until the start of the academic year.'

'You seem to have thought of everything Mr O'Shannessy,' said Kate.

'Yes I do rather. Please call me Richard.'

'Thank you so much for this,' said Brian.

'Yes,' said Kate. 'This has removed our biggest worry.'

'Happy to oblige, now run along the pair of you. I have work to do.'

<center>~~~§~~~</center>

Back out on the street, the full implications of O'Shannessy's offer were still sinking in. Brian had always doggedly trusted to luck that his finances would fall into place but even he had quiet moments of deep uncertainty about his future. Kate had always been more down to earth and up until that moment had not really believed that Brian would actually earn enough to get him back to university. Now the uncertainty was over and the year had proven to be a brilliant success for both of them.

'I think Dad might have had something to do with this,' said Kate. 'Something he said to Mum and me a few weeks back. We must go back to Denistone soon and find out. They've hardly seen you since you got back from picking apples.'

They were sauntering down Jamieson street, hand in hand and full of the joys of life when they heard an excited shout from behind them.

'Brian! Brian!!'

They turned round and saw a little man in a too large gabardine overcoat, dark glasses and a fedora hat. 'It's me, Tom!!'

'Why so it is. Sorry Tom I didn't recognize you all dressed up. Why the disguise?'

'There are people in this city who don't have my best interests at heart. People with turf connections.'

'Curiouser and curiouser.

'Anyway, Tom this is my girlfriend Kate. Kate this is my friend Tom, the philosopher from Hollybank. Remember I was telling you about him.'

Tom doffed his hat and then shook Kate's hand.

'I'm very pleased to meet you Kate. You're a very lucky girl. Brian is without a doubt the wisest man on earth.'

'You mean **this** Brian,' said Kate, smiling a smile of pure delight at the absurdity of it all.

'Without a doubt Kate. Without a doubt. I used to take all my problems to him at Hollybank. He has a gentle way of listening that always puts you at your ease. No conundrum is too large or too small for him to understand. He confirmed my theory about the spaces between our fingers.'

'Why don't you show Kate?'

'Why certainly. If you'd care to hold up one hand Kate. Either one, left or right. All my theorems have universal application. Now how many digits counting the thumb?'

And so Kate was duly initiated into the mysteries of Tom's unique view of the world.

'Who would have thought,' she enthused, 'five digits but only four spaces and it's the same on the other hand as well. I couldn't resist checking.'

'Like I was saying Kate, universal application. You needn't have doubted.'

'Have you checked to see if a similar universal law applies to our feet?'

'Why bless me, no I haven't.

'You clearly have the mind of a natural born philosopher. Now since Brian and I are both wearing shoes and socks (although not necessarily in that order) and you Kate are wearing those lovely little 'Atlantean' sandles I suggest we examine your feet immediately. Brian would you do the honours. I wouldn't presume to perform any kind of calculation on the gentle flesh of your beloved. Did Brian paint your toenails that exquisite shade Kate?'

'No. I let him try once and he proved most untrustworthy.'

'OK Tom,' said Brian. 'We'd better do both feet and be empirical about it.'

He solemnly began to count Kate's toes.

'This little piggy went to market. This little piggy stayed home.'

'I'm warning you McInerney!' said Kate vehemently under her breath. She was pathologically ticklish.

'This little piggy had roast beef.'

A few onlookers had gathered by now but the experiment was suddenly rudely interrupted.

'Tommy Madigan what have I told you about bothering complete strangers with your crackpot, woolgathering, bullshit!!!'

'Molly dear, these are no strangers. This is Brian, one of my most treasured friends. He used to be at Hollybank disguised as a cleaner but he was really an under-cover doctor and this is his lovely girl friend Kate.'

'Hallo. I hope he hasn't been giving you any trouble with his cock and bullshit.'

'On the contrary,' said Brian. 'We've been having an interesting philosophical discussion.'

'He **has** been giving you trouble, either that or you're as silly as he is. And you can piss off!' she snapped at a bystander who had showed no sign of moving on. 'The show's over. G'arn! Shoo!!'

Sensing the need to pour oil on troubled waters, Kate suggested a coffee at the Bluebird, which was close by. 'We've just had some wonderful news and you can celebrate it with us.' On the door of the Bluebird, Brian noticed with some concern that there was a poster for Tex Buchanan, appearing that night.

In the relative seclusion and privacy of the cafe, Tom's wife calmed down and her mood lightened. She was a vibrant little diamond of a woman in her mid forties, small like Tom with a dazzling smile and brilliant dark blue eyes. She had a mane of very long, wavy, black hair tied back but always threatening to break loose.

'And tell me Brian, were you working at Hollybank or were you a patient like his Nibs?'

'I was working Molly but as a cleaner not an under-cover doctor.'

'Ah' said Tom with a knowing smile, 'but I was able to see you as we all appear on the other side. I saw your astral self.'

Molly snorted. 'More of your tommy rot.' But she was smiling in spite of herself.

'Now tell me Brian,' said Tom, 'Where did you get to after apple picking?'

'I came back to Hollybank. I had to work in the laundry for a while 'til the cleaners had a vacancy. By the time I got back to cleaning you were long gone. Where did you get to?'

'The enlightened ones decided that all my threatening demons had been well and truly vanquished, so they let me go back home to Ross where Mollie and I live with me old Mammy.'

'I'll be living in Ross next year too. That's the good news Kate and I are celebrating. I'll be going back to uni.'

'As a Doctor of Philosophy?'

'No' said Brian when Kate had her laughter under control. 'Just a humble undergraduate.'

'But he'll be studying to become a teacher,' said Kate.

'All is well then,' said Tom. 'All the necessary balances will be restored and I will be able to rest easy. One by one all my most vexing conundrums are being sorted.'

'What's been vexing you Tom?'

'Giraffes mainly.'

'In what way?'

'It's their necks. Why are they so infernally long? To be sure it's an excess beyond the bounds of common decency in any man's language or terminology.'

'What does Darwin have to say on the subject?'

'Don't talk to me about Darwin! Darwin is a blackguard and a scoundrel! He couldn't lie straight in bed.

'Do you know what he did when he was in Australia? He shot and killed a poor little platypus – the most divine and blessed little conundrum in all the whole of the animal kingdom. God be praised that Darwin never came to the Cumberlands. That's all I can say and a lot more beside.'

'Now what's all this about you being a wanted man? Why are you incognito?' Tom drew an expansive breath and prepared to give a lengthy explanation but Molly cut him off.

'I'll tell them Tom, otherwise we'll be here all day. Tom is a very good jockey, or rather he used to be. But he was injured in a fall during a race. The horse wasn't hurt. She got straight back up but Tommy had head injuries and was in a bad way for a while. Doctors were worried about brain damage. That's assuming there ever was a brain inside his skull to start with.

'Anyway he woke up eventually and at first, he seemed to have recovered completely. I mean he's always away with the fairies so it was a little bit hard to be sure. But after a while it was clear that he was different. He started getting these bad headaches. It turned out he had "the sight". He probably gets it from his Mammy. But he only got it after his fall. It started interfering with his races. It started tellin' him when things were going to go wrong in a race – and he lost his nerve. He had to give race riding away and now he works with me as a stable hand and only rides trackwork to exercise the horses same as I do.

'Then he got the bright idea of using '"the sight" to pick winners and make his living as a punter but that didn't work out very well at all. "The sight" can be a fickle mistress. He went about it like a bull at a gate and made a killing at three race meetings in a row. He won a lot of money in a couple of weeks. Unfortunately for Tommy he backed a couple of 100 to 1 shots that nobody was "supposed to know about" and attracted the unwonted attention of a gentleman by the name of Tickler Murphy. Tickler is a Bookmaker but he is happy to plunder his fellow Bookies with huge betting plunges of his own, on long shots that nobody is "supposed to know about."

'If Tom had just shown a little common sense and spread his bets around no one would have noticed, or minded probably. It was just bad luck and stupidity on his part that he placed all his bets with Tickler. To cut a long story short, a couple of "consultants" came round to our place one night to warn Tom that if he ever did anything to irritate or upset Tickler Murphy ever again, Tickler would personally come round and geld him with a blunt butter knife. It was also around this time that the "philosophisin" started.'

'We really should adjourn this conversation to a public house to lubricate the cogs and sprockets of our cerebral thrombosis with some spirituous liquor,' said Tom who was suddenly looking very pale and eager to change the subject.

'Over my dead body, Tom Madigan. You're still on your tablets.'

'Molly dearest! Tablets, physic and single malts are all but strings on the same harp.'

'Well if that's the case, you can just come home with me and make do with your tablets.'

'Molly dear! You have the wisdom of Solomon and the compassion of Joseph Stalin. If you weren't so good in bed, I'd slit my own throat, as true as I'm standin' here.'

'You're sitting down actually but if you don't start behaving yourself I'll put you across my knee. Now say goodbye to Kate and Brian. We've got a train to catch.'

'Goodbye Kate. I see that Brian hasn't put a ring on your finger yet. Should I have a word to him do you think?'

'Enough of your nonsense Tom. We'll miss the train.'

'And did you solve the giraffe question?' Brian called out as the Madigans started running back down Jamieson Street.' 'Oh yes I did,' Tom called back over his shoulder. 'Obvious once you know the answer.'

'Well why are their necks so long?'

Tom tapped the side of his nose with a knowing finger, 'It's because their heads are so far up in the air.'

<p style="text-align:center">~~~§~~~</p>

On Wednesday December 23rd the 'conspirators' met at O'Brien's for the last time that year. Hugh and Lucy would be going up to Middleton on the Down Train the next day for Christmas and Brian would travel with them as far as Denistone where Kate would be waiting for him. Robert had work next day at the supermarket after which he would spend Christmas as usual with his family.

There had been a good crowd in the bar during the day with various office Christmas parties turning up but by the time Robert arrived only the usual old regulars were still there. However there was still plenty of Christmas cheer in evidence. Madge was putting decorations up and enlisting help from the more able-bodied patrons as required. At about nine o'clock she was satisfied with how everything looked and she called the room to attention.

'All right everyone, now I normally do this on Christmas Eve like Dad used to do but the regulars are all here and as you kids will have gone on your holidays tomorrow I'll bring it forward a day. She produced a bottle of Chivas Regal and the requisite number of glasses.

'OK kids, welcome to the inner sanctum. You old lags know the drill.' Glasses were charged and toasts were drunk, first to Madge's Dad and Mum, then to the Pub, then to present company and then to Christmas. And may we all still be here next Christmas.'

This was one of the few times in the year when Madge came out from behind the bar and had a drink with the punters. The doors were locked and everyone there became an honorary member of the O'Brien Clan. By 9.30 people started to go home. Madge and Lyle started cleaning up. The only punters left were Hugh, Lucy, Brian, Robert and Alf.

'Are you kids going to let me in on your top secret discussions tonight?' he asked. Robert was the only one who looked uneasy about this prospect. By this time Hugh and Lucy had come round to Brian's point of view about opening up their enquiry to other people but they hadn't floated the idea with Robert yet. In spite of the look of alarm in his friend's eyes, Brian took matters into his own hands.

'Robert here believes there were people already living in the Cumberlands before the wreck of the Dryad.'

'Ah. The Nonesuchers.'

'You mean you've heard of them!'

'I've heard of them. Whether or not I believe everything I've heard is another matter.'

'Who were they exactly?'

'Exactly, I can't say. I heard about them when I was a kid. Dad thought they were some kind of church. They kept to themselves. There were a few small religions about in those days, outside the main ones, Bretheren mainly. When I was in my teens I knew a bloke who grew up in a Nonesuch family. He didn't believe in it himself but he told me more or less what they believe.'

'And what do they believe?'

'They call themselves the 'Half Elven'. They believe that there is an angel living amongst them. His name is Norian Fairchild. It was his father who made them the Half Elven in the distant past, because one of their kids had died trying to rescue Norian in a boating accident. Being Half Elven means they can go to Heaven without dying. They call Heaven the 'Deathless Realm'. Getting there involves a sea journey. Norian takes them on his boat 'Dandillion,' the white ship and if you believe that you'll believe anything.

'My friend didn't believe a word of it. He said he'd never seen hide nor hair of Mr Fairchild. His family told him that Norian sometimes went on long voyages and could be away for many years at a time but he always returns as long as you believe in him. My friend wasn't convinced so he 'dropped out' as you kids would say, a bit like a lapsed catholic. He reckons a lot of young Nonesuchers did the same but they usually respected the secrecy and didn't talk about it to others.

'I suppose, when you think about it, that sort of belief is not much different to any other religion. Christians believe Christ is God. He holds the key to eternal life and he lives among his people. "Wherever two or more people are gathered in my name I am with them," or something like that. The Nonesuchers were no big secret back then but over the years they've been making themselves scarce. You've left your investigation about fifty years too late.'

Alf paused for breath and a sip of 'Chivas' while his dumbfounded listeners sat there absorbing what he had just told them. Robert in spite of his initial resentment had been as fascinated as the others. Brian was the first to find his voice.

'I told you we were being too secretive.'

'That's not to say that what they believed is true,' Robert was finally able to say. 'It doesn't prove there were people here before the Dryad was wrecked.'

'You're right there son,' Alf continued. 'They're just another mob who think they're the chosen few. That's what's wrong with the world. It's full of all these different groups who think they're the only ones that matter.'

By some unspoken understanding they didn't tell Alf any more about their quest that night. Even Brian wanted time to digest the new information. They thanked him very much for what he had told them.

'Any time kids. Now I'd better get off home before the missus sends out a search party.'

Madge called time and the 'kids' made their goodbyes. Alf's disclosures had taken the wind out of everybody's sails. When they left the pub they all went back to Gracechurch street for a cup of coffee and a post mortem. The general consensus was an enormous sense of anti-climax.

'I mean,' said Robert, 'how many years have we spent puzzling and searching and then Alf makes it all seem so matter of fact and no great secret at all.'

'He described Norian as an angel,' said Hugh. 'There's nothing matter of fact about that.'

'Alf obviously doesn't believe it Hugh. And it turns out that all along, this mysterious secret society is just another crackpot religious sect. It's no big secret. People have just forgotten about it.'

Brian suggested telling Alf about "Dandillion". 'I wouldn't bother,' Robert replied. 'He's probably got it on his bookshelf, published by Penguin or something. It's probably no great secret out there in the *real* world.'

'I suppose,' said Lucy, 'it was bound to happen if we learnt all the answers. However secretive they were they'd still just be people going about their everyday lives. If we got to know them they wouldn't be mysterious anymore.'

'Come on everyone! Don't let's all start dropping our bundles,' said Brian. 'Nothing Alf told us disproves any of our theories. Although he doesn't believe Norian is some kind of mystical being, he still gave us a pretty succinct summary of "Dandillion". The thing is, we know heaps more about Norian than Alf does. What about Kate's grandad and the Penruddocks?'

'I'm not dropping my bundle,' Lucy sighed. 'It's just that our secret 'quest' isn't quite the secret we thought it was I suppose and that's a bit disappointing. But you're quite right about Norian. There's still a lot to learn about him I guess.'

'That's getting into immortality and stuff,' said Robert. 'You know how I feel about all that bullshit.'

'But just think Robert,' Brian went on. He had the bit between his teeth now. 'What if we were able to track Norian down and meet him in the flesh. Wouldn't that change your mind?'

'We might meet someone with that name but I don't see how he could prove his immortality. More than likely he'd just be a boring ordinary person living a boring ordinary life like all the rest of us. What's an angel supposed to look like anyway? I didn't see any wings in the picture in Mrs Malleson's room. I'll leave that side of things to you blokes and get on with my own research – Maps and documents, bricks and mortar.'

'What about your grocery deliveries to the old families in the cul-de-sacs? Did you have any luck with them?' asked Lucy, concerned that Robert seemed to be in the early stages of a mood-swing.

'Not really Lucy. There isn't much chance to talk. I'm in and out pretty quickly.'

'You actually go inside the houses!'

'Yes Brian! A week's supply of groceries is too much for some of them to carry. Sometimes a carer comes to the door and takes them from me. When that happens, I don't get inside at all.'

'Well whenever you do get inside, keep your eyes peeled for anything out of the ordinary. Obviously there wouldn't be anything photographic from before the wreck of the Dryad but there might be old paintings and stuff. See if you can get them talking.'

'Brian you know I'm not good at talking to strangers and anyway Alf has told us all we need to know about the 'Nonesuchers'. Norian must be away on one of his journeys at the moment, which is a pity. Some of the poor old sods could do with a quick trip to Heaven without having to die.'

~~~§~~~

On Christmas Day, Jim came home from hospital. His physical injuries were healing well. He needed a walking stick in the short term but his prospects of regaining full mobility were good. All the bandages and plaster casts had been removed. His hair was starting to grow back where it had been shaved prior to surgery, giving his head an exotic patchwork appearance. Apart from that, to the untrained eye, he would have appeared to be fully recovered.

However, those who knew him well could see subtle changes, a certain slowing down or perhaps a calming down. His facial expressions weren't quite as mobile as they used to be. Also his speech, although steadily improving, was hesitant and at times appeared to be struggling to keep up with his thoughts.

During the latter part of his stay in hospital, fragments and scraps of memory had begun to return but nothing substantial or cohesive. Pictures from his past appeared in his mind but he did not perceive them as pictures from his past. They were entirely without context. He had no clear recollections of anything that had happened to him before he woke up in hospital. He now recognized and knew his mother and Lucy and understood who they were but he couldn't recall any of his experiences with them from before his accident.

The hope was that on returning to the only home he'd ever known, he would be met by an avalanche of old associations, impressions and feelings that would stimulate the recovery of his memory. The doctors had
~~~

advised Mrs Lovegrove to leave him to his own devices and let him re-discover the house for himself while she carried on with her usual domestic routine.

Jim followed his mother into the warm, bright kitchen and automatically sat in his usual place at the kitchen table. He savoured the familiar smell of freshly baked bread while his mum put on the kettle to make a pot of tea. A leg of lamb was sizzling in the oven for Christmas dinner and she added the potatoes, pumpkin and parsnips to commence baking. Then she poured the tea.

Jim watched his mother intently.

'Why don't you get up and stretch your legs for a bit Son. The doctor said you needed to start exercising but not too much all at once.'

Jim got up from his chair and wandered aimlessly from room to room around the house. There was nothing of interest in his mother's room. He didn't recognize himself in the baby pictures on the dresser. The parlour with its black and white television set and family photos was a little more interesting.

Then he wandered into his own room. It wasn't a homecoming exactly. He didn't recognize or remember anything but he was fascinated by everything he saw. The bookshelf with its collection of 'Just William', 'Biggles', 'Treasure Island' and even a few Enid Blyton books, was like an Aladdin's Cave, demanding to be explored.

On top of the chest of drawers were the two 'Airfix' models he had assembled when he was twelve years old – a Spitfire and a Messerschmitt 109. On a stool in the corner was a teddy bear. He didn't think of them as his own, he was simply enchanted by them. Half an hour later, his Mum found him curled up, sound asleep on his bed with "William in Trouble." He hadn't seen the copy of "Dandillion" which had fallen under the bed when Mrs Lovegrove had aired the bedding.

1972

25: After the Quest?

On the evening of June 20th 1972 at the Mahoney's' place in Denistone, there was a small dinner party for Maggie McInerney's 20th birthday. There were three couples present. Mr and Mrs Mahoney, Brian and Kate, Maggie and Boy Upson. While it was generally assumed that Brian and Kate would marry when they graduated, what the future held for Maggie and Boy was anybody's guess.

The exact nature of their connection was the subject of much conjecture within their circle of acquaintance. As a couple they were not overtly demonstrative of any kind of physical connection. Maggie was fond of Boy because he treated her with gentle courtesy and he had made no physical demands on her during the two years they had known each other. Boy's feelings were harder to fathom. It is true that his personality had changed dramatically since meeting Maggie but observers like Kate and her mother disliked and distrusted the new, quietly reserved Boy even more than his loud, brash and abrasive former self.

Mrs Mahoney had invited Boy to the dinner at Maggie's suggestion, to make up the numbers. It seemed that they spent a fair amount of time in each other's company but they were seldom ever alone together. Boy would often take Maggie to the races, particularly if Nostromo was running, and they mixed with his friends from the landed gentry. They would occasionally see a movie together but Boy always kept his hands to himself. Once or twice they flew to Darlington and dined at

Montini's but on each occasion, at Boy's insistence, they stayed at separate hotels, all paid for by Boy.

There were two weekends when he invited Maggie to stay with him on his estate but he also invited Brian and Kate. On both occasions Maggie and Kate were expected to share a room and Brian slept in a room on his own. Boy had said that this was to avoid scandalising Mrs Morgan, his housekeeper. Maggie seemed to be comfortable with the arrangement but Kate's suspicions increased.

The birthday dinner passed pleasantly enough and the Mahoney women were on their best behaviour, for Maggie's sake. Boy had given Maggie a bottle of Chanel No 5 as well as a huge bunch of flowers all of which overshadowed her other presents. After the meal, the grazier made his goodbyes to the party at large and Mr Mahoney saw him to the door. A discreet silence was maintained in front of Maggie. But in their bed that night Madelaine kept her husband awake for some time trying to fathom Boy's motives. Kate would wait till next day at uni to share her concerns with Brian.

They met for coffee in the ref.

'I don't know what she sees in him Brian. I would have said once that it was obvious what Boy saw in Maggie but from what I hear, it's strictly platonic. It wouldn't surprise me if Boy is queer and he's just passing Maggie off as his girlfriend to disguise the fact.'

'That's a possibility I suppose. I know he takes her dancing at 'Rural Youth' socials. All old fashioned stuff - foxtrot, quickstep and the like. But that doesn't mean he isn't queer. Lots of queers dance. Look at Nureyev and Fred Astaire.'

'Weren't Fred Astaire and Ginger Rogers an item?'

'Just dancing partners I suspect. Fred doesn't strike me as being overly hairy chested.'

'Don't change the subject. Boy buys her dresses to wear at the dances. He lets her choose them and he foots the bill.'

'I hope she isn't just taking advantage of him.'

'Oh no. She's been very scrupulous about that. He was pestering her for ages before she finally relented and she only let him buy three. She modelled them for me. They all suit her perfectly but then she'd look great in a spud bag.'

'That would be a bit too basic, even for a 'Rural Youth' social. Come to think of it Kate, you'd look good in just a spud bag yourself – very back to nature.'

'Berk! Don't keep changing the subject. Boy's latest folly is the Graziers' Annual Ball. It's held in September. That's when all the silvertails and land barons come out of the woodwork in their ostentatious best. He wants her to have an expensive gown for that.'

'Is she getting to know any of his friends among the gentry?'

'There's two couples they go to the races with - the Pirbrights and the Anstruthers. They are joint owners of Nostromo with Boy.   He tried to introduce her to his female cousins once. They were perfectly beastly to her and as good as called her a gold-digger to her face.'

'Maggie would have been furious about that.'

'I think she was deeply hurt. She told Boy never to put her in that situation again.   He grovelled in mortification and to the best of my knowledge there have been no further lapses.   I think he was just showing Maggie off to his cousins to piss them off which was hardly fair to Maggie. It beats me why she persists in his company.'

'I guess it's a style of life she's not accustomed to and there's a bit of glamour mixing with the 'bluebloods'.'

'Boy's no blueblood. He arrived with a suitcase remember.'

'You never know. He might be something quite exotic – a royal bastard or the illegitimate son of an archbishop.'

'More likely he's the result of a phantom pregnancy.'

The eleven o'clock bell rang and they parted with a mutual peck on the cheek, Kate to a lecture and Brian to a history tutorial.

Brian had made a comfortable and successful return to university life. He was back in his old room at Trinity College. Maxwell Tynan, who was now in his final year, was up on the next floor. The Insects still gathered at Insect Corner but a few of them now had women in their lives by this time so their behaviour (and to some extent their drinking) had moderated somewhat. Brian joined them occasionally but he remained focused on his studies and his cleaning job.

Much to his own surprise and that of everyone else, he completed his first year with three distinctions and a high distinction. Half way through his second year, all the signs were that he was on course to achieve similar success this year as well. He now found that lecturers and tutors like the dreaded Dr Spotswood in the English Department weren't his 'adversaries' after all.

They had only appeared in this light to Brian in the past when he fronted up to tutorials with a hangover and attempted to bluff his way through proceedings, having done zero preparation. In fact on closer acquaintance,

Brian and the good Doctor began to enjoy each other's company and each developed an appreciation of the other's wit and intellect.

Maggie was now in the third and final year of her degree. Although Brian, to everyone's' surprise, was giving her a run for her money in terms of academic achievements she still relished her seniority. She would graduate a year before him and Doctor Spotswood was urging her to considers doing Honours next year. Kate meanwhile was completing her Diploma of Education.

With Brian's return to academia, the focus of his world shifted from Darlington and Gracechurch street, to Ross. He and Kate still spent the occasional weekend with Hugh and Lucy but as time passed, such visits became less frequent. Brian was constrained by the demands of his cleaning job. There was no lessening of the friendship they shared but their interests and preoccupations began to diverge.

The biggest unifying factor had been the 'quest' but Alf Prentice's revelations about Norian Fairchild and the 'Nonesuchers' had taken the wind out of everyone's sails. Each of the 'conspirators' retained their own particular opinions and theories about the matter but the 'quest' had lost its appeal and importance. It no longer required weekly meetings at O'Brien's to update progress.

Robert in particular became very disillusioned and for a time, gave up on the 'quest' altogether. He showed signs of slipping into a depression. Lucy was becoming quite concerned as were his parents until his father hit on the idea of teaching him how to drive. This opened up a whole new sphere of interest for him. In the past, his mental issues had been seen as an impediment and driving lessons had not been a high priority. After a few preliminary lessons in the driveway at home and then in the grounds of a local school, he began to grasp the basics and his father considered him ready for lessons with the RACC.

Robert became fired with new enthusiasm. A driver's licence would open up all sorts of possibilities. In time he could do deliveries for the supermarket which would mean more pay. The supermarket had expanded its delivery service to include all and sundry, not just the frail and elderly. He could buy a van (colloquially known as a Shaggin' Wagon) and camp in the back of it. Then, with his own vehicle, he would have greater independence and freedom to travel around the Island.

On Friday September 22nd at his third attempt, Robert successfully passed his driving test. He had raided his life's savings and, with the help of a generous birthday gift from his parents, had recently become the proud owner of a blue, 1962 Ford Anglia van. In the euphoria of the moment, the only concern of Lucy and his parents was that he didn't become hyper-excited and end up back in Hollybank. But common sense carried the day and he remained grounded and sensible.

It was at about that time that Robert reconnected with Jim. Lucy figured that Jim was sufficiently recovered. His hair had all grown back so he looked normal again. Also, given the remarkable changes in his personality since the accident, there would be nothing about his behaviour that would distress Robert unduly. Jim took Lucy's word for it that he had known Robert in the past but the past still meant nothing to him. They were virtually meeting for the first time and quickly began to form a new friendship that was the polar opposite of what their relationship had been in the past.

Jim was now fully recovered from his physical injuries except for a slight limp which would probably be permanent.   His personality and temperament were dramatically changed, Lucy thought for the better. He had become gentle and affectionate towards those around him. There were still big gaps in his memory and he was occasionally troubled and terrified by flashbacks and nightmares. In particular there was a recurring dream of being alone and adrift in the sea, miles from anywhere. He would wake up terrified, but there was no context to the dream. He had no memory of the fact that he had spent most of his working life at sea.

Mrs Lovegrove took some comfort from the fact that her son now seemed to be afraid of the sea. She hoped he would never remember that part of his life and regain an appetite for it. Lucy wondered to herself about the therapeutic potential of helping him work through his nightmare and possibly remembering his rescue by Norian Fairchild. But she was eventually able to dismiss the idea, reminding herself that she was no psychiatrist. It was probably better to let sleeping dogs lie.

Jim had found the copy of 'Dandillion' under his bed when he was looking for a lost sock. He got about half way through it, then lost interest and never gave it another thought. His needs and interests were much more simple and basic than they used to be. He took a shine to Robert and began to look upon him as a companion. Together they would go for long drives in the van and they became inseparable. By November, Robert's proficiency as a driver was such that he was promoted to driving a grocery delivery van. He then successfully contrived to have Jim employed in his old job of stacking shelves. The job was well within Jim's capabilities and it did wonders for his confidence and self esteem.

For the first time ever, Mrs Lovegrove found that her house was becoming a little hub of social activity. Just like her son she was revelling in getting to know an engaging group of friends, effectively for the first time since her childhood. Lucy was there most days. Robert drove Jim to and from work every day and often stayed for the evening meal. On one or two occasions Brian and Kate had dropped in with Lucy and Hugh. It was an amazing change for Mrs Lovegrove, from the long, painful years of isolation and ostracism inflicted upon her by her family.

Hugh was as pleased as anyone that Jim had recovered to the point where he could enjoy life, albeit a less complex life than he had lived previously. Like Robert and Lucy he had nursed his own little package of guilt because of past unpleasantness and they were all sincerely supporting him in his recovery. Hugh took pride in Lucy's compassionate care and concern for their injured friend. Healing was her profession after all.

<div style="text-align:center">~~~§~~~</div>

In late November the academic year ended. Kate had successfully completed her Diploma of Education. Maggie had finished her degree with a swag of distinctions and would do honours in English Literature next year. Brian had passed year two with a credit, two distinctions and a high distinction. Everyone was quite content with their year's work.

However the celebration for Kate and Brian was overshadowed by concerns about the year to come. Since Kate was now a fully qualified teacher, the Education Department would expect her to start teaching somewhere. The Department had a habit of posting unmarried first year teachers to out of the way places which could mean Brian and Kate being separated for at least a year while he completed his degree. For some time now they had planned to marry after they had both graduated but in Brian's case that was still twelve months away; two years if he did a Dip Ed. He had visions of Kate being posted to Green Island, Lesser C or somewhere even more remote.

One night when he was cleaning O'Shannessy's chambers, he had an insight into the blindingly obvious. If he was to marry Kate straight away, the Education Department wouldn't post her any great distance from her husband. It was only single and unattached teachers that got posted to the ends of the Earth. He and Kate were very happy in their relationship and marriage was the ultimate aim but it had never been an urgent priority. It was always seen as a thing for the future. Well now there was a high degree of urgency. Although he was yet to graduate, Brian already had a secure job of a kind and could at least share the expense of putting a roof over Kate's head.

At 6.30 there was a knock on the front door. It was Kate. She was all dressed up for the Folk Club end of year "Do". 'Are you all done here then?'

'Yep if you can whisk me back to Trinity I'll change into something more elegant and we'll head off. But there's something rather important I want to discuss with you first.'

'Oh yes. And what might that be?'

'I want to ask for your hand in marriage?'

'Just my hand?'

'Obviously not. I want the whole sensual, tantalizing package.'

'When did you have in mind?'

'As soon as possible. Don't you see, if you're married to me, the Department will be less likely to send you to Timbuktu next year.'

'Well alleluia the penny finally drops.'

'What do you mean?'

'At last you've identified the solution which has been staring you in the face all year.'

'Well why didn't you say something if you'd already thought of it?'

'It's the gentleman's place to propose.'

'Are you serious?

'What a quaint old fashioned little thing you've become Miss Mahoney, hardly the fearless young 'Today's Woman' who ensnared my heart.'

'If you don't keep a civil tongue in your head I might turn you down.'

'Don't do that Kate. As I've told you once before, it would be cutting off your nose to spite your face. Lets wind back the conversation and start again.'

'What, here in O'Shannessy's chambers? Let's find somewhere special, somewhere romantic. I know just the place.'

The Folk "Do" became an impromptu celebration of Kate and Brian's engagement. The radiant couple arrived at about 8.30 and their glad tidings spread like wildfire. *For they are Jolly Good Fellows* was sung more than once during the night as different people learnt the news. Mark Denham congratulated them and asked after Maggie.

'She certainly keeps to herself these days doesn't she.'

'Yes,' said Kate. 'She's in danger of turning into a crusty, dusty old academic.' Maggie was actually out with Boy that night but Mark didn't need to know about that.

Angela Moriarty also congratulated them. She and Kate knew each other well from boarding school and had always gotten on well. Angela was well on the way to becoming a doctor which was her primary ambition but in the interim, her five to seven spots on the CBC had become a permanent fixture and a useful source of extra income. Colin, the former Hollybank cleaner was proving highly successful as the producer/director of her film clips in exotic and atmospheric locations around the Cumberlands. There was talk of an hour long feature programme and sales to overseas television networks.

Kate drove Brian back to 'Trinity' as the "Do" ran out of steam. 'When are you going to ask Dad for my hand?'

'I hadn't thought that far ahead.'

'He'll be working from O'Shannessy's chambers tomorrow. He's there most Fridays lately unless there's a flap on in Darlington. I suggest you see him after lunch. He's usually pretty mellow after Friday lunch, not that you need worry. He's a baa lamb. We can spend the morning looking for a ring.'

'What here in Ross? I thought you'd prefer to go to Darlington.'

'No we should strike while the iron's hot. We're not in the market for the Crown Jewels or anything like that – just something simple and tasteful. There's a lovely old jeweller's shop here in Ross where Dad got Mum's engagement ring.'

The meeting with Kate's Dad was a friendly and relaxed affair. After readily giving his blessing, Mr Mahoney poured two whiskeys to seal the deal and then amazed Brian with a question. 'Tell me Brian is this all your own idea or did Kate put you up to it?'

'Of course it was my idea,' said Brian, a little defensively.

'Good man. Don't get me wrong. I'm not doubting your feelings for Kate, far from it. The thing is Madelaine and Kate got it into their heads that you would have waited two more years, til you finished uni, before you proposed unless they put the idea into your head. But in their typical contradictory fashion they were being very old fashioned and insisting that the proposal must be entirely your doing.

'I had every faith in you Brian and I had wagers with both of them that you would propose of your own volition. I'll be collecting a fiver from Kate and a bottle of vintage port from her mother. It must have been a closely run thing. They had a deadline no doubt and if you hadn't proposed by then they'd have forced your hand. Planning for the wedding has been in train for a couple of months.

'It will be in the second week of January next year. That will allow time for a honeymoon before school goes back in February. If you have anyone in mind to be your best man you'd best stake your claim at the earliest opportunity. I think they have young Max Tynan in mind. Maggie's in on the secret too.'

'Thanks for filling me in. I guess for a long time I felt that I couldn't get married before I had a full time job. But in the end I couldn't bear the thought of Kate spending the next two years at the other end of the Archipelago.'

'I think you'll find that Kate feels exactly the same way. But I'll add a word of caution. Bureaucracy is an ornery and contrary beast. In two years time when you're fully qualified the Department might transfer you both to

Dark Tor for the rest of your days. Now let's drink a toast to the women in our lives and then I'd better get back to work.'

As Brian walked back to the uni some pennies began to drop. He'd been shopping with Kate many times in the past and it was usually an exhausting and exhaustive process but the quest for an engagement ring had been uncharacteristically swift and targeted. She had obviously already been into the shop and made her choice. There was a show of letting him have a browse of what was on offer but the purchase was made in under fifteen minutes. He smiled to himself; that had to be a world record.

Kate and Maggie were waiting for him in the ref.

'See the conquering hero comes,' said Maggie. 'Is Kate being premature wearing this lovely ring or has your suit been successful?'

'Never in doubt,' said Brian with a smile. 'I didn't know your Dad was a betting man Kate.'

'What do you mean?' asked Kate, trying unsuccessfully to stop her cheeks from colouring.

'He didn't go into details but he landed two wagers today apparently, a fiver and a bottle of vintage port. He said the outcome was a vindication of his judgment and discernment. Now, who to pick as best man? I thought at first it would be a simple choice. Hugh is one of my oldest friends, but with you as the obvious choice for bridesmaid Maggie, that wouldn't work very well under the circumstances.'

'The thought had occurred to us,' said Kate.

'And much to your amazement no doubt, it has occurred to me also. Fear not, I have a plan B.'

'The girls looked apprehensive.

'Not one of the Insects,' said Maggie.

'No an older man, a more settled and solid citizen than any of the Insects will be for some years yet. He lives locally too which will be handy for rehearsals.'

'Not Dr Spotswood?' said Maggie.

'He was my second choice. My preference is Mr Thomas Madigan Esq.'

'Mad Tom from Hollybank!!'

'The very same Kate. That way we won't have to pay for any entertainment and don't worry. Molly will keep him in line.'

'Who are these people?' Maggie wanted to know.

'Nothing you need worry about, sister mine. I'm sure you'll be very favourably impressed when you meet them. Come on Kate. Because I left it so late to propose we've hardly any time left to organize things if we want to have a wedding in the second week of January. Tom will be perfect,' said Brian ingenuously.

'Watch it Buster!' said Kate, not quite succeeding in suppressing a smile. She appreciated a good 'Checkmate' when she saw one and there was plenty of time ahead to even the score. 'OK Tom it is. We'll go and ask them when we're finished here. When are you going to tell your parents the good news?'

Brian and Maggie shared a wry smile.

'Ah!' said Brian, 'The children! What do you think Maggie? Does it warrant the cost of an overseas phone call?'

'You could always reverse the charges.'

'No! Dad went ape-shit last time I did that. He said with my cleaning job on top of my studentship I can easily afford it. I suppose we ought to tell them.'

'What is it with you two and your parents?'

'It's a long story Kate. They're not normal parents. Maggie and I were left to our own devices growing up. They stuck it out until Maggie turned 14, put us both in boarding schools and then they ran away from home and went back to England.'

'It wouldn't surprise me if they've split up,' said Maggie. 'I can't remember the last time they were on the phone together.'

'Surely they'll come back for the wedding?'

''I wouldn't bet on it Kate. One of them might. They'll probably cry poor and say they can only afford one airfare.'

'They might cry even poorer than that,' said Maggie 'and not even pay one airfare.'

'I think that's very sad for both of you.'

'Don't jump to conclusions Kate,' said Brian laughing. 'You haven't met them yet.'

'It's unconventional,' said Maggie. 'But I think we've done pretty well actually bringing ourselves up. Although really, I suppose I've brought the pair of us up.'

'That I could well believe,' said Kate.

When they'd finished their coffee, Brian and Kate left Maggie alone with her thoughts. She had a few things on her mind. The talk about Hugh had been unsettling. In spite of thinking otherwise, she clearly wasn't really over him yet. Given their childhood history it should have been a perfect fit to have herself and Hugh both participating in Brian's wedding but clearly there was too much baggage now. Presumably Lucy would go to the wedding with Hugh. Maggie hadn't met her yet and that would be another difficulty. At least she could rely on Boy to partner her on the day and that would shield her to some extent. They had provided that service for each other on a few occasions now.

Maggie had become quite comfortable in Boy's friendship and she had accepted his strange ground rules: separate beds, separate hotels even and absolutely no sex. But lately she had detected signs of unease in his manner. He continued to play the role of the quietly spoken, platonic gentleman friend but she sensed a growing tension in him.

A couple of times in the 'Tea Rooms' on the previous evening, he had seemed to be on the point of introducing some new topic into the conversation only to draw back at the last minute. She had tried to encourage him to open up but each time he passed it off as just business matters and tried to change the subject.

After a silent drive back to 'Madelaine', he finally spoke, sounding like he had reached some kind of conclusion.

'I'm afraid I won't be able to see you again for a while Maggie. I'm going to be tied up with business affairs for the foreseeable future and I'll be off the Island for quite some time.'

'Oh. Nothing wrong is there?'

'Not at all. It's just routine business stuff.'

The temporary separation didn't bother Maggie personally but she was a little concerned about Boy. She wasn't dependent on him for anything but she was fond of him and worried about him. On more than one occasion during the evening, she had noticed some fleeting but pained expressions that momentarily dulled the sparkle in his innocent, peri-winkle blue eyes.

Because of the transformation she had caused in Boy's behaviour, Maggie had no experience of what a loud and obnoxious individual he used to be before they met. For that reason she could be forgiven for being slow to pick up on his inner conflict. People, like Kate and her Mum, who had known him for much longer were not only unconvinced by his new persona, they were sure that it couldn't last.

Giacomo Montini marvelled at the tension that must be building up inside him as he sought to restrain all that bullshit and hot air for which he was so famous if not notorious. Like Kate and Madelaine, he felt that it couldn't go on forever. It was little short of miraculous that he had kept it up for two years. Eventually, and sooner rather than later, there was going to be an almighty explosion.

<div align="center">~~~§~~~</div>

Back in Gracechurch Street, a melancholy Hugh was taking stock of the closing year with the help of a bed time glass of sherry. In many ways 1972 had been very good to him. His career was going ahead in leaps and bounds. He had received further promotion to a level 5 position which involved more responsibility and much more mental effort. He was in good odour with his boss and also making new friendships among his colleagues. Needless to say he was happy with the substantial increase in his salary.

His promotion had also helped to fill the vacuum left in his life when the 'quest' was more or less debunked by Alf Prentice nearly two years ago in O'Brien's. It had been the 'quest' that had brought them all together. Since its demise they had slowly but inexorably begun to drift apart and be absorbed by different preoccupations.

Robert was all taken up with his van and the independence of mobility. Brian was back at uni and he and Kate were thriving. The arrival of the invitation to their wedding had been a bitter sweet moment for Hugh. There was a time, not too long ago when he and Lucy, Brian and Kate had been a very closeknit and vibrant little foursome. But these days, Lucy was becoming increasingly distracted by other interests and issues - Jim and his recovery in particular.

As 1971 had drawn to a close, Hugh had found himself wondering when Jim's recovery would be regarded as complete and life could revert back to its old routine. Half way through 1972 he became resigned to the fact that life would never return to the way it was. Lucy still lived at home with her family and the times she could share Hugh's bed with him were limited by this fact and the vagaries of her shift roster. Added to this, she was now spending a lot of her spare time at the Lovegrove house. Hugh felt that she was spreading herself too thin.

Christmas was getting close and he had assumed that he and Lucy would spend it with his family in Middleton. They had been alternating between families from one Christmas to the next. He'd mentioned it to Lucy a week ago, suggesting that his mother would need to know in plenty of time for catering purposes.

Surprisingly, Lucy didn't automatically concur. She had been thinking about Jim and his Mum. 'Christmas must be a lonely time for them.'

'It'd be no lonelier than any other Christmas they've had.'

'I've been thinking of asking Mum and Dad to invite them to our place for Christmas lunch.'

'What about my family?'

'We can go up to Middleton on Boxing Day. We've both got plenty of leave built up.'

This compromise resolved the matter but it had unsettled Hugh, particularly when he thought back to the excitement that surrounded their previous trips to Middleton.

As it happened, Lucy's proposal didn't gain acceptance. Her Mum had said perhaps it could be done but would the Lovegroves really want to come? Tom O'Rourke didn't mince words.

'I think it's a bloody stupid idea. It's nearly two years since Jim got out of hospital. I'll grant you they needed a lot of moral support back then but he is as recovered as he ever will be now and holding down a job for Heaven's sake! He comes round here often enough for Sunday lunch. Let's just leave it at that. I think you're becoming obsessed with the Lovegroves and anyway it's your turn to spend Christmas up on the coast with the Conroys. I take it you are still going to the Conroys for Christmas?'

'Yes Dad. If you had agreed to invite the Lovegroves here for Christmas Day, we would have gone up to Middleton on Boxing Day. I cleared it with Hugh first and he was OK with it.'

That had pretty much been it. The proposal was abandoned. Lucy's initial reaction was one of complete surprise followed by a wave of guilty embarrassment as if she had been caught out in a deception. Had she been deceiving herself? Until that moment she had thought everyone was on the same page where Jim was concerned.

~~~§~~~
~~~

Viney's Farm
Lesser Cumberland
11/12/72

Dear Mervyn

Not long to go now before Christmas. I'm getting quite excited. It will be my first time off the Island and my first plane trip. I'm really looking forward to seeing Trinity Island. You make it sound like a fascinating place.

I've finished up at Business College now and it's good to be back on the farm full time again. Those two years have flown by and I'm glad that I took your advice and did the course. I passed everything with flying colours and my typing speed is getting better all the time.

Thanks for the new strings you sent me last week. I've tried to talk Dave into using lighter gauge strings but he reckons they're only for sissies. That's typical of his bullshit.

Everyone here is fit and well and sends their regards. Do you reckon you'll get down again for a week in May next year? It was great seeing you this time and the music was good fun.

Well that's all my news for now. Looking forward to seeing you soon.

Ever yours
Elsie.

PS Are you sure your parents won't mind about you changing your name? I understand now why you want to do it and I think it's a great idea.

PPS Bob is now walking out with Elaine, one of the Berechree girls from the dairy. Whatever next!! Dave calls him Romeo these days. I'll keep you posted.

Elsie xx

1973

26: Boy

As a small child, Boy Upson was regularly and systematically groped, fondled and interfered with by one of his father's employees. It started when he was six years old. To begin with there were inducements: sweets, silver coins and tractor rides, generally to isolated places where more abuse would happen. The scale of abuse gradually increased til it ended in rape.

Whenever a particularly egregious rape occurred, he would be given a ten shilling note with the warning that if he ever betrayed their 'little secret' he would have to pay all the money back. He kept the money hidden in an old tea caddy that he buried in the bush far away from the homestead.

It hadn't taken long for Boy to become badly damaged by what was happening to him. What seemed to start out as pleasant tickling games quickly degenerated into painful and humiliating intrusions. He hated everything about the abuse, especially the parts of his body that had been handled. They continued to ache with the vile sensations for days afterwards. Then there was the horrible scent of the abuser especially his foul breath.

Boy was completely alone in his suffering. He felt constrained to keep the matter secret, partly out of shame and partly out of fear of his abuser. Even if he had wanted to tell someone, he didn't have the vocabulary to name the parts of him that had been attacked or the procedures he had been subjected to. The few crude colloquialisms he knew to describe his ordeal could never be used in a conversation with his mother and definitely not with his father, who once famously knocked an employee down for swearing in front of Mrs Upson.

Finally, after the abuse had been going on for about four years, a day came when Boy's father caught the paedophile in the act. It was in a little used barn on the remote outskirts of the estate. Mr Upson had been checking boundary fences and was surprised to see the tractor parked there in such an isolated spot.

He was alerted by the sounds he heard coming from the barn and crept quietly up to a window. One look was enough. The offender hadn't even bothered to lock the door and the first he knew of his apprehension was when Mr Upson grabbed him by the scruff of the neck and threw him against the stone wall. He collapsed there cowering on the flagstones.

'Put your clothes back on Son. Go home and tell Mum to run a bath for you. I'll be home directly and we'll talk. You're not in any trouble. Off you go now quickly.' Mr Upson had spoken in a calm, quiet voice trying to allay Boy's fears but he couldn't conceal his anger.

As soon as his son had gone, Mr Upson laid into the paedophile, boots and all, repeatedly and viciously kicking his exposed genitals and beating him black and blue. The grim assault went on and on without a word being spoken other than the pathetic whimpers of the child molester.

Boy hadn't gone straight home. He couldn't leave without knowing the outcome. He crept up to the window and witnessed his father's retribution. He felt some gratification at seeing his abuser so savagely beaten up but first and foremost he was terrified, to see that his father was capable of such violent anger. He also feared that his father would punish him in the same way. Instead of going home, he went into hiding.

When eventually his parents found Boy, cold and hungry two days later, hiding and still terrified under a mass of blackberry vines, they did their best to reassure him that he wasn't to blame: that he was an innocent child and none of it had been his fault.

Even though they did not blame him for what had happened and they did their level best to love and comfort him, Boy quickly realized that the consequences of his injuries were a problem he had to face on his own. His Mum and Dad would never be able to really understand or share how he felt. When he told them how long the abuse had been going on, his mother held him close and tried to comfort him but even that loving embrace felt tainted and he pulled away from it.

<div align="center">~~~§~~~</div>

Sadly he realized in time that the damage he'd suffered couldn't be erased or forgotten. He also found that various forms of sexual predation were never far below the surface wherever he went. Two years later at the convent school, he was sitting at a table with four other children for a history tutorial with Sister Joseph. Without warning, the only other boy in the group reached under the table and squeezed Boy's testicles. All the old outrage and fury flared up inside him. He stood up and punched his assailant in the face breaking a tooth and causing a copious nose bleed.

Sister Joseph was furious and demanded an explanation. Of course there was no way that Boy could tell her what had just happened to him so he maintained a smouldering silence. He received six strokes of the cane on his hands while the whole class looked on and his assailant smirked from behind his bloodied handkerchief.

Boy took one bitter comfort from the incident. He realized that he was handy with his fists. That was how you dealt with perverts.

At home that night, in an effort to erase the past, he dug up the tea caddy, took out the 27 crumpled ten shilling notes, one for each rape, and set them alight. When the flames had consumed them, he pissed on the ashes.

For the rest of their lives, Boy's parents tried to compensate him for the loss of his innocence by showering him with gifts and gratifying his every material whim. They lacked the vocabulary and understanding to counsel him in any other way. This largesse helped turn Boy into the loudmouthed young squire he eventually became. Bravado, bluster and swagger became his shield and his escape.

Understandably Boy became convinced that sex was a negative and predatory thing. It had caused him nothing but suffering. While he was drawing these conclusions from personal experience he was also being inculcated at school with the doctrine of Original Sin and man's natural tendency to evil. Consequently when his own sexuality began to emerge with puberty, its flowering was stunted and diseased. He saw his natural healthy sexual impulses as impure thoughts and feelings: a manifestation of his natural inclination to sin and depravity.

He accordingly tried to exclude any further sexual encounters from his life. This worked fairly well for a number of years until the night he met Maggie. She had looked so beautiful and vulnerable. Something about her fragility spoke directly to Boy's heart in a way that no other voice or idea had ever done before. It penetrated all the layers of brag and bluster he had built around himself to shut out his painful past but as a consequence those long suppressed feelings of trauma and guilt were rekindled.

To begin with, Boy was able to keep the conflict at arms length by thinking and acting in strictly platonic terms about his feelings for Maggie. This was made a little easier by the fact that she wasn't trying to seduce him and only offered him platonic friendship in return. However, over the two years of their friendship, Boy became increasingly conflicted. He lived for the times he spent in her company but became increasingly wracked with guilt and frustration when they were apart. His life had assumed the combined torments of a straitjacket and a hairshirt and he was getting near the limits of his endurance.

<center>~~~§~~~</center>

Boy was included on the guest list for Brian and Kate's wedding when the invitations went out in early December but, much to everyone's surprise, he didn't R.SV.P. Christmas came and went and Maggie didn't receive the customary Christmas card and present from him. She rang his number a couple of times only to be answered by his estate manager who said his boss was out of the country on business at the moment.

Early in the new year, Mrs Morgan answered the phone and told Maggie that Boy was doing a Novena and Retreat with the Benedictines at their monastery on Green Island. Maggie took some reassurance from the fact that he was at least back in the country. Kate and her mum found the idea of Boy observing nine days of contemplative silence hilarious if not downright impossible. Be that as it may, all concerns about Boy were forgotten in the final days leading up to the wedding.

The Ceremony took place at four o'clock on the afternoon of Friday 12th January at the Church of St Francis, the parish church in Denistone. It was a beautiful, mild summers day with just a few white clouds to provide occasional shade from the afternoon sun when required. High in the branches of the old pine trees in the churchyard, a small group of crows formed an alternative reception committee and watched the arrival of the guests: making the occasional comment as they did so. Brian smiled a nervous smile. He was pleased to see them there and regarded them as a good omen. He could still hear odd snatches of corvine commentary after he and Tom had entered the church.

The celebrant was Father Hanratty, an old priest who had known generations of the Mahoney family. He had been at school with young Jack Mahoney, married Kate's parents and baptised Kate and her two siblings, as well as giving them all their first holy communion. He chatted in an undertone to Brian and Tom as the church filled and the congregation settled and waited expectantly for Kate's arrival.

Madelaine shed a quiet tear as Kate, on her Father's arm, walked down the aisle and took her place at Brian's side. She looked perfect and a smile from behind her veil suggested she shared the nervous excitement that was coursing through Brian's veins.

When Father Hanratty challenged anyone knowing of any impediment to the marriage to 'speak now or forever hold their peace', nobody in the church spoke but one of the crows outside launched into a vehement tirade which seemed to go on forever.

'That bird just likes the sound of his own voice,' said Father Hanratty with a wry smile, when people had stopped laughing. 'He's one of my regulars. We'll take his comment as a No.'

The service proceeded without further incident. When the vows were exchanged more people than just Madelaine shed a tear. Even Kate's Dad was a little watery around the eyes.

As best man, Tom was on his best behaviour, except for one piece of sleight of hand when he was asked to proffer the wedding rings. He made one ring disappear and then retrieved it from behind Brian's left ear. After the ceremony, walking down the aisle with Maggie on his arm, he whispered something unexpected in her ear that elicited a loud peal of laughter from her. She was in stitches the rest of the way out of the church. She had just learnt the identity of the antichrist. Tom's wife Molly looked on, shook her head and smiled a resigned smile.

The reception was held in the grounds of the Mahoney family home. Everything was in readiness as the guests made their way from the church. Boy wasn't the only notable absentee. Brian's parents had sent their apologies on the grounds of distance and expense. Hugh was there with Robert but interestingly Lucy wasn't with them. This fact wasn't lost on Maggie.

Kate's two brothers, Tim and Martin were both there. Tim had brought his new girl friend, Raewyn McCleod, from New Zealand. She looked a robust, athletic sort of girl: well capable of keeping Tim in his place. Martin was recently returned from Australia having completed degrees in law and economics at the ANU. He was about to embark on a career in politics: the first Mahoney to do so since his grandfather. The Labour Party in the Cumberlands had been in the wilderness for fifteen years and there was to be an election next year. The incumbent conservative government was looking tired and there was a whiff of change in the air.

As the guests mingled, the extraordinary contribution of the crow during the ceremony was a popular topic of conversation. It led Tom into a debate with Father Hanratty. He was arguing that, if you knew of an impediment to the marriage you could either declare it or hold your peace. Either option was valid so if you chose to hold your peace, the marriage could still go ahead. 'Well Tom,' said the priest, 'when you become Pope you can clarify the point in an Encyclical'.

'Indeed I will Father. I'll put it on my list of things to do when I move into the Vatican.'

'Are you sure Molly would let you become Pope though Tom?'

'Well if all the Cardinals voted for me there wouldn't be much that Mollie could do about it Father.'

'Anything to get him out from under my feet,' said Molly.

Elsewhere, Hugh and Robert were feeling a bit isolated and out of place, not knowing anybody there apart from the happy couple. For that reason, Hugh was particularly gratified when Kate's grandad sought him out.

'It's Hugh isn't it. Kate told me you'd be here. What did you think of "Dandillion" when you finally got a chance to read it?'

'To be honest I don't know what to think. We were hoping that behind all the imagery it might relate to events that happened here in the Archipelago. But I'm more inclined these days to think of it just as a piece of literature.'

'I don't think it is reliable as a historical document,' said Robert when he was introduced. 'All that stuff about Elves and immortality doesn't wash with me.'

'It does sound a bit far-fetched doesn't it,' Jack replied. 'Mind you I believe that each of us has an immortal soul. But I don't know what Norian was trying to say about immortality. Your guess is as good as mine.'

'What was he like as a person?'

'He was a charming young man and a dear friend. He could be very witty at times and yet there was an underlying sadness about him that sometimes showed through. Mind you when I knew him, the first world war was still very fresh in our minds. He drove an ambulance in France and we all saw a lot of terrible things over there. He was a conscientious objector I believe. One thing I do know, he was very popular with the ladies. They all loved him. The second book of his poems that he gave me is mainly poems about women.'

At that moment Kate and Brian came up to them.

'So you found him Grandad. Well spotted.'

'I never forget a face Kate, part and parcel of being a politician. That's a skill young Martin will have to acquire very soon.'

At six o'clock a bell rang to summon the guests to their seats for the formal part of proceedings. 'No Lucy?' Brian enquired as they filed into the marquee.

'She couldn't make it,' said Hugh with a fleeting grimace. 'Congratulations by the way. It was a beautiful service. Kate looks lovely.'

~~~§~~~

The 1973 academic year in the Cumberland Archipelago began on Monday February 5th. From the
~~~

smallest Kindergarten to the university, students of all ages were embarking on new beginnings. It was also a new beginning for Kate as she embarked on the first year of her teaching career. She had been posted to the high school in Ross to teach English and History to years 7 and 8. She had enjoyed the sessions of prac-teaching during her Dip-Ed year and quickly found the right balance between discipline and entertainment to hold her students' attention while she educated them.

Life was good for Kate at that time and she was brimming with self-confidence. She and Brian had enjoyed a wonderful honeymoon on Lesser C. It was the first time she had ever been there. They based themselves at the Shipwright's Arms, a comfortable hotel in Cork and, when they could drag themselves away from the delights of the bridal suite, they explored those parts of the Island within a comfortable day's drive.

This had included a day trip to Woodfield and the orchard country. Kate had built up an imaginary picture from Brian's letters, of what the countryside and people there were like and she was keen to see the reality for herself. Brian took her to Murphy's' Orchard. The packing shed was deserted at that time but it was unlocked and he was able to give Kate a guided tour. Then he showed her his picker's hut, which was also unlocked and he felt a nostalgic rush of warm memories being back there again after so long. Riley's hut was locked but he dared a look through the window. Inside it was unchanged.

Their next stop was the little post office.

'Well if it isn't young Brian,' said old Mrs Townsend 'and this must be Kate. We heard a lot about you when Brian was down here picking.' She invited them out the back into the parlour and called her husband in from the garden. After a cup of tea and a chat, the honeymooners took their leave with promises to look in next time they were down that way.

They took to the back roads in search of the ancient orchard near the old cemetery with its pre-convict gravestones from 1782 (all of which took some finding on the winding back roads with their almost total lack of signage). As luck would have it, Elsie Viney was there at the cemetery, with Brutus and Fang, tending to her uncle's grave. She was dressed in skimpy little yellow shorts and a Mickey Mouse tee-shirt. Her long red hair was untied and fell freely round her face and shoulders and she was barefooted. She was thrilled to see Brian again and charmed to meet Kate as well.

They sat beside Uncle Terry's grave, which now boasted a proper head stone, and caught up on the news. Elsie was still full of excitement about her recent trip to Trinity for Christmas with Mervyn's family, and she was eager to share it with them. Brian listened to this with great interest and dared to hope that something had kindled between her and Mervyn, but he didn't say anything specific.

'How was Mervyn? I haven't seen or heard from him since the day we got back from apple picking.'

'He's fine. He works for the PMG these days: an office job on Trinity and he lives with his parents. His dad is a wizard pool player.'

Elsie insisted on them coming back to catch up with the rest of the family. This resulted in a dinner invitation and some music afterwards. All the Vineys were there as well as Elaine Berechree, Bob's new girlfriend. Brian was impressed to see how competent Elsie had become on Mervyn's guitar and he complimented her and Dave on their finger picking. He was also very interested to hear that Mervyn had spent a week with the Vineys in May last year but again he kept his hopes to himself. He didn't want to put a jinx on any possible romance or have his fond hopes for Mervyn dashed.

Mindful of the long drive back to Cork, Brian and Kate had to make their goodbyes at eight o'clock. As they drove back in the twilight, Brian kept his eyes peeled for any sign of a light where the Penruddocks' house should be. He was in luck and they stopped the Mini for a moment to look at the faint light flickering through the trees in the distance. They both wanted to try and find the old house but they knew there wasn't time. 'Next trip,' said Kate and re-started the engine.

<div align="center">~~~§~~~</div>

The honeymoon couple arrived back in Ross on January 22nd and prepared to set up house in a cottage owned by Tom's mother. It was next door to where the Madigans lived and quite near the local racetrack, where Molly and Tom rode trackwork.

Tom's 'Mammy' was a strikingly handsome woman with an impressive head of long silver hair which she wore up and braided in an Edwardian style. She was much taller than her son but her eyes contained the same chaotic glint. Her customary facial expression was a frown teetering on the brink of breaking into a smile. Apparently she supported herself and, when necessary her son and daughter-in-law, by playing the stock market. Brian and Kate could well believe that she had 'the sight', as Molly had told them.

Mammy, as Mrs Madigan senior preferred to be known, had drawn up a two year lease. The cottage was furnished which was very convenient since neither Brian nor Kate had anything in the way of furniture themselves, except for a few items donated by Kate's parents. They were looking forward to having the Madigans as neighbours and had become close friends: in fact Tom and Molly had done the cleaning of O'Shannessy's chambers, for Brian while they were on honeymoon. Also, unbeknownst to Kate, Tom had been giving Brian driving lessons in an old Vauxhall belonging to Mrs Madigan senior!

Upson Downs
Tues Feb 27th

Dear Maggie

At last I've got my head above water again. I've been incredibly busy these last few months. I have had a lot of issues to sort out, both business and private. I think I've got everything pretty much under control now and it will be back to business as usual.

I think it's high time we caught up again. The Darlington Cup will be run on Saturday March 10th and Nostromo has been set for it. He is looking the best I've ever seen him. If you're up for it, we could fly down on the Friday afternoon. After the races, we could catch up with Jack Montini for a meal on the Saturday night like old times and then fly back on the Sunday.

I'm sorry I missed the wedding but like I said I've had a lot on my mind lately.

How are you getting on in your Honours year? You'll have to tell me all about it when we catch up.

That's all my news for now.

Kind regards
Boy.

27: Rites of Passage

As it happened, Boy and Maggie didn't get to Montini's on the night of the Darlington Cup. Shortly after sending his recent letter to Maggie, Boy learnt from Sally Anstruther about the formal celebrations that connections of the winning horse would be expected to attend; including a dinner and a ball. In the event of Nostromo winning it would be very poor form for the connections not to show up. Boy accordingly sent Maggie a follow up letter advising of the change of plan and urging her to let him buy her a gown for the occasion. She was excited by the prospect and agreed. The result was a tastefully simple creation in emerald green, made to measure, which suited her to perfection.

When Cup day came, Nostromo was the shortest priced favourite ever to start in the history of the two mile classic: this was in spite of the fact that he had drawn a very wide barrier and was also carrying the heaviest weight. His jockey had two options: he could sprint Nostromo from the starting gate, head off the other horses and cross over to the fence and then put the brakes on and save himself 'til later in the race; or he could save Nostromo's energy and cross over to the fence behind the field and bide his time.

He chose the latter option and steadily wove his way through the field as the race progressed. As they approached the turn into the straight he was in seventh place but he was blocked for a run with horses all around him. The commentator and the crowd alike thought he couldn't possibly win from that position.

It wasn't until half way down the straight when some horses began to sprint towards the finish and others began to flag, that a gap opened for him and Nostromo produced a withering run: bursting free of the pack and leaving them in his wake, winning by three lengths and drawing away.   The crowd was relieved, amazed and ecstatic.

The festivities continued well into the night, long after Nostromo was sound asleep in his stall. Maggie had a thoroughly enjoyable time; the Ball had been a glittering affair. Boy was in his element and seemed to be perfectly at ease. They had danced every dance together although she received a number of requests from other men. By midnight she was sitting up in bed in her hotel room with a cup of hot chocolate and looking forward to a good night's sleep. They had decided to stay an extra night in Darlington and dine at Montini's on the Sunday night. Sunday was Giacomo's night off but the restaurant would still be open and the food would still be great.

<div align="center">~~~§~~~</div>

To begin with at the restaurant next evening, they talked about Nostromo's triumph and the ensuing celebrations. Maggie was a little concerned that Boy's manner was rather subdued compared to the previous day and put it down to a sense of anti-climax or possibly a hangover, but he hadn't seemed to drink too much yesterday and he was sober enough to drive her to her hotel after the Ball.

Later, during the meal, Boy began to reminisce about the time they first met. Maggie wondered where the conversation was heading. As yet Boy hadn't said anything to explain exactly what 'business' worries had kept him out of the country for so long. Nor did he mention the time spent on Retreat with the Benedictines on Green Island.

He talked instead about Maggie's failure to reconnect with Hugh that had brought her to Montini's the night they met. For the first time ever, he talked about sex. He was disturbed to learn that Maggie and Hugh had been lovers 'out of wedlock.'

'Well Boy, given I was only thirteen at the time, marriage wasn't really an option.'

Boy was silent for a while, apparently having trouble digesting and accepting this.

'Boy I told you here that first night that Hugh and I were lovers.'

'I thought you just meant sweethearts.'

'We were that too, obviously. Look, I hope you're not going to start thinking of me as some kind of a fallen woman.'

'No no of course not but you were so young.'

'Perhaps we were but it was love and it was beautiful. I'm not ashamed of it. I hope this isn't going to be a problem between us. Hugh is my only lover if that's any consolation to you. Tim was all over me like a rash but it didn't get him anywhere. Let's change the subject.'

The conversation soon petered out and half an hour later Maggie was back in her hotel room with plenty of food for thought. Things became awkward between them for a while after that.

<p style="text-align:center">~~~§~~~</p>

They next met one evening two months later in May at the 'Old Cumberland Tea Rooms' in Ross. Boy began by apologizing for intruding on her past, last time they met.

I'm sorry if I seemed judgmental. Your past is none of my business and I know you well enough by now to know you would have acted with integrity and a clear conscience.'

'So I'm not a fallen woman then.'

'Of course not and it wasn't me who used that expression.

'Your relations with Hugh were obviously very positive. My experience of sex was anything but positive.'

'I'm sorry to hear that. Is it something you want to talk about?'

'Most definitely not,' he snapped. 'I've never told a soul.' Maggie gave him a look of gentle compassion that began to melt his reserve. 'Sorry I didn't mean to snap. It's very painful for me to even think about. Perhaps, one day I might be able to tell you some of it.'

As Maggie went back to the library that night to resume her studies a multitude of pennies began to drop. Up until then, she had always inferred from Boy's behaviour towards her that his interest was strictly platonic. The thought had crossed her mind that perhaps he was queer but she had no problem with that. She was happy with a platonic friendship while she concentrated on her studies.

Boy played the role of the platonic, slightly older, disinterested gentleman friend very convincingly for a long time. It was reinforced by the separate hotels and separate beds policy he maintained; similarly the 'chaperoned' weekends at his estate with Brian and Kate. Maggie remained blissfully unaware of Boy's suffering until she began to detect signs of tension and conflict in his manner late last year. What if he had been in love with her all the time?

Then she thought of the dresses he had bought her and the beautiful gown, specially made at such short notice, for her to wear on Cup night. She could say with a clear conscience that she had vigorously discouraged him from buying the three dresses until his dogged persistence carried the day. The ball gown was a slightly different kettle of fish. It was probably a once in a lifetime opportunity to participate in such a glamorous and prestigious event; and once again Boy was particularly insistent.

Maggie had never known anyone so wealthy before and assumed that such largesse was par for the course among people like that, but what if he had been in love with her all along? How mortifying was it that she didn't notice and even more so that she didn't love him? She thought his chivalrous, flamboyant generosity was how he treated everybody except perhaps his female cousins; yet how often had Kate and her Mum told her that Boy had been acting completely out of character ever since he met her?

<div align="center">~~~§~~~</div>

As Boy drove home that night, his heart was full of an exciting new possibility. Perhaps there was a way to vanquish his demons and rid himself of the contamination of his childhood trauma. Apart from talking about it to priests in the confessional, who simply told him he was not a sinner but someone grievously sinned against, he had spoken to nobody about the constant shame of his sexual past and the guilt he felt when contemplating any sort of sexual future; that is until tonight with Maggie.

Instead of appearing scandalised or critical she had shown him compassion and invited him to share it with her. Talking about his wounded past with Maggie (the woman he loved so desperately) might be the first step towards healing. It might lead to marriage and a sexual union that would not trouble his conscience: a sexual union that would cleanse and heal him completely.

A quarter of a mile from home, on a blind corner, a drunk truck driver on the wrong side of the road, who hadn't turned his headlights on, slammed into Boy's burgundy coloured jaguar crushing it beyond recognition. Boy was killed instantly.

In the 11:00 p.m. news bulletin on CBC radio that night, there was a report of a fatal accident on the Denistone road but no names were mentioned. Word of mouth eye-witness accounts soon began to circulate and the full story was on the front page of next morning's paper. 'Well known grazier dies in road accident'. The truck driver had been charged with causing death by dangerous driving and driving under the influence of alcohol. He had been released on bail but he was more than likely going to receive a substantial prison sentence when the case came to court.

Maggie woke up next morning, showered, dressed and had breakfast, unaware of the accident but still sorely troubled about her friendship with Boy and her failure to read the signs. How was she going to deal with him and spare his feelings? Indeed what were her own feelings? Brian was waiting for her on the steps of Madelaine.

'Have you heard the news about Boy?'

'What news?'

'He's dead - killed in a road accident last night.'

'But I was only talking to him last night. There must be some mistake.'

'No mistake. It's on the wireless and in the paper.'

Maggie became unsteady on her feet and fell into her brother's arms. He guided her over to a park bench where they sat down together and he held her in a protective embrace. There were no tears, just a stunned and dreadful silence.

'Perhaps you should take the day off.'

'No. It's not as if I loved him although I think now he might have loved me. What happened? Was it his fault? It wasn't suicide was it?'

'No, the other driver was in the wrong – drunk at the wheel, no lights and took a blind corner on the wrong side of the road. There was nothing Boy could have done.'

'That's terrible! Poor Boy! What time did it happen?'

'About nine o'clock last night.'

'We were together at the 'Tea Rooms' til 8.30. I'm probably the last person he ever spoke to.'

Boy's funeral took place on the following Wednesday. It was a big affair with a requiem mass. The church was packed with friends and associates. There were quite a few members of the Upson family there, including some of the 'harpie' cousins, but they didn't officiate in any way. Proceedings seemed to be in the hands of Father Hanratty, Boy's business manager and Mrs Morgan. Maggie thought the Upsons were only there to make sure that Boy really was dead and buried.

When Boy had been adopted, the rest of the Upson clan had looked on him as an interloper, a grotesque young cuckoo chick, rudely transplanted into their midst. They had all lusted after the considerable estate and fortune of Boy's (til then) childless parents; and then Boy had appeared, usurping their prospects and shouldering all their aspirations out of the nest to their doom and destruction on the stony ground below. They felt that the estate, which had been in the family for generations, would now revert to them. Exactly how it would be shared out remained to be seen.

After the burial, the mourners mingled for a while outside the church. Kate and Brian had been with Maggie for moral support. She was also comforted and gratified by the fact that the co-owners of 'Nostromo', the Anstruthers and Pirbrights, made a point of seeking her out to offer their condolences. As the mourners began to file into the hall for the funeral breakfast, Brian and Kate took Maggie home to their place for a private funeral breakfast of their own.

They were joined by Tom, Molly and Mammy who managed to rally her spirits and bring a smile to her face. Among other things she was initiated into the mysteries of the human hand with its five digits separated by only four spaces Brian and Tom also took the opportunity to complete the previously interrupted experiment to determine if a similar universal principle applied to the human foot.

A quick 'digital' survey of both of Kate's feet, followed by a similar examination of Maggie's feet, confirmed that the same universal principle did apply to feet as well. Five toes per foot separated by only four spaces. It also emerged that, like Kate, Maggie was pathologically ticklish. When Kate suggested broadening the sample by checking the feet of Brian and Tom, they felt that the theory had been adequately proven and that any more sampling would be a waste of time.

At about four o'clock that afternoon, Kate drove Maggie back to Madelaine College.

'Thanks for being there today Kate. I couldn't have faced it on my own.'

'Happy to do it Maggie. Fortunately the Upson Harpies kept a low profile.'

'Yeah they certainly didn't have anything to do with conducting the service. Mrs Morgan's eulogy was wonderful and so heartfelt. I was trying my hardest not to cry but that was the last straw.'

'I think, after his parents, Mrs Morgan probably understood Boy better than anybody. I never realized his faith was so important to him.'

'A few things he said to me in our last couple of conversations gave me the impression that he was quite religious in a very old fashioned way. I don't think any of us really understood him.'

'Perhaps there were hidden depths. It doesn't mean he wasn't a crashing boor a lot of the time but he definitely treated you well. Poor bloke. Nobody deserves to die like that.'

<div align="center">~~~§~~~</div>

Back in Darlington, Lucy found herself becoming increasingly conflicted. She was fully aware of her growing affection for Jim and, out of loyalty to Hugh she did her level best to suppress it. She tried to spend less time with Jim and more with Hugh and made a point of sharing Hugh's bed with him more often than she had done of late. It had always been enjoyable making love with him and she did her best to pleasure him and evoke memories of their happy past. However it **was** now definitely the past and the harder she tried to reassure Hugh, the harder she found it to convince herself.

The changes in Jim since his accident had been profound. The tricky, manipulative character of the past had been erased along with his memory. In recent months his new personality had blossomed. He radiated an extraordinary calm and just being with him could have an inspirational and exhilarating effect on others, Lucy in particular.

Detailed memories of life before his accident still eluded him but memories of another kind were flooding back into his consciousness; he was reliving the experiences of whatever part of his consciousness had remained aware and awake during his coma; be it his conscious mind, his unconscious mind, his soul or whatever. Some part of his being had been on a journey while his broken body struggled to stay alive. The impressions from that mystic journey sustained and enlightened him now. They couldn't be seen, touched or heard; nor could they be put into words; but they imbued every atom of his being with a deep sense of belonging.

However, Jim's sense of well-being wasn't with him all the time. There were occasional terrifying flashbacks or panic attacks which took him by surprise. Often it was the sense of being abandoned at sea. During these visitations he became as frightened and fragile as a tiny child. Once when Lucy was with him during one of these attacks she held him in a comforting embrace. In his vulnerable state he melted into her arms and in time was comforted by her touch. Increasingly Lucy used her body to comfort him and inevitably they became lovers.

Once she had crossed that line with Jim, Lucy realized that deceiving Hugh or keeping him in the dark was not an option. She still had a deep and abiding affection for him and she would never deceive him. Her problem was how to end their relationship but not their friendship. She thought of putting it in a letter but dismissed that as cowardly. On a cold Monday evening in late June, she rang Hugh and told him she was coming round to discuss something serious with him. That would prepare him so that it wasn't a complete surprise.

'I think I know what you've come to tell me,' Hugh said as he greeted her at the street door. 'It's about Jim isn't it?'

'Yes, is it that obvious?'

'To quote Madge O'Brien, it's been sticking out like dog's balls. Come upstairs, we'll have a sherry.'

Lucy was immensely relieved that Hugh was taking it so well. 'I've been dreading this moment Hugh. I fought the attraction to Jim as hard as I could and for as long as I could. But I can't control it. Are you sure you don't mind?'

'I was incredibly pissed off to begin with especially since you had such a low opinion of Jim before his accident but I've had time to get used to the idea. Mum said she sensed something wrong during our last visit. Have you told your parents?'

'Not yet but I think they suspect. They are both very fond of you and Dad is particularly grateful for the strings you pulled to get his bigger kiln approved.'

'Yeah I like them both.'

'And I hope you'll still come round for Sunday lunches. You're little Lucinda's favourite uncle. She dotes on you.'

'That might be a bit awkward. Perhaps in time. Have you thought about what sort of future you'll have with Jim. He is still basically an invalid you know.'

'He is almost childlike but I don't see him as an invalid. Since he woke up from the coma he seems to have found a kind of enlightenment.'

'That's getting a bit hippyfied and mystical isn't it?'

'I honestly don't know where it will lead Hugh but surely you've seen the change in him.'

'I haven't seen as much of him as you have lately.'

'Please don't be bitter about this Hugh. Your friendship is still very important to me.'

'We'll always be good friends Lucy because of what we've shared in the past and you never know, I may even still be here to pick up the pieces if you and Jim come to grief.'

'Can we go to bed one last time?'

'That would be cheating on Jim. We'd better start out now as we mean to carry on.'

'At least a parting kiss,' said Lucy and she took him in her arms before he could resist. It was a long and sweetly bitter kiss as kisses went. 'Now I'd better go home and break the news to Mum and Dad. I'll be sure to get it in the neck from Dad.'

'Good luck with that. I'll see you down to the street.'

Five minutes later Hugh was back upstairs in front of the fire with another glass of sherry. 'What an absolute pain in the arse life can be sometimes.' He heard a scratching at the kitchen door. It was Mrs Malleson's cat. 'Hullo Puss, did you come up the stairs with Lucy? Well you are very welcome. You can keep me company for a little while before bedtime.' He raised his glass. 'Here's to absent friends.'

Lucy's assumption about her father's reaction to the news was correct. He was livid.

'Well that's brilliant that is; throwing away the chance of a life with a thoroughly decent bloke with a good steady job and a heart of gold for a bloody invalid. Is that what you meant by taking up nursing as a career because that's what you'll end up being with Jim; a bloody nursemaid.'

Mrs O'Rourke tried to calm things down, knowing full well her husband's belligerence would only get Lucy's back up.

'Now then Tom, getting angry won't help matters. Are you sure you've thought this through Lucy?'

'It's been coming on since Christmas before last,' said Tom. 'Ever since Jim was in hospital.'

'Yes Mum of course I've thought about it and anyway Dad I don't need your permission. Hugh has been much more mature about it than the way you're carrying on!'

'It's not Hugh's maturity that's in question,' Tom snapped.

'Precisely!' said Lucy, laughing in spite of herself.

'I suggest we postpone this discussion til heads are cooler. When things calm down we may even realize there's nothing to discuss. Now Tom go and find something to do in the pottery and Lucy you come and help me unpack the groceries. Robert brought them round on his way home from work.'

28: Bequest

The winter of 1973 was proving to be particularly severe. Both Brian in Ross and Mervyn on Trinity thanked their lucky stars that they weren't picking apples on Lesser C that year, as a particularly frosty month of June came and went. On Murphy's orchard, Charley Flint still complained about the cold: in fact whenever Charlie eventually went to meet his Maker, some shivering vestige of his being would probably remain wailing and cursing round the fire pots in the orchard for all eternity.

On Friday July 6th Maggie received a letter from Richard O'Shannessy advising her that she would learn something to her advantage if she attended his chambers in Ross on Wednesday next at 11:00 a.m. Maggie had no idea what this letter could portend and duly attended chambers at the appointed time.

When she arrived for the meeting, she was wearing faded blue jeans and tan riding boots, a mainly blue fair-isle jumper, tweed jacket and a blue beret and scarf that matched the brilliant pale blue of her eyes. Her impressive mane of wavy, red hair was tied back in a pony tail. As usual she looked stunning and Mr O'Shannessy, on meeting her for the first time was suitably stunned.

'Ah Miss McInerney thank you for coming. You're probably aware that your brother and I are business associates of a kind. It now appears that there may be an opportunity for us to transact some business of a different kind. But first can I interest you in some elevenses? Maggie said yes, her curiosity intensifying as she did so. A Devonshire tea was duly served while O'Shannessy made small talk. When his secretary left the room the Lawyer cleared his throat.

'Now Miss McInerney I understand you were an acquaintance of the late Mr Boy Upson.'

'Yes we were friends but no more than that.'

'Really! Well it may surprise you to know that I am the executor of the late Mr Upson's will and in that capacity it is my pleasant duty to inform you that you are the sole beneficiary of that will.'

Fortunately for Maggie, she was sitting down when she heard this pronouncement. She hastily tried to collect her thoughts as O'Shannessy set about pouring the tea.

'There must be some mistake.'

'I can assure you there is no mistake my dear. We drew up this revised will in August last year and it is very specific and unambiguous in stating that you are the sole beneficiary.

'You have become a very wealthy young woman Miss McInerney. I appreciate that it is a lot to take in. In fact Mr Upson was mindful of that eventuality and he appointed me and his estate manager to advise you in the management of the property and its assets but strictly with a view to implementing your wishes; not to direct or control you in any way.'

'This is insane,' said Maggie, shaking her head in disbelief. 'It can't be happening.'

'Such strokes of good fortune are extremely rare but they do occur, I can assure you.'

Mr O'Shannessy had anticipated Maggie's reaction and allowed an hour and a half for this appointment to help her come to terms with the dramatic change in her fortunes. He stressed that nothing had to happen straight away and no big decisions were called for until she had given the matter careful consideration. He also suggested that Maggie might want to enlist the support of people she knew to help advise her.

'I am given to understand that you and your brother don't seem to rely on your parents for any form of guidance or support. On the other hand, you do have a close connection to the Mahoney family, your brother having married into that clan so to speak. I'm sure his Father-in-law would be a very knowledgeable and unbiased advisor.

'Now this has obviously come as a tremendous shock to you and you will need time to absorb it all. I suggest we meet at the same time next week, after you've had a chance to get used to the idea, and I can answer any questions that occur to you in that time. I need hardly say that this is a life-changing stroke of good fortune but don't rush into any rash, spur of the moment decisions. Don't be in a hurry to change anything in the short term.

I understand that you are well advanced in a brilliant academic career at the moment. I would suggest seeing your studies through to completion. I would also urge you not to make your windfall common knowledge. Do that and you'll be plagued by all sorts of would be parasites and speculators.'

'That's just the thing. It will be hard to keep it completely secret. Who exactly knows about it at the moment?'

'Apart from the late Mr Upson, only myself, your good self, Mrs Morgan and my secretary. Those two ladies witnessed the document.'

'What about the rest of the Upson family? They'll challenge the will won't they? I don't want any of them to get a single penny of Boy's money.'

'Spoken like a true heiress. Those were Boy's sentiments to a tee. They were uppermost in his mind when he gave me his instructions in drafting the will. The Upsons may challenge it but they won't succeed. As I said before, it is a specific and unambiguous document.

'I can see that your mind is already starting to come to grips with the ramifications of your change of fortune. Keep it a secret from all but your closest associates and swear them all to secrecy. Now can I interest you in that last remaining scone?'

'What? Oh no be my guest. Could you answer a question for me Mr O'Shannessy?'

'Certainly, if it is within my power.'

'When Boy made this new will last August, did he behave like someone who expected to die soon?'

'Not a bit of it. He was full of the joys of life and looking forward to a long and prosperous future.'

'What was in the will it replaced?'

'I'm not really at liberty to share that with you Miss McInerney. Suffice it to say that the previous will favoured other branches of the Upson family, in the event of Boy dying without an heir. It was broadly based on the last will his parents made and he didn't put a lot of thought into it at the time having just come into his inheritance.'

'Do I inherit a share in the ownership of Nostromo?'

O'Shannessy's eyes lit up. 'You most certainly do. He is a most impressive animal. It's just bad luck that he contracted a virus when they took him to Melbourne last year. The Australians didn't see him at his best. I still think he is capable of winning a Melbourne Cup. That all depends on what his owners decide to do with him – but of course that decision will now include your input. Have you met the Pirbrights and the Anstruthers?'

'Yes we used to go to the races together; hopefully we still shall. They've kept in contact with me since Boy died. Poor Boy was always worried that the tracks in Australia would be too hard for a horse used to Cumberland conditions.'

'If they have a wet spring over there, that shouldn't be a problem.'

'And what about Mrs Morgan?'

'What! Are you planning on entering Mrs Morgan in the Melbourne Cup?' Maggie burst out laughing for the first time in the meeting.

'Has she been provided for?'

'Your concern does you credit. Fear not. Boy set Mrs Morgan up with a secure income for life, not long after he came into his inheritance. That includes a well set up cottage for if or when she chooses to retire from her position at Upson Downs. It looks to me from our conversation that you are not going to be daunted by the challenges of your inheritance and I look forward to addressing whatever new questions and concerns you raise at our meeting next week.'

With that they shook hands and the meeting was concluded. When Maggie had gone, O'Shannessy returned to his desk and buzzed his secretary to come and clear away the morning tea things. He smiled thoughtfully. He was very favourably impressed by Maggie's forthright intelligence and maturity and captivated by the enchanting fragrance of her perfume. 'Although barely twenty one years old, that young lady would be quite capable, with a little bit of mentoring, of running the

Upson estate as well as Boy, if not better,' he thought to himself as he lit a cigar.

~~~§~~~

As she walked back to the campus, Maggie continued to process this latest complication in her life. She still hadn't forgiven herself for misreading Boy's intentions towards her and inadvertently fuelling his passion. His old fashioned 'celibate' approach to their friendship, while unusual in that day and age, had suited her own desire for celibacy at that time while she threw herself into her studies and tried to forget about Hugh.

She hadn't consciously taken Boy for granted but he had been so assiduous in maintaining a presence on her radar that it was inevitable she should do so. She was happy to entertain his 'disinterested' friendship while devoting most of her energy and attention to her work. There had never been a possibility of her falling in love with Boy. She found his friendship a charming old fashioned distraction and she returned that friendship in good faith but it was just friendship no more than that.

Had she been too self-obsessed? She couldn't be blamed for not knowing about the mental anguish and conflict Boy had suffered because of his sexual past or his religious scruples about possible sex, in or out of wedlock, in the future. But would she have noticed that mental anguish and conflict if she had been less self-centred? And now by bequeathing his entire fortune to her, Boy had made (to use O'Shannessy's words) a specific and unambiguous statement of his love for her.

By the time she returned to Madelaine College, Maggie had almost persuaded herself that she couldn't accept Boy's bequest. She went upstairs to her room, put
~~~

the kettle on for coffee and collapsed on her bed. It was all too much. Surprisingly, she left the arguments and counter-arguments whirling around in her head and escaped into sleep.

She slept deeply until around three o'clock and woke feeling refreshed and light of heart until she suddenly remembered that she was now a millionaire. She re-boiled the kettle, made a cup of coffee and sat at her desk while she gathered her thoughts. Through her window she could see a pair of native doves in the old plane tree outside.

'The birds of the air they neither reap nor sow, or was that the lilies of the field?' she mused. Perhaps misremembering quotations was a McInerney family trait.

When she left O'Shannessy's office she had resolved not to tell a soul about her inheritance, not even Brian and Kate, until she had come to terms with all its implications. This resolve wavered and fluctuated throughout the afternoon until, at five o'clock, she found herself with a bottle of champagne, knocking on Brian and Kate's front door. It was opened by her sister-in-law.

'Hullo Maggie. Why the bubbles?'

'Is anyone else here apart from you and Brian?'

'Brian's at work. It's just me and Tom why?'

'I've got some important news but it is strictly confidential, so you better put the bubbles in the fridge til Tom goes home.'

'OK. Stay and have dinner with us when Brian gets back. He'll only be an hour or so. But come in. Come in.'

Tom was seated at the kitchen table with a cup of tea. He had been unblocking the kitchen sink. 'Ah 'tis my favourite bridesmaid herself,' he said, getting up and kissing Maggie's hand while Kate put the champagne in the fridge.

'Tell me Maggie,' Tom continued. 'What are your feelings about the misleading theory of evolution.'

'I take it from your tone of voice that you are a sceptic,' said Maggie.

'I have my doubts. I have my doubts. It's such a hit and miss affair. Take the three legged spider for example.'

'If it hasn't got eight legs it isn't a spider.'

'There's always an exception. This particular spider used to have eight legs but five of them have shrunk to little spiky stumps through lack of use. They gave up spinning webs you see and they live in hollow trees or old cigarette packs.'

'I've never heard of such a creature.'

'That's not surprising it's very rare. It's only found in the central highlands of Tasmania. Do you know where that is?'

'Tom! Don't patronise,' said Kate. 'Of course she knows where Tasmania is. She's doing Honours.'

'Forgive me Maggie. I was forgetting you're a Doctor of Philosophy like your eminent brother. Of course you'd know Tasmania is part of New Zealand. Now getting back to the triantula.' Both girls burst out laughing.

'I'm quite serious. That's what the Tasmanians call their three legged spider. They're quite proud of it. It's on their national flag.

'As I was saying, another unique fact about the triantula is that the male consumes the female after intercourse. Now you have to admit, that trait alone would pose a pretty serious threat to the survival of that particular species, or any species for that matter. But no! The Darwinists will tell you that the triantula evolved a way around the problem. They decided that five of their legs were surplus to requirements and through lack of use they degenerated into little spiky stumps.

'These spikes cause great discomfort to the male triantula when he consumes the love of his life. In fact they cause gastric reflux and nine months after conception the proud father vomits up the eggs. At least that's what the Darwinists say and if you believe that you'll believe anything.

'For one thing how could the species exist in the first place if the male eats the female after the act? And even more to the point how did the first male and female triantula come into being? Realistically the species would have gone extinct in the time it took for the five surplus' legs to degenerate into little spiky stumps.'

'You'd better go home Tom before Mollie comes looking for you. My head is spinning from all your philosophising. Thanks for fixing the plumbing.'

'It was my pleasure Kate. Good evening to you both ladies. Charmed as always.'

When he had gone both girls collapsed into helpless laughter.

'Is he always like that Kate?'

'Some days more than others. It pays not to encourage him. Brian eggs him on whenever they get together. They're as bad as one another.'

'But does he believe any of what he says?'

'I honestly don't know. Your guess is as good as mine.'

By eight o'clock that evening, dinner was complete, the washing up done, the champagne bottle was empty and Brian and Kate were still digesting Maggie's news.

'When are you going to tell the 'children?' Brian asked.

'That's not a high priority,' his sister replied. 'They'd soon be back here if they got wind of it.'

'But they **are** your parents Maggie,' said Kate. 'Surely you'll tell them.'

'Not until everything is sorted out and they can't have a say in how I dispose of it. You've seen what they are like now. They couldn't be bothered coming to your wedding.'

Kate shook her head. 'I still think it's very sad.'

'I still can't believe that Boy would leave you absolutely everything. He must have really loved you,' said Brian.

'That's the hardest part of the whole business for me,' said Maggie. 'I was fond of him. He was cute and kind to me but I didn't love him in the romantic sense. I still feel that if I take his money it will be under false pretences.'

'Well you could give it all to charity if that makes your conscience more comfortable,' said Brian. 'But I think you owe it to Boy to respect his wishes. You would be denying him his grand statement of love for you from beyond the grave. You at least owe him that. I think it would be unkind of you not to accept his gift.'

Brian's wife and sister both looked at him in surprise as if to make sure it was **their** Brian and not some enlightened stranger sitting there offering this strangely sensible advice. Maggie gave him a rare but heartfelt hug and a kiss, while Kate looked on approvingly.

On the first Saturday in September, having completed his housework, Hugh went round to O'Brien's for a beer and a chat with whoever happened to be there. It was a beautiful spring afternoon which meant that Alf Prentice and Vern Talbot would be busy working in their vegetable gardens. There were only a few punters in the bar but Hugh was quite happy with that. What he really wanted was a good down to earth chat with Madge.

'Hallo Hugh - the usual?'

'Thanks Madge. It's a beautiful day out there.'

'Thank God for spring. It was a hard winter. June was a shocker.'

'It certainly was. In more ways than one for me.'

Madge poured a brown ale for Hugh and one for herself.

'Yes. I must admit I was disappointed when I heard Lucy had left you. Do you see anything of her these days?'

'No. She spends all her free time with Jim and Robert tends to hang out with them mostly. Now he's got a car, they use him for transport. To tell you the truth I think Robert has been carrying a torch for Lucy all along. Lucy's mum once said that she seems to attract boys that are emotional lame ducks, because of her empathetic nature.'

'Well you're no lame duck. Back in your sherry drinking days you might have been but definitely not any more. You're climbing up the greasy ladder of success at the Council.'

'The first promotion was largely down to Lucy's coaching but I guess the next one was all my own work.'

'Exactly. You've grown up in the time I've known you.'

'Thanks Madge.'

'How's your social life?'

'Pretty quiet. I socialize with people from work more than I used to.'

'I bet you miss having Brian around the place. He's a livewire that one and no mistake.'

'Yeah and he's happily married now. They get down occasionally and there's a long standing invitation for me to go up to their place for a weekend.'

'Will you take it up?'

'One day I might. When I get my driver's licence and buy a car it will be much easier to get around.'

'But you don't want to risk running into Brian's beautiful sister. What was her name again?'

'Maggie.'

'That's right - Maggie. Is she the Maggie McInerney who inherited the fortune in that disputed will case that's been in the papers lately?'

'The very same; which is another reason for keeping out of her way. If she's successful in court she'll have no end of freeloaders and gold diggers trying to sponge off her. And after the way I rebuffed her a couple of years back, it would look pretty shabby of me if I started moving in the same circles again.'

'And she's more than likely still grieving for the chap that left the fortune to her,' said Madge.

'Very probably. I think it's a poor show that the press got hold of the story.'

'Anything to sell papers I suppose. She's done very well to keep her picture out of the papers. That's probably down to her lawyer, O'Shannessy. He is one of the best in the business. They're expecting a decision to be handed down fairly soon but these cases can drag on sometimes.

'I think it's just sour grapes on the part of the Upson family,' said Brian. 'From what I hear, the deceased wasn't a blood relative. He arrived with a suitcase and the rest of the family used to treat him like shit. Here's hoping the decision goes in Maggie's favour and the other mob have to pay the costs.'

'I'll drink to that,' said Madge'

They clinked their glasses and Hugh considered ordering another drink.

<center>~~~§~~~</center>

On Trinity Island, when Mervyn got home from work on Friday October 12th there was a letter for him which heralded the beginning of a new chapter in his journey. The letter advised that his application for the position of Assistant Postmaster at Whiteford on Green Island had been successful. He was to start work on November 5th. He took the letter out into his vegetable garden in the afternoon sunshine of daylight saving, to digest and absorb its implications.

Like his garden, Mervyn had become well established at his childhood home over the past three years. He was very happy there and it was tempting to put down permanent roots and live the rest of his days on the Island. But there were certain limitations that had begun to chafe. There were no prospects for promotion on Trinity and his salary was only modest. If he ever wanted to buy a home of his own he would need to be earning much more.

Something about the postal side of the PMG's operations appealed to him more than the telephonic and telegraphic branches and about six months previously he had begun applying for vacancies in the postal service.

Now he had been successful and it was time to spread his wings. His parents had loved having him at home for the past three years but they appreciated the fact that one day he would need to reassert his independence.

They had been very favourably impressed by Elsie and Mervyn's mum in particular hoped that something might develop there. She had holidayed with them twice now and Mervyn had reciprocated twice by going to Lesser C. Mrs Purvis and Elsie exchanged letters on a regular basis usually to exchange recipes. In fact she was using Elsie's rhubarb and apple crumble recipe for that night's dessert. Mervyn's dad was also very taken with her and found her an apt and enthusiastic pupil at the pool table.

On her second visit, Elsie had brought her guitar and she and Mervyn spent many happy hours playing together; not cooped up in Mervyn's room but on the verandah where it could be shared with his parents and the occasional visitor. Mervyn revelled in showing off Elsie's sublime singing voice to all and sundry. The songs they played were mostly from the repertoire of the Viney household and more accessible to the Purvis family than some of the more esoteric numbers in the song list of Mervan Mithras.

He re-read his acceptance letter a few times to let it sink in and then did an inspection of his garden. Being October the spring was well established and a full range of vegetables was starting to thrive: broad beans, brussel sprouts, lettuce, carrots, parsnips, pumpkin, sweet corn and (under glass) tomatoes. With a view to his parents being able to take over the running of the garden when he moved on, he had raised many of the beds.

He surveyed his handiwork with a sigh of satisfaction, read his letter again and went in to have a beer with his parents and break the news about his new job.

1974

29: Hugh and Maggie

The year 1974 was a landmark year for the Mahoney family. The general election in April had seen the Labour Party swept back into power after fifteen years in the political wilderness. Kate's brother Martin had won back the seat that had formerly been held by his grandfather and before that by his great grandfather. Young Jack Mahoney had come out of retirement to campaign for his grandson and to his great satisfaction found that the Mahoney 'Brand' still held its value.

In Ross, Kate was growing in confidence as a teacher and starting to enjoy her work. One boy in year 7 clearly had a crush on her which was sweet but not without its problems. While Kate was negotiating these pitfalls and educating herself and her pupils, Brian and Maggie were struggling through their Dip Eds. Compared to what they studied for their degrees, they found the subject matter esoteric, overly philosophical and deadly boring. The one positive was the classroom experience gained through supervised prac teaching sessions. They both did well in these sessions and were in agreement that they were the only worthwhile part of the course.

For Brian, a Dip Ed was a necessary evil that had to be endured because he had chosen to become a teacher. Maggie's situation was different. She didn't **need** to become a teacher. She didn't particularly **want** to become a teacher. Thanks to Boy's bequest, she didn't **need** to become anything. She was now financially independent and free to pursue whatever interest happened to take her fancy.

Richard O'Shannessy had counselled her to complete her studies to keep herself grounded while she came to terms with her changed circumstances. Kate's parents had offered similar advice and it had made sense to Maggie at that time. Acting on their advice, she had enthusiastically embarked on her honours year.

The life and work of Anne Bronte, the subject of her honours thesis, was a topic very close to her heart. She happily threw herself into the work and graduated with first class honours. It had been hard work that she found stimulating, rewarding and (best of all) very enjoyable. As a consequence, she was now conducting English tutorials for Doctor Spotswood's pupils, when the constraints of her education studies allowed. Her education studies, on the other hand afforded her no such satisfaction or stimulation.

<div align="center">~~~§~~~</div>

In Darlington, Hugh continued to live in splendid isolation; except for the occasional visit from Mrs Malleson's cat and the occasional cup of tea with Mrs Malleson herself, usually on rent days. Work was busy and for three months he was acting in a higher position while a senior colleague was on Long Service leave. This provided a temporary but substantial increase in pay.

He had made use of this increase to purchase a car; a red VW Beetle, 1965 model. He had taken driving lessons and qualified for his driver's licence earlier in the year. The car afforded him greater freedom and mobility and he would now be able to drive home to Middleton for weekends and other holidays.

It was a four hour drive, much quicker than the eight hours taken by the Up and Down trains which took a more circuitous route to service numerous remote country hamlets and villages along the way. It was feasible to drive home to Middleton after work on Friday afternoon, and back to Darlington on Sunday evenings.

One Thursday evening at about 8.15, while he was contemplating the pleasant prospect of spending such weekends in Middleton with his family and reconnecting with the environment of his childhood, there was an unexpected ring on the door bell. Since the split with Lucy, that hardly ever happened. Wondering who it could be, he went down to the street door, where he found Robert looking awkward and sheepish.

'Robert! Long time no see. Come in.' Hoping that his visitor wasn't in the middle of an episode, Hugh led him upstairs.

'Yes I'm sorry it's been so long,' said Robert. 'How have you been?'

'Busy at work but fine apart from that. What have you been up to?'

Hugh hadn't seen Robert in more than a year; in fact not since the split with Lucy. This fact had reaffirmed his conviction that Robert's universe revolved around Lucy. They went upstairs and made themselves comfortable. Hugh poured a sherry for his guest and another one for himself.

'So Robert what can I do for you?'

'I wanted to apologize for staying away when you and Lucy broke up. I didn't want to take sides or anything but we couldn't all be together after the split, not like the old days.'

'But there was no hostility between Lucy and me. It was all very civilized.'

'No hostility but it was very awkward.'

'How is Lucy?'

'Oh she's happy enough. She and Jim are busy disappearing up each other's backsides. There's no room for me anymore. Not like when she was with you. Jim became someone else after his accident and now he's making someone else out of Lucy.'

'Do you think it will last?'

'It's looking pretty permanent at the moment. She's lost all interest in Norian Fairchild and the pre-convict inhabitants of the Cumberlands. Jim reckons that stuff is just an ephemeral distraction, whatever that means. He says you have to concentrate on being - "be here now".'

'When I first got the van he was keen to go exploring and stuff like that but now he reckons it interferes with his inner stillness.'

'Is he still working at the supermarket?'

'Yeah. It's simple mindless work and he makes a meditation out of it. What I call "mindlessness" he calls "mindfulness." '

'And Lucy goes along with all that? That could make working as a nurse a bit tricky.'

'No! Nursing the sick is nurturing the 'life force'. The great Guru has given that the tick of approval.'

'It all sounds a bit like Buddhism to me.'

'A bit like Bullshit more like.'

Robert was clearly unhappy. Hugh wondered if he was working himself up into an episode or if he was just understandably and quite rationally disappointed and pissed off. He decided to change the subject and started talking about his car. The diversion worked.

'So that little red beetle outside is yours. I'm impressed. Beetles have got real class.'

They finished their sherries and went outside to look at their two vehicles, making comparisons and trading compliments. Hugh's inner prayer was answered and Robert decided not to come back upstairs but thankfully he had definitely cheered up.

'I'd better be getting home. Thanks for the sherry by the way.'

'That was my pleasure. Haven't seen you at the pub for months.'

'Alcohol was banned by the guru. It does bad things to your "Aura" apparently.   It affects other peoples' perception of you – like interference on a TV screen. I ask you!!'

'Well it hasn't killed either of us yet. Come back to O'Brien's some time soon. Madge would love to see you again. So would Alf.'

'We could revive Wednesday nights.'

'If you like. I'll see you there next Wednesday.'

'That would be great.'

Hugh went back upstairs to the flat and, inspired by the prospect of reviving Wednesday nights at the pub with Robert, he hunted out his long neglected copy of "Dandillion" and read it again for the first time in nearly four years.

<div style="text-align:center">~~~§~~~</div>

While Hugh was pleasantly re-engaging with "Dandillion", Maggie, in her room at Madelaine College was wrestling with the final assignment for the term. She was struggling with an American textbook on child psychology and hating every bit of it; especially the jargon.

'Anne Bronte could express herself much more eloquently and intelligently than any of this garbage and I'd back her experience with children as a governess over this bullshit any day,' she thought to herself in her frustration. She made herself a cup of tea (from a teapot, not a tea bag) and forced herself back to her assignment. For company, she had a little transistor radio on her desk.

The events of the previous year: Boy's death, his will, the Upson family's court challenge, on top of the demands of her Honours year had all taken their toll and Maggie was still feeling mentally and emotionally exhausted after all this time. She had nothing but contempt for the paper she was writing and the jargon she was expected to use. An inner voice (possibly her native common sense) was wheedling and pleading with her.

'You don't have to bother with this crap. You can pay off your studentship debt to the Education Department and be free. Spotswood wants you to do a Master's and you can do tutoring to keep your hand in – not that you need the money. You're rich remember!!!'

These ideas were comforting and disturbing at the same time. She had been guided by O'Shannessy and by Kate's parents ever since she learnt of her inheritance and unbeknowns to her they had been impressed by the maturity she had shown in addressing her changed circumstances. But this decision to drop Education! What would they think about that?

'Sod what they think,' said the inner voice. 'It's your life and your money. It's time to make an independent decision. The sky won't fall in if you do.'

Maggie was not so dismissive of her advisors but the inner voice did have a point. Was it time to make an independent decision? Would the sky fall? Or was she just throwing in the towel because of the stupid paper she had to write? She suddenly felt very alone.

At the same time she became vaguely aware of the voice of Tex Buchanan serenading her, courtesy of her transistor.

"Pretty girls can pick and choose.
Who they want to be their man.
While lonely people sing the blues
And look for something second hand."

She thought for a moment, as she often did now, about Boy. He had made himself a constant in her life, by leaving his entire fortune to her. This had changed her life forever and he would always be a part of it because of his legacy. Now, unlike most other students, Maggie no longer had to learn a trade and work to earn a living. She was financially secure for life and free to pursue whatever interests took her fancy.

She had never loved Boy when he was alive but she had always been fond of him. He now occupied a profound and revered place in her affection and she more fully appreciated the depths of his feelings for her. That in itself was also very troubling as she wondered if she would ever be able or free to give her heart to anybody else.

"Lonely people sing the blues
Wonder if they'll ever score.
Think there's nothing left to lose
And then they lose a little more."

For some time now, Maggie had realized and accepted that Hugh, was still the love of her life and probably always would be. As much as she wanted him back, she was convinced that those bridges had been well and truly burnt; writing all those heavy letters and challenging him to meet her at Montini's – and look what that led to.

At Brian and Kate's wedding, she and Hugh had studiously avoided each other.

She knew about the split with Lucy but derived no comfort from the fact. It was time to rule a line under that unfortunate saga. All she could salvage from it was the bleak, heroic consolation that Hugh had been her only lover. She had never shared her body with anyone else.

Maggie had never assembled a large circle of friends and was generally fairly self-sufficient, so long as she had enough interests to keep her mind occupied. Nevertheless she dearly loved those closest to her and drew strength from their love. Brian and Kate had always made her very welcome. Kate was the sister she had always longed for but after the wedding, when the newlyweds were busily setting up a home of their own, Maggie became mindful of not intruding too much on their privacy. To begin with, they would be busy working out their ground rules and learning how to function as a self-sufficient couple.

Maggie had no prospects of ever forming such a partnership. Sometimes, if she was feeling a little flat or despondent she was haunted by visions of a future spent in lonely academic spinsterhood – a perennial gooseberry haunting the happiness of others.

"Pretty girls can pick and choose."
Who they want to be their man.
While lonely people sing the blues
And look for something second hand."

Very suddenly, Maggie picked up the transistor and hurled it at the wall. 'What the fuck would you know about anything you dreary, bloody hillbilly!!' She heard no more from Tex that evening.

Immediately feeling pangs of remorse, she picked up her little broken transistor and carefully put it back together. After waiting a reasonable time for Tex to vacate the airwaves, she tentatively turned it back on. Thankfully it still worked. She switched to the classical station and listened to Mozart until bedtime.

It may have been the influence of Mozart, but whatever the cause, Maggie's mind gradually became calm and she began to see things with a new clarity. There was a potential confidante: a compassionate intelligent person who was uniquely placed to help her understand and deal with Boy's impact on her life. Why hadn't she thought of him before? At the earliest opportunity she would arrange to catch up with him.

She also reached an understanding with her inner voice and the problems of a few minutes ago ceased to trouble her. She **would** give up the Dip Ed and pursue her real academic aspirations and interests. She would go to the studentship office and end it all, but, just to prove that she was more than capable of completing the stupid Dip Ed, she would finish the stupid assignment before she went to bed. They wanted jargon so she gave it to them in spades but it was all done with a calm detachment.

'Well done,' said her inner voice as Maggie's head sank into her pillow. 'No sign of the sky falling. Sweet dreams.'

<div align="center">~~~§~~~</div>

On August 18th for the first time in over a year, Hugh found himself treading the familiar path to the O'Rourke family home for Sunday lunch. After the split with Lucy, Tom O'Rourke had taken pains to assure Hugh that he was still a valued family friend in his own right. The fact that he was no longer Lucy's boyfriend didn't signify.

He had come round to Gracechurch Street more than once in the weeks following the break up to express his regret and his frustration about his daughter's 'hare-brained stupidity'. They had also gone to O'Brien's for a beer a couple of times. Hugh appreciated Tom's concern and his continuing friendship as he tried to explain how further contact would be awkward for him in the short term. Lucy's mum had also been trying gently to explain to her husband. Eventually Tom got the message but he still hoped in his heart of hearts that his daughter would see sense and go back to Hugh.

Hugh was gratified by Tom's solidarity and also by the birthday and Christmas cards he had received from Lucy's mum. For that matter, Lucy herself was missing Hugh's friendship; not pining for his love by any means but missing the social contact. With these thoughts in mind, she had come round to Gracechurch Street unaware of Robert's visit the previous evening. Thinking 'it never rains but it pours,' Hugh had ushered Lucy and Jim upstairs.

They politely declined the offer of a sherry but accepted a cup of tea.

'I hope you don't mind us coming here Hugh. I've come with an invitation. It's Dad's birthday on Sunday and I know he'd love you to come for lunch. I think we've all moved on enough now and neither Jim nor I want to lose your friendship.' Jim hadn't spoken as yet. He had been looking intently around the room.

'I remember this place.' He said suddenly. It was the first time he'd been in the flat since his accident.

'Do you Jim? Really!'

'Yes Lucy. Gracechurch Street. Mrs Malleson lives downstairs. Hugh and I had an argument here once.'

The awkwardness in the room vanished instantly. Jim had remembered Hugh, not as someone he'd met since he woke up but as someone he knew from earlier in his life. 'We drank a bottle of rum. You said you didn't like it at first but we drank it all.'

'And do you remember me from back then Jim?'

'I do now Lucy! Though we all used to go to O'Brien's more than here.'

'That's right. We did! You used to round us all up.'

'Did I?'

A whole lifetime of memories started flooding back, too many to process all at once. After a few more minutes of excited conversation, Lucy and Jim made their goodbyes and hurried off to share the news with Mrs Lovegrove.

Hugh hadn't seen them since then but he had been doing a lot of thinking about them. Jim's apparent recovery posed some interesting questions. Robert had said that Jim became someone else after his accident. Lucy had fallen in love with the person Jim had become. If Jim's memory returned fully, would he revert fully to his old character? And if so, would Lucy still love him?

Then thought Hugh, as he opened the O'Rourke's' front gate, 'If she goes off Jim, will she want to get back with me?' He found himself realizing that he didn't necessarily want Lucy to be his lover again. To use her words, 'I think we've all moved on.' Hugh had fond memories of their relationship if he reflected on its high points but the same could also be said of his relationship with Maggie.

He rang the doorbell and instantly heard Tom's roar of acknowledgement from inside. In a few seconds the door opened and there was Tom with his little granddaughter Lucinda riding on his shoulders. She was now four years old and quite capable of walking but enjoyed being carried or riding piggy-back.

'Well Lucinda. Look what the cat dragged in. It's Uncle Hughie.'

'Where have you been Uncle Hughie? Were you lost?'

'I've been away on business.'

'What sort of business?'

'Grown up business.'

'I'm grown up!'

'Old peoples' business.'

'Boring! Don't do it again. I missed you.'

She reached out for Hugh and he in turn gave her the bottle of red he was carrying.

'This is Grandad's birthday present. Don't drop it whatever you do.' Lucinda gave Tom the bottle and then settled herself on Hugh's back as they went inside.

'Look what the puss dragged in,' she announced as they joined the rest of the party out the back.

The party consisted of the usual suspects: Lucinda's parents Ted and Elizabeth, Lucy's younger brother Trevor and Jim. Luke, Lucy's twin, now lived and worked on Green Island. Everyone was pleased to see Hugh again. Ted quickly provided him with a glass of red as Mrs O'Rourke and Lucy wheeled in the roast lamb and all the trimmings.

'Do you know Jim, Uncle Hughie?' asked Lucinda as she slid down from Hugh's back to take her seat at the table.

'Yes I know Jim. Good to see you again.' Jim reciprocated in kind and the awkward moment passed. The meal was served and as always, it was excellent. In Hugh's opinion Mrs O'Rourke's roasts were second only to his Mum's in terms of perfection.

When the first course was mostly done, Tom found his voice. 'Here's to the return of the wayfaring stranger,' he said and Hugh's health was drunk. Lucy and Jim toasted him with lemonade. 'And have you heard about Jim getting his memory back? Leastways most of it. However he doesn't seem to remember that he used to be as fond of alcoholic beverages as the next man, in his misspent youth.'

'Perhaps it's because I gave up alcoholic beverages that I've gotten my memory back,' said Jim with a broad smile.

'Touché,' said Elizabeth.

'Hear hear,' said Lucy. 'Put that in your pipe and smoke it Dad.'

'Smoking tobacco is not one of my vices, Daughter mine, as you well know. But I'd be prepared to wager that you and Jim will both be back on the sauce by Christmas time.'

'Right' said Lucy. 'You're on. How much do you want to bet?'

'Ten bob or its equivalent in grog and you can share it with me when the time comes.'

'I'll bet you ten bob as well' said Trevor, speaking for the first time since Hugh's arrival. He had grown much taller in the intervening months and his voice had broken. His appetite for baked potatoes remained undiminished. If anything it had more than kept pace with his burgeoning physique.'

'You're still a minor Trevor and anyway I don't want you to lose ten bob like Dad is going to.'

Dessert was served and consumed and those not involved in preparing the meal took care of the washing up. Lucinda commandeered Hugh and Mrs O'Rourke to join her in a walk around the garden. She was feeling very proprietorial both of Hugh and a row of broad beans she had planted under Tom's supervision.

'It's nice to see you again Hugh,' said Lucy's mum. 'Don't leave it so long next time. You know you're always welcome here.'

'He's been doing old peoples' business Nan,' said Lucinda sagely. 'I told him it was boring.'

'Did you indeed!'

'Don't worry. I told him not to do it again.'

'Well there you are Hugh. Consider yourself told.'

'She also told me she is grown up now,' said Hugh.

'Ah! That must have happened without my noticing. Kids grow up so quickly these days. I don't know about you two but I could really do with a nice cup of tea.'

'So could I Nan.'

The broad bean plants having been duly admired, the little threesome went back inside.

~~~§~~~

On the following Saturday evening Maggie had dinner at Montini's. When she made the phone booking she had told Giacomo she needed to talk to him about Boy. With this in mind the little Italian had reserved a table in a secluded corner where they would not be disturbed. He left the running of the restaurant in the hands of his very capable staff for the evening and shared a private meal with his young guest.
~~~

Maggie had realized that Giacomo was the ideal person to fill in the gaps in her knowledge about Boy. He had vouched for the grazier's character on that first night there in the restaurant, all of which now seemed so long ago.

'I feel terrible because I misread Boy's intentions.'

'I don't think you can be blamed for that. I think he kept his true feelings hidden even from himself a lot of the time.'

'Did he ever talk to you about me?'

'A couple of times. Until the first time he did, I had thought he was probably homosexual. He had never seemed to show any interest in women before he met you.'

'I'd wondered about that too. I've heard they sometimes cultivate friendships with women to disguise their true sexuality.'

'Yes. Sometimes they even marry. I know one politician who did that. But there was no pretence in Boy's case where you were concerned. Although I didn't understand its significance at the time, he changed from the moment he met you. Before then, he was a loud self-centred sort of person; not a bad person but very full of himself. But I never heard him raise his voice after he met you.'

'Yes, my friend Kate and her mum kept telling me how loud and abrasive he was but I never saw that side of him and so I never quite believed them.'

'There was no way you could've known what he was like before you met him. But those of us who knew him from before, marvelled at the change. To begin with I wasn't sure what his intentions were towards you. He was acting more like a kindly uncle than a lover but then one night he told me everything. He was totally in love with you but judging by the way he spoke he seemed to be conflicted about it and trying to repress his feelings.'

'He never gave me that impression; what with always staying in separate hotels and so forth. I stayed at his place a couple of times but I was always chaperoned and always we slept in separate bedrooms. He never once tried coming on to me. He was more like you said, a kindly uncle. That's why I was happy with the friendship. I wasn't interested in a relationship at that time and he didn't seem to be either.

'He always seemed quite comfortable in my company and I never detected any stress or tension in him until the last few months. He suddenly said he wouldn't be able to see me again for some time because he'd be out of the country on an extended business trip. Then I heard from his housekeeper that he was doing a novena and retreat with the Benedictines on Green Island but novenas only last nine days.'

'He did a lot of novenas, the more troubled he became. The Benedictines were always very kind to him. There was a time when I thought he might join them permanently.'

'Really! Anyway I didn't hear from him again until just before the Darlington Cup.

'He wrote saying he had sorted out all his business problems and we arranged to go to see Nostromo run in the cup. We had a wonderful day with the Pirbrights and the Anstruthers and that night we went to the Cup Ball. Boy was as happy as Larry. As usual he dropped me off at my hotel afterwards and I didn't see him again until he brought me here next evening.

'By that time his manner was quite strained and tense. He started talking about the first night we met here when I was waiting for Hugh and he didn't show up.'

'Hugh! Your ex boyfriend's name was Hugh. Not Hugh Conroy by any chance?'

'That's right.'

'He used to be quite a regular here – him and Lucy and Brian and Kate.'

'I knew he came here a lot. That's why I arranged to meet him here. Brian is my brother and Kate is now his wife and my sister-in-law.'

'It's a small world. I don't see much of Hugh these days, not since he and Lucy split up last year. She's been here once or twice since with her new chap.'

'Yes. I'd heard from Brian that they'd split. But getting back to what I was saying, that last night here with Boy was the first time he ever talked to me about sex.'

'About his sexual past?'

'No about my sexual past, not that it was any of his business! It was the closest we ever came to having an argument. He was very upset that Hugh and I had been "lovers out of wedlock." He was quite old fashioned about it.'

'How often did you meet him after that conversation?'

'Only the once, the night he died. I'm probably the last person he ever spoke to. I feel creepy about that.'

'And what did you talk about?'

'He started by apologising for appearing judgmental the last time we met. He had obviously given my actions a lot of thought and come to the conclusion that I'd acted with integrity and a clear conscience (albeit out of wedlock). It was as if he had been weighing up my actions on some kind of moral scale to see if I had sinned or not. He concluded that my experience of sex was entirely positive.'

'Did he talk about his own experience of sex?'

'Only to say that it was anything but positive. I asked him if he wanted to talk about it but he clammed up. Pretty soon after that we went our separate ways. When was the last time you spoke to him?'

'Two days before he died. He sat where you're sitting now and told me everything: all about his negative sexual experiences. His childhood was an absolute horror story.'

Giacomo told Maggie the full story of the sexual abuse Boy had suffered; the resulting feelings of guilt and contamination; his quest for cleansing and purification through religion and celibacy; the moral crisis he experienced when he met Maggie and became sexually attracted to her.

'He wanted you desperately but his desires were in complete contravention of the shield of morality he had used to protect himself from his past. The more he fancied you the more wracked with guilt he became.'

'That's absolutely heartbreaking. The poor man. I had no idea he felt that way. He always went out of his way to create the opposite impression. He was very hands off and he never laid a finger on me, not so much as a peck on the cheek.'

'Yes,' said Giacomo. 'He would keep up the kindly uncle facade when you were together and then be tortured by guilt and frustration later when he was alone. It was driving him mad.'

'That last night, when I asked if he wanted to talk about his sexual past, for a split second he looked like he wanted to. There was a pleading look in his eyes but then the shutters went up and he bit my head off saying 'no'. He apologized straight away but the moment was lost.

'It was only after those last two conversations I had with him that I began to realize that he might have feelings for me other than just platonic friendship. I felt awful for not realizing sooner and also because I didn't reciprocate those feelings for him. I liked him a lot and he was very kind to me, especially here in the restaurant that first night, but I definitely didn't love him; not in the sexual or the marital sense. On top of all that, if I needed any further proof of his love, he left his entire fortune to me. If only he had been more forthcoming sooner it could have all been nipped in the bud.'

'There was a girl in my village back in Italy that I was crazy about. Very beautiful she was and I adored her. I took every opportunity to spend time with her, inventing silly excuses to be where she was. I hung on her every word and smile but I never put my feelings into words because deep down I knew that if I did, her answer would be no. Not that I admitted it to myself at the time. But men in love do stupid things to torture themselves.'

'Not just men. Thank you for this chance to talk Jack. I understand poor Boy much better now. He deserved more, someone better than me.'

'Now don't start beating yourself up over this. He disguised his true feelings too well. To use his words, you acted with 'integrity and a clear conscience.' Now we'd better finish up so they can clear the table. Where are you staying tonight – not the Y?' They both smiled with fond sadness, remembering Boy's reaction to that suggestion the first night they met: it was probably the last time he ever really, wholeheartedly raised his voice.

'No I'm staying in a hotel, the one Boy always booked me into. I can afford that sort of thing now but I'm not looking forward to it because of the associations.'

'Are there any friends here in Darlington that you could stay with?'

'Not really.'

'No old acquaintances?' Giacomo smiled mischievously while wishing Maggie all the best and flatly refusing to take any payment for the meal. 'What's the world coming to if a man can't provide dinner to a charming young Lady, free of charge, in his own 5 Star restaurant?

'Good night Maggie my dear and the very best of good fortune. Dine here whenever you want and with whoever you want (within reason). Can I ring a taxi for you?'

'Thanks but no. I'll walk. The Duke of York isn't far from here.'

'There's a good shortcut if you go via Gracechurch Street.' Giacomo smiled another mischievous smile as he turned and went back into the restaurant.

'It's only nine o'clock,' said Maggie's inner voice. 'That's not too late. Mrs Malleson will probably have gone to bed but Hugh is more a ten thirty person from memory. Not that that's got anything to do with the price of eggs. But use Gracechurch street by all means as a short cut back to the hotel. That was a good suggestion of Jack's wasn't it. I wonder what made him think of it.'

'Shut up,' said Maggie in an undertone.

A very light drizzle, of atomized rain had began to settle on everything. Maggie had always felt something comforting and cheering in the touch of such gentle and considerate rain on her face and in her hair. Gracechurch street looked unchanged and it felt strange to walk past the familiar houses again after so long. With interest she noticed the smart red VW parked outside the old place. WBA 577 was the number plate. Downstairs the house was in darkness but there were still lights on in the upstairs flat.

'Go on I dare you to,' said the inner voice.

'Shut up!' said Maggie again in a more emphatic undertone as with some bemusement she witnessed her hand opening the front gate and ringing Hugh's doorbell.

'Now you've done it,' she said to her inner voice. 'I hope you're bloody satisfied.' She turned around to run for her life but the hall light had come on. What would be worse, standing waiting at the door or being seen, hightailing it off down the street? Warning her inner voice to expect retribution, Maggie stood her ground and prepared to face the music.

'Maggie! What on earth are you doing here?'

'It's a long story Hugh. Let me start by saying I have a swanky room booked at the Duke of York, so you can say no. Now I know there's been a lot of water under the bridge but the fact is I love you more than ever. I've also grown up a lot and I want to come home. There! I've said it now do your worst.'

'That rain's getting heavier. Come here.' Hugh gathered her up in his arms and shepherded her in out of the elements. 'Quietly,' he whispered, 'So we don't wake Mrs M.'

Neither of them quite believing what was happening, they tiptoed up the carpeted stairs, still somehow in each other's arms and tumbled through into Hugh's flat.

'Maggie this is such a wonderful surprise.' They held each other in a close embrace for the duration of a long and hungry kiss. 'And yes of course you can come home.' Mrs Malleson's cat bounded in from the lounge room where he had been studying the fire and wrapped himself somehow around and between their legs.

30: Reunion

On the Wednesday evening following Maggie's 'homecoming', a very contented and satisfied Hugh strolled round to O'Brien's for his meeting with Robert. Madge noticed a new spring in his step but as yet didn't know the cause. The reason for Hugh's sunny disposition had gone back to Ross that morning to finalise her severance from the Education Department and to negotiate a continued tenure at 'Madelaine', which she would now pay for herself. Hugh was going to join her in Ross on Friday after work and they would spend the weekend with Brian and Kate.

He and Maggie had enjoyed a wonderful few days re-connecting. Maggie was thrilled to be back in the beloved flat. They caught up with Mrs Malleson who remembered Maggie fondly. She asked them in for a cup of tea.

'I've really missed your garden Mrs M. There is something deeply magical about it and it's lovely to see it again. It's looking great.'

'Thank you dear. I do my best but it really needs a thorough sprucing up. It's all getting a bit much for me now. The vegetable beds need a good digging over by rights. I've missed the early spring planting this year and that's never happened before.'

'You should have said something,' said Hugh whose heart, like Maggie's, was full of the milk of human kindness just at that particular moment.

'Hugh and I will give you all the help you need. I don't have to go back to Ross till Wednesday and it would be a shame to waste this beautiful spring sunshine.'

They finished their cups of tea and then, under Mrs Malleson's direction, they spent the rest of the afternoon gardening. Hugh's back would feel it next day but at least all the heavy digging was done and Mrs M's worries were all taken care of.'

'My poor back,' said Hugh as they went upstairs to the flat.

'Don't worry Hugh,' said Maggie with an enigmatic smile. 'That doesn't have to be a problem.'

~~~§~~~

By Wednesday evening, most of Hugh's aches and pains were gone as he sat at the bar and savoured a brown ale while he surveyed the room with a contented smile on his face.

'Well young man,' said Madge. 'You're looking like the cat that ate the cream. Have you won the lottery or something?'

'No Madge. I just feel happy.' He hadn't worked out how to break the news to Madge as yet. Fortunately he was let off the hook by Robert's arrival.

Robert was also looking pleased with himself. He had forgotten how much he enjoyed it at O'Brien's. The revival of Wednesday nights had given him a new interest and a new lease of life. He had dusted off all his notes and maps relating to 'the quest' that had been gathering dust since Alf Prentice's Christmas bombshell back in 1970 and brought them along for Hugh's perusal.

'Here he is, the man himself,' said Hugh. 'What's your poison?'

'I'll have a half of lager thanks,' said Robert. Now that he was a licensed motorist he was more careful of
~~~

how much he drank, not that he was ever a really heavy drinker.

'I've brought that stuff about rivers and drainage I was telling you about last week.'

Hugh was impressed by the work Robert had done; in particular his assumption that, for the purpose of the exercise, the River and the Parfentine should be treated as one and the same.

'That was good work Robert. You deserved a better outcome. One problem we've got is that we don't know the time in which "Dandillion" the poem is set. It could be in ancient times, thousands of years ago and rivers and their tributaries can change over time.'

'I don't see how.'

'Ice ages and stuff like that.'

'That's more like ten thousand years ago.'

'I guess so. But all we can really look for is man made changes like the rivulets that have been built over. What say I make a few enquiries at work. The oldest maps we have would be in the Council archives. I'll see if you can get a look at those. They should provide a record of all the man made changes at least.

<center>~~~§~~~</center>

Hugh was as good as his word and spoke to the head of records first thing next morning. He was able to ring Robert that evening with an invitation to visit the council archives at lunch time next day. Robert turned up punctually and Hugh introduced him to Sharon, the head of records. Sharon was a lady in her early forties with greying dark hair tied back in a bun. She viewed the world through very thick and rather severe looking spectacles but the illusion of severity vanished instantly when she spoke or smiled.

'Hugh's been telling me about your research project and I think you're in luck.'

While Sharon inducted Robert into the mysteries of the Council archives, Hugh ducked out to buy some lunch.

The archive contained some of the earliest maps ever made of the Islands in the archipelago. The oldest was a map of Darlington commissioned by Governor Jamieson in 1822. It was huge and took up most of the wall where it was hanging. Robert was enchanted. This old document was a tangible link with the past. It took him back to the wreck of the Dryad and the days of Governor Jamieson. He was studying a map that Jamieson had commissioned. He may have even handled it and used it himself.

'This is the good stuff,' he thought. 'None of your bloody fairies or immortals. Maps are quantifiable statements of fact.'

He rejoiced in the fact that he had stumbled into a vast repository of solid information. It could contain the answers to all kinds of questions. It didn't matter if archive documents didn't confirm the authenticity of "Dandillion". He still hoped they would enable him to prove, once and for all, that there was a significant, thriving settlement on the site of Darlington before the wreck of the Dryad.

To begin with, Robert looked for place names, in particular the Parfentine and the Cypress Gate but with no success. He then turned his attention to the rivulets that ran down off Mount Cameron. They were depicted in much greater detail than on the recent maps he had bought from the Lands Department.

There were a few tributaries that appeared much bigger on the old map. Some had jetties and warehouses and other infrastructure that didn't appear on the modern maps. In fact the two largest rivulets, the Kingfisher Rivulet and Mountain River, didn't appear at all in the modern maps. Robert had plenty of data to digest.

After about twenty minutes, Hugh returned with some packets of mixed sandwiches. Sharon brewed a pot of tea and joined them in their search. Robert asked Sharon what she knew about the Kingfisher Rivulet and Mountain River.

'They were diverted into a large man-made reservoir over here in the 1920s.'

She pointed to a large blank space on the old map. The reservoir was also shown on two of Robert's Lands Department maps.

'Their old watercourses were eventually swallowed up and buried in the growth and spread of new suburbs,' said Sharon.

Reluctantly as two o'clock edged closer, Robert was obliged to make his goodbyes and head back to the supermarket.

'Thanks so much for this Sharon. You're lucky being able to work in such a fascinating place.'

'It has its moments,' she conceded with a warm hearted smile.

'I don't suppose I could come here more often for my research.'

'Something could be arranged. I often work on Saturdays when there's less distraction. Leave it to Hugh and me. I'm sure we'll be able to come to some arrangement.'

With that, Hugh saw him out onto the street.

'Well that was interesting, plenty of food for thought.'

'Yes,' said Robert. 'Particularly about Kingfisher Rivulet and Mountain River, or at least what's left of them. That's my next project.'

'Well good luck with it. I'm off to Ross for the weekend, so I'll see you next Wednesday if not before. It'll be good to give the Red Terror a bit of a workout.'

'Yeah. Say hullo to Brian and Kate for me and I'll see you next week.'

<div align="center">~~~§~~~</div>

Meanwhile Maggie was eagerly awaiting Hugh's arrival. She had arrived back in Ross on the Down Train on Wednesday, bursting with her news. She tracked Brian down on campus and suggested a coffee. As soon as he heard her news he said coffee wasn't appropriate and took her to the Old Bohemian for a glass of champagne. They shared a half bottle and when he heard the pretext, Lionel Moriarty (Angela's Uncle) waived the cost. He'd never met Maggie before and was favourably impressed.

'You've certainly been hiding Maggie under a bushel, Brian. No question who inherited the looks in the McInerney clan.' He poured what was left in the half bottle into a glass and joined them in a toast. 'I only hope this Hugh Conroy character deserves you.'

'It's more the other way around,' said Maggie with a blush.

'Surely not. Surely not.'

Brian had a lecture to attend and Maggie went to Madelaine College to make arrangements for her future tenure.

Kate was thrilled when she heard the news that afternoon. When Kate's Mum was told by phone later that evening, she was concerned and sceptical.

'Is Hugh suddenly interested in her now because of her money?'

'No Mum she hunted him down herself. She's been pining for him for years. You should see the difference in her.'

'Ah well if you're sure that's the case. She has shown a lot of maturity about her inheritance so far so hopefully she knows what she's doing. I've always been very fond of her.'

Kate didn't bother to tell her mum that Maggie was discontinuing her Dip Ed studies. She probably wouldn't think that was the mature thing to do especially with only one term to go.

'Maggie can break that news to Mum herself,' she said later to Brian.

<div align="center">~~~§~~~</div>

Maggie faced some resistance from the Education Department when she declared her intention to buy her way out of her studentship at such a late stage. The Education officer felt that regardless of paying back the cost, she had gained an excellent education and owed a moral debt to the Department. Maggie had politely begged to differ and stuck to her guns.

'Good girl!' said her inner voice. 'That put him in his place. Congratulations!'

The decision to buy her way out of the studentship was the first major incursion into her inheritance that she had made so far.

She had a special arrangement with O'Shannessy. The running of the Upson Estate would continue as usual until a buyer could be found who would keep it as a going concern. Maggie didn't want any employees to lose their job because of her, nor did she want the hard work and planning of Boy and his parents to be broken up and liquidated. Until such time as a suitable buyer was found, she would draw an allowance of 100 pounds a week from the business. That was considerably better than the living allowance she had received from the Education Department and would also cover the cost of her accommodation at Madelaine. Any larger expenditure would be cleared first with O'Shannessy.

Over Devonshire tea on Friday morning, she told him of her plans to pay out her studentship. He was surprised and a little concerned at first but Maggie's cogent argument, reinforced by the news that Doctor Spotswood had employed her as a tutor for the English Department, beginning next year, soon put paid to his concern.

'Very good Miss McInerney. Now there is one scone remaining.'

'Oh no that's yours. I'm going to have start watching my figure.'

'Surely not. There's hardly anything of you. But back to business.'

He wrote a cheque for the cost of the Studentship, consumed the scone and wiped his fingers on a napkin; before shaking hands with his client and wishing her good day.

'As always a pleasure doing business with you Miss McInerney.'

'The feeling is mutual Mr O'Shannessy.'

<center>~~~§~~~</center>

Hugh arrived outside Brian and Kate's' place in the dusk at 6.30. The 'Red Terror' had performed perfectly and hadn't missed a beat. He rang the doorbell and was soon greeted by a small man he recognized as Brian and Kate's' best man.

'No thank you. We're not in the least bit interested in the Jehovah's witnesses. Everyone in this house is a devout, card-carrying Buddhist so we'll have none of your foot in the door evangelizing here thank you very much.'

Fortunately Maggie had forewarned Hugh about Tom and although he couldn't think of a suitably witty riposte he was not taken completely by surprise. Molly came to his rescue, woman-handling her husband by the scruff of the neck and the seat of his pants and slinging him back down the hall.

'Behave yourself Tommy Madigan. Can't you even perform a simple task like answering the door without making a song and dance of it? I'm sorry. You must be Hugh. Brian and Kate have just gone out to get fish and chips and pick Maggie up from college. They won't be long.

'Tom make yourself useful and fix Hugh up with a drink.'

'But Molly dear, Jehovah's Witnesses don't partake of intoxicating liquor.'

'As God is my witness Tom, if you don't fix Hugh up with whatever he wants to drink this very instant, I'll withdraw my favours for the next ten years.'

This threat had the desired effect and Hugh had a beer in his hand within seconds.

Seated comfortably in the kitchen Hugh enjoyed ten minutes of verbal sparring between the Madigans. At first he felt sorry for Molly as she weathered the onslaught of her husband's relentless absurdity. But as he sat there trying to keep a straight face, he noticed the occasional sparkle in her eyes and twitching at the corner of her mouth that suggested that she enjoyed the repartee too, although perhaps not as much as Tom did.

Peace of a kind returned when Brian, Kate and Maggie arrived. They sat around the kitchen table and unwrapped the fish and chips.

'I've made a fruit salad for dessert to make up for this junk food,' said Kate but it's Friday and I couldn't face the thought of cooking after a week at work.'

'For what we are about to receive may we be truly hungry,' intoned Tom and the meal commenced. Maggie had bought two bottles of champagne and the meal became a celebration.

Kate was keen to hear the details of Maggie's negotiations with the Education Department and Madelaine College, all of which was news to Tom, not that it was really any concern of his.

'I bet the chap from Education wasn't best pleased.'

'No Kate he wasn't but I'm sure he'll live. He tried to take the moral high ground, talking about my indebtedness to the Department for the wonderful education I received.'

'And Madelaine College, how did that go?'

'Nothing simpler. Continued residence is assured and from now on I'll pay the rent, instead of the Education Department doing it.'

'Does this mean you won't become a doctor of philosophy like your illustrious brother?'

'That's right Tom. I won't finish my Dip Ed but next year I'll start on my MA.'

'And what's an MA when it's at home and not roaming around the countryside at all at all at all?'

'Master of Arts. I'm not going to be a school teacher like Kate and Brian. I'm going to specialize in the study of English Literature. I might even write books on the subject.'

'Aha! A lady of letters. A girl after my own heart. I too am a devotee of the written word and I love literature in all its manifestations. Many's the cold winter's night I've spent happily curled up with "Gray's Anatomy in a Country Churchyard". I see and applaud the wisdom of your strategy.'

'Thanks Tom,' said Maggie struggling in vain to keep a straight face. 'That's a load off my mind.'

By nine o'clock the meal was over and the champagne had been drunk. The Madigans, who had to be up early next morning to ride trackwork, had gone home at eight thirty and things quietened down considerably.

'Is he like that all the time?' Hugh wanted to know.

'Everybody asks that, the first time they meet him,' said Brian. 'It varies. Some days he's more hyper than others. And you'll notice please Kathleen that I didn't give him any encouragement tonight.'

'No Brian, credit where it's due, your behaviour tonight was exemplary for a change. Normally you're as bad as he is. Molly thinks his medication might need adjusting but she's not really keen on the idea. Apparently when he first came back from Hollybank he was so drugged up that he was like a zombie. Molly said it nearly broke her heart. They've been trying to get the dosage right ever since.'

'Apparently Tom's always been away with the fairies to a certain extent,' Brian said to Hugh. 'His behaviour became more flamboyant and eccentric after he suffered head injuries in a race fall back in his jockey days. But there's nothing negative or aggressive about him when he gets excited. Rather there's a joyous innocence about his humour; an almost enlightened and mystical absurdity.

'Interestingly there aren't corresponding bouts of depression when he isn't high. He just becomes tranquil and serene. There is isn't a negative bone in his body. He's got a heart of gold and he'd do anything for you.'

'I agree with everything you say Brian,' said Kate, 'but too much of him can be bloody exhausting sometimes.'

'You're right Kate. You can have too much of a good thing. Molly is a marvel, the way she copes.'

'Yes,' said Kate with a broad grin, 'but even Molly has her moments. On more than one occasion, I've seen her chase him out of their house and round the backyard with a broom.'

'Have you? You should keep a camera handy.'

The conversation then moved on to other topics. Brian and Kate wanted filling in on Hugh and Maggie's reunion.

'How did it come about? We had no inkling that a reconciliation was in the offing.'

'Neither did we Brian,' said Hugh. 'Out of the blue on the Saturday night my doorbell rang and there she was and very glad I am that she was too.'

'I'd been to Montini's to have a long talk to Jack about Boy,' said Maggie. 'I'll tell you more about that in a minute. After the meal, Jack asked me where I was spending the night. I said the Duke of York because that was where Boy used to put me up while he stayed at the Royal. I said I wasn't looking forward to it because of the associations. He asked if there was anyone I could stay with in the City and I said no. Then, when I said I would walk to the hotel instead of getting a taxi, he suggested that I take the short cut via Gracechurch Street.

'Come to think of it, he had this funny little smile on his face when he said that. Anyhow that's how I came to be in Gracechurch street at that time of night. Jack wouldn't know you live in Gracechurch street by any chance, would he Hugh?'

'I honestly don't know Maggie. It could have come out in conversation at some time I suppose.'

'The man's a mine of information,' said Brian. 'He has sources and contacts everywhere. One would almost think he was playing cupid. But how would he have known about you two and your history?'

'That came out in our conversation over dinner,' said Maggie. 'I happened to mention that my (then) ex boyfriend's name was Hugh and he said "not Hugh Conroy by any chance" and everything fitted into place for him.'

'What was he able to tell you about Boy?' Kate wanted to know.

'Quite a bit actually and we were able to fill some of the gaps in each other's understanding of him. Jack reckons Boy was always crazy about me but spent months trying to suppress his feelings, and keep them secret from everyone, even himself. It wasn't until very late in his life that I realized he had feelings for me other than just platonic friendship. It came as quite a shock to me. I had never seen our friendship as anything **but** platonic. If he had shown his feelings a bit sooner, I could have nipped it in the bud.

'But Boy's troubles started long before he ever met me. In his last conversation with Jack he revealed an absolutely dreadful secret from his early childhood.' Maggie proceeded to tell them the story of the years of prolonged sexual abuse that Boy had suffered as a small child; about his attempts to cleanse himself by religious practices and celibacy and how the stirring of his feelings for her had revived all the old feelings of guilt and contamination from his childhood. 'The stress of it all was doing his head in.'

Maggie paused for breath, and got herself a glass of water while her words sank in. Of everyone in the room, Kate had known Boy the longest. Brian and Hugh only knew what they had observed of his loudmouthed and conceited behaviour in the restaurant. Those impressions had been reinforced by Kate's expressions of loathing. They sat for a while in stunned silence.

Kate was mortified. 'How awful! I had no idea. I feel terrible now for the way I used to talk about him. Mind you Mum was just as bad. The poor man. The poor little boy.'

'Don't beat yourself up over it Kate. How could you have known? The family kept the matter secret. Apparently Boy's father caught the paedophile in the act and beat him up so badly he nearly killed him. Boy thought he would get the same punishment and ran away from home. It took a couple of days to find him and reassure him.'

That night as they got into bed Kate felt very fragile and insecure. 'Hold on to me tonight Brian and don't let go. That news about Boy has really upset me. Nobody deserves to suffer like that. I was never very nice to him.'

Brian gathered her up in his arms and watched over her as she fell into a shallow and troubled sleep. With time the sleep became deeper until finally the tension broke and with a deep sigh she drifted off into true sleep and relaxed completely. He continued to watch over her tenderly for about half an hour until finally he too began to fall asleep. The last thought to flash through his mind was the memory of 'Gray's Anatomy in a Country Churchyard.'

<div align="center">~~~§~~~</div>

On a sunny Sunday in mid December, Lucy and Jim were enjoying a cruise on an old Edwardian ferry, the 'Miranda'. She had been lovingly restored and renovated. Her steam engine had been replaced with a modern diesel engine and she now earned her keep on pleasure cruises. A small but talented trad jazz band (Teddy Moncrieff and his arse-about syncopators) entertained the passengers with a nostalgic mix of memories of the twenties, thirties and the old days of music hall. There was a small and well patronized dance floor in front of the band.

Passengers were treated to complimentary champagne on the outward journey and port on the return. Lucy and Jim were frequent patrons of the cruise and to begin with they dutifully abstained from the alcohol and drank lemonade but over time, first Lucy and then Jim succumbed to the temptation.

The return of Jim's memory seemed to be complete. It hadn't been just Hugh who had speculated about him possibly reverting to his old character if that happened. Lucy had also been anxious about the possible return of some of his less likeable old traits. Mrs Lovegrove had dreaded the thought of him remembering his seafaring days and going back to sea but her fears proved groundless. He remembered it all but had no desire to return to it. Cruises on the Miranda and long walks on the sands of Ocean Beach, with an occasional paddle in the shallows, were as much of the sea as he needed to experience now.

The Miranda sailed out beyond the mouth of the River and a little way up the east coast of Greater C to Kempton, a small resort village on a sheltered bay, which boasted a number of excellent restaurants and cafes. Three hours later she made the return journey to Darlington harbour. Lucy and Hugh used this time to walk on Ocean Beach, which was separated from Kempton Bay by a low headland. Sometimes they took Jim's mum with them but she had no desire to be a gooseberry and generally declined their invitations.

Robert had only come on one cruise with them. At dinner one evening Lucy had bemoaned the fact that she hardly saw anything of him these days.'

'Well what do you expect,' said her father, none too gently. 'The poor kid is sick of hanging around like a spare prick at a wedding.'

'Language Tom O'Rourke!'

'Sorry mother but it's true nonetheless.'

As Lucy and Jim walked on Ocean Beach that sunny December Sunday, they talked about Robert.

'He has become a casualty of the quest Lucy. That's what brought us all together, you me, Robert and Hugh. We didn't have enough common interests outside that and so now Robert has drifted away, for the time being at least, like Hugh did.'

Since getting his memory back, Jim was given to making such pontifications and usually, Lucy was persuaded by them; but she felt pangs of guilt on hearing this remark. She had known Robert far longer than she had known Jim but she let it pass.

Jim had now remembered his encounter with Norian Fairchild aboard Dandillion but it hadn't reawakened his interest in the quest.

'He is someone definitely not of this world and he saved my life but he has his own life to lead. I became aware of other beings like him when I was asleep.'

That was his euphemism now, for the coma.

'Our meeting served its purpose. Because of it I'm here with you today and that's enough. He might well be an immortal but then again we all are really. Death doesn't actually stop anything. I had a birds eye view of the whole thing and it doesn't frighten me in the least.'

These days, Jim seemed to remember a lot more of what he experienced during his coma . Tom O'Rourke, was quite sceptical about it all but even he had to admit that there had been a seismic shift in Jim's personality since his recovery; but he still took it all with a grain of salt. Although Lucy had inherited a lot of her father's healthy scepticism, it didn't seem, to apply where Jim was concerned. But even she had started to become a little uneasy about some of the changes that occurred in him.

When he first woke up there had been a gentle innocence about him and he regarded the world with a childlike awe and trust; but with the return of his memory he had become more assertive and dogmatic. It only showed up in occasional flashes of insight but this newfound confidence lacked the enraptured sweetness he displayed when he first came home from hospital.

Back on Ocean Beach Lucy and Jim amused themselves by making a huge sand castle. It was a drip castle festooned with tapering, gothic spires of wet sand trickled by hand onto every available corner of the superstructure. The finished product looked magical and fairy-like. They viewed their handiwork with mutual satisfaction and contentment. 'I should have brought my camera,' said Lucy. 'This is our best yet.'

It was time to head back to the ferry. Hand in hand they walked along the wet sand; the ceaseless boom of the breaking waves would continue to sound in their minds long after they returned to Darlington, probably into their dreams that night. Jim's mood was gentle, tranquil and affectionate again and Lucy's anxiety subsided.

A small complication occurred back on board the Miranda. They were lining up for a glass of port when the barman recognized Lucy. 'Aren't you Tom O'Rourke's daughter?'

'I have that dubious distinction, yes!'

'I thought so. Does he know you're back on the sauce?'

'I don't know what you mean.'

'He was telling me how he was expecting to win ten bob or its equivalent in grog come Christmas time.'

'Shit and I suppose you'll tell him.'

'Not a bit of it. That wouldn't be very gallant of me would it?' He said laughing. 'I'll just leave it up to you and your conscience.'

Lucy fully appreciated the fact that she had been caught out fair and square and she could see the funny side of it. Her Dad would be bloody insufferable with his crowing. Should she suffer in silence until Christmas time or 'fess up straight away? She decided on the latter option and by way of consolation, she danced every slow dance with Jim on the way back to Darlington.

She had taught him to dance, to help him savour every experience the Miranda had to offer. He was a quick learner with the slow dances, which were virtually just opportunities for vertical smooching; achieving the maximum surface contact permissible within the limits of social decorum. She loved the look of innocent delight on his face whenever their eyes met, and the feeling of being held close to him.

1976 - 1977

31: *New Beginnings*

At the end of November 1976, Maggie moved out of the room in Madelaine College that had been her inner sanctum throughout her university career. She had successfully completed her two year Master's Degree. Her thesis had been based on the novels of Eliza Denmeade, an obscure and (in Maggie's opinion) sadly underrated Cumberland novelist who lived and wrote in the same years as the Bronte sisters.

Denmeade's work was typically Victorian in many ways but it also contained exotic elements looking back to an imagined, non European heritage: among the typically Victorian gentry and lesser nobility were people of colour, a kind of Oceanic or Polynesian element, totally integrated and in no way socially inferior, that reminded Maggie of the Gondal and Angria characters in the 'juvenilia' of the Bronte's.

As part of her research, Maggie gained access to contemporary portraits stored in the National Art Gallery and Museum. She found a number of portraits of Miss Denmeade and also several portraits of Oceanic Gentry who could have been models for some of her characters. In time Maggie planned to write an extensive biography and study of all of Denmeade's work - novels and poetry.

Between the years 1840 and 1845, Miss Denmeade had taught at Iona College, a venerable old academy in the leafy suburb of Mill Farm that was still regarded as the most exclusive girl's school in the country. Because of a referral from Dr Spotswood to Miss Carstairs, the school principal, Maggie had been given access to the college's records and archives.

Miss Carstairs (a descendant of Eliza Denmeade) was so thrilled to meet a young person who held her ancestor in such high regard that she also gave Maggie access to private family heirlooms including much of the novelist's correspondence, her diaries and notebooks, none of which had been made available to researchers before. This information had helped Maggie to break important new ground in her thesis.

During the course of Maggie's research, Miss Carstairs became very fond of her and more than once hinted that she would be very welcome to follow in Eliza Denmeade's footsteps by teaching English Literature at Iona. Maggie was flattered but she wanted a break from academia for the time being. She wanted to just enjoy reconnecting with Hugh and coming to terms with the dramatic change in her fortunes.

A buyer had been found for the Upson estate in 1975. A Tasmanian consortium led by the Van Diemen's Land Company paid two million pounds for it. The administration of Boy's estate was then finalised and Maggie's substantial fortune had been invested conservatively in reliable and secure old enterprises. The interest earned by these investments provided her with a stupendous annual income far in excess of anything she had ever dreamt of. She had it deposited in a special bank account from which a fortnightly sum was paid into her regular bank account; roughly double what she would have earned teaching. It was more money than she knew what to do with.

Her principal financial advisers, Mr O'Shannessy and Kate's Dad had applauded and facilitated her wishes to keep the fortune invested in a safe and modestly productive way. Maggie had no starry eyed entrepreneurial ambitions and planned to live a simple and private life. In early December she moved in with Hugh and made Gracechurch St her home.

Shortly after moving into Gracechurch street, she received a formal offer of employment, from Miss Carstairs for when school resumed in February next year. She was anxious not to over-commit herself while she found her feet as an independent woman but she felt indebted to Miss Carstairs whom she regarded as a friend. Eventually she agreed to a trial run. She would, teach the senior classes English Literature on Tuesdays and Fridays for the first term to see if she had what it takes to be a teacher and also to see if she enjoyed it. Then she and the principal could consider their options.

One of the first things Hugh did when Maggie moved in was to propose to her.   She promptly accepted his proposal and they went to Montini's that night to celebrate. The little Italian was pleased to see them, even more so when he saw the ring on Maggie's finger.

'The wine tonight is on the house my friends.'

He ordered champagne, pulled up a chair and proposed a toast to their future happiness. It was a busy night and a full house so he could only spare a few minutes to sit with them, but he had been following their progress with considerable interest and was very happily satisfied by this latest development.

<div style="text-align:center">~~~§~~~</div>

The happy couple planned to spend Christmas with Hugh's family in Middleton. When Hugh's mother first heard that Hugh and Maggie were not only together again but engaged to be married, she had misgivings;

remembering the 'conceited little Miss' from 18 years earlier.

She had further misgivings about the fact that Maggie was now a wealthy heiress whose inheritance had been the subject of an acrimonious legal challenge, that had been covered extensively in the press. Exactly what had been her relationship to the deceased Mr Upson? Fortunately those misgivings were largely dispelled upon meeting Maggie again and seeing how she had matured beyond all recognition. She was therefore prepared to give her prospective daughter-in-law the benefit of the doubt.

Nevertheless she had been surprised to hear that Hugh hadn't asked Maggie's father for his daughter's hand and even more surprised to be told by Maggie that, her parents weren't a lot of use at the best of times. 'They virtually abandoned Brian and me and ran away to England as soon as we were old enough to put into boarding schools.' But she had said it in a quite matter of fact way without any apparent bitterness or regret. Mrs Conroy thought back to the few years that the McInerneys had been her next door neighbours. There *had* been something decidedly odd about them.

Hugh's sister Annie, who was now 19, had only just been born when the McInerneys had moved to Green Island in 1958, so she was effectively meeting Maggie for the first time and without any negative preconceptions. They hit it off immediately which was just as well as they had to share a bedroom.

Annie had embarked on a career as a dressmaker with a view to becoming a fashion designer. She had tried to follow her mother into nursing but found that she didn't have the stomach for it. Her parents were philosophical, if a little sceptical, about her new career path but they were in no hurry for their baby to fly the nest.

On their first night together in her bedroom, Annie had shown some of her designs to Maggie. Preparing to be tactful and diplomatic, Maggie got the shock of her life when she saw how amazing Annie's designs were.

'These are fantastic Annie! Who else have you shown them to?'

'Just Mum and Mrs Hardcastle, the lady I work for. They're polite about them but really they think they're too daring and way out; Mrs Hardcastle's stock in trade is very conservative - wedding dresses mainly, first communion frocks and twin-sets in sensible tweed for middle aged ladies.'

'There's a school of design in Darlington. People there would be more appreciative. I think you've got a real talent. We'll have to get you down to Gracechurch St for a while.... after the wedding.'

'That would be cool but let's not say anything about it to mum just yet. We'll have to prepare her for it.'

They talked softly and enthusiastically until nearly midnight and Annie went to sleep with a commission to design and make Maggie's wedding dress and bridesmaid dresses for herself and Kate.

In their bedroom at the end of the hall, Hugh's parents carried on a whispered conversation 'til well after midnight, comparing impressions of Maggie. Mr Conroy had been very favourably impressed, not least because she was a part owner of Nostromo, a horse he greatly admired. (That particular equine gentleman was now eleven years old and a successful sire standing at stud, with a Cox Plate, a Caulfield Cup, Wellington Cup and four Darlington Cups to his credit.)

'Maggie has turned out very nicely,' said Hugh's dad. 'I always found Brian more approachable when they were little but she's very agreeable and easy to get on with now. No airs and graces about her and Hugh seems to be very contented with her which is the main thing. Against all the odds our boy has grown up. He's holding down a pretty senior position at the City Council these days on a good salary. He has done much better than we could have hoped for in the beginning and he and Maggie seem to be very happy together.'

'Yes I suppose you're right. They are very happy. When he first brought Lucy here, I hoped she'd be the one for him. I was so disappointed when she left him for that other chap. She seemed such a nice down to earth sort of girl.'

'She still is and it's far better that she changed her mind before things were set in concrete. We were spared the unpleasantness of a divorce. If it turns out this other chap who had the accident is the right bloke for Lucy, then nobody loses out and everyone is happy.'

'Do you know where Maggie is living? You don't suppose they're living together already?'

'So what if they are, they'll be man and wife in May.'

'Things have certainly changed since our day Max.'

'In this case for the better. Don't raise the subject with them Maureen, whatever you do. What we don't know can't hurt us.'

'Yes I agree.......and after all we jumped the gun ourselves didn't we Max? Remember?'

'How could I forget. Five times counting that night on the beach.'

'No Max not five times. It was seven times at least. They're all marked in my old diary, in code.'

In his room and by himself, Hugh was sound asleep without a care in the world.

~~~§~~~

Christmas Day had dawned fine and clear at the O'Rourke household. Mrs O'Rourke and her eldest daughter Elizabeth were busy in the kitchen. Tom, little Lucinda and her dad Ted were setting the table in the dining area out the back. Trevor and his older brother Luke were sorting out the drinks. Lucy and the Lovegroves hadn't arrived as yet.

There had been a certain amount of perturbation on the part of their respective mothers when Lucy moved in with Jim. Lucy's mum was a little troubled that there had been no talk of marriage but accepted that that was increasingly 'the way of things these days'. Tom had been blasé.

'Try before you buy. It's about time Lucy put her money where her mouth is. And speaking of money, it's usually the parents of the bride that foot the bill remember.'

For Mrs Lovegrove it was more complicated. The mental conditioning imposed by her religious upbringing was very stark and unyielding where sex and marriage were concerned but she had rebelled against all of that by marrying Jim's father. The harsh punishment of ostracism with which she had been threatened by her family hadn't been enough to dissuade her from marrying the man she truly loved. She had realized in choosing his love and suffering the consequences, that her family and their church had no love to offer.

When her husband died at sea, she had wondered at first if it was a judgment. She had no doubt that her family
~~~

would have seen it as such (as vengeance even) but she believed that her husband's love lived on in her infant son and she devoted the rest of her life to him. It hadn't always been easy for her as Jim had often been remote and uncommunicative both in childhood and early adulthood.

He had persisted in working on fishing boats in spite of her pleading and now it seemed, after his terrible accident, that the sea had given her son back to her and he had grown somehow. He spoke with a new authority and conviction about religion and morality and spirituality; all of which seemed more credible and wholesome to her than the strictures of her childhood.

Now Jim and Lucy were proclaiming their love for each other in frank and unambiguous terms and she realized what she had known all along. It wasn't the external ceremony or the social ratification that made a marriage, it was the mutual love of the couple involved; that's what her own marriage had been. Who was she to stand in the way of such love? Of course it meant having another woman under her roof but she and Lucy had formed a very close bond. During Jim's time in hospital, they had become the best of friends. For much of her life, before Jim's accident, she had been lonely and now she began to thrive on company.

Lucy and the Lovegroves arrived just before midday, laden with gifts and sweets for dessert. Jim and Lucy's mums had also become very good friends and to begin with, Tom went out of his way to show Mrs Lovegrove gentle hospitality until she became sufficiently acclimatized to witness, and even participate, in the rough and tumble of his table talk. That had taken about 6 months.

At 12:30 the womenfolk, except for Lucinda, had all withdrawn to the kitchen to ready the meal for serving. Jim was sitting at the table with a beer in his hand enjoying a typically lively conversation with Tom when suddenly the glass slipped from his nerveless hand and shattered on the paving stones. He cried out then slumped in his chair. His body began to twitch convulsively in violent spasms.

Ted quickly handed Lucinda to Tom. 'Take her inside Tom and get Lucy. Bring a pillow and a blanket too.' He then laid Jim gently on the ground on his side to help his breathing. Trevor found a dustpan and broom to clear away the broken glass. Ted continued to sit by Jim's side speaking to him in gentle and soothing tones.

Tom and Lucy hurried out, Tom carrying a pillow, a blanket and a carpenter's pencil.

'I'm telling you Dad you shouldn't put anything in the mouth during a fit. It's not possible for a person to swallow their tongue. Tell him Ted.'

'She's right Tom. Put a pencil in his mouth and he could damage his teeth or his jaw. But don't worry. It's only been four minutes and he's starting to come round already.'

'They could still bite their tongue off, or chew it to shreds.' Tom persisted.

'Don't worry Dad,' said Lucy. 'Leave it to the experts.' But she said it gently, relieved to see that the seizure already appeared to be over. Ted let Lucy take his place. 'We'll just let him lie there til he is properly awake and then we can sit him up in a comfortable chair. Did Lucinda say anything Tom?'

'She asked what was wrong. I told her that Jim had a very big sneeze that couldn't get out, so it went round and round in his head and made him dizzy.'

'That was inspired Dad, do you think she believed it?'

'No Lucy. She told me her Dad was a doctor so she'd ask him. She was very gentle about it though, in a condescending sort of way, and told me not to worry. Just like you did a minute ago.'

An hour later they were all seated at the table, the food had been kept simmering and was still very palatable in spite of the delay. Jim ate a little but drank no more alcohol that day. He was a bit quiet for the rest of the afternoon but there were no further seizures. Presents were shared mid afternoon and then at around four o'clock Tom drove Lucy and the Lovegroves home.

At 11:35 that night, Jim suffered a much stronger seizure. Lucy rang for an ambulance. She and Mrs Lovegrove accompanied him to the hospital where eventually the fitting stopped and he was stabilized. He was put on medication and remained in hospital for a few days for observation while various tests were run. It seemed likely that the seizures were a delayed consequence of his accident and the coma. There were a few smaller seizures before he was discharged but these were brought under control after his medication was adjusted.

<div align="center">~~~§~~~</div>

At 2:15 on the morning of Monday 3rd of January 1977, after a six hour labour, Kate McInerney gave birth to a little baby girl, Gwyneth Marie. Brian was present at the birth which fortunately was quite straightforward as

labours go and without any undue complications. One of the midwives placed the baby in her father's arms while the nurses looked after Kate and made her comfortable.

Brian took his tiny little daughter over to the window. He waved the curtain back and forth in front of her and her eyes seemed to be following the movement. He pulled the curtain back; a crescent moon, ten days past the full, and climbing up the eastern sky shone into the room. Brian's eyes filled with tears and he treasured that moment for the rest of his days.

When Kate was settled, he put the baby back in her arms and the midwife handed him the phone. Kate's parents had been on tenterhooks since 8:00 p.m. when she was admitted to hospital and they said to call them as soon as there was any news. Madelaine swooped on the phone halfway through the first ring and the glad tidings were shared and savoured. She also received instructions to ring Gracechurch street and let Maggie know.

The midwife took some photos of the little family group. Normally Brian tended to look awkward and self conscious in front of a camera but on this occasion he was positively beaming: a radiant smile that didn't leave his face for the next ten days at least. Kate's eyes were dull with exhaustion but to her husband she radiated a deep and mellow contentment. He was in awe of what she had just achieved and never lost a deep sense of wonder and admiration for her and all of womankind.

They were served a late supper of sandwiches which tasted like manna from Heaven and they washed it down with cups of tea that were pure ambrosia. Eventually, at about 4:30 a.m., Brian arrived back home. The Madigan's were early risers because of riding trackwork, so their lights were already on. In any event he was under strict instructions to wake them up if necessary. He took a bottle of champagne from the fridge and duly knocked on their door.

'Aha it is the young patriarch himself. Soon his offspring shall be as numerous as the grains of sand on the seashore. They shall march in ranks like locusts with heads on them like mice.'

'Shut up Tom if you can't say anything sensible,' said Molly. 'Boy or Girl Brian and how is Kate?'

'A little girl Molly and she's every bit as beautiful as her mum. They're both doing fine.'

Tom opened the champagne and Molly found glasses. Because they had to be sober to ride trackwork, the Madigans drank only one glass each while Brian drank three. He was too excited to sleep and, at their invitation he went along to the racetrack to watch his neighbours in action.

Brian had never been this close to racehorses before and he was impressed by their size, beauty and power. He was also very surprised to see an instant change in Tom's behaviour and demeanour. Once in the saddle he became the consummate professional. He was only a tiny little scrap of a man but in the saddle he was the master. There was no eccentricity or whimsy about him and he exuded a sense of control. Skittish and excitable horses became calm and tractable when Tom was in the saddle. It was no less of a surprise that Molly was equally competent and professional. She was no bigger than her husband but she too controlled these large and powerful creatures with the same 'apparently' effortless confidence.

When all the horses had been ridden, groomed and fed, the Madigans realized Brian was nowhere to be seen. After ten minutes or so, one of the other stable hands found him curled up among the bales of straw in a vacant stall, sound asleep and still with a radiant smile on his face.

~~~§~~~

Kate's mum waited till 6:00 a.m. to ring Maggie with the news. Hugh had answered the phone because he was already up and about, getting ready for work. He took the news into Maggie with a cup of tea and sat beside her on the bed while they digested the glad tidings. They decided that it was too early to call Kate at the hospital and rang Brian at home around eight o'clock to congratulate him.

Brian wasn't long back from the stables. He was almost delirious with fatigue and jubilation and wasn't making a lot of sense. He chattered away happily for about ten minutes revelling in Maggie's congratulations.

'You should see her Maggie. She's perfect and so tiny.'

Hugh offered his congratulations and then told him to get his head down and catch up on some sleep because Kate would want him back at the hospital soon. He readily complied and went to bed, while Hugh and Maggie sat down to breakfast. At 8:30 Hugh left for work and Maggie, after washing up the breakfast things, went back to bed for a while to do some reading.

~~~

32: D.M.Fairchild.

Maggie's first year out of university proved to be memorable, challenging and rewarding in many ways; a case in point being her first term trial of teaching at Iona college. She had found it most enjoyable. Miss Carstairs was more than satisfied, Maggie's pupils likewise. Because she was considerably younger than the other teachers and much more modern in her attitudes, dress sense and tastes in music, the students tended to regard her as one of them. It was agreed that she would complete the year teaching two days a week and consider her options at year's end.

As her wedding day drew closer, she became increasingly engrossed in the preparations. She was thrilled with the wedding dress Annie had made for her. It was a pre-Raphaelite creation with a hooded cloak instead of the conventional veil. Annie also made dresses for herself and Kate. She had wanted her brother and Brian to be dressed in something 'medieval' to suit the theme but Hugh and Brian were quietly firm, insisting that simple dark suits would be adequate. In their opinion it was all about Maggie and her bridesmaids. They were both happy to be understated foils to the beauty of the ladies.

The wedding took place on Saturday May 21st. There was an interesting assortment of guests Hugh's parents and some uncles, aunts and cousins were there; also Kate's parents, Jack Mahoney, the Madigans and Mammy, Madge O'Brien, Mr O'Shannessy and his wife, Dr and Mrs Spotswood, Miss Carstairs, Mrs Malleson, Giacomo and Mrs Montini, the Anstruthers and the

Pirbrights. Hugh and Maggie had weighed up the pros and cons of asking Lucy, Jim and Lucy's parents and eventually did so.

One guest who's invitation was never in doubt was Robert. For all his bashful behaviour in the presence of women, he had taken a great shine to Maggie. She had shown an immediate and unfeigned interest in his belief that there was a well established, but now invisible community in the Cumberlands before the wreck of the Dryad. Maggie had enthusiastically told him about finding elements in the writing of Eliza Denmeade which pointed to some kind of non European heritage in the Cumberlands. From that moment they pooled their resources and shared their research.

Robert's partner for the day was Sharon from Council. She had found him a job in archives. This had meant an increase in salary and a potential ladder for future promotion in work that he loved and thrived on.

In due course Hugh and Brian took their places in front of the altar and the priest waited with them. Maggie arrived outside the church. Kate's Dad was waiting to accompany her up the aisle. Once it had been clearly established that Maggie's father most definitely would not be present, he happily accepted the invitation to give her away.

A crowd of interested onlookers waited outside to watch as Maggie entered the church. Closest to the door was a cluster of girls from her English class. They looked on with a mixture of admiration, adoration and affectionate support; tinged a little in some hearts by a trace of envy. She gave them a quick, nervous but grateful smile as she passed them. The girls stayed where they were, armed with boxes of confetti, to cheer her on when she and Hugh emerged as a married couple half an hour later. She had looked stunning and stately entering the church but absolutely transcendent when she returned.

The official photographer was very busy and there were some press photographers there as well to record the nuptials of the 'wealthy heiress'. Molly Madigan took some snaps with her 'instamatic' and she was not the only guest to do so.

Seeing the bridal party assembled on the steps, Hugh and Annie's parents were most impressed by and extremely proud of their daughter's handiwork. The wedding would feature in the social pages and Annie's design skills would benefit from the public exposure. With some surprise, Max and Maureen began to realize that perhaps their little girl did have a future in the Rag Trade after all.

~~~§~~~

Early next morning after spending the night at an undisclosed location, Hugh and Maggie flew out of Darlington airport on a Qantas flight to Melbourne where they would board a jumbo jet travelling first class to London for a two week honeymoon.

~~~§~~~

They had returned from their honeymoon totally enchanted with the United Kingdom and both in agreement that a fortnight was not long enough. A lot of their time had been spent in Bronte country. Unfortunately Hugh picked up a cold on the plane that had settled on his chest and as they wandered through the Bronte parsonage, he was wracked with a rattly and wheezy cough.

'You must be channelling the girls,' said Maggie with a wry smile. 'Just be thankful it isn't consumption.'

In spite of that bit of levity she was in awe of the parsonage and the church and cemetery, seeing the rooms where the sisters had lived, worked and slept; pieces of their actual handwriting, drawings and other artefacts. To Maggie, all the Bronte's were very much there with them in the present.

The last thing on their list for Haworth was a drink at Branwell Bronte's local, the Black Bull. It was less than a stone's throw from the Parsonage. The compulsive temptation must have been torture for Branwell. Later on they also visited Scarborough, to lay flowers on Anne Bronte's grave.

In the meantime Robert had been busy in his new job as well as his private research. There was a lot of overlap between the two but Sharon didn't seem to mind. In fact she was very supportive. He had been gratified to learn from Maggie that the Parfentine was the name of a river flowing through Casterton, the principal town in the three Eliza Denmeade novels.

During her studies Maggie had used editions of the novels that had been reprinted in the 1920's. However Miss Carstairs had shown her original editions of all three books and each of them contained a map of Casterton, drawn by the author, that was omitted from later editions. It was unmistakably based on a representation of Darlington at some much earlier time – a river town watched over by a rugged mountain. Unfortunately there was no reference to the Cypress Gate.

~~~§~~~
~~~

On the first weekend in August, Jack Mahoney played host to Maggie and Hugh. It was a longstanding invitation made by Jack at their wedding reception. It was the first time Hugh had been there since the night of the Carlingford concert which now seemed so long ago. Maggie of course had made her two nefarious visits to make a copy of 'Dandillion' when Jack was overseas and that too, now seemed long ago. However she had been back a few times since then with Maggie and Brian.

They arrived at about eight on the Friday evening. Mrs Sullivan had prepared some salmon patties for their supper. Jack shared the meal with them and afterwards they adjourned to comfortable seats around the fire in the lounge room.

Jack was keen to hear about their trip to England and they happily compared notes.

'Two weeks was nowhere near long enough,' said Hugh. 'I could have spent a month in the Natural History Museum alone and I wouldn't have seen everything.'

'And then there's the Victoria and Albert practically next door,' said Jack.

'Yes we only spent a couple of days in London,' said Maggie, 'because I was keen to get up north on the trail of the Brontes.'

'What did you think of the parsonage?'

'Amazing. It felt like they were still there – in the next room or just gone out for a ramble on the moors.'

'Yes they were altogether a remarkable family. So much genius under one roof but also so much heartache and tragedy and their poor father buried them all. Even Branwell was gifted but I don't think much of his paintings. Who knows what he might have been capable of writing but for the demon drink. Speaking of which, can I interest either of you in a night cap.'

Hugh joined him in a single malt while Maggie opted for some Irish Mist.

Later the conversation turned to Maggie's job at Iona and the school's links with Eliza Denmeade. Jack was sure that he had all of her novels somewhere; original first editions that had belonged to his grandmother. They adjourned to the library which was very chilly because the fire hadn't been lit. Jack quickly found the novels and they retreated to the warmth of the lounge.

He had never looked closely at the books before and he was fascinated when Maggie showed him the map of Casterton with the river Parfentine.

'Well I never. That's the river in "Dandillion". That's very interesting. I wonder if there's some factual basis to the poem after all.'

'Robert reckons he won't believe a word of "Dandillion" unless he can physically locate and identify the only two believable place names in it and they are the river Parfentine and the Cypress Gate. Remember Robert? He was at the wedding.'

'Yes I talked to him then and earlier at Kate and Brian's wedding - only believes in cold hard facts.'

'That's right. Well thanks to Eliza Denmeade's novels he is almost persuaded that 'the River' in Darlington and the river Parfentine are one and the same.'

'In this map, Casterton looks like a very early version of Darlington,' said Hugh.

'It does,' said Maggie. 'Robert hasn't seen the books or the map yet. Hopefully there will be original editions in the National Library and he can look at them there.'

'Don't worry about that,' said Jack. 'You two are family now and I'm quite happy to lend them to you; especially since you're well on the way to becoming *the* leading authority on Eliza Denmeade, Maggie. I can trust you to take care of them. In fact I'll make them a wedding present. I know I got you a toaster (one of a number as it happens) but this will be something you'll treasure.'

'Thank you so much Mr Mahoney,' said Maggie, giving him a hug and a kiss.

'Call me Jack,' he said with a chuckle. 'Now what was that other place Robert wants to find? Did you say the Cypress Gate?'

'Yes. It's the place the Dandillion used to sail from. "In secrecy to make our way, From rivulet to open sea" and then on to the Islands of the moon.'

'You sound quite conversant with the poem."

'I've read it a few times but Robert is fond of quoting that bit.'

'I seem to remember reading about the Cypress Gate somewhere but exactly where escapes me at the moment. Well who's for a mug of cocoa to take to bed?'

Mrs Sullivan had already retired so Jack did the honours in the kitchen. Half an hour later everyone was comfortably tucked up with their cocoa. Mrs Sullivan had planted hot water bottles in the beds for everyone's comfort.

<center>~~~§~~~</center>

By the time Jack had returned from mass next morning his guests were up, showered, dressed and helping Mrs Sullivan get breakfast ready. It was a clear sunny morning and there was still a heavy frost on the ground.

'I've remembered where I'd heard of the Cypress Gate before. If my memory doesn't deceive me, there's a poem by that name in my other book of Norian's poetry; it's a collection of his shorter verses, love poetry with this one exception.'

After the breakfast things had been washed up, Jack took them back to the library, went to the glass cupboard that housed his most precious editions and took down the two Fairchild volumes.

'I don't know if you remember seeing the originals that first time Maggie. From memory Kate mainly got them down to show Hugh.'

'Yes I have seen them before,' said Maggie, colouring slightly.

'Oh well here they are again. He made the paper and bound the books himself and everything is in his own handwriting. He was a very clever young man.

'This is the book we want.' He leafed through the book slowly so they could see clearly. Each of the love poems was about a different woman and there was a pencil portrait of each girl, for they were all young girls, seemingly late teens to early twenties.

To Maggie it seemed that the poems and their subjects spanned a considerable period of time. There were twelve in all. Judging by the hairstyles, the most recent seemed to date from the 1920's while the earlier ones could have been from antiquity, but of course that could just be artistic license.

'Do you recognize any of them Jack?'

'I'm pretty sure that girl number twelve is Melanie Davidson. She did classics at university the same time as Norian. A very pretty girl as you can see and highly intelligent. I don't know what became of her but she was a lovely, gentle soul. I remember that Norian was quite taken with her. But here we are, poem number thirteen, 'The Cypress Gate'.'

This poem had a drawing of a house partly hidden behind three huge old cypress trees. There was silence for a few minutes while they took it in turns to read the poem. On a first reading it seemed to echo what they could remember about the Cypress Gate from 'Dandillion'. It was a point of departure for a sea journey. The house in the drawing seemed to be a brick building. It looked quite old but it was hard to determine the exact age and style because a lot of the house was obscured by the trees.

Maggie knew in her heart that Jack wouldn't part with either of Norian's books even on a temporary basis so there was no point asking for a loan, but she also appreciated the use that Robert could make of a drawing of a place purporting to be the Cypress Gate.

She asked Jack about the possibility of getting the drawing photocopied but he went one better and offered to copy the drawing himself.

'If I don't get it finished before you leave I'll post it on to you next week some time. I used to be a bit of an artist myself you know, back in the day. Nothing good enough to hang on the wall mind you but a pencil sketch this size I can manage.'

That afternoon, while Maggie and Hugh took cuttings from his garden, Jack set to work copying the drawing of the Cypress Gate. The sun was sinking and the biting cold was intensifying when they gathered in the warm kitchen for a cup of tea. It seemed that everyone was satisfied with their afternoon's work.

Maggie had taken cuttings of Daphne, Buddleia, Liquid Amber and the towering Lombardy Poplars. This time the cuttings wouldn't end up in a rubbish bin at Denistone station. Maggie knew exactly where they were going, back in Gracechurch Street. Mrs Malleson was steadily handing over control of that large garden to her young protégé who was a willing recipient of all she had to teach her. It was a mutually satisfying arrangement.

Jack was also pleased with the results of his labours and his guests were impressed. The picture was nearly complete and it compared very favourably with the original.

'This is beautiful Jack,' said Maggie. 'You're far too modest! Nothing good enough to hang on the wall, indeed!'

'Thank you my dear. I am a little rusty but I think it will serve. And will Robert really prowl the streets of Darlington comparing every house he sees with this drawing?'

'You don't know Robert,' said Hugh. 'He has that kind of mind.'

After breakfast next morning, Hugh and Maggie made their farewells and headed for Denistone where they were invited to lunch with Kate's parents. Brian, Kate and Gwyneth would be there too. Then it was back home to Gracechurch Street with their cuttings and Jack's drawing.

~~~§~~~

On the following Wednesday night as he turned up for the usual meeting at O'Brien's, Robert was blissfully unaware of what lay in store for him. Hugh and Maggie were already at the bar chatting with Madge. Alf Prentice and Vern Talbot were also sitting at the bar playing crib as
~~~

usual and drifting in and out of the general conversation. Madge and Maggie were discussing cuttings.

'I don't think you'll be able to plant your Lombardy Poplars Maggie love. Council by-laws won't permit it.'

'That won't be a problem Madge. Hugh made a few discreet enquiries and it turns out that the Tree By-law was one of a number that the Council repealed back in 1972. Apparently some councillors wanted to cut back on government red tape. But they didn't publicize the fact very well so most people don't know about the change.'

'Well there you go then. It pays to have friends (or husbands) in high places.'

'It sure does and anyway, the garden at the back of Gracechurch street is huge. The poplars won't encroach on anything. Here's Robert. What are you drinking?'

'A half of lager thanks Maggie.'

'Make it a pint Madge.'

Wondering what was in the offing Madge duly poured the pint and recharged Hugh's brown ale and Maggie's moselle but they went off to a secluded table before Maggie sprang her surprise.

'Look what we found in Carlingford on Saturday.' She handed him the drawing and when he saw the title, his eyes nearly fell out of his head.

'Now stay calm mate,' said Hugh, sounding a note of caution. 'Don't let this make you high again. That hasn't happened in ages.'

They filled him in on all they had learned at Jack's place about the second book of Norian Fairchild's poetry.

'It was all love poems which wouldn't have interested you, all except the last poem, "The Cypress Gate". It's clearly talking about some kind of departure point. Jack has written out the poem as well, as you can see. But the bonus is the drawing. The house is partly obscured by the Cypress Trees but hopefully there is enough of it showing, to give an idea what it looks like.'

'Yeah! I can see at least four chimneys and that exposed corner is clearly made of bricks. This is magic. It's the final piece of the puzzle.'

'Jack has visions of you walking down every street in Darlington.' said Maggie.

'No it won't take that long. The house we're looking for needs to have access to a tributary of the 'River' slash 'Parfentine', large enough to be navigable by ocean going vessels; if not now then at some time in the past. I'd put my money on the Kingfisher rivulet and that's where I'll start. Ah!! Everything's coming together. If we can find concrete evidence of places and things described in "Dandillion" – the actual sites, that will change everything. I see now why you got me the pint Maggie and don't worry Hugh I'm not getting high over it. This is too important. I've already got maps of the streets that cross or intersect the original course of the Kingfisher rivulet. They are at work, so I'll start with those. Sharon has been a great help.'

'There's one last surprise for the night,' said Maggie. 'This is an original edition of 'Lucinda Harkness', it's Eliza Denmeade's first novel.'

She opened it at the map of Casterton. 'There's the river Parfentine.'

Robert examined the map. 'That's just a map of Darlington. The course of the Parfentine is exactly the same as the "River". And that's definitely the profile of Mount Cameron, whatever Miss Denmeade has called it……. "The Mountain". That's not very imaginative. But who cares, it's all valuable evidence.

'Thank you so much Maggie and you as well Hugh and Old Jack Mahoney too, fancy him helping us.'

'It's young Jack Mahoney actually Robert. His father was old Jack. Now promise to keep on your tablets.'

'I will Hugh. Don't worry, Sharon makes me keep some spares at work. She watches me like a hawk.

$$\sim\sim\sim\S\sim\sim\sim$$

On August 11th Angela Moriarty returned from South Australia, where she had been working in a hospital since completing her medical degree in 1975. She had been back a few times to catch up with her mother and record more 5 to 7:00 spots with Colin at the CBC, but now she was coming home more or less permanently to join her mother in her medical practice in Mill Farm.

Colin was eager to capitalize on the recent introduction of Colour television to the Cumberlands, to produce a new range of programmes with Angela. He had already had considerable success marketing their work overseas where Angela's looks and talent had created a lot of interest: but, despite his persistent pleas, Angela could not be persuaded to return to 'Show biz' full time. Even though she had now begun to write quality songs of her own that were uniquely her own, she regarded music as a hobby. Medicine was her profession.

Angela's mother was happy that her daughter was coming back home to share the practice with her. It was something they had both looked forward to since Angela was a little girl. She would also resume living with her Mum, although they both realized a time would possibly come when Angela might want to set up house with someone else. There didn't appear to be anybody on the horizon as far as Dr Moriarty senior was aware but Angela played with her cards close to her chest.

She had been beating off suitors with a stick for as long as she could remember and often regarded her looks as a liability. She longed for the quiet obscurity that she hoped awaited her in the leafy and reserved confines of Mill Farm; although she wasn't blind to the blatant contradiction of frequent appearances on national television, where Colin endeavoured to highlight and exploit her physical beauty to the utmost. As her plane made its approach to Darlington airport, Angela wondered if it might not be time for Colin to find himself a new protégé.

<center>~~~§~~~</center>

For the September school holidays, Brian and Kate planned a holiday on Lesser Cumberland. They hadn't been back since their honeymoon. Gwyneth was doing well and now had her first few teeth. She had a happy temperament and was a good sleeper. She enjoyed travelling in the car and had made a few trips to Darlington and back quite happily, so her parents thought she would be up to the sea voyage and the tour of Lesser C. She was too young to realize it but she had her father wrapped round her little finger, although as a first child and first grandchild the same could probably be said of a few other people as well.

They sailed from Carlingford on the evening of September 5th. The day had been spent with Jack who welcomed the opportunity to get to know his little great granddaughter who shared a name with his late wife. The seas were kind and the journey went smoothly. Gwyneth obliged by sleeping quietly beside them in a little portable basinet while they had a meal in the restaurant. They didn't make a late night of it and soon all three were sound asleep in their cabin while the ship ploughed through the light seas on its way to Cork.

The ship arrived on time and passengers disembarked around eight thirty next morning. It took a little longer to get the vehicles unloaded. Kate would never part with her Mini but with Gwenyth's arrival they needed a bigger car; so they became a two car family with the acquisition of a Ford Cortina. Brian had almost surprised his wife by qualifying for his driver's licence in May.

The surprise had been spoiled to a certain extent when Kate happened to see him at the wheel of Mammy's little brown Vauxhall with Tom beside him, bunny hopping down a quiet backstreet in Ross. It had become a familiar sight to local residents and a source of much amusement.

However, there was some method in Tom's madness and Brian began to grasp the basics of driving. The little Vauxhall was not without its idiosyncrasies. Tom was convinced it had been a combine harvester in a previous life. Finally a time came when he felt his task was done.

'Brian my friend and comrade I have given you the basic instructions. I now suggest that you take some lessons with the RACC and allow them to hone your newly acquired skills and make them truly sparkle. The RACC has vehicles that aren't possessed by poltergeists and allergic to holy water.' Brian took this advice and duly qualified on May the 11th. Despite his frequent efforts to appear otherwise, Brian was no fool and he proved to be a very capable and competent motorist.

So with Brian at the wheel, they drove from the wharf to the Shipwright's Arms and settled into their room. After lunch they decided to drive to Woodfield and catch up with Mr and Mrs Townsend at the little post office near the orchard. They were in for a sad surprise. When they pulled up outside, the Townsends' name was no longer on the front door apparently the new proprietors were a D M and E.M Fairchild.

Full of apprehension and curiosity they got out of the car, unpacked the baby from her car seat and walked into the post office where they were met by Elsie Viney.

'Brian, Kate what a lovely surprise and who's this you've brought with you?'

She hurried round from behind the counter. 'Boy or Girl?'

'Elsie meet Gwyneth,' said Brian proudly.

'She's beautiful. Can I hold her?' She cradled the little one tenderly in her arms, her green eyes shining with delight. 'But don't stand out here come out the back and we'll have a cup of tea.' She handed Gwyneth back to Kate and ushered them out to the parlour. 'Make yourselves comfortable and I'll put the kettle on.'

Mystified they sat down on a sofa, while Elsie went out into the kitchen. Where were the Townsends? Who was D.M. Fairchild?

'Elsie's wearing a wedding ring,' Kate whispered.

'Is she Mrs Fairchild?' Brian whispered back. 'Poor old Mervyn' he thought to himself as Elsie came in with the tea things on a tray.

'There's so much to tell you I don't know where to start.'

'How are Mr and Mrs Townsend.'

A sad look momentarily clouded Elsie's face.

'Of course, you wouldn't have heard. We lost them both two winters ago, to pneumonia. The winters down here have been fierce lately. They died two weeks apart. Mrs Townsend went first and he wasn't going to hang around after she had gone. They were dear old things.'

'And who is D.M. Fairchild?' Brian wanted to know.

'He's the new postmaster. He's out in Mr Townsend's wonderful garden. I'll go and get him,' said Elsie with a slightly mischievous smile. A few minutes later she returned with Brutus, Fang and a puzzled looking Mervyn.

'Brian Kate!! Why didn't you say Elsie?'

'I wanted it to be a surprise for you too.'

'D.M. Fairchild?' said a nonplussed Brian. 'What's going on here? It's great to see you again after so long but obviously a lot has happened I don't know about. You're looking great by the way.'

'Never better Brian and life seems to be treating you very well too,' said Mervyn with a smile for Kate and Gwyneth. How long are you down for? Can you stay for dinner?' Kate had acquired the habit of carrying an extra day's worth of supplies for Gwyneth when they went anywhere but she was mindful of the long drive back to Cork.

'What do you think Brian?'

'It should be OK.'

'You could always stay the night,' said Elsie.

'Thanks for the offer but most of our baby supplies are back at the hotel. Dinner would be lovely though.'

'Now,' said Brian, 'So many questions. Why the name change?'

'I've told you in the past how I hated my name. It always left me open to ridicule. Back on Trinity, growing up, I was always called 'Purve' or 'the Purve' and the fact that it rhymed with Merv made me a sitting duck. When I went back to Trinity after apple picking my contemporaries still called me that. If you only knew how much I hated it.'

'It's OK Davey,' said Elsie soothingly, 'you've changed your name and made a new beginning with me – problem solved.' She kissed him lightly on the cheek. 'The only worry was his family, but his mum and dad were very understanding, weren't they Love?'

'They were brilliant.'

At 4:00 p.m. D.M Fairchild packed the bag of the day's outgoing mail and put it out in the post box ready for collection and closed the post office. Then they adjourned to the kitchen and sat around the table and talked while Elsie prepared dinner. There was so much to catch up on. The news was mostly good and when Brian thought back to how vulnerable and fragile Mervyn had been at times during that memorable apple season (particularly where Elsie was concerned) the outcome was nothing short of miraculous. The two of them were thriving.

Elsie didn't look a day older. She had retained her lissome and slender figure and still wore her hair long. She had also retained her distinctive dress sense although, where she used to dress up for dinner, she now dressed up during business hours and reverted to her more knockabout casual style after hours. Brian fondly recognized the Bugs Bunny jumper and skinny jeans she changed into before she started to prepare dinner.

'And have you seen or heard anything of Riley since we last met?'

'Of course you wouldn't have heard about that either,' said Elsie. 'We hadn't seen hide or hair of him since he left our end of season dinner that you came to, the night Davey gave me his guitar. Now I don't know if you remember, but there used to be a lot of roadside blackberries back then, huge hedges of them ten or twelve feet high. Well two years ago the Council tried to get rid of them using a poison spray. It worked and killed off the blackberries and they lost their leaves and there was only their long bare stalks left. Then you could see lots of old stuff just lying there that had been hidden for years.

'Just down from our place they found Riley or his skeleton at least. He was still wearing his old tweed overcoat and the bottle of whiskey he had at our place that night was in the pocket. It was still nearly full. He was curled up like a baby with a picture of a beautiful girl next to his chest.

'I reckon when he left our place that night he must have just walked twenty yards down the road and then decided to burrow down under the blackberries and go to sleep. Or perhaps he knew he was going to die then. I'm sorry Brian. I know how much you liked him. We all did. Mr Riley was one of a kind.'

Brian was silent for a moment as the realization sank in. In his heart of hearts he'd always thought that Riley was indestructible.

Up until that point, except for a beer with dinner, no alcohol had been consumed. Sensing the need for a gesture of respectful commemoration, Elsie got down some glasses from the cupboard and a bottle of whiskey.

'Here's to Riley. God rest his soul.'

'Thanks Elsie,' said Brian at last, 'for letting me know and for the toast. There are friends of his back on the Big Island that will need to be told. Was there a proper funeral?'

'Oh yes. His brother is a priest. Father Riley says mass here in Woodfield sometimes although his parish is up in Buckton. He conducted the service and they buried him later, up in Buckton. I would never have guessed that they were brothers but there you go.'

The evening was slipping by and Kate was mindful of getting back to Cork.

'We'd better think about making tracks pretty soon.' She had just fed Gwyneth and after letting Elsie hold her for a while she had settled her down to sleep.

'I'll just make a pot of tea for the road,' said Elsie.

'Mervyn, sorry, I mean David, how did you arrive at your new name?'

'Well Brian, David is my middle name so I swapped them round – David Mervyn instead of Mervyn David.'

'That way he was able to keep two of the three names he had from his parents,' said Elsie. 'They were very understanding when we explained it to them and never realized how much he had suffered from teasing. It was really quite spiteful.'

'I know,' said Brian. 'I see it every day in the schoolyard. But isn't it confusing having two Daves or Davids in the family?'

'Not really,' said Elsie. 'We usually call my man David or Davey and as for my brother, he is just plain Dave: Although mostly these days I call him 'Faceache', which is what he used to call me when I was little. He's become the baby of the family now; the only one of us who isn't married. Bob and Elaine tied the knot two months after us.'

'And where did you come across the name Fairchild?'

'Ah now that is an interesting story. When I left Darlington to go apple picking I couldn't afford the train fare to Carlingford so I hitch hiked. The chap who picked me up on the outskirts of town took me all the way to Carlingford. He looked very young, late teens, and he was driving an old black rover.

'I was still feeling very fragile then because I wasn't long out of Hollybank and I was hoping I wouldn't have to say much; but he had such an easy, 'interested' way about him and we were soon chatting away quite freely about all sorts of stuff – things I would never have told the shrinks in Hollybank, spiritual and mystical things. The more time I spent with him, the better I felt. When we got to Carlingford there was a couple of hours before the ferry sailed so he shouted me dinner in a little French restaurant. After dinner he drove me to the ferry terminal.

'Now when I was admitted to Hollybank I was a mess. When I was discharged I was stabilized but I was still all at sea. I am quite convinced that I was healed during the time I spent with him. He healed me or at least he set the wheels in motion but Elsie is my real saviour.' He fondly clasped her hand and she gave it a gentle squeeze.

'But the guy in the car,' said Brian with mounting excitement. 'What was his name?'

'He never told me but the waiter at the restaurant called him Mr Fairchild.'

'And what did he look like?'

'Now that's an interesting thing. The moment I set eyes on him he reminded me of someone and I was wracking my brain trying to remember. The penny didn't drop 'til I was walking up the gangplank of the ferry. He was the spitting image of Angela Moriarty even the same moonstone eyes.

Half an hour later on the road back to Cork an impenetrable sea fog appeared out of nowhere. Brian had no option but to pull over to the side of the road and wait for it to pass. It was a cold night so they huddled together on the back seat under a couple of blankets, to keep Gwyneth warm. It was surprisingly comfortable and they were all soon sound asleep. An hour later the mist began to clear and a late crescent moon was visible in the eastern sky.

The light of two lanterns appeared in the misty distance. If the MacInerneys had been awake, they would have seen two grey horses emerging from the fog, drawing an old cart. Harry and Maude Penruddock, with Norian the sheepdog on the seat between them, passed them by on their way home from business that was entirely their own.

33: A Teacup Toast

On a lovely, sparkling Wednesday morning in mid September, Maggie made her way downstairs to Mrs Malleson's apartment. She had just finished preparing next Friday's lessons for her English classes at Iona and was ready to help her neighbour wage war on the burgeoning weed growth of early Spring.

As she approached Mrs M's door which was wide open to welcome the morning sun, she heard an unfamiliar and disturbing sound. Mrs Malleson, who was usually so calm and serene was sitting at her kitchen table crying her eyes out.

'Mrs M! Whatever's the matter?'

The older woman tried to compose herself but the effect of Maggie's concern made more tears flow. Maggie held her in a comforting embrace and waited for the storm of tears to pass.

'I'm sorry dear I'll be all right in a minute. It's nothing to concern you so don't worry about it.' She managed somehow to stop the tears and put on a brave face. 'I'm sorry love. I've had some bad news and I let it get the better of me but I'm all right now.'

'Are you sure? How about I put a kettle on and make you a cup of tea?'

'That would be lovely Maggie, just what I need,' she said wiping her eyes and blowing her nose.

When she had made and poured the tea, Maggie suggested sitting outside in the sunny garden. 'You'll feel much better there.'

'Thank you dear, you might well be right. You're always telling me it's a healing place.' After their second cup of tea, Mrs Malleson had herself under control. Maggie had tactfully refrained from asking any probing questions but her understandable curiosity was soon satisfied anyway.

'It's my son dear, my son James in Australia. He's been in the Australian Army for many years. Some of them he spent in Vietnam and that was a great trial to me. He has been back in Australia in a training role these last few years and I was able to breathe easy. But I received word this morning that he was killed in a helicopter crash during a training exercise two days ago. His commanding officer rang this morning to tell me.'

'I'm so sorry. Do you have any other family to be with you?'

'My older sister lives up near Carlingford. When I'm feeling a bit stronger I'll ring her and tell her; then I'll probably go and stay with her for a bit.'

'What about a funeral?'

'That's where it gets complicated and possibly expensive. His commanding officer is going to call me again in a few days when I've had time to consider. They could ship his body back to the Cumberlands.'

'If it's a question of cost, you don't have to worry.'

'That's very kind of you Maggie but I think the Australian Army should pay for it. I'll let you know if I need any help. A cheaper option would be for the army to give him a military funeral in Australia, cremate him and send his ashes to me.

'It's a lot to take in. We didn't share the same beliefs about death and beyond or anything else much. He was always on at me to go and live in Australia but my home is here in the archipelago. I've never been anywhere else. I still think it was very brave of you and Hugh, flying all the way to England and back. I could never have done that.'

'It was quite an adventure and it was tremendous fun. Have you never wanted to travel?'

'There's only one journey I want to make and I'm not ready to set out yet.'

'I hope that's not the journey I think it is. There's definitely no hurry for that. Now have you had any breakfast?'

'No I couldn't eat anything just now love. Perhaps I'll be up for a dry biscuit or two a bit later on; but look at the time; we'd better get a move on, this garden won't weed itself.'

<p style="text-align:center">~~~§~~~</p>

At last Robert was ready to get out in the field to locate the Cypress Gate. With Sharon's help in analysing maps, he had been able to focus on the old course of the Kingfisher Rivulet as it made its way through the suburbs. This had proven difficult at first and he was frustrated until Sharon suggested tracing the rivulet's old course over the modern street map. Once the two images were precisely lined up, this approach worked well. He was able to narrow down his research to specific sections of relevant streets and intersections in the immediate vicinity.

The next step had been to look at property maps in the target area to identify individual property boundaries which included or intersected parts of the old watercourse. When that was done the next problem would be getting the approval of property owners to access their back yards and gardens to carry out the search.

'One step at a time Robert,' Sharon used to say as they shared cups of coffee in the office after their colleagues had knocked off for the day.

All of that changed when Maggie gave him the copy of Jack's drawing of 'The Cypress Gate.' All he had to do now was walk down all the streets in the target area, looking for a house that matched the one in the drawing. He was hoping that things hadn't changed too much since the original drawing was made by Norian Fairchild back in the 1920s. Buildings could be knocked down or added to and trees could be cut down. The fact that the cypress trees obscured a fair bit of the house was another complicating factor. But this was still his best lead yet, so he persevered.

One Saturday afternoon his efforts were rewarded. It was in Havelock Road, a residential street on a fairly steep hill. It was clear that the road was following the course of the valley of the old rivulet. The houses were all on steeply sloping blocks and across the way, houses and their yards climbed up the other side of the valley.

Robert carefully made his way down the street, methodically scanning each house. There were no big cypress trees to be seen. The houses were of varying ages. There were some very old looking timber homes that appeared to be farm houses. Sharon had told him that the valley used to contain apple orchards and a goat farm. Some houses were timber bungalows from the 1930s and 40s. Others were more recent but there were very few brick houses.

The gradient of the hill flattened a little at a point where another street, Oriole Avenue, ran up into Havelock Road. On his left hand side, opposite that junction, there was a red brick house that was clearly much older than anything else in the street. He compared it with Jack's drawing. It had the requisite number of chimneys; parts of it matched what was visible amongst the Cypress trees in the drawing. But Robert could see no Cypress trees. In the front garden of the house there were a couple of young oak trees. An old black rover was parked in the driveway.

Along the side of the house closest to Robert, a pathway led down out of suburbia, through a surprisingly green field into the old bed of the rivulet. As he came up to the house itself, his heart leapt. Fronting onto the footpath were three massive tree stumps corresponding to the positions of the old cypress trees. They had been cut very close to the ground and had almost been reclaimed by the surrounding vegetation.

Inside the house someone was using a floor sander. Robert knocked several times but couldn't make himself heard. It was too good an opportunity to miss so, with his camera at the ready, he walked down into the quite substantial bed of what was once the Kingfisher Rivulet.

Set into the bank he found an ancient looking stone wharf. It looked much older than any of the stonework in the older parts of Darlington that Robert was familiar with. He took pictures of the jetty and the old watercourse. He was so engrossed in what he was doing that he didn't notice that the floor sander had gone silent. Nor did he notice the young man who had come outside for a breath of fresh air. The man was of medium height and slight build. Most of his features were obscured because he was wearing blue combination overalls, a black balaclava and goggles to keep out the dust from the sander.

'Can I help you?' he asked as he removed a cloth from around his mouth and nose and shook the dust out of it. 'This path doesn't lead anywhere and strictly speaking its private property.' Robert got the shock of his life but fortunately the man's voice didn't sound aggressive. Much to Robert's surprise he found himself conversing quite easily with the stranger.

'I'm interested in the Kingfisher Rivulet or rather, what's left of it. It looks much bigger in the maps commissioned by Governor Jamieson. It must have been navigable by quite substantial boats in its day.'

'A long time ago it was. The rivulet was diverted to help create the city reservoir. A victim of progress I guess. Why the interest?'

'I'm fascinated about the past. I think the history of the Cumberlands goes back further than the wreck of the Dryad. I'm trying to build up a picture of what the Island looked like before 1807.'

'That's an obscure interest. Are you a student?'

'Strictly amateur. I work in the City Council archives and before that I worked in a supermarket.'

'I see. So you're just a natural born philosopher.'

'Nothing so flash. I'm just curious I guess.'

'Well there's nothing wrong with that. It's proof that you're an intelligent human being with an enquiring mind. You're quite right, there definitely was life on earth before 1807, but what made you come to this particular property to look for it?'

'I was looking for a place called the Cypress Gate. I've got a drawing of a place that goes by that name and I've been looking to see if I could find it in this area.'

'Mind if I have a look?'

'Of course not, help yourself.' Robert handed the drawing over. For a moment the stranger seemed taken aback.

'This is quite well drawn but it isn't the original.'

'No it's a photocopy.'

'You misunderstand me. The drawing that this is a photocopy of, isn't the original. It's a copy of another earlier drawing. Do you know who drew it?'

'Young Jack Mahoney.'

'Young Jack Mahoney! Well I never. You have friends in high places.'

'His granddaughter is a friend of mine.'

'I see.

'Look I'm just about to have a drink. This floor sanding is very dusty and thirsty work. Would you care to join me?'

'Sure.'

'Just wait here. I'll be back in a minute.'

The stranger went back inside and returned a few minutes later with a green bottle and two glasses.

'So is this place called the Cypress Gate?'

'Yes that's its original name. There used to be a brass nameplate on the front door. Some vandal must have purloined it one New Year's Eve.'

'Do you live here?' asked Robert.

'I stay here sometimes. At the moment I'm doing it up for a friend.' He busied himself pouring a clear sparkling liquid into the two glasses.

'Is this champagne?' Robert wanted to know.

'Something suspiciously like champagne but much older. Nothing better for cleansing the palate and soothing a dry and dusty throat.'

Robert took a tentative sip and found the taste much to his liking and they sat there for a while in silence. Then Robert, rather uncharacteristically, became aware of the tranquil beauty of the afternoon; the soft breeze, the fragrance of lilac blossom and the bird song. These were things that he was usually only vaguely aware of as 'background stuff.' But at that moment they became particularly vibrant and articulate.

'It certainly is a beautiful afternoon. Much too nice a day to be cooped up indoors sanding floors.'

'Yeah,' said Robert. 'It certainly is.' After a few more minutes of lazy, contemplative peace he remembered his mission.

'The stonework in this jetty looks incredibly old. I've never seen anything like it anywhere else in the City.'

'I have. If you ever get the chance you should check out the network of tunnels under the city. You'll find some even older stonework there that is much, much earlier than the wreck of the Dryad. Perhaps that's where you should look next in your research.'

'Thanks I might. There'd be council maps of the underground at work.'

'They might not show everything. But look at the time. I better get back to sanding this floor. It's been nice talking to you. You can have the rest of this bottle if you like. Good luck with your research.'

And with that the stranger was gone. A few minutes later the sander started up again. Robert emptied the bottle into his glass. It didn't feel like alcohol and he certainly didn't feel pissed, just very energetic all of a sudden. He got up and took some more pictures of the jetty, the old river bed, quite a few of the house itself and the stumps of the cypress trees. Then he ran out of film so he went home.

On the Monday after Robert's discovery of the Cypress Gate, Mrs Malleson returned from visiting her sister in Carlingford. Hugh and Maggie had arranged to pick her up from the station when the up train arrived that evening. She was very tired and grateful for the lift.

'How was your sister?' asked Maggie.

'She was good dear and a great comfort, not that you and Hugh haven't been just as great a comfort. But there was family business and decisions to make that only she and our advisor could help me with. We've sorted everything out and some big decisions have been made but I'm too tired to go into it all with you now. It'll keep until tomorrow.'

'Nothing to worry about is there?'

'No Maggie dear, nothing at all.'

'Good. Now I don't know if you're hungry but I've left a casserole on your kitchen bench; a cross between a thin casserole and a very thick soup, that's if you've got your appetite back.'

'Yes I'm eating again thank goodness. That sounds lovely, that and a slice of toast and a cup of tea and then the land of Nod. I'll tell you everything tomorrow.'

Because Maggie had teaching next day, it wasn't until Wednesday that she and Mrs Malleson could talk.

'The fact is Maggie dear, I will be leaving you very soon. Don't be upset it isn't what you're thinking. When I told you about the death of my son, I told you there was only one journey I wanted to make but it wasn't time yet. I know you thought I meant death but it definitely isn't that.

'Now that James is dead, my sister and I are the last survivors in our family. She is older than me and getting quite frail. Our advisor says that, with the right change of climate and location, she can be made quite strong and well again and so the two of us are going to make that change.'

'Didn't your son have any descendants?'

'No dear. He wasn't the marrying kind. Now stop looking so worried this is nothing to be sad about. It's quite exciting really. My sister and I will be starting a new life where her health can improve.'

'We'll miss you.'

'At first you might but separations of one kind or another are the way of life. After a bit of sadness, what we've shared will never leave you and I'll always be here with you in the garden.

'Now we have some business to discuss. When I go, this place will be put on the market. Your landlord has made that decision. Because he has always been happy to have you as tenants, he has asked me to give you first option on the place before making anything public. He is aware of your inheritance but, more importantly, he is also aware of how much you love the place.'

'I'll buy it,' said Maggie without hesitation. 'But when will you make the move?'

'It will be very soon Maggie, now that we've made the decision, but I'll know I'm leaving the place in good hands. Now you will want to discuss the matter with Hugh of course.'

'Oh yes, definitely. But we both know how he feels about the place don't we! I still wish you didn't have to leave us though.'

'It's for the best love. Our advisor has made that very clear to me and my sister.'

'Who is this mysterious advisor? You've never mentioned him or her before.'

'He is a very important person in our lives; something like a parish priest but not from any church you would recognize. He is also your landlord.'

'Will I meet him when we sign the deeds of sale for this place?'

'I very much doubt it dear. We'll do it in a lawyer's office and I am authorised to sign on his behalf. He is a very private person you see.'

'Sounds like it.'

Maggie was unhappy about the situation and it showed.

'Cheer up Maggie it is for the best. It will give my sister a new lease of life and I should be there to share it with her. Anyway I better get back to my packing. You accumulate so much stuff over the years. A lot of it will go to charity I think. Maggie went upstairs to start work on dinner. She and Hugh had a lot to talk about.

Hugh was also saddened by Mrs Malleson's news but he was philosophical about it as well: both he and Maggie realized that Mrs Malleson's sister's health clearly took priority. They also began to feel excited about being the owners of No 9 Gracechurch Street. This is exactly what Mrs Malleson wanted them to focus on. They even considered getting themselves a cat. Sadly Mrs M's cat, who had ruled both flats, upstairs and down, had died just over a year ago.

~~~§~~~

That night at the pub, Robert was feeling triumphant and he brought Sharon along to share his big moment. He had been rehearsing how he was going to break the news but after ten minutes of chit-chat as
~~~

Sharon was introduced to Maggie, he lost patience and blurted out his news.

'I have found the Cypress Gate. Jack's drawing worked a treat. It's in Havelock road.'

'Fantastic,' said Maggie. 'That's an incredible achievement. Out of a whole city you found a single house in no time at all, from an incomplete picture.'

'You're sure it's the right place?'

'Yes Hugh and I've got photos to back it up.' He proudly spread out a dozen photographs on the table.

When the excitement subsided a little, Hugh asked a question. 'Do you remember Robert, you once said that you wouldn't believe a word of "Dandillion" unless you could verify the physical existence of those two places, the Cypress Gate and the River Parfentine. Does that mean you're a believer now?'

'I've proven that the poem is at least partly located in the Darlington area but it could still be a work of fiction. I mean I found the Cypress Gate but I didn't see any immortal elves there.'

'Did you see anybody while you were there?'

'There was a bloke sanding floors in the house. I tried knocking on the door but he couldn't hear me. There was a pathway down the side of the house which led into the old watercourse. That's where I found the jetty, although I suppose it's more a wharf than a jetty, made of really old looking stone work.'

'From before the wreck of the Dryad?'

'Yes Maggie, definitely pre the Dryad.'

'Well what with that and the 1782 gravestones that Brian found on Lesser C, you've just about proven that there was some kind of settlement here before the convicts arrived.'

'Yep and the guy doing the sanding told me there's even older stonework in tunnels under the city.'

'You mean you actually spoke to him!!' said Hugh with increasing excitement. 'I thought you said he didn't hear you knocking.'

'He came out later for a break from sanding, scared the life out of me. I was too busy taking photos.'

'And? What was he like?'

'He was just an ordinary bloke. He was wearing overalls, a balaclava and goggles to keep the dust and stuff out of his eyes – just an ordinary tradesman. I asked him if he lived there and he said he stays there sometimes. He's doing up the house for a friend of his. He told me the house is definitely called the Cypress Gate. It used to have a brass name plate on the front door but it got stolen.'

'Tell us everything he said to you,' said Hugh who felt that Robert should have been much more excited; at least as excited as he was. Robert accordingly tried to remember as much of his conversation as he could. He was a bit frustrated because he thought his photographs were all the evidence he needed to verify his discovery. Then he remembered showing Jack's drawing to the stranger and his reaction to it.

'He said it wasn't the original drawing. I told him it was a photocopy but he said it was a photocopy of a drawing that wasn't the original.'

'Robert! Didn't that strike you as significant?'

'No. Why should it? He was right.'

'How could he know it was a copy without having seen the original which has been sitting on a bookshelf in Jack Mahoney's house since the 1920s? That book of poetry was handmade and hand written. It is probably the only copy in existence. How old was the guy with the sander?

'It was a bit hard to tell, what with the balaclava and goggles but he sounded quite young and his hands didn't look like an old man's hands.'

'Robert my friend, I think you might have had a conversation with Norian Fairchild.'

'This was no fairy prince Hugh. He was just an ordinary bloke in daggy old overalls doing house renovations. If he'd been what you say he wouldn't have been slaving away with a floor sander. He would have just waved a magic wand or something wouldn't he?'

'Not necessarily. Even if he is an immortal living in the Cumberlands in the latter half of the twentieth century that wouldn't prevent him from using modern appliances. Immortality doesn't necessarily mean magic.'

By this time Sharon was looking confused.

'There is obviously more to this business than plain old fashioned map work. What's all this about immortal magicians using floor sanders?'

'Hasn't Robert told you?'

'No Hugh, nothing more than a search for a once navigable tributary of the River (which might also be called the Parfentine) with a wharf at a place called the Cypress Gate. It was a purely geographic assignment.'

'I deal in facts,' said Robert doggedly, feeling cheated in a way because Hugh's assumptions seemed to have trumped his discoveries and his photographic evidence.

Hugh quickly gave Sharon a potted history of the Norian Fairchild saga and his poem "Dandillion". 'And Robert here has verified our theories, not that he seems overly excited about it.'

'He was just an ordinary bloke. All I did was find the house and the wharf.'

'All you did! You've proved there is some factual basis to "Dandillion" the poem. You've also found the wharf from which the ship Dandillion most likely used to sail and I think you have almost certainly met and spoken to Norian Fairchild himself. You're a genius Robert.'

Robert began to cheer up. His efforts were certainly being appreciated even if he hadn't immediately remembered more of the encounter; but now he began to remember other things such as his heightened awareness of the beautiful afternoon as he sat there at the Cypress Gate drinking something 'suspiciously like champagne'. He was pretty sure the drink wasn't alcoholic perhaps it was the man's company that was intoxicating.

It also struck him, in retrospect, that the floor sanding stranger had been very easy to talk to. Normally, Robert was ill at ease making conversation with strangers but on that occasion, he had been remarkably chatty and chummy; especially considering he'd just been caught trespassing.

By the time the little gathering broke up and he had driven Sharon home, Robert was feeling very pleased with himself and the enthusiastic appreciation his efforts had received. As he drove home to his parents' place he felt like crowing to somebody. Perhaps it was time to drop in on Jim and Lucy again sometime soon. He might even take Sharon.

<div style="text-align:center">~~~§~~~</div>

On the following Friday, the McInerneys arrived for the weekend, to celebrate Hugh's birthday on the Saturday. It had been a while since they had seen one another and there was plenty of news to catch up on. After Gwyneth had gone to sleep and they had eaten dinner it was time for sherry and conversation.

The big news was Robert's discovery of the Cypress Gate and his apparent meeting and conversation with Norian Fairchild himself.

'So Grandad's drawing came good.'

'It certainly did Kate,' said Hugh 'and Norian gave himself away by what he said about it; that it was "a good drawing but not the original".'

'The whole business has captured Grandad's imagination. He has been going through that second book of Norian's poetry with a fine tooth comb. He has made some notes to pass on to you Maggie. It seems that there's a common theme running through all the poems other than the obvious love elements. They are all about preparing for a long voyage to another realm or world and the final poem, "The Cypress Gate" describes setting out on that journey. They are poems of painful separation and exile but all with the hope of eventual reunion.'

'Do you think he'd believe that Robert has actually spoken to Norian Fairchild, here and now in 1977?'

'I honestly don't know Maggie. And I don't think we should even tell him. They were dear friends in the twenties but he has long since assumed that Norian is dead and he has done his grieving. I think he'd find it all unsettling and it would go against all his beliefs.'

'I agree Kate,' said Brian. 'If Norian had wanted to reconnect with your grandad he would have done it long ago. But I don't think that's his way. What was that line in Dandillion, "A second exile then I chose and hid from them my agelessness." It'd be a pretty rotten trick now that Jack's an old man to turn up again, not looking a day older than he did when they were both young men half a century ago. It's strange, that after all those years of secrecy he should make that slip about Jack's drawing not being the original.'

'I think it came as a tremendous shock to him,' said Hugh, 'seeing a copy of his drawing again after so long. Robert told him who had made the copy so he would definitely have made the connection. Grief over old friendships can cut both ways. He probably still misses Jack's companionship and grieves for the loss of it, more in a way because there is nothing stopping him from going up to Carlingford at any time and knocking on Jack's door; nothing but common decency and compassion.'

'You're right. I'd never thought of it like that before. Perhaps immortality isn't all it's cracked up to be.'

Hugh handed copies of Robert's photos to Brian and Kate.

'Here are the results of Robert's brilliant investigation.'

One of the photos of the house clearly showed the old black Rover parked in the driveway. It jogged Brian's memory.

'Shit! I'd completely forgotten. On lesser C we met up with Mervyn Purvis but these days he calls himself David Mervyn Fairchild.' Brian then told them Mervyn's tale about the inspirational stranger who had given him a lift to Carlingford; about the waiter in the restaurant addressing him as Mr Fairchild and his striking resemblance to Angela Moriarty.

'And seeing this photo has brought it all back to me. The car that the inspirational stranger gave Mervyn a lift in, was – wait for it – an old black Rover!!'

Everyone looked at everyone else in amazement.

'Well,' said Maggie at last with quiet emphasis, 'That just about clinches it.'

Hugh brewed a pot of tea and everybody settled down with their drinks as the sensation abated. It was at that point that Maggie dropped her twofold bombshells about becoming the new owner of No 9 Gracechurch Street and Mrs Malleson's imminent departure. There was great excitement about the real estate news but the excitement was tempered by the sadness of losing Mrs Malleson as a neighbour and friend.

This news affected Brian deeply at first and he questioned Maggie closely about everything Mrs Malleson had told her. Kate wasn't as deeply affected because she had only met Mrs M a few times but she was mindful of the value Brian attached to parental and grand-parental figures in his life, like Riley and her own mum and dad, in the absence of any real nurture or guidance from his own parents.

Happily after some minutes of intensive interrogation, Brian's mood lightened suddenly.

'Hang on a minute. Aren't we forgetting something? Mrs M is almost certainly a 'Nonesucher'. It was in her cellar that you found all the exercise books. Because we've gotten to know her over the years, what with being co-tenants and all, we've lost sight of the fact. We've just treated her like an ordinary person.

'Now what was it again that she told you Maggie? "There was only one journey I wanted to make but it wasn't time yet. I know you thought I meant death but it definitely isn't that." Were they her exact words?'

'Yes,' said Maggie, 'or near enough.'

'Well, in the words of the lovely Madge O'Brien, 'the truth of the matter is sticking out like dog's balls'. Mrs M and her sister are going to take a voyage on the Dandillion. That's who her mysterious advisor is, Norian Fairchild Esquire.'

'Of course!' said Maggie, that's it and that would explain why she is so excited about it. Fancy me not spotting that straight away.'

'You were probably too busy coping with your own grief at the thought of losing her company, sister mine.'

'So now we know the secret,' said Hugh, 'What do we do next?'

'Absolutely nothing,' said Maggie. 'We'll respect her secret just as we love and respect her. We've got lives of our own to lead and we're doing just fine.'

'Hear Hear' said everyone else and the sentiment was toasted in cups of tea.

'So are Mrs M and her sister Norian's children?' asked Kate after a minute or two of thoughtful silence. I originally thought the people he transported on Dandillion, were children that he had fathered with women other than his wife over the years but I re-read the poem recently and now I'm not so sure. It actually says in 'Amnesty', 'Though I can take them to those Isles, I myself can't go ashore where Madelaine, made young again, welcomes *our* descendants home.'

'That could mean all his descendants and all Madelaine's descendants,' Hugh suggested. 'But then again, Mrs M and her sister could just be ordinary citizens of Nonesuch covered by the Covenant of Nonesuch and not Norian's children at all.'

'And that's another thing I spotted in "Dandillion",' Kate continued, 'the description of the children Norian had with Madelaine. "Two healthy sons were born to us, the image of their mother's kin, and then two daughters elven fair, sweet echoes of the Deathless Realm." Is Angela Moriarty a sweet echo of the Deathless Realm? She told me at boarding school she has no idea who her father is and her mother has always flatly refused to discuss him.

'Can you really believe we're having this conversation? I sometimes have to pinch myself to see if I'm dreaming it all and speaking of dreaming I'm ready for bed.'

The feeling in the room was unanimous and by eleven they were all sound asleep, while downstairs Mrs Malleson continued with her packing.

34: Mrs Malleson

Mrs Malleson left Gracechurch Street the following Wednesday September 28th. On the previous afternoon in a Lawyer's office, she and Maggie completed the sale of 9 Gracechurch St and all the necessary documents had been signed and witnessed. Maggie had asked Mr O'Shannessy to act for her and he was there for the signing. He told Maggie later that she had bought wisely and picked up a bargain.

On the Wednesday morning, a removal van from a local charity took away all of Mrs M's furniture except for some pieces she had given to Maggie and Hugh. The rest of her things had been packed up and removed the night before. When it was all done she asked Maggie to give her a moment alone to say goodbye to her home, with an assurance that she'd come upstairs for a farewell cup of tea before she left.

'You've really put your stamp on this kitchen Maggie,' said Mrs M appreciatively. 'The bunches of dried herbs are a lovely touch. I know that you and Hugh will be very happy here. I can feel it in my bones.' They made light, pleasant conversation about surface things, as the inevitable and final separation crept closer.

At 3:00 p.m. precisely, they heard the sound of a car horn.

'That's my lift. Don't follow me out Maggie. We'll make our goodbyes here in your lovely kitchen. Say goodbye to Hugh for me and give him my love. Now let me give you a goodbye kiss. My dear Maggie, it has been a privilege to know you and see you blossom and grow into such a gentle and caring young woman. I will always treasure the time we have spent together and you will live in my heart forever.'

Then she quickly left the room and the house to hide her tears. Maggie was tempted to go to a window to try and catch a glimpse of who was driving the car but she stood firm. She cried a little as she heard the car drive away.

That evening over dinner, Maggie and Hugh felt Mrs M's absence very acutely, even though she seldom ever came upstairs and they mostly met downstairs in her kitchen or out in the garden.

'I guess it'll feel a bit odd for a while Maggie. It's probably a good thing that it's pub night tonight, although we won't make a late night of it.'

Sharon and Robert were already at a table when Hugh and Maggie arrived. Robert was still feeling very satisfied with his recent achievements but a hint of anti-climax had begun to trouble him. He *had* gone around to Cranwell Street to share his news about the Cypress Gate with Lucy and Jim. To begin with, Lucy had been very enthusiastic and excited about the news; after all she had been an integral part of the quest for a long time. Jim's response, on the other hand, had been rather muted and low key. Robert put this down to sour grapes on Jim's part because he was no longer the only one of the group who had met and spoken to Norian Fairchild.

Lucy then appeared to take the lead from Jim's response and they both seemed to lose interest. The conversation drifted on to more mundane topics. After about half an hour of small talk Robert left them to it and drove round to Sharon's place feeling quite deflated.

Sharon cheered him up considerably. While reassuring him that his finding the Cypress Gate was a brilliant success, she flatly refused to believe any talk of Norian Fairchild being an immortal and strongly urged him to do the same. It didn't take him long to revert to his earlier view that the various reported encounters with Norian Fairchild had been encounters with the grandfather and great great grandfather of the Norian Fairchild who had rescued Jim at sea.

<div align="center">~~~§~~~</div>

Following the 'teacup toast' with Brian and Kate at the weekend, Hugh and Maggie believed they had learnt all they needed to know about Norian and the quest was fulfilled. Their theories had been proven to their satisfaction and they were now committed to keeping Mrs Malleson's secret.

This meant that, although they shared their news about having bought No 9 Gracechurch St, they were not specific about where Mrs M had gone. They merely said that her sister needed a change of climate for her health and Mrs M was making the move to keep her company.

'Ah,' said Robert, 'I reckon they've gone somewhere in tropical Australia, Queensland maybe.'

'That sounds reasonable,' said Maggie. 'She didn't say where specifically.'

And so it was that all of the 'conspirators', for their own different reasons had laid the quest aside. For a time they alone of all the population of the Cumberlands had been caught up in an ancient mystery. Each of them had penetrated that mystery only so far as their individual personalities had allowed, and to varying degrees of satisfaction. All of them now felt that it was time to get on with the rest of their lives.

Robert had become very interested in the ancient stonework under the city that the man with the floor sander had told him about. He would still draw on Maggie's advice about literature and art for clues about a pre-convict society in the Cumberlands – but he believed it was a society of flesh and blood mortals like himself and no 'supernatural bullshit'. For Robert, having something to search for was more important than actually finding it.

For Hugh and Maggie the 'quest' had been completely successful. They had gone home from the pub that night quite content. They didn't go downstairs into Mrs M's flat until the weekend but the first thing they did after breakfast on Saturday morning was to go down into the cellar. It was the first time Hugh had been back down there since the original incursion which now seemed so long ago. It proved to be a bit of a disappointment. The room had been swept clean: there wasn't an exercise book in sight and the mysterious lantern had been removed.

Mrs Malleson's flat was similarly spotless. In her bedroom there was a tall sideboard she had given them. The charity workers had shifted it to one side as they removed the other furniture. Together, Hugh and Maggie moved the sideboard back into its correct place and saw that it had been concealing a framed picture.

'Maggie' said Hugh, 'allow me to introduce you to Norian Fairchild.' Maggie was fascinated. The image in the photograph stared at them calmly with a slightly amused and affectionate expression. It had the appearance of an icon. The photograph had been hand coloured to emphasise the fair hair and pale, almost transparent, moonstone eyes. It was a head and shoulders portrait, vignetted in an oval frame. It was not possible to distinguish the subject's clothing and there were no clues as to when the photograph had been taken.

'Brian was right,' said Maggie. 'He's the spitting image of Angela Moriarty.'

Finis.

© Neil Gardner 20/1/2023.

Because the maternity hospital in his home town of Smithton, on Tasmania's North-West coast, was temporarily closed in June 1949, Neil Gardner was born in nearby Wynyard. His first notable literary achievement was "A day in the life of a fish", a one page composition in early primary school set in a creek on his grandparents' farm. It began with the words "My home is a quiet, country stream" and concluded with the confession of a yearning desire to make a proposal of marriage to Miss Mary Mullet. The nun who was Neil's teacher at that time kept the manuscript among her most treasured possessions for the rest of her days.

Sixty years later, after a varied career as a clerk, an ore-sampler, an apple picker, a student, a cleaner and a public servant, but mainly as an obscure singer-songwriter with ten albums to his credit, Neil is now returning to literary pursuits. He is attempting to release the half dozen novels and plot lines that have been swimming around in his head, each in search of its own Miss Mary Mullet, for the last forty years or so.

9 780064 578 0 802